ANCHOR
IN THE
STORM

Books by Sarah Sundin

WINGS OF GLORY

A Distant Melody
A Memory Between Us
Blue Skies Tomorrow

WINGS OF THE NIGHTINGALE

With Every Letter
On Distant Shores
In Perfect Time

WAVES OF FREEDOM

Through Waters Deep
Anchor in the Storm

ANCHOR IN THE STORM

A NOVEL

SARAH SUNDIN

Revell

a division of Baker Publishing Group
Grand Rapids, Michigan

Published by Revell
a division of Baker Publishing Group
P.O. Box 6287, Grand Rapids, MI 49516-6287
www.revellbooks.com

Printed in the United States of America

Library of Congress Cataloging-in-Publication Data
Names: Sundin, Sarah, author.
Title: Anchor in the storm : a novel / Sarah Sundin.
Description: Grand Rapids, MI : Revell Books, [2016] | Series: Waves of freedom ; #2
Identifiers: LCCN 2015044002 | ISBN 9780800723439 (pbk.)
Subjects: | GSAFD: Historical fiction. | Mystery fiction. | Romantic suspense fiction.
Classification: LCC PS3619.U5626 A85 2016 | DDC 813/.6—dc23
LC record available at http://lccn.loc.gov/2015044002

Scripture quotations are from the King James Version of the Bible.

This book is a work of fiction. Names, characters, places, and incidents are the product of the author's

Published in as

16 17 18 1

60946761

To Zander and Anna Cameron—

What a joy to watch the pursuit, the resistance, the persistence, the melting—as our daughter slowly fell in love with one of her brother's best friends. Many blessings to you in your marriage.

1

Vermilion, Ohio
Sunday, December 7, 1941

Lillian Avery's dream couldn't have come true at a worse time.

In the pale afternoon sun slanting through the kitchen window, Dad sat at the table building a model ship while humming "On Christ the Solid Rock I Stand," and Mom gathered kitchen gadgets.

"Here. A flour sifter." Mom added it to Lillian's pile on the counter.

"Remember, Mary Stirling said I didn't need to bring anything for the apartment in Boston."

Mom rummaged through a cabinet. "But do they have a flour sifter? You'll need one. And last Christmas Jim gave me a new one." Her voice cracked.

Lillian's heart clenched. At the table, Dad stopped humming and gave Lillian a look that said, "At a time like this, take the flour sifter."

Mom already had reason to be anxious, with the United States tilting on the brink of war and the three oldest Avery boys serving as naval officers. But now? Two weeks after Jim's destroyer—a neutral ship!—had been sunk by a U-boat? Two weeks of not knowing if he was alive or dead?

How could Lillian leave home at a time like this?

She squeezed the handle of the flour sifter so it made the "shugga-shugga" sound she loved. "Sure, Mom. But if you fill my trunk with gadgets, I won't have room for clothing and I'll have to walk around Boston naked." She winked at Dad.

He smiled and resumed humming and tinkering.

"Lillian Avery! What am I going to do with you?" Mom extracted herself from the cabinet, her hazel eyes misty. "Rather, what am I going to do without you?"

"You'll manage, same as you did when I was at Ohio State."

"I know." Mom tucked a graying lock of hair back into the roll at the nape of her neck. "But I do wish you'd found a job closer to home."

Lillian suppressed a groan. Even excellent grades hadn't shielded her from six months of unemployment. Thank goodness Jim had found her a position in Boston. Of course, she'd still have to prove herself. In the acceptance letter, Cyrus Dixon had stated he didn't want to hire a girl pharmacist but that the peacetime draft limited his choices. She could imagine how he felt about hiring a cripple.

"I'll be fine, Mom." In time, she'd win over crotchety Mr. Dixon.

"I know. You have my spunk." Mom squinted at a turkey baster.

"I don't know, Erma." Dad tied a miniature sail to a miniature mast. "With Lillian's spunk and Mary Stirling for a roommate, she could get in all kinds of trouble."

"Isn't that something?" Lillian plucked the turkey baster from her mother's hand and slipped it into the drawer. "I didn't know her well growing up, but she was always so quiet and sensible, and off she goes—"

"And catches a saboteur." Mom stashed the baster in Lillian's pile. "Well, young lady, see you don't get caught up in such shenanigans."

"I'm working at a drugstore, not an ammunition plant." To distract her parents from the truth that drug addicts did rob drugstores, Lillian grabbed the baster, held it to her mouth like a trumpet, and squeezed the rubber bulb in rhythm to her words. "Don't make me go to Massachusetts. That's where Thanksgiving started. Do you know what they do to turkeys there?"

"Goofy girl." Mom laughed. She actually laughed, for the first time since the telegram came. "But what if you need—"

"They have stores in Boston. I—"

The doorbell rang.

Everyone sucked in a breath. It was only three-thirty. Lucy and Martin weren't arriving until five. Who else would come on a Sunday afternoon?

A telegram would.

"I'll get it." Lillian kept her voice light. She turned too fast, and her prosthesis pinched the skin around her knee, but she moved at a steady and calm pace for her parents' sake.

"Oh, George." Mom's voice wavered.

Grasping the doorknob, Lillian squeezed her eyes shut. *Lord, please let Jim be all right.*

Her two younger brothers, Ed and Charlie, pounded down the stairs behind her.

Lillian twisted the doorknob and faced the boy from Western Union and whatever news he had. After she tipped him and he departed, she leaned against the doorjamb, the door wide open, chilly air nipping at her good leg.

"Read it," her father said, deep and firm.

She slipped a shaky finger under the lip of the envelope. How could one tiny slip of paper hold the power to change their lives forever?

Lillian scanned it, read it, read it again to make sure she comprehended, her breath chuffing out faster and faster, pushing up a smile. "It's from Jim."

"Yes . . . ?" Mom said, her eyes anxious.

"No, Mom. Not from the Navy. From Jim. He's alive."

"Oh, hallelujah." She sagged against the wall, eyes shut, hands clasped under her chin.

Dad grabbed the telegram. "Here you go. 'Alive and whole. Back in Boston. Thirty-day survivor's leave. Might come home for Christmas. Might bring Arch.'"

"He's alive, and he's coming home." Mom smiled toward heaven.

"Might come home, he said." Lillian tugged her old maroon sweater tighter around her.

"He's bringing Arch," Dad said. "Such a nice young man."

"Might bring him." Lillian hadn't met Jim's best friend, Archer Vandenberg, who came with a pedigree as hoity-toity as his name, but she didn't relish the thought of sharing Christmas with some snooty society boy.

At the base of the stairs, Ed and Charlie sang about the unsinkable Avery boys and danced a bad jig with their too-big feet and their too-long legs and their too-deep voices.

A smile burst onto Lillian's face. Why was she fussing about Christmas? Jim was alive, and nothing else mattered.

She reached outside to pull the screen door shut. Martin Freeman's Chevy parked on the driveway, and Lucy opened the car door and dashed up the walk.

Lillian frowned. Lucy never opened a door for herself.

Her identical twin sister's dark blonde hair bounced around her shoulders as she trotted up to the porch, her hazel eyes round, her face pale and drawn. "Did you hear?"

They must have seen the Western Union car and followed it. Lillian smiled to ease her sister's fear. "It's good news. Very—"

"How could you?" Lucy's face twisted and reddened. "You've always been coldhearted, but this—"

"Lucy." Dad set his voice down like a rock and clamped his hand on Lillian's shoulder.

At that moment, Lillian's heart felt anything but cold. "Jim's alive." Her tone came out clipped. "I suppose it is coldhearted of me to consider that good news."

"Lillian." Dad squeezed her shoulder.

Lucy's lips parted, and her gaze swam between family members. "Jim . . . he's alive. Well, that explains . . . but haven't . . . oh, you aren't listening to the radio."

Martin stepped to his wife's side. "You need to sit down, sweetie."

"Oh yes. In my condition." She curved one hand around her belly.

Lillian's shoulders softened in Dad's grip. After four years of marriage, Lucy was finally carrying a child into her fourth month of pregnancy. With her emotions in turmoil, outbursts were expected. Still, would an apology be too much to ask for?

Martin guided Lucy to a wing chair as if she were fragile and precious.

Familiar jealousy wormed inside. Men never treated Lillian that way. Since she was already shattered, they gaped at her in shock, then swept her into the corner and walked on past. She would never be precious.

Lillian thrust the door shut and left her self-pity outside in the cold.

"Such news," Lucy said. "So awful."

Ed fiddled with the radio knobs, and voices broke through the static, somber and strident.

The Avery family gathered in the living room as words organized into sentences, and sentences clarified into truth. Horrible truth about the tropical land of Hawaii and the naval base at Pearl Harbor and Japanese planes with blood-red spots and American ships in flames. Ships sinking. Lots of ships. Good strong ships. And men killed. Lots of men. Good strong men.

Lillian's oldest brother, Dan, was on a cruiser somewhere in the Atlantic. The second-oldest brother, Rob, served in San Diego. Jim was back in Boston after surviving a sinking. What would happen to them now?

"We're at war," Lucy said with a sob.

Mom leaned on Dad. Lucy gripped her belly and Martin's arm. Charlie sat on the rug by the radio, his back straight as a gun. Ed's good strong hand formed a fist on top of the radio cabinet.

And Lillian tugged her blood-red sweater around her, knowing she could never wear it again because it would bring back memories of that day.

★ ★ ★

Friday, December 19, 1941

Arch couldn't shake the dream.

He shifted in the train seat and stretched his eyes wide. Anything to stay awake and avoid the nightmare. Conversation would help, but Jim Avery and Mary Stirling sat across the aisle, cooing at each other. How could Arch complain? It had taken months for the couple to admit their love, and now they reveled in it.

His eyes drifted shut. No, he couldn't fall asleep. Not in public.

With a solid shake of his head, he adjusted the jacket of his newly tailored dress blues. He'd lost most of his possessions when the *Atwood* went down.

The shudder of the torpedo piercing the destroyer's skin. The shouts of the men in the engine room as they fought to keep the ship underway. The second torpedo. The list to starboard. The call to abandon ship.

As an officer, Arch had insisted his men get out first, but the watertight hatch was stuck. Could they open it in time?

No, he wasn't trapped. He was on a train in Ohio, but his fingers trembled in his lap.

Arch rubbed his hands together, as if cold. He'd lick this. He had to. His future depended on it.

"Here we go—Vermilion, Ohio." Jim leaned over and grinned at Arch. "Ready for a home-cooked supper?"

"Absolutely." Why hadn't he noticed the train's deceleration? He fetched his coat from the overhead rack. Two weeks in the heartland should set his head back on straight.

Better than two weeks at the Vandenberg estate in Connecticut, with long-legged Elizabeth "Bitsy" Chamberlain working her wiles on him. He'd spent three days at home after the sinking, and that was three days too many.

Arch buttoned his coat.

Ironic that Bitsy had broken up with him in high school when he insisted on attending the Naval Academy, but now her interest had reignited, potent and deadly. With the United States at war, landing a naval officer had risen in status in their society. But Arch knew her. After the war ended, she wouldn't rest until she'd trapped him in a position at Vandenberg Insurance, trapped him in the mansion she deserved.

He'd rather go down with the ship.

Arch followed Jim and Mary off the train. The evening cold stole his breath. Not as brisk as the North Atlantic convoy route, but close. On the platform, puffs of steam from the engine glowed in the lamplight.

A middle-aged couple dashed forward, laughing, and pulled Jim into an embrace and a session of face-patting, as if to affirm he was really alive.

Then Mrs. Avery embraced Mary, a girl she'd known from

childhood, exclaiming how happy she was that Mary was willing to put up with her Jim.

Mr. Avery shook Arch's hand. "Good to see you, Arch. It's been a while since we saw you at graduation. We're glad to have you."

"Thank you, sir. I'm glad to be here."

"Let's get the luggage." He led the way. "Lillian's keeping the car warmed up, Ed and Charlie are back at the house, and Lucy and Martin promised to come by and make sure the boys left us some dinner."

Arch chuckled, but his head spun. As an only child, how was he going to keep the Avery clan straight? Seven children! He knew Dan and Rob, Jim's older brothers, from the Academy, but he hadn't met the others, and he never could remember the names and relationships.

Out on the street, Mr. Avery opened the trunk of a late-model Pontiac sedan, large and serviceable, and they loaded the luggage. Then Arch slipped into the backseat on the driver's side, with Mary in the middle and Jim on the right.

On the passenger side, a light-haired young lady leaned over the front seat in an awkward embrace with Jim. "So glad you're alive. What would I do without you?"

"I got you a job. You'd be fine."

The girl grasped Mary by the arm. "I can't wait to join you in Boston."

Arch squinted. Boston. Yes, the sister who was a pharmacist, of all things. Thank goodness Mr. Avery hadn't shut the front door and snuffed out the overhead light, because she was a rather pretty pharmacist, with a delicate face and large dark eyes.

Jim set his hand on his sister's shoulder. "Lillian, you haven't met my friend Arch."

"How do you do, Lillian? It's a pleasure to meet you." He put on his best smile and stretched out his hand.

She gave him a brief handshake. "How do you do?"

Mr. Avery sat in the driver's seat. "Home again, home again—"

"Jiggety jig!" Jim and Lillian said in unison and laughed.

What would it have been like to grow up with a large family like this? A normal middle-class family in normal middle America?

Lillian twisted around in the front seat. "Mary, tell me about the apartment."

"Yes," Mrs. Avery said from beside her daughter. "Do you have everything you need?"

"A flour sifter? A turkey baster?" Humor ruffled Lillian's voice.

"Oh, you." Her mother nudged her.

"I think so," Mary said, a smile visible in the dim light.

"See, Mom. I told you Boston was civilized." Lillian looked back over her shoulder. "Jim, tell me more about Dixon's Drugs. How big is the store? Is it clean and modern? How many employees? Do they have a soda fountain?"

Jim put his arm around Mary's shoulder. "Yes, no, yes, yes."

"Smart aleck," Lillian said.

"I can be of some help." Arch leaned forward. Time to turn those large eyes his way. "It's rather old-fashioned, like stepping back to the turn of the century."

"Yes," Mary said. "I shop there because it's on the way home from the El station, but sometimes I have a hard time finding things."

"Good." Lillian seemed to grow a few inches. "That means I'll have a job to do. I learned so much in school, and I can't wait to apply it."

She went on to describe things she'd learned, proper practices for running a store and serving patients. Her voice was low in tone and precise in pace, her words intelligent and informed, and her bearing lively without giddiness.

A pleasant sense of warmth filled Arch's chest. Jim had held out on him. Never once did he mention his sister was so bright and lovely.

Mary patted Lillian's shoulder. "Before you make too many plans, wait and see the store and get to know Mr. Dixon."

Jim grumbled. "He does seem set in his ways. I told you—"

"I know. He doesn't want a woman pharmacist, but the draft is siphoning off the men, so now I have a chance to fulfill my dream."

"A chance?" Arch put his full charm into his words. "I'd say it's a done deal."

The car stopped at an intersection, and a streetlamp cast light on Lillian's strained smile.

His charm didn't . . . charm her? Arch sat back, but then that warmth stirred into full appreciation.

This woman wasn't like the society girls angling for the best husbands or the shopgirls digging for gold.

Not Lillian Avery. She'd gone to college to learn, not to snag a man. She had a career and plans and dreams and didn't need Archer Vandenberg or his wealth. And his good looks and charm didn't seem to affect her.

If he could win the heart of a woman like her, it wouldn't be due to his name or looks or money, but due to who he was inside.

That would mean something.

Mr. Avery pulled to a stop in front of a modest-sized two-story brick home.

Now was the time to act. Arch bolted from the car and circled to the passenger side, careful not to slip on the icy pavement. He opened the door and bowed his head. "Miss Avery."

She glanced up with those large eyes. Guarded eyes. She swung one leg out. A shapely leg.

My, he liked a good set of legs on a lady.

Then she swung out the other leg. A strange line stretched below her knee. Her leg looked stiff. Fake. An artificial leg?

Jim's plethora of stories bounced around in Arch's head. Something about a sister who lost a leg and never let it slow her down. This sister?

Oh no. He was staring.

He shifted his gaze to Lillian's face. Her cool, appraising face.

"Jim didn't tell you."

Arch wiped his hand over his mouth, wiped away gaping rudeness. "I—well, he—I think—"

She closed her eyes, shook her head, and marched away, a slight hitch in her step.

Arch's breath turned to icicles. Win her heart? At this point he'd be happy to make peace.

2

Lillian tugged her old green stocking cap over her ears, swung the tail around her neck, and escaped the house. Mom wouldn't approve of her wearing Dad's work coat in public, but it was so warm and Dad-scented, she didn't care.

She sniffed the afternoon air on Main Street. No sign of snow in the overcast sky, but plenty cold. A few blocks to her left, Lake Erie lay gray and deceptively placid, but across the street lay her haven—Dad's boatyard on the Vermilion River. She crossed Main to the long brick building, passed the office where Mom ran the business end of things, and entered the workshop.

Oh, the wonderful smell of sawdust and varnish. Four sailboats rested in scaffolding in various states of construction. Dad stood at the bow of one, squinting down the length and brushing sandpaper over the surface as if stroking a child's hair.

"Hi, Dad. Want some help?"

He blinked, then raised a slow smile. "Are you calling my workshop untidy?"

"Is it ever not?" She mock-frowned at the sawdust on the floor.

"You know where things are."

"Good." She dashed to the corner and grabbed the big push broom.

"Where's the rest of the family?"

"Mom took soup over to poor Mrs. Cassidy. She's still sick. Jim's at Mary's, and Ed and Charlie went to the movies with their buddies."

"And Arch? Our houseguest? Don't tell me you left him alone."

Lillian ducked her head to conceal her grimace. "He was reading, last I saw. Besides, I'm sure he relishes his own company. He thinks he's quite charming."

Dad chuckled. "Give the poor fellow a chance. He's a nice young man."

She jabbed the broom into the far corner, but it was too large. She should have started with the smaller broom, but she liked the satisfaction of handling the large one. "Rubs me the wrong way."

"Did I catch him staring?"

Jaw-to-the-pavement gaping was more like it. She shrugged. "Everyone stares. I'm used to it. But the way he tried to apologize. 'I'm afraid I got off on the wrong foot.' Then he got a mortified look and apologized again—for putting his foot in his mouth. Honestly. I'm not sure if he was mocking me or if he thinks I'm so frail I can't bear to hear the word *foot*."

No response. Lillian looked up from her pile of shavings.

Dad's shoulders shook with silent laughter. "I wish I could have seen. Poor, poor fellow."

"Pompous fellow. We put him in Dan, Rob, and Jim's

bedroom, the biggest in the house, and he called it a 'cozy little room.'"

In the cavernous workshop, the swish of her broom on concrete echoed the scratch of sandpaper on wood. Tension built inside Lillian. She'd gone too far, and now she'd hear it.

"Would you like to know what I think?" Dad asked, his voice as gentle as his touch on the wood.

Did she have a choice? And did she really want to discount her father's wisdom? "Go ahead."

"First, remember he's been Jim's best friend for a good six years. Your brother's an excellent judge of character, and any friend of his deserves our respect."

All her indignation flowed out, down through the broom bristles. She really was coldhearted, wasn't she? "I know."

"Second, he's an only child thrust into the Avery Aviary with all our squawking and twittering and cawing."

A smile nudged her lips. "We are overwhelming, aren't we?"

"Third." Dad met her gaze, his dark eyes amused. "He couldn't take his eyes off you last night. I think he sees a lovely young lady, and he's working hard—too hard—to overcome a horrible first impression."

Lillian's face scrunched up, and she swept under the scaffolding. Only a stupid man would want her, and she didn't want a stupid man. Or a twisted man. A shudder rippled through her. Never again.

She had to distract Dad, and the broom handle inspired her. "Say, have you given any thought to my crutches? Did you look at my drawing? You're so clever. I'm sure you could make them hinge or telescope."

"So you can fit them in your trunk."

"I hate carrying them on the train. Hate it. I only need them at night when I take off my prosthesis. And it looks odd to carry them."

"Lillian," he said in that low rolling way of his when he wanted to soothe her. "You'll be fine."

She jerked up her gaze, but he'd resumed sanding. She'd be fine? What did he mean by that? Didn't he realize she didn't want to step off the train in Boston carrying the emblem of her weakness? Not when she'd have to be stronger than ever, living with roommates she barely knew, working for a boss who didn't want her, and pulling fully away from her family's security.

She loved her family, but depending on them was beginning to chafe like her prosthesis at the end of a long day.

"You'll be fine." Dad ran a bare hand over the plank, one eye closed. "Lean on the Lord, and you'll be fine."

"I know." She dragged more shavings from under the scaffolding. Everyone else in the family seemed to have faith that was warmhearted and alive. Hers felt mechanical and wooden.

A knock sounded. Lillian bonked her head on the scaffolding and rubbed it.

Arch Vandenberg stood by the door, wearing his navy blue overcoat and service cap and a smile that said, "You missed me, didn't you?"

She didn't.

"Hello, Arch," Dad said. "You wanted to see the shop?"

"You did say I could come down. Is now a good time?"

"Of course. You're always welcome."

"Thank you." He nodded at Lillian. "Hello, Lillian."

"Hello." Her hands twisted around the broom handle. She wasn't done sweeping, but she needed to leave. She headed toward the entrance, even if she did have to pass Arch. One step past him, two, and soon she'd reach the door.

"Don't leave on my account."

She spun around. She'd misjudged. He stood only one pace away, several inches taller than she, his bright blue eyes twinkling a challenge. If she left now, he'd know she'd most certainly left on his account. Stuck. She was stuck.

"I . . ." She gestured to the back corner. "I need to switch brooms."

"May I help?"

"Switch brooms?"

His smile surely made girls swoon up and down the Eastern Seaboard. "Sweep. May I help sweep?"

He didn't look like the sweeping sort, which could be amusing. She handed him the broom. "That's called a broom. You may have heard of them."

Arch frowned at the item in his black-gloved hands. "Yes. Yes, I've heard of such things." Then he winked. "And *that's* called sarcasm. You may have heard of it."

Lillian inclined her head in appreciation. At least he could take teasing. She grabbed a regular broom. She'd follow him and take care of all he missed.

"What are you working on, Mr. Avery?" Arch pushed the broom with vigor and decent technique.

"A yacht for a client in Columbus. She won't be needed until summer, so I have time. Her name is *Isabella*, and we're still getting acquainted."

Arch removed his cap and bowed from the waist. "Good day, Isabella. An honor."

Lillian peered at the officer. No sign of condescension or mockery. He simply shared her father's love of boats, understood his mystical connection.

Arch pulled his cap on over his blond hair and resumed sweeping, as he and Dad discussed the sailboat's specifications. Since sailor boy was doing a passable job with the push broom, she'd let him manage the open spaces while she cleaned under the equipment.

Lillian poked the broom under the woodstove, the only source of heat in the workshop, and she sniffled in the cool air. If Arch thought her lovely last night, he'd change his mind now that he'd seen her in a man's work coat, heavy gloves, and the ugliest hat in Ohio.

"Good," she whispered.

"I'm sorry it isn't sailing season," Dad said. "I'd love to take you out."

"That's all right." Arch's voice sounded stiff.

"I know how it is with sailors and the sea."

"The sea was always my refuge."

Lillian pushed the dust from under the stove into Arch's path. Oh brother. Why on earth would a rich, privileged boy need a refuge?

"Was?" Dad said.

Arch stood up straight. "Pardon?"

Dad refolded his sandpaper. "You said the sea *was* your refuge, not *is*."

Arch's broom paused. "I—I mean—of course, the sea's never been safe. I knew that, but—"

"But now you've seen firsthand."

A cloud passed before Arch's eyes.

Lillian couldn't look away, but she refused to stare. With effort, she ripped her attention to sweeping around the wood box.

A sudden chuckle from Arch. "Yes, now I've seen firsthand, and I have renewed respect. I'll be a better officer for it."

"I'm sure you will," Dad said.

"The country will need all the good officers she can get. Things aren't going well."

"No, they aren't. Seems the Japanese land somewhere new every day. The Philippines, Borneo, Malaya. We've been caught unaware."

"We sure have." Arch's broom shushed over the floor. "The only good thing the war has done is to shut down talk of isolationism. We're all in this together."

"Even here in little Vermilion." Lillian swept under the workbench. "We have a Home Defense Guard Unit, the Boy Scouts are holding a paper drive, the Red Cross is stepping up work, and the Civic Club donated the money for Christmas lighting to local defense. People are scared but determined."

Dad cleared his throat. "Mrs. Avery would like for us to dine at Okagi's tonight, partly so she doesn't have to cook so close to Christmas, and partly to support Mr. Okagi. But Arch, we won't go if it bothers you."

"Why would it?"

"Mr. Okagi is Japanese."

Lillian stood her broom straight and clutched it like a standard. "He's been here over a decade, and he wants to become a citizen, but the United States won't let him, and his wife is French, and everyone in Vermilion loves them. Their restaurant is the finest in Ohio. We used to go into the city to dine, but now city folk come out here, and it's all because of Mr. Okagi."

Arch stared at her, but a different stare from the night before, his eyes warm and his mouth bent in a slight smile. "Sounds like a fine man."

"He is." Her breath huffed out. She probably sounded like a silly schoolgirl.

"The FBI came the day after Pearl Harbor." At the workbench, Dad exchanged the sandpaper for a finer grade. "Closed down the restaurant and investigated him. He's clean, so the FBI let him reopen the next day."

"I'm glad," Arch said.

"Well, we don't want to put you in an uncomfortable position. The Navy took the brunt of it in Hawaii." Dad rubbed the sandpaper between his fingers.

"Yes, but it sounds like Mr. Okagi has an airtight alibi." Arch grinned at Lillian. "And I wouldn't want to get in the way of you and that broom."

She allowed herself to smile.

"Besides, I believe in judging a person on words and actions and character." His expression sobered and homed in on Lillian. "Not on background or appearance."

Lillian sucked in a breath and swept around the workbench. Did he mean he wouldn't judge her for her leg? Or was he asking her not to judge him by his wealth? Or both?

The Navy had better assign Ensign Archer Vandenberg somewhere other than Boston.

3

Arch had never seen such a Christmas. Mr. and Mrs. Avery, five of their children, and Lucy's husband, Martin, jumbled up on the furniture and on the floor in pajamas. Presents changed hands in no predictable order, yet the braided rug in the center of the living room bore neat piles of boxes, paper, and ribbon.

Chaotic, confusing, and beautiful.

On the floor by the Christmas tree, Lillian hugged a book to her chest. "Agatha Christie's *Evil Under the Sun*. Thank you, Jim."

"Mary picked it out. She loves mysteries too. Obviously." Jim laughed and plucked at the red and green ribbons Lillian had transferred from packages to her hair. "Don't let my girlfriend give you ideas about solving your own murder mystery."

"Silly boy." Lillian swatted Jim's hand and readjusted the ribbons in her amber hair. "I'm a pharmacist. It won't be a murder—it'll be a drug ring."

26

Arch grinned and set his new handkerchief next to his chair with his other gifts. What was it about that woman that drew him?

He repeated the reasons he shouldn't be attracted to her. She was Jim's sister, and if anything went wrong, the friendship could be marred. She was also crippled, and he ordinarily wouldn't give her a second look.

Yet reason was foundering. Why would Jim stand between his best friend and his beloved sister? And how could Arch use the word *crippled* to describe a young lady who let nothing impede her dreams? No, he'd describe her as strong, determined . . . enchanting.

However, she didn't seem to like him. He needed to orchestrate more time together, preferably in a romantic setting. And he needed to show her he wasn't a snob.

Charlie, the youngest Avery, pulled eight flat boxes from under the tree. "From Arch. One for each of us. Wow."

Arch settled back in the chair while Charlie distributed the boxes. "Jim told me your sizes. If they don't fit, I can exchange them."

"Oh my." Lucy pulled out her pair of gloves in the finest russet leather, lined with cashmere. "These are beautiful."

Mrs. Avery stroked the leather. "Goodness. You shouldn't have spent so much on us."

"Nonsense. I'm consuming your food, heat, and hospitality for two solid weeks. It's the least I could do."

She raised bewildered eyes. "But you already gave me a lovely hostess gift."

"Not to mention you sprang for the lot of us at Okagi's." Jim's smile teased Arch for spending like the Vandenberg heir.

Jim was wrong. Arch didn't use money to get his way. Not anymore.

He gave the family a sheepish look. "Have pity. I don't

have brothers or sisters to treat. Besides, if I can't be generous on Christmas with my best friend's family, when can I?"

"Of course." Mrs. Avery gave him a look full of compassion—pity even. "And they're lovely. Thank you."

Lillian inspected her glove-encased hand and tipped a smile to him. "Thank you."

That smile paid him back tenfold. "You're welcome."

From his armchair, Mr. Avery pointed under the tree. "You missed one, Lillian."

She peeled off the glove. "For me? Thank you, Dad."

Arch couldn't stop watching her, how the honey-colored waves of hair swished down her shoulder as she bent over the package, how her cheeks rounded, how unadorned lips spread in a winsome smile.

That day in her father's workshop, when she gave an impassioned plea for Mr. Okagi while dressed like a peasant in an oversized coat and a stocking cap, he'd tipped over the edge. He'd been in free fall ever since.

"How pretty." Lillian lifted a gold necklace. "An anchor to remind me of my nautical heritage when I get to Boston."

Mr. Avery rested his forearms on his knees. "To remind you of something deeper. Jesus is your anchor, your hope in any storm, your sure refuge." He stretched out the last word so it reached all the way to Arch.

Jesus was his refuge, his anchor. He knew that, but did he believe it?

Arch had grown up with an aloof stained-glass Jesus, but Jim had introduced him to the rugged carpenter in the fishing boat, genuine and straightforward. Arch's faith had become personal in the past few years, but it must not be enough.

If it were, the shakes would be gone by now.

In thirteen days, his survivor's leave would end. Would he be ready to return to sea, to go below decks?

A tremor built in his hands, and he laced his fingers together. He had to be ready. How could an officer in the US Navy plead anxiety while soldiers and sailors fought and died throughout the Pacific, while U-boats devastated Allied shipping in the Atlantic and Japanese subs sank ships off the California coast?

Lord, help me do this.

"I know I can do it." Lillian clasped the golden chain behind her neck. "I'm so excited about my new job. The store, the patients, everything. I can't wait."

"All right, girls." Mrs. Avery stood. "Let's clear the breakfast dishes, and then we can all get dressed."

Lillian headed for the dining room, her brown oxfords in contrast to her creamy bathrobe. She always wore oxfords, probably because of the prosthesis.

Lucy eased up from the couch as if expecting her child tomorrow rather than in May, and she cradled her hand around her flat belly. "I'm coming. I can't move so fast now."

Arch rearranged his laced fingers. Jim said Lillian was born big and healthy, while Lucy was small and sickly. They'd almost lost her a few times. Coddled, most likely.

Lillian seemed to think Arch was coddled too, a rich boy accustomed to servants clearing the table.

That thought propelled him to his feet. He'd show her he could clear dishes.

Lillian carried a stack of plates into the kitchen, and Lucy followed with some glasses. Arch grabbed a platter and set serving bowls on top.

"Your new job will be a stretch for you," Lucy said in the kitchen.

"Why? I've worked in pharmacies since high school."

"But you'll have to work with sick people, and you've never had any compassion for the sick."

What on earth? Arch stopped in the doorway.

Lillian stood at the sink with her back to him, her shoulders pinched together. "I was four years old."

Lucy placed the glasses on the counter. "You never wanted anything to do with me when I was sick, only thinking of yourself, playing with the boys, leaving me—"

"Girls!" Mrs. Avery set her hands on her hips. "Enough of that. You're twenty-two years old. And it's Christmas."

"Sorry, Mom," Lucy said.

"Sorry." Lillian turned for the door and met Arch's gaze, her eyes wide.

"Just bringing in the dishes," he said.

Mrs. Avery dashed to him and took the stack. "Oh, you don't have to do that. You're our guest. Lillian, show him back to the living room. Lucy and I can manage the dishes."

"Yes, ma'am," he said.

Lillian led him through the dining room and paused at the door to the living room, her eyes guarded. "See? A big family isn't always so swell."

He spotted a crack and wedged it open with a smile. "So it isn't true what they say about identical twins being inseparable?"

"Not us." She glanced back, her voice low. "My fault mostly."

He leaned against the doorjamb, sank his hands into his bathrobe pockets, and willed the moment to last. "You were only four years old."

"Old enough to know I was being mean."

"And twenty-two is old enough to know you're being mean." He tilted his head toward the kitchen.

She dipped her head, and the green and red ribbons flopped forward. "Apparently not."

Arch swallowed hard. Why did he want to hold her? He'd known her less than a week.

Lillian lifted her chin. "Is it true about only children being spoiled brats?"

30

He chuckled. Yes, she had pluck. "Not in my case. My parents gave me chores, put me in public school, and refused to buy me everything I wanted."

Those large eyes dissected him, allowing him to study the rich mix of greens and golds and browns. "Did you have a pony?"

"A horse. Can you forgive me?"

One corner of her mouth edged up. "Without brothers, you needed someone to play with, I suppose."

"I was lonely." He gave her his most pitiful frown.

"I doubt that." She strolled into the living room.

Yes, he was falling hard. And that conversation had gone well. If only the Navy would keep him in Boston, but they were transferring much of the fleet to the Pacific. This last week in Ohio might be his only chance with Lillian. Come New Year's, they could be separated by thousands of miles.

Lillian sat on the couch and leafed through a book, while Jim and his brothers sorted the wrappings on the floor.

Arch sat on the opposite end of the couch. "Say, Jim, do we have plans for New Year's Eve?"

"We don't do much here."

Mr. Avery gathered his pile of gifts. "Don't worry about us. You young folks ought to go out and have fun."

"That's what I was thinking." Arch leaned forward on his knees. "Cleveland isn't far. What do you say, Jim? Martin? Would Mary and Lucy like an evening of dining and dancing? Lillian?" He turned to her.

Her face went flat. "I don't dance."

Inside, he groaned. For heaven's sake. Of course she couldn't dance. Somehow he had to recover. "You can still enjoy an evening out. As for the dancing, I'll sit out with you."

"No, thank you." She raised her book. *Evil Under the Sun* indeed.

"Well, I'm going to get dressed." Jim stood and ran his hand over his rumpled dark hair.

"I should too." As he changed, he'd think of an alternate plan. Why hadn't he said dinner and a show? That would have worked.

He followed Jim up to the room they were sharing and shut the door.

Jim faced him and crossed his arms over his blue bathrobe. "What are you doing?"

"Doing?"

"With Lillian. You're flirting with her."

Arch's mouth went dry, and he wet his lips with his tongue. "Would that be so bad?"

Jim scrunched up his face and shook his head. "Don't."

A slow measured breath. "I understand you want to protect your sister, but you know me."

"Yes, I know you. I've watched you date half a dozen women and discard them all."

"They were gold diggers. You know that. They only loved me for my money. Lillian—I know she isn't like that. In fact, if it makes you feel better, she doesn't like me at all."

"Good."

A burning sensation filled his chest. Apparently loyalty to a sibling ran deeper than loyalty to a friend.

Jim groaned and plopped onto his bed. "It's not just you. It's Lillian."

"What do you mean?" Arch sat on the other bed.

"She hasn't dated much. She's only had one boyfriend, when she was at Ohio State. I don't know the details, and she won't talk, but it ended badly."

"Oh." Arch folded his hands between his knees.

"I do trust you, buddy. I do, but . . ."

But not with his sister. Arch gave a stiff nod. "I respect both of you too much. I'll back off."

A long sigh. "You know what, though? Lillian could really use a friend. She hasn't had lots of those either." Jim's mouth bent in a smile, repentant and warm again.

"All right." Most likely, Lillian would reject his friendship as she had his flirtation. But if she accepted his friendship, perhaps he could earn her trust. And Jim's too.

4

Lillian stood on the sidewalk across from Dixon's Drugs, her only chance to be secure and independent.

A neon sign on a brick storefront, a striped green awning over the door, and windows plastered with ads. Typical but garish.

Her breath formed icy coils before her, and her fingers found the anchor necklace under her scarf. "Jesus is your anchor, your hope in any storm," Dad had told her.

If only it were true for Lillian, but it wasn't. Not God's fault, but hers. *Please be my anchor today, Lord. Please help me make a good impression.*

She tucked in the necklace and rearranged her scarf over her bottle-green overcoat, the russet gloves warm on her hands.

Since the gloves were a gift from Arch, she hesitated to wear them, but they were so fashionable and supple and toasty. Besides, since Christmas, Arch had only been polite and kind. He'd abandoned the phony flirting he'd adopted as some strange way of apologizing for staring at her leg. As if acting attracted to her was preferable to staring.

He was much better company now that he acted normal.

Then she pulled herself tall. Only with cheer and confidence could she succeed.

Lillian opened the door, and bells jingled. In dim light, rows of shelves marched like soldiers, and a soda fountain ran along the right side of the store.

"May I help you, miss?" A matronly woman stood behind a cash register at a counter to the right.

"Hi, I'm Lillian Avery, the new pharmacist."

"Oh yes. Mr. Dixon's expecting you. I'm Mabel Connelly. Miss Felton isn't here today—she's the other cashier."

"I'm looking forward to working with both of you." Lillian headed down the center aisle, past shelves crammed with goods. No signs labelled the rows, which explained why Mary had a hard time finding things. That would be easy to fix.

At the back of the store, the prescription counter sat on her left, with a door straight ahead. In the prescription area, shelves were lined with bottles and boxes. The top shelves displayed colorful old apothecary jars with their marvelous Latin names.

Behind the counter stood a gentleman in his sixties with a round belly, glasses, and thick silver hair. That had to be Mr. Dixon. He handed a paper bag to a young lady and then held out a jar of marbles to the little boy at her side and told him to choose one.

How sweet. She'd like working here.

When the patients departed, Lillian approached with her most confident expression. "Mr. Dixon? Good morning. I'm Lillian Avery."

He grunted and glanced at his wristwatch. "You're five minutes early."

"Yes, sir." Why did he sound disappointed?

He opened the door and pointed to the stockroom to her right. "Put your things in here. Not happy about hiring a girl. Customers won't like it, won't like it at all. But you'll have to do."

Apparently Mr. Dixon reserved his warmth for little boy customers. She stuffed her gloves in her pockets and hung up her coat, scarf, and hat. "I assure you, I'm a hard worker. You won't be sorry."

Another grunt, and he gestured back between the shelves. "This here's Albert Myers. He's my main delivery boy, stock clerk, and soda jerk. Reggie's my other clerk. You'll meet him tomorrow."

Albert stepped forward. He wasn't a boy, but a man in his thirties, with deep red hair and a friendly freckled face. "Hello, Miss Avery. Welcome."

"Thank you. I'm glad to be here." She straightened her white coat over her brown skirt and cream-colored blouse. "Where should I start?"

Mr. Dixon poured tablets onto a counting tray. "Go learn your way around out front. I expect my employees to know where everything is."

"Of course, sir." She had to be prepared to answer any question.

Lillian returned to the main store and puffed out a breath. So the man was grumpy. She'd manage.

She strolled the perimeter of the store to note the general layout. After she finished, she'd study each aisle to become familiar with the stock.

Halfway down the side aisle, Albert caught up to her and set down a cardboard box. "Don't let old Dixon get under your skin, miss."

She smiled at him. "I won't."

"Good." He set boxes of razor blades on the shelf. "He ain't as bad as he sounds. I was a no-good scoundrel, and he took me under his wing and gave me a job when no one else in town would."

Lillian scanned the shaving supplies. "I like how he gave that little boy a marble."

"Yeah, he likes kids. Never had any of his own. Never married, you know, but he dotes on his nephew. That's why I'm here. Me and his nephew go way back. Used to run with a bad crowd, but he never gave up on us."

Yes, she'd like working here, indeed. "Thank you, Albert."

She continued around the perimeter, envisioning improvements. Signs, better lighting, and pleasant displays up front. Strip away some of the posters on the windows to let in the sun and show off the wares. But not for a few weeks.

First, she had to win over her boss with hard work.

At the rear of the store in front of the prescription counter, she studied the last row of goods, the proprietary medicines. She'd receive the most questions about them.

Laxatives, antacids, liver pills . . .

"Miss Avery!" Mr. Dixon hissed from behind the counter.

She spun around. "Yes?"

His jowly face went pale, but fire lit up his eyes. He jerked his head to the door. "Come here this instant."

What had she done wrong? Her stomach squirmed, but she went to her boss.

He glared at her prosthesis. "What's wrong with your leg?"

Jim had told Mr. Dixon, hadn't he? She cleared her throat. "I lost it in an accident when I was five, but—"

"That's an artificial leg."

"Yes, sir, but—"

"You didn't say you were a cripple."

A sick feeling wormed around her windpipe. "I—I thought my brother told you."

Mr. Dixon's upper lip curled. "He failed to mention that. How am I supposed to get by with a cripple?"

She couldn't lose confidence, not now. "I've worked in pharmacies since high school, and I'm used to being on my feet all day. My references can vouch for me. I work as hard as any other pharmacist. Harder, in fact."

He closed his eyes and shook his head. "Don't you see? A drugstore represents good health to the community. How can someone so . . . so . . . disfigured represent good health?"

Lillian's eyes tingled, but she kept her chin high. "On the contrary. I represent overcoming adversity. Patients say I give them hope."

A deep grumble emanated from his throat. "I can't have you out front. You'll scare the customers away. Stay behind the counter."

Lillian gripped the hem of her white coat. Behind the counter? She'd only be half good behind the counter.

Mr. Dixon marched to his counting tray. "Finally get this position filled. Finally, and now I have to start looking again. Now we're at war. All the men will be drafted."

That sick feeling clamped her windpipe shut. He wanted to replace her, and she hadn't even started.

"Well, what are you waiting for?" He gestured to the shelves. "Learn your way around."

"Yes, sir," she choked out and headed for the farthest shelf. Thank goodness she'd trained herself not to cry, because her eyes burned.

She poked around the shelves, willing her brain to learn the layout, all very orderly. It wasn't hopeless. It couldn't be. As always, she'd be cheerful, work hard, and find a way to make herself indispensable. A month from now, he'd forget he ever wanted to replace her.

Lillian swept her hand down the shelf, memorizing the medications, and she paused.

Phenobarbital, one-half grain, in five-hundred-tablet bottles. Ten bottles.

"My word," she whispered. Why on earth would the store need over five thousand tablets of the sedative?

She opened her mouth to ask, then shut it. Asking questions today didn't seem wise.

Probably a simple ordering error, an extra zero. Poor Albert had meant to order one bottle and ordered ten. Mr. Dixon must have hated that.

He hated everything. A dark wave plunged through her, but she wrestled it back. No, he loved children and he had given Albert a chance.

If only he'd give her a chance too.

5

Boston Navy Yard

How could Arch's palms sweat when the temperature was below freezing?

He and Jim strode down the pier at the Boston Navy Yard toward their new destroyer.

"What a great assignment." Jim grinned in the morning sunshine. "We're serving together again, and in Boston."

"Yes, great." Arch tried to return the grin. Yes, he was glad of those things as well, especially with the intriguing Lillian Avery in town. But why a bucking little destroyer that could snap like a twig? Why the frigid U-boat-infested North Atlantic? Some said U-boats were on their way to the East Coast, but the Navy hadn't said a word about instituting coastal convoys.

"The USS *Ettinger*." Jim paused beside the Gleaves class destroyer, same class as the *Atwood*. "We saw her launching almost a year ago, the day I started falling in love with Mary."

Arch barked out a laugh. "Took you a while, old pal."

Jim knocked on his temple with a gloved fist. "Tough noggin."

Perhaps thick skulls ran in the family. When Arch flirted with Lillian, she shut him down like a leaky boiler valve. But when he didn't flirt, she relaxed. How long would it take her to trust him? He wasn't used to waiting for a woman's affection, but Lillian was worth the wait.

Jim hiked up the gangway, and with a steadying breath, Arch followed. He needed Jim's friendship now, his cheer and his faith.

The gangway bounced and jangled underfoot, and the tremors returned to his hands. He gripped his seabag with both hands to make it stop.

The deck of the *Ettinger* resembled the *Atwood*—the bridge superstructure and two funnels, with two 5-inch guns at the bow and two at the stern. Only this deck wasn't tilted at a grotesque angle and covered in flames, spilled fuel oil, and mutilated bodies.

Arch slammed his eyes shut and mumbled a prayer. He couldn't make a bad impression today.

On the quarterdeck, Arch and Jim faced aft and saluted the flag, then saluted the officer of the deck.

"Ensign James Avery, reporting for duty, sir."

"Ensign Archer Vandenberg, reporting for duty, sir."

The officer, a tall, trim man with sandy hair, took their orders. "Welcome aboard. I'm Lt. John Odom, first lieutenant. The captain's on the bridge. Palonsky, escort Mr. Avery and Mr. Vandenberg to the captain."

"Aye aye, sir." The seaman marched toward the bridge superstructure. He glanced over his shoulder at Arch and Jim. "Say, you fellows don't look as dry and dull as the other officers. Something tells me you like a good laugh."

And something in Palonsky's eyes told Arch that if they gave this man any slack, he'd turn it into a vaudeville show. "Nothing wrong with a good laugh—after your work is done."

"And done well," Jim said with as stern a look as his face could muster. Which wasn't very stern.

"Yes, sir. Aye aye, sir." Palonsky sauntered down the deck with an exaggerated swing to his arms. "I'll do my job well, sir. Only laugh during liberty, sir. Anything else, sir?"

"Carry on, Palonsky." Arch glanced at Jim, whose face contorted with restrained laughter. At least one man on this ship would be entertaining.

The men entered the bridge superstructure and climbed the ladder to the pilothouse.

A wiry little dark-haired officer accepted their salutes and their orders—Lt. Cdr. Alvin Buckner. Despite his size, he had a forceful air about him, like Humphrey Bogart, but with a butter-smooth patrician voice. A fellow New Englander.

"Very well." Captain Buckner examined their orders. "Both of you served on the *Atwood*. A shame. I know Captain Durant. I'm pleased to hear he was given command of a cruiser."

"Yes, sir," Arch said. "We're pleased too. A fine man."

"Yes." Small dark eyes bore into Jim. "Mr. Avery, you've already served in gunnery. You'll be my assistant engineer under Lt. Emmett Taylor."

Poor Jim, assigned to the deep bowels of the ship.

"And Mr. Vandenberg." That riveting gaze turned his way. "We need an assistant first lieutenant. You'll serve under Lt. John Odom."

"Thank you, sir." Arch gave the first genuine smile he'd felt all day. The first lieutenant and his assistant supervised the deck gang in the open air.

"Get settled in your cabin and report to duty at 1000. You are dismissed."

None of the warmth they were used to with Captain Durant, but what did that matter?

Jim and Arch trotted down the ladder to the wardroom.

"I'm jealous," Jim said. "While I slave in the engine room with the 'black gang,' you'll work on your suntan."

"That's why tourists flock to Boston in January—the sun."

"Why else?"

They crossed the wardroom and filed down the narrow passageway into officers' quarters. A typical cabin, with a double bunk, two lockers, a sink, and a desk. Spartan, simple, and right.

Arch plopped his seabag on the lower bunk as always, since Jim liked the top bunk. Why did the cabin seem smaller, more restrictive? Why did the overhead press down on him?

His breath quickened, ragged and shaky. What was wrong with him? Why couldn't he pull himself together?

"Say, buddy. You all right?" Jim shrugged off his overcoat. "You look pale. Are you coming down with something?"

That was it. Surely, that was it. "I—I might be."

Jim chuckled. "Buckner won't like it, but you'd better see a doctor."

"Yes." His forehead did feel clammy. "I will."

★ ★ ★

"Nothing wrong with you." Dr. Blake hunched over Arch's chart and scribbled in it. "Your exam is normal. It's all in your nerves."

Arch tried not to shiver while sitting in his skivvies on the exam table in the Navy Yard dispensary. "I'm fine most of the time, but sometimes I shake. And I have a hard time sleeping. The nightmares."

"The sinking was back in November. You should be over it by now."

Arch's lips pressed together. Didn't he already know that?

The Navy doctor pulled a prescription pad from his desk

drawer. "We don't usually see such weakness of nerves in officers. It's concerning."

Weak? Arch squared his bare shoulders. "Sir, I assure you I can perform my duties. I'm stronger than whatever this is."

"I hope so." He ripped a prescription from the pad. "Give this to the nurse. She'll give you some pills to help you sleep. Be careful. They're habit-forming. And don't drink while taking them."

"I'm not a drinking man, sir."

"Too bad." Dr. Blake raised a wry smile. "You might have licked this by now. Wine, women, and song are quite effective. The sailor's favorite remedy since the dawn of time."

Arch returned the smile. "Right now I'll have to settle for song."

"Sing a lot, then. I see no reason to intervene at this time, but if this continues . . ." He tucked the prescription pad in a desk drawer. "I'd hate to survey you out of the Navy with our country at war."

Arch's face went ice-cold. Surveyed out? He could lose his commission? After going against his father's wishes and attending the Naval Academy? After graduating near the top of his class? After serving with distinction on the *Atwood*? He could be discharged because his hands shook?

Nonsense. "It won't come to that, sir."

The doctor gave a noncommittal grunt and left the exam room.

Arch put on his dress blues. He'd earned the right to wear this uniform. He loved everything it stood for. He loved the Navy life. He couldn't return to where he'd been, to the superficial snobs using other people for personal gain. *Lord, help me lick this.*

He knotted his tie. If he couldn't lick it, he'd hide it.

6

Why had she told Mr. Dixon she could work on her feet all day?

Lillian trudged up Monument Avenue, trying not to limp. Her previous employers had allowed her to rest her left knee on a stool, relieving the pressure on her stump. She didn't dare ask Mr. Dixon if she could use one, but if she wasn't careful, soon she'd have sores. Then she'd have to use crutches while they healed. How could she work on crutches?

She hated taking off her prosthesis before bedtime, but tonight she had no choice. She'd hobble on her stupid crutches, heat up a can of soup, and curl up with a book. Not how most girls her age spent a Friday night, but she'd never been like girls her age anyway.

The brick building sported white wood trim—similar to her home in Vermilion, yet so different. The shade of brick perhaps, or the cut of the trim? Or simply the lack of a lawn.

Lillian mounted the granite steps and paused on the landing to open the door to her right.

The door in front of her swung open. An elderly lady stopped in the doorway, wearing a fur-edged black coat, and she smiled. "You must be the new girl downstairs."

"Yes, ma'am. I'm Lillian Avery. I moved in a week ago."

"I'm Opal Harrison."

Lillian peered past Mrs. Harrison to the bank of stairs. "You have a piano, don't you?"

"Oh dear. You must have heard my grandchildren the other day. I'm sorry they bothered you."

"Not at all." She smiled into the lady's clear blue eyes. "I come from a big family. Someone was always banging on the piano. It makes this place sound more like home."

"If you'd ever like to play . . ."

Lillian tensed. Did she sound like she'd been fishing for an invitation? "I couldn't impose. I didn't mean—"

Mrs. Harrison laid a black-gloved hand on Lillian's arm. "Nonsense, dear. I can't play anymore with my rheumatism, and my grandchildren—well, they don't visit often. Only my dear Giffy, but he never did learn to play. I adore music, so you'd be doing a lonely old lady a favor. Please?"

How could Lillian say no to such a sweet face? "Well, if you really wouldn't mind—"

"Tomorrow then? Eleven o'clock?"

"I'll be there. But I'll warn you—I'm not that good."

Those blue eyes lit up. "Even better. I used to give piano lessons. Good-bye now."

"Good-bye." Lillian chuckled as she unlocked the door. What had she gotten herself into?

Inside the apartment, a different kind of music greeted her—mingled male and female laughter.

Oh no. Company.

Jim and Mary, Arch Vandenberg, Quintessa Beaumont, and Quintessa's new boyfriend, Clifford White, filled the sofa and chairs in the living room.

Quintessa dashed to Lillian with her blonde curls bouncing. "Congratulations! You survived your first week of work. We're taking you out to celebrate."

"Dinner and a movie." Arch draped his arm along the back of the sofa.

"Oh, I'm afraid not. I'm so tired." She sent Jim a pleading look and pressed her hand to her left thigh in a silent message. "All I want is to sit down."

Her brother grinned. "You can sit down for dinner, sit down at the movies."

How could such an intelligent man be so thickheaded? "I really don't—"

"No arguing. We made reservations for a party of six." Quintessa grabbed her arm and guided her toward the bedroom Lillian shared with Mary. "Let me help you pick out a dress."

"Chinese food," Jim called after her. "Your favorite."

Lillian glared at him over her shoulder. He knew she couldn't resist Chinese food.

Quintessa shut the bedroom door and opened the closet. "Ooh, I like this emerald one. Dressy but not too fancy." She clutched the dress and faced Lillian, her eyebrows tented. "Please come. It'll be less awkward with Jim."

Lillian sighed and shed her coat and work clothes. The details were sketchy, but Jim had been infatuated with Quintessa in high school. Apparently the blonde had come to Boston to reignite the flame—but Jim and Mary fell in love instead.

If Lillian's presence would help, how could she decline? "All right, then."

"Good girl. You can keep Arch company." She winked at Lillian. "He's cute, isn't he?"

"He certainly thinks so."

"Oh!" Quintessa gasped and laughed. "I take that back. You're a naughty girl."

Lillian reached for her dress. "Be kind to me, or I'll stay home."

"He's really a nice fellow, you know. A gentleman, but down-to-earth."

Wiggling into the emerald wool jersey allowed her to make a face unseen. Even if he were the finest man in the world, she couldn't indulge in a crush.

★ ★ ★

Lillian dug the serving spoon into the plate of chop suey. "I was heartbroken to learn chop suey isn't true Chinese food. I love it."

"As long as you use chopsticks, you're fine." Arch took the platter and served himself.

Although she didn't want to sit next to Arch, it was better than having him across from her and in her line of sight.

Lillian took the plate of sweet-and-sour pork from Clifford, a brown-haired businessman in his early thirties. Quintessa had met him at Filene's when she'd sold him a scarf for his mother for Christmas.

Across the round table, Jim gave her an expectant look.

She'd skirted questions about Dixon's Drugs on the cab ride, and she planned to continue skirting. "How are things on the *Ettinger*?"

"Different from the *Atwood*, that's for sure," Jim said.

"In what way?" Lillian poured hot tea into her cute little round teacup.

"Hmm." Arch squinted at Jim. "The officers are more distant. The captain's all business, and the crew takes his lead."

Mary rested her hand on Jim's forearm, her eyes starry. "If I know you two, you'll warm things up on that ship."

"That's our goal," Arch said. "We saw excellent leadership from our previous CO. He believed in cooperation and mutual respect between officers and men. But he was also firm and decisive in a crisis. It works."

"Sometimes." Clifford used a fork and knife. "But a boss needs to be tough and distant at first to establish authority."

Jim shook his head. "That must be Buckner's philosophy, eh, Arch?"

"Apparently." His clipped tone said he agreed with Jim but was too polite to disagree with Clifford.

Lillian studied Arch out of the corner of her eye. His double-breasted navy blue jacket fit perfectly, the sleeves exposing a quarter-inch of his white shirt. A narrow band of gold braid above the cuff designated his rank of ensign, and a gold star denoted him as a line officer, in the line of command. Strong, nimble fingers worked the chopsticks with ease.

"Since Buckner and the senior officers keep a cool distance, Jim and I, as junior officers, want to bridge the gap. Someone in command needs to listen to the men." Arch's wavy blond hair gleamed in the light of the silk lanterns, and his expression gleamed more. With that combination of strength and compassion, he'd make a fine officer.

Lillian jerked her attention to her chop suey, the crunchy vegetables and savory sauce.

Clifford shrugged. "If you're too friendly at first, they'll walk all over you."

Jim pointed a chopstick at Arch. "Keep a tight rein on that Palonsky."

Arch laughed. "I will."

"Palonsky?" Lillian asked.

"Warren Palonsky." Arch turned those bright blue eyes to her. "He's on my deck gang. A born actor and comedian. I'm told he already does a mean impression of me."

Lillian could imagine the nose in the air, the raised pinky, the measured high-class tones, but that didn't truly capture this man who wanted to listen to those under his command. "You're told? You haven't seen it?"

"I don't want to." Humor crinkled the corners of his eyes.

Lillian focused on eating her fried rice with her chopsticks, a difficult task.

"Here. Try it this way." Arch held his chopsticks close together and used them like a fork to scoop up his rice. "Much easier."

Lillian tried, and it worked. "Thank you."

Next to her, Clifford and Quintessa conversed, and Lillian's throat clamped. If Jim and Mary began a private conversation, she'd be stuck with Arch.

"Lillian." Mary came to her rescue. "I wonder if your boss is also being tough to establish authority."

Only a partial rescue. "Maybe."

"Mr. Dixon?" Jim's forehead creased. "Are you having a difficult time?"

How could she state this diplomatically in public? "He isn't pleased to hire someone with my . . . condition. Apparently he didn't know." She skewered her brother with her gaze.

"Didn't think it mattered. It's never been a problem before."

Her heart softened at Jim's faith in her. "But it does matter."

Arch wiped his mouth with his napkin. "I disagree. When it comes down to it, the only thing that matters is whether or not you can do the job."

Lillian's stomach squirmed. She never liked discussing her condition with anyone outside the family, but she also wasn't used to no-nonsense support from outside the family. "No, when it comes down to it, the only thing that matters is whether or not Mr. Dixon *believes* I can do the job."

"Then you'll just have to show him." A firm nod and a flash of a smile, and Arch returned to his meal.

Lillian sipped her tea, and her good foot jiggled. No matter how sweetly he talked, she knew what men were like. Even if he was Jim's best friend.

"You'll win him over in nothing flat," Quintessa said with a big smile. "I know the type. A grumpy old man with a heart of gold."

Lillian harrumphed. "More like a grumpy old man with a heart *for* gold."

"Goodness," Quintessa said. "You say the funniest things."

"It's true." Lillian lifted one shoulder. "They're customers to him, not patients. Sales, not prescriptions. Yes, you need money to run the store, but the main purpose of a drugstore is to help sick people get well. That's why I became a pharmacist."

Arch gave her a look too long and appreciative for her comfort.

She fixed her gaze on Jim. "I'll give you an example. Today we received a prescription for two hundred tablets of phenobarbital. Two hundred!"

"That's high?" Jim winked at her.

"Yes, Jimmy. It's a big number." She gave him a teasing tip of her chin. "It's a habit-forming drug, and it can be dangerous. So I asked Mr. Dixon, and he didn't bat an eye. The doctor wrote the prescription, he said, so the patient must need that many. Besides, the patient could pay, so why worry?"

Quintessa's mouth twitched in a smile. "You won't have to worry about your salary."

Lillian scooped up some fried rice. No, she wouldn't. Until Mr. Dixon hired her replacement.

7

Off Montauk Point, Long Island
Wednesday, January 14, 1942

A good stiff wind, a brace of chill sea mist, and Arch felt awake for the first time all day. It was almost noon.

He stepped closer to the forward funnel to allow sailors to pass as they swept the deck.

Later today, he'd flush those pills down the head. Phenobarbital. Habit-forming, the doctor had said. Dangerous, Lillian had said. Worse than being drunk, in Arch's opinion.

He'd avoided taking the pills until last night, his first night at sea since the sinking. When he was still tossing and turning at 0200, he'd succumbed to temptation, and he'd slept. Boy, had he slept, but the kind of sleep that left him more exhausted than the night before.

After Mr. Odom caught him fast asleep over his paperwork earlier this morning, Arch vowed never to take the fool medicine again. Better a fitful night than this.

Arch passed two seamen scrubbing their laundry. Although he'd dreaded going back to sea, perhaps this was the best way to conquer his nerves. Getting back on the old horse and all that. Besides, at sea, he felt God's presence most keenly—the enormity and depth, the mystery and beauty, the peace and power.

He peered north. A cloudy sky, but with good visibility. Not good enough to see Boston and the lovely Lillian Avery, though.

His mouth puckered. He should feel guilty longing for port. The U-boats had arrived. Two days before, the British passenger ship *Cyclops* had fallen prey to a German torpedo only three hundred miles east of Cape Cod.

The Navy had issued a warning of ten U-boats off the East Coast, and just that morning, they'd closed the ports of Boston, Portsmouth, and Portland due to the threat. The *Ettinger* wasn't on official patrol, only testing her sea legs with her new crew, but Buckner felt it wouldn't hurt for the Germans to see the might of the US Navy.

The might? Arch ducked some flapping laundry. The few warships in eastern ports were officially assigned to convoy escort across the North Atlantic to England, and the number and quality of ships assigned to coastal patrol would make Hitler laugh. Nowhere near enough to institute coastal convoys.

Despite the threat, despite the dire need at sea, Arch longed to sit next to an amber-haired pharmacist in a green dress.

She should always wear green. It brought out the color in her hazel eyes and made her hair glow. Granted, he'd like her in mousy gray. So lively and genuine, a woman who didn't need him or even want him. Yet sometimes he saw a flash of fear and insecurity. Perhaps someday she wouldn't mind a man to stand by her side, a man to lean on.

A group of sailors stood by the davits of the whaleboat, inspecting the tackle, the system of lines and pulleys that lowered the boat to the sea.

"I tell you, boys. It's only a matter of time." Seaman Winters ran his hand along a line. "It'll be worse than the seas off Iceland."

"I heard over eighty men went down with the *Cyclops*. And what are we doing? We're swimming laps."

"Yeah, and did you see the shore lit up like Christmas last night? Why don't they order a blackout, huh?"

"The Nazis will turn this shore into a shooting gallery, and we ain't got nothing to shoot back with."

Arch winced. While he agreed with every word, grumbling was bad for morale. He stepped forward.

"Say, fellas." Warren Palonsky scowled and raised his hands as if brandishing a tommy gun. "You wanna see a shooting gallery? I'll show you a shooting gallery." His voice managed to mix Buckner with Bogart, and he sprayed imaginary bullets out to sea.

The men laughed and whooped, and Arch smiled. Palonsky always lightened the mood.

"What's going on here?" Lieutenant Odom strode over in his overcoat with his own scowl in place. "Pipe down and do your duties."

The men snapped to attention. "Aye aye, sir."

Odom glanced Arch's way. "Mr. Vandenberg. You were about to tell them the same thing, were you not?"

Arch gave him a noncommittal smile. "May I have a word with you, Mr. Odom?"

"Very well." He followed Arch to a quieter section of the deck. "Yes?"

"Just so you know, that was the tail end of that exchange. The men were grumbling, and Palonsky wanted to lift their spirits."

Odom shifted his jaw to one side. "They were goofing off."

"Only for a minute, sir. The men are on edge. They've served on convoy duty. They've seen ships go down, bodies in the water. Some of them rescued the survivors of the

Reuben James and the *Atwood*. Some of them were on those ships. They're nervous, and Palonsky took their minds off the danger."

"Maybe. But he also took their minds off their work."

"I'll talk to him, sir."

"Good." Odom departed.

Arch huffed. How did the man get through the Naval Academy without a sense of humor?

"Palonsky?" He waved over the seaman.

"Yes, sir?" The sailor stood rigidly at attention.

"At ease. You have some comedic skills."

He shrugged. "Trying to boost morale, sir. The men are wound tight, and Buck—" His gray-blue eyes went wide.

"Please speak freely." Arch angled his shoulders toward Palonsky. "This is confidential."

Palonsky's mouth worked, and his gaze darted around. "It's just . . . Captain Buckner and Mr. Odom are hard men, sir. The boys can't work like this. They'll snap, now that we're at war."

"I know. However, the comedy needs restraint. The purpose is to aid the men in their duties, not to interfere, correct?"

"Yes, sir."

"So why don't we confine the outright comic routines to quarters and the mess? When you're at light duties, perhaps a few jokes."

A spark of mischief lit. "Want me to run the scripts past you first, sir?"

Oh boy. Arch would certainly be the subject of the next comic routine. He smiled and clapped the man on the shoulder. "Not necessary. I trust you. Carry on."

"Aye aye, sir." Palonsky returned to the tackle.

The alarm clanged. General quarters!

Arch's heart careened into his throat, his knees bent, hands splayed wide, braced for impact.

"All hands to battle stations."

Dear Lord, a U-boat. Arch knew what to do, where to go, but he froze, braced, immobile, while men scurried to their stations.

"Lord, help me." He broke free, stumbled forward. "I'm not below decks. Not trapped."

Before him, in the doorway to the bridge superstructure, Mr. Odom talked to the executive officer, Lt. Ted Hayes. Odom beckoned to Arch.

He worked his way to them, pulling himself together. "What's going on? Sound contact?"

"Message from Newport. A Navy patrol plane reported a sunken tanker sixty miles southeast of Montauk Light."

"U-boat." Arch swallowed hard. "We're chasing it."

"No, we're searching for survivors. A lifeboat and a raft were spotted."

"Then we're chasing—"

"No." Odom's face scrunched up as if he'd eaten something sour. "Those are not our orders. Our orders are to rescue survivors."

"It's stupid." Hayes crossed thick arms. "This is a destroyer. Designed to destroy U-boats. But we'll be good little boys and do as we're told."

"Better hope that U-boat crosses our path. Then we can sink it," Odom said.

"Yes." Arch put false cheer into his voice. "Better hope."

By the time Arch reached the quarterdeck, Chief Boatswain's Mate Ralph Lynch had gathered the men in the damage control repair party—a machinist's mate, a gun captain, a talker, and repairmen for machinery, electrical, and structural integrity.

Arch briefed them on the situation. Although the *Ettinger* was performing a rescue, with a U-boat in the vicinity she had to be ready for combat.

The crew set Condition One, closing and dogging hatches and doors and preparing tools, first-aid supplies, and fire-fighting equipment.

A few minutes of rushed activity. Then watching and waiting. Arch scoured the horizon through binoculars. A periscope, a wake, a lifeboat, a signal flare, a column of smoke, oil on the surface—anything to guide them. Deep in the hull below, the sonar crew would be monitoring for a submerged submarine.

Arch's vision through the binoculars blurred. Stupid shaking hands. He flexed and clenched his hands, over and over, as if he only wanted to warm them.

An hour passed. The stewards brought up sandwiches and coffee from the mess. While the communication, navigation, and propulsion divisions would be humming with activity, the deck gang and the gunners watched. Waited. No opportunity to act. No opportunity to relax.

"Ahoy!" a lookout cried from the signal bridge, pointing to port.

Arch spun and pressed the binoculars to his eyes. A lifeboat. *Thank you, God. Not a sub.*

"Away fire and rescue party," sounded over the loudspeaker, and the destroyer slowed, the familiar pitch of engines telegraphing the precise speed to Arch.

The rescue party gathered by the whaleboat, including Mr. Odom and the ship's medic, Pharmacist's Mate Parnell Lloyd. The whaleboat had already been loaded with blankets, first-aid supplies, and rum.

Arch returned to his station. U-boats sometimes lingered near their victims to prey on rescue ships. They couldn't lower their guard.

In the lifeboat, hands waved above blond heads.

"Lower the cargo nets," Arch ordered the sailors by the rails. "Prepare to aid the survivors."

They heaved the nets over the side, then tossed lines to the lifeboat to help them heave to.

Arch grasped the lifeline. Twenty-four survivors, it looked like, if they'd sit still long enough for him to count. But they waved and cheered and called out in a Scandinavian language. "Anyone speak English?" he shouted.

"*Ja!* I do." A stout middle-aged man pulled on the line. "*Takk. Tusen takk.* Thank you."

Arch ordered three sailors to climb down the net and assist the survivors. "What happened? Where are you from?"

"The Panamanian tanker *Norness*. But we are *norsk*."

Arch addressed the talker behind him. "Call the bridge. Find out if anyone on board speaks Norwegian." He turned back to the survivors working their way up the net. "What happened?"

A long string of Norwegian hit his ears, and it wasn't happy. "U-boat. Three torpedoes."

Arch glanced out over the waves, straining to see the enemy. "How many men?"

"Forty. Here we are twenty-four."

"Mr. Vandenberg, sir?" the talker called. "Captain got word from New Bedford. A fishing boat picked up nine survivors. Still one raft unaccounted for."

"Thank you." Seven more to find. He grasped a hand and heaved a man onto the deck.

"*Takk. Takk.*" A young man in nothing but an undershirt and shorts shivered hard.

Two crewmen wrapped the survivor in a blanket and poured rum down his throat.

Arch shuddered. Not even two months earlier he'd been the waterlogged flotsam wrapped in blankets and soaked in rum.

He dragged another man on board, the English speaker, splattered head to toe in black oil. Someone tossed Arch a blanket, and he flung it around the man's trembling shoulders. "You're cold."

"We are from Norge. We are not cold." The man's blue lips broke into a quaking grin.

Arch chuckled. "When were you sunk? How long were you in the lifeboat?"

The Norwegian downed the rum a sailor offered him and wiped his mouth. "First torpedo at 0130."

Arch yanked up his coat sleeve to see his wristwatch. It was 1330. Twelve hours. Thank goodness the men of the *Atwood* had been rescued immediately. Destroyers only had two whaleboats, and the life rafts consisted of a rubber ring with netting in the center, useless in frigid waters.

"You are cold?" The Norwegian sailor hunkered in the blanket.

"Me? No."

"You . . . you . . ." He held out one hand and wiggled it.

Arch shook. Yes, his hands shook. He forced a smile. "Maybe a little cold. Let's get you somewhere warmer."

A sailor escorted the man below, and Arch hauled another survivor to safety. Arch had survived too. He was safe. But when would he be free?

8

A man with thinning gray hair and a droopy mustache handed Lillian a prescription. "Mr. Dixon's never had a clerk at the counter before."

A common misconception, despite her white coat. "I'm actually a pharmacist."

"But you're a . . ." His nose wrinkled. "Girl."

"Yes, and a pharmacist too." She hefted up her sweetest smile, one her twin sister Lucy might wear, and examined the prescription for digitalis. "Everything looks in order."

Gray eyebrows drew together. "It's for my heart. I'd rather have a real pharmacist fill it."

"Don't worry, Mr. Barnes," Mr. Dixon called from the back, where he was compounding an ointment. "She does a fair enough job. Would I hire an incompetent?"

Mr. Barnes's face relaxed. "Of course not."

"I'll have this ready in ten minutes, sir." Lillian typed out the prescription label. That was the closest Mr. Dixon had come to a compliment in the last two weeks, and Lillian smiled. She'd win him over.

After she finished the label, Lillian shook a few dozen digitalis tablets onto the counting tray, counted them by fives into the collecting chute, poured the extra back into the bulk bottle, then poured thirty tablets into an amber glass vial. She gummed the back of the label and applied it to the bottle, nice and neat.

"Mr. Fenwick, your medication is ready." Mr. Dixon stood at the counter with an ointment jar. "Ah, good morning, Mrs. Harrison. I'll take your prescription in a minute."

"Thank you, Mr. Dixon."

At the sound of her neighbor's voice, Lillian peeked around the wall. "Hi, Mrs. Harrison."

"There you are, sweet girl. I tell you, Cyrus, you're blessed to have this young lady. Smart as a whip."

Mr. Dixon grunted and peered around. "Mr. Fenwick?"

"Cyrus, when you're done, would you please help me find an antacid?" Mrs. Harrison tapped her glasses. "I can't seem to read the labels."

"May I help her?" Lillian gave the vial of digitalis to her boss. "Mr. Barnes would prefer if you dispensed this to him, and it's ready."

Mr. Dixon narrowed his eyes at Lillian's prosthesis and heaved a sigh. "I suppose you'll need to go out front sometime."

"Thank you, sir." She was making progress today, and she darted out the door before he could change his mind. If only calf-length dresses were fashionable as they were when she was in high school. The knee-length hemlines in vogue didn't hide the top of her prosthesis or the hinged steel bars connecting it to the leather strap around her thigh.

Mrs. Harrison handed Mr. Dixon her prescription, asked for Albert to deliver it, and led Lillian to the antacid section. "It's too dark in here for my old eyes."

Lillian pulled a bottle of calcium carbonate off the shelf and lowered her voice. "It's also too dark in here for my young eyes. Makes the whole store look dingy and old-fashioned too."

"You should tell Mr. Dixon."

"I don't dare. He doesn't like having a lady pharmacist, especially . . ." She shook her head. Best not to talk of that.

Mrs. Harrison squinted at the shelves. "Maybe if your suggestions brought in customers, he'd see your worth. I've known Cyrus for years. Bedrock of the community, that man, but he does like money."

Lillian's mouth twitched. "Yes, he does."

"I only shop here because it's on the way home from the City Square station, and I trust Cyrus. But when I just want to do some shopping, I go to Morton's on Winthrop Square. So bright and modern."

Lillian rotated the bottle in her hand. Perhaps that would be the best tack to take.

After Mrs. Harrison selected her antacid, she headed to the front cash register with her purchase, and Lillian returned to the prescription area.

Mr. Dixon was mixing an elixir. "Did you help her?"

"Yes." Lillian took the bulk bottles back to the shelves. "She has a hard time reading the labels because it isn't bright enough in here. We wondered if we could improve the lighting. It would increase sales."

"I doubt that. It would only increase my electric bill."

Lillian set the bottles on the shelf and put on her cheeriest voice. "I think it would be worth it. A bright store is so inviting, especially on a rainy day like today. And I'm sure Mrs. Harrison isn't alone in her difficulties, but most people are too proud to ask for help. They'll just go to another store."

"I've never had complaints. My father established this store in 1878. It's a Charlestown institution, and our customers are loyal. Extra lightbulbs? Do you want me to take that out of your salary, young lady?"

Not a bad idea. Perhaps they could make a deal where she swallowed the cost, and if sales increased, she could earn back her salary. "I wouldn't mind."

"Foolish naïveté of youth." He poured liquid from a graduated cylinder into a glass bottle. "A customer's coming. Man the counter, please."

"Yes, sir." She sighed, then smiled for the patient, a light-haired man in his thirties. "Good morning. How may I help you?"

"I need this filled. Have it delivered, please."

Lillian frowned at the prescription for Harvey Jones for three hundred tablets of phenobarbital. Goodness, they received lots of prescriptions for large quantities of phenobarbital, all from Dr. Maynard Kane. What she'd seen as an unusually high inventory of the sedative seemed to be the store's normal usage.

"Is something wrong?" Mr. Jones asked.

On Dr. Kane's printed form, his handwritten order was complete and used proper abbreviations and terminology. Lillian gave a flimsy smile. "I was worried we might not have that much in stock, but we did get a delivery today."

"All right."

"Albert will deliver it in his afternoon rounds." Lillian pulled down a stock bottle.

Why did Dr. Kane write so many prescriptions for this medication? Her education told her to call and ask. Lillian stepped to the telephone and dialed the physician's number.

"Let me guess," Mr. Dixon said. "The doc forgot the sig."

She stuck her finger in the dial for seven and swung it around. "No, the directions are there. But the quantity is extremely high."

"Hmm. Let me see."

Lillian nestled the receiver in the cradle and brought the prescription to Mr. Dixon. "Three hundred tablets. I've seen several prescriptions for high quantities of phenobarbital from Dr. Kane."

Mr. Dixon gave her a look as if she were daft. "Some patients require higher doses."

"But why all from Dr. Kane?"

"His office is across the street. And what are you going to do? Question his judgment? He'd be furious."

Lillian shifted her weight off her bad leg. "Not if I word it tactfully."

"Tactfully? Doctors hate it when we disturb them and question their orders. Choose your battles. Call if the prescription is incomplete. Call if a patient could be harmed."

"But the medication is habit-forming."

Mr. Dixon waved his arm toward the door. "The doctor knows the man's condition better than you. He knows the proper treatment. Besides, did that man look like a drug addict?"

"No, but . . ." What did a drug addict look like, anyway?

"First rule . . ." He lowered his thick gray brows and thrust the prescription back in her hand. "Never turn away a paying customer."

Lillian's muscles stiffened, but her spine felt limp. "No, sir. I won't."

The prescription was legal. Filling it wasn't wrong. And she couldn't afford to lose her job. It was hard enough to get this job as a crippled woman. It would be impossible to find a job if she were fired.

Her stomach squirmed. She'd have to keep a low profile for a while to undo today's damage.

★ ★ ★

Saturday, January 24, 1942

Lillian played Chopin's "Mazurka" on Opal Harrison's piano. The tension of the week pulsed into the piano keys—the worry over her job and the dread of the coming evening.

The *Ettinger* was in port. Jim and Arch would want to go out. If only Lillian had something else to do, but she didn't have any other friends in town. Arch hadn't flirted with her since Christmas, but she couldn't take any chances. She couldn't let herself become incapacitated again, weak again, hurt again.

"Softer, Lillian. Softer." Mrs. Harrison leaned back in her wing chair, her eyes shut and her gnarled hands in her lap. "It takes more strength to play softly than loudly, more control."

"Yes, ma'am." She finished the piece.

Mrs. Harrison picked up her eyeglasses from the end table. "You're a fine technical player. Out of practice, of course, but you have good technique and know your scales. A bit zealous in the allegro sections and impulsive in the adagios."

The same traits that had gotten her in trouble as a girl still plagued her piano playing, even though she tempered them in real life.

Mrs. Harrison put on her glasses. "Yes, a fine technical player."

Lillian sighed. She'd heard it since childhood. "But no heart."

"Oh? Why do you say that?"

"My playing is cold, no heart. I know." She ran her finger over the smooth keys.

"Mm." Mrs. Harrison sipped her tea. "Why do you play?"

Lillian traced the black keys in their patterns of twos and threes. "After my accident, I couldn't run or climb. But I couldn't sit still and play tea party with my twin sister. My mother understood, so she started me on the piano. At least my hands could be active."

"I have just the piece for you." She eased out of the chair and opened a cabinet.

"Nice and hard, I hope. I love a challenge."

"Oh yes, it'll be a challenge." She set the music in front of Lillian—"To a Wild Rose."

So much white. She liked her music as black as she liked her coffee, with lots of notes and complications. "I could play this without thinking."

"Ah yes. You can play it without *thinking*." Mrs. Harrison tapped her chest. "But you can't play it without *feeling*. You need to open your heart."

"My . . . heart?" Why not ask her to dance the rumba? "I can't."

Mrs. Harrison shuffled back to her chair. "I think you can."

Lillian's head wagged back and forth. Her heart was as ugly as her stump, and both needed to be concealed.

"Oh, sweet girl. You may be able to hide your feelings from people, but you can never hide them from the Lord."

Lillian spun to the older woman. She kept a polite distance from God. If she opened up to him, he'd see just how cold her heart was.

But didn't he know that already?

Her fingers gripped her necklace, and her mind flicked to the Bible verse Dad had tucked in the jewelry box, Hebrews 6:18–19: "We might have a strong consolation, who have fled for refuge to lay hold upon the hope set before us: Which hope we have as an anchor of the soul, both sure and stedfast."

Lillian stared at the music that required so much of her.

Consolation. Refuge. Hope. God promised those things if she held on to him.

Could she pay the price?

9

Off Cape Cod, Massachusetts
Monday, January 26, 1942

Arch laid his mackinaw on his bunk. How many men survived a sinking only to freeze to death in their underwear in the lifeboat? Not Arch. He slept fully clothed with his outerwear in reach.

Seated at their desk, Jim picked up an envelope, sniffed it, and grinned. "Still haven't opened it, eh? It's perfumed. From Miss Elizabeth Chamberlain."

Arch groaned. "Bitsy. My high school sweetheart who dumped me when I chose the Navy over the glittering life. That isn't love."

Jim held the envelope over his mouth and batted his eyelashes like a girl. "I've changed my tune, Archie-poo."

Best to ignore that nickname lest it take hold. Arch loosened his belt for his nap during the forenoon watch. "Yes, she changed her tune. Dating an officer is patriotic now. But if this war ever ends, she'll sweet-talk me into resigning my commission and joining Vandenberg Insurance."

"Maybe she sees your worth now and regrets her actions."

Arch plopped onto the lower bunk. "You have a woman who loves you for who you are, for richer or poorer, right?"

"Yes." Jim tapped the envelope on the desk.

"I want the same. What's wrong with that?"

"Nothing, but why not give Bitsy another chance? It's been a few years. We've all changed. Come on, read it." Jim flashed another grin and flung the envelope to Arch.

He let it fall to the deck. "You just want Bitsy to distract me from Lillian."

The laugh lines disappeared from Jim's smile. "I thought you'd given up."

"I promised to back off, and I have."

"But you haven't given up." Jim went to the sink and squeezed toothpaste onto his toothbrush.

Arch chose his words with care. "I'm getting to know her as a friend and letting her get to know me."

Jim grunted and stuck his toothbrush in his mouth. The most easygoing and congenial man in the world until it came to his little sister.

"Jim."

His friend faced him, scrubbing at his teeth.

Arch rested his elbows on his knees. "You said men reject her because of her leg."

He nodded.

"She probably wants someone to love her in spite of her leg, don't you think?"

Jim nodded but turned back to the sink.

"Maybe she dreams someone could love her *because* of her leg, love her because adversity has made her stronger."

Jim's gaze snapped back to him, his eyes wide.

Arch's jaw edged forward. "Please don't rule out the possibility that I could do so."

He choked, spat toothpaste into the sink, and swiped a washcloth over his mouth. "I didn't mean you weren't capable—"

"It's all right. You love your sister and want what's best for her."

One corner of Jim's mouth flicked up. "You know, she doesn't like you."

Arch stuffed his shod feet under the sheets and burrowed in. "See? You have nothing to worry about. Except the toothpaste on your chin."

Jim inspected his face in the mirror. "Makes me look distinguished."

With the air cleared, a warm breakfast in his stomach, and his survival gear in reach, perhaps he could sleep for once.

General quarters clanged on the alarm.

Arch bolted to sitting, his feet tangled in the blankets, his heart thudding so hard it hurt.

"GQ again?" Jim groaned and pulled on his mackinaw. "Three times yesterday and twice last night."

"Wonder what it is this time." Despite his effort to keep his voice light, it came out thin and strained. He grabbed his mackinaw and punched his arms through the sleeves.

Jim squinted at the overhead as if it held the answers. "Sound contact with a pocket of cold air? Sub sighting by a beachcomber with bad eyesight and an overactive imagination?"

Arch fastened his life vest. He tried to laugh but couldn't. Most of the emergencies had been nothing, but twice they'd raced out to sunken merchant ships. Too late. Always too late. The U-boat gone, half the men dead, the other half soaked in oil and shivering in lifeboats.

The men dashed out of their cabin and through the wardroom. Thirteen ships had been sunk off the Eastern Seaboard in the past two weeks, over five hundred merchant marines and passengers had died, and the US Navy hadn't inflicted any damage in return. No convoys had been instituted. No blackouts ordered. Air cover was weak. And the few warships available performed fruitless patrols like the *Ettinger*'s.

Arch climbed to the main deck and freedom. As a strong swimmer, he stood a better chance of survival topside.

He and Jim joined the flow of sailors to battle stations. Maybe Arch's bad nerves made him overly sensitive, but the men didn't look well—some looked jittery, some looked exhausted, some looked terrified.

Arch found Lt. John Odom on the quarterdeck. "What's the word?"

"SSS from a British merchant ship, the *Traveller*, at 0842."

Sub sighted on the surface. Most of the British merchant ships were armed, but few had sunk U-boats. "What's her position?"

"Hundred miles southeast of us."

Arch winced. Even at flank speed, the *Ettinger* wouldn't reach the coordinates for three hours. "Another rescue mission."

"We hope." With a grim set of his jaw, Odom went to the starboard whaleboat.

Arch's left eyelid twitched. They'd be at general quarters for three hours en route, plus several hours at the site of the attack. Such a long time at heightened alert frayed the men's nerves.

Soon the *Ettinger* stood at Condition One, ready for battle, surging through the rough gray seas, a thin white wake angling from her bow. Arch scanned the horizon with the binoculars and wandered among his men, encouraging them and keeping them alert.

The sun rose but yielded no warmth. They headed south, not southeast, and after two hours, the course shifted east in a zigzag pattern and the ship slowed to two-thirds speed to allow sonar readings.

Buckner wanted to nail the head of a U-boat over his mantel, and Arch didn't blame him. If the U-boat had headed out to sea as would be prudent, the *Ettinger* wouldn't catch her.

But if she were bold, if she sought prey exiting New York Harbor, she might cross the destroyer's path, a path strewn with depth charges.

A mess attendant handed Arch a cup of coffee. Arch thanked him, downed the brew in one swig, and handed back the cup. He needed to stay alert, but the coffee intensified the twitching. Arch pressed a gloved finger to the muscle in his eyelid until it stopped its mad jitterbug.

Take it away, Lord. Help me do my job. If only Arch had more faith, he wouldn't be like this.

The sailors around him kept up the watch, indulging only in short conversations. But Hobie McLachlan, a lanky dark-haired seaman with a history of disciplinary infractions, leaned against the aft superstructure, his arms crossed and his head slumped forward.

"McLachlan." Arch tapped him on the arm with the back of his hand.

His eyes opened, glassy and unfocused. "Wha . . . ?"

Arch frowned. Most men caught dozing startled and blurted out apologies. "McLachlan, we're at general quarters."

He kneaded his face with his hand. "Gen'rul. Should be adm'ral quarters. We're in the Navy."

If Arch didn't know the ship was dry, as were all ships in the US Navy, he'd think the man was drunk. Besides, he couldn't smell anything on his breath. He put steel in his voice. "McLachlan, pull yourself together."

His wide mouth twisted into a smile, and he raised a sloppy salute. "Seaman McLachlan 'porting for duty, sir."

The man wasn't fit for duty. Arch rubbed his hand over his mouth. What was he going to do with him? Sick bay? Confine him to quarters?

"All right, boys. This is it." Buckner's voice.

Arch spun around.

The captain charged down the deck in his cold-weather gear. "You, keep a look out. You, snap to it. We're going to get this German kraut-boat, be the first American ship to do so. You, get to work."

Oh no. McLachlan.

Captain Buckner's gaze fell on Arch, then shifted to McLachlan and hardened. "You—leaning on the job? We're at general quarters."

"Yes, sir." McLachlan pushed off from the superstructure and wobbled.

"What's wrong with you? Are you drunk?" Buckner leaned forward and sniffed the man's breath.

Arch stood straighter. "Sir, I was about to send him to sick bay."

"Nothin' wrong with me. Just resting. General quarters is bad for the nerves."

In the old days, that would have earned a flogging. Or worse.

Buckner's gaze was sharper than a cat o' nine tails. "Resting? By all means. Don't let me stand in your way." He directed his lethal stare around the deck. "Anyone else want to rest your poor little nerves?"

"No, sir!" The cry rose in unison from a dozen stunned faces.

Buckner returned his ire to McLachlan. "This is war. Think of your brothers battling the Japanese on Bataan. They don't get any rest. They *live* at general quarters. They'd kill for a few days' liberty in Boston, you lazy—" He shook his head. "No, that word's too good for you. You're confined to quarters. After we secure from general quarters, report to the Captain's Mast for your discipline."

"Aye aye, sir." Another sloppy salute, and McLachlan ambled away.

Arch made a face. McLachlan would get his rest after all.

"And you, Mr. Vandenberg."

"Yes, sir?" His breath froze in the iciness of that glare.

"Make these men buck up." The CO charged down the deck. "Snap to it, boys. Don't let that U-boat get away."

Arch's posture collapsed. How could he make his men buck up when he couldn't buck up himself?

★ ★ ★

Six hours later, the *Ettinger* was secured and McLachlan had been sentenced to five days in solitary confinement. Arch trudged down to the tragic emptiness of sick bay. When they'd reached the *Traveller*'s coordinates, they'd found wreckage and bodies. Not one survivor.

Nor any sign of the U-boat.

In the passageway, Arch pressed the heels of his hands against his eyes. This would be hard on the men. It was hard on him. All those bodies.

He flung down his hands, removed his cover, and marched into the pharmacist's mate's office.

Parnell Lloyd stood. "Good afternoon, sir."

"Good afternoon, Doc." Arch shut the door. "Do you have a moment? I have a question."

"Of course, sir. Please have a seat." Doc motioned to a chair and sat at his small steel desk covered with medical texts. Above his desk hung four sketches signed by Parnell Lloyd, mimicking the works of Rembrandt, Monet, Van Gogh, and Picasso.

Everyone on board knew Doc had joined the Navy to see the world, but he'd discovered a love of medicine and now hoped to put his dexterity to use as a surgeon.

Arch sat. "I'm concerned about my men."

"In what way?" Doc picked up a clipboard and a pen.

"They're anxious, shaky, on edge." He used his cover to shield the shakiness in his own hands.

"Shell shock, they called it in the Great War. Now we call it combat fatigue, combat neurosis." His brown eyes shone with concern.

"How does one treat it?"

Doc ran his hand through his light brown hair. "They don't really know. Sedatives work to some extent, but I only have a small stock on board for emergencies, if a sailor gets hysterical or dangerous."

Arch licked his lips. "So what can we do for them?"

Doc barked out a laugh. "You want to know the treatment of choice? The men are surveyed—kicked out of the Navy. Can you imagine the disgrace in a time of war? The men know what awaits them, so they don't ask for help. Don't want to be labelled as cowards or malingerers."

"I—I don't blame them." The exact reason Arch wouldn't seek help again. Besides, all Dr. Blake had done was give him those pills. "You said sedatives work to some extent. How would they affect the men?"

Doc set down his clipboard and opened a textbook labelled *Pharmacology*. "They're quite interesting medications, the barbiturates."

Why did he sense a lecture on the horizon? He offered a smile. "In layman's terms, please."

"Oh, of course." The textbook closed. "In layman's terms, the men would act drunk."

"Drunk." Like McLachlan.

"Yes, sleepy, relaxed, uninhibited, unsteady."

"One of my men acted like that this morning. Captain Buckner and I smelled his breath. I smelled nothing but bacon and eggs."

"But I haven't dispensed a single tablet." Doc's gaze skittered around the office. "Come to think of it, I've seen other men acting groggy. I thought they were tired. No one's sleeping well, including me. Do you think . . ."

"I don't know what to think."

Doc stood and rubbed his chin. "I want to help the men. I want their anxiety relieved so they can do their jobs and stay in the Navy. It isn't right to put men in combat then punish them for their humanity. It isn't right."

"I agree."

Doc's eyes brimmed with emotion. "I'm glad you think that way. The captain doesn't."

Arch stood and snugged his cover back on his head. "I'll let you know if I see anything else."

"Thank you, sir."

Arch headed toward his cabin for his long-delayed nap. Had McLachlan taken a sedative? If so, where had it come from? From a Navy physician? What about the other groggy men Doc had noticed? Were they simply exhausted, or had they taken something?

If only Arch could find out the truth, but the enlisted men wouldn't open up to an officer for fear of disciplinary action.

A sailor burst through the door to the main deck, his hand wrapped in a rag.

"Palonsky," Arch said. "What happened?"

He squinted at his hand. "You know, sir, I felt bad for Doc, not having anyone to fix up today. Being a man of compassion, I decided to remedy that. Sliced open my thumb securing the whaleboat."

"How thoughtful of you."

"Yeah?" His wide-set eyes glittered. "'Cause you said that, I'm going to be extra thoughtful and ask Doc to name all the bones in my hand. He'll like that, don't you think, sir?"

Arch lifted a wry smile. "As a man of compassion, you're sure to use that information to cheer the men in a comedy routine."

"Ah, Mr. Vandenberg, you've got me pegged." He sauntered down the passageway.

75

Arch chuckled and stepped out to the main deck. If he had Palonsky's rapport with the men, he could find out anything he wanted.

He stopped in his tracks. The setting sun spilled orange light over the gray waves.

What if he could use Palonsky as an intermediary?

"Use?" He spat out the word. Wasn't that why he'd rejected the life of wealth? Because he'd used people and discarded them? People who loved him?

He'd hated the boy he'd become, and he'd vowed never to become a man he would loathe.

No. Arch wouldn't use his rank to get his way. He wouldn't use Palonsky or anyone else ever again.

He'd have to find another way.

10

Boston
Saturday, February 7, 1942

"Such a treat." Quintessa sat by the bay window across from Lillian. "The sailor boys are here when Clifford finally gets to spend the weekend in town. Isn't it swell?"

"Yes, swell." Clifford perched on the arm of the chair and squeezed Quintessa's shoulders, but his voice sounded stiff.

"Too bad Dan won't join us." Lillian settled back in her armchair and sent Jim a wink.

"Dan, Dan, Dan." Squished between Mary and Arch on the couch, Jim laughed and shook his head. "All work, no play."

"What are we going to do with him?" Lillian fingered a pleat in her brown-and-gold plaid dress. Their oldest brother's ship, the cruiser USS *Vincennes*, had been sent to the Pacific, but Dan had been assigned to an Anti-Submarine Warfare Unit the Navy was establishing in Boston. Dan was not pleased. He wanted to go to sea.

"So," Arch said. "What should we do with our day?"

"I had the best idea." Quintessa fairly hopped in her seat.

"One of the girls at Filene's told me she'd gone ice-skating at the Public Garden downtown. We could rent skates. Doesn't that sound fun? I used to love skating on the Vermilion River."

Mary tilted her brunette head in Lillian's direction. "I don't think skating is a good idea."

Lillian shrank back. She hated to be excluded, but she also hated to be singled out.

"Oh." Quintessa's pretty face stretched long in both mortification and disappointment, but then she smiled. "That's all right. Let's think of something else."

The usual suggestions of movies and walks circled the room, and Lillian groaned inside. If only she could beg out and let them have fun without her, but they'd never allow that. Why did she always have to be the wet blanket?

"No." Lillian sat up straight, her jaw firm. "You're going ice-skating."

"Nonsense," Mary said. "We want to do something together."

"Since I came to town, you haven't even gone dancing, and I know you love dancing. It isn't fair. I refuse to hold you back."

Jim pressed his lips together. "We want you to come too. We want—"

"I'll come. I'll watch. Like watching a movie. In fact, watching you on skates is better than a Hollywood comedy." She gave her brother a teasing grin.

It worked. An hour later, Lillian sat on a pier by the pedestrian bridge in her bottle-green coat and matching hat. Frost-covered trees sparkled under a clear sky, and Boston's cityscape rose on the far side of Boylston and Arlington Streets. Her friends zipped by on the vast frozen lagoon. As enjoyable as a movie.

Jim and Mary made such a darling couple, skating with linked arms. Arch skated with masculine ease, greeting her when he passed but never lingering. And all the children were adorable in their oversized snowsuits, tottering and slipping and falling. Longing tugged at her heart. She'd only had one winter of skating before her accident, and she'd loved it.

Clifford and Quintessa stood to the side of the lagoon in conversation, and Clifford looked annoyed. Something about that man made her uneasy. What was it?

A skater shushed ice in front of her, and she startled.

Arch grinned down at her. "What are you watching so intently?"

Her cheeks warmed. How could she admit she was snooping?

But he'd already followed her line of sight. Clifford motioned over his shoulder with his thumb, and Quintessa planted her hands on her hips and shook her head.

Arch plunked onto the pier beside Lillian. "I don't like that fellow."

"You don't?"

"I don't like how he pressures her. He wants time alone with her, and she wants to stay with her friends."

"You were eavesdropping?"

Arch shrugged, his eyes impossibly blue in the sunshine. "We're in public."

Clifford took Quintessa's elbow, but she shook him off, and then he gave her a big smile and spread his hands wide, as if pleading.

Lillian's stomach turned. That's what she didn't like—the pressure, the controlling. "I don't either."

"Don't what?" Arch gave her a quizzical look.

Why did she have to be so bad at conversation? "Clifford. Something about him . . ."

"Mm-hmm. I'll keep an eye on him."

"Good."

Arch crossed his ankles, the blades of his skates flashing in the sun, and he watched the skaters pass.

The silence wasn't uncomfortable, but she didn't want him to feel obligated to keep her company. Nor did she like the idea that he might *want* to keep her company.

"I've been meaning to ask you about . . ." Arch stopped, and a smile spread. "Never mind. I have a better idea."

"What? What were you going to ask me?"

"Another time." His face grew serious. "But I do have something to ask. Why can't you skate?"

Lillian gripped her hands together. "What do you think?"

"I *was* thinking. Your foot—pardon me, please—but your foot bends when you walk, as if it were hinged."

"It is." Her shoulder muscles tightened. No one asked about her prosthesis except small children—who were rebuked by their mothers.

Arch stared at her prosthetic foot, not with morbid curiosity, but like a boy inspecting a gadget. "How does it . . ." He glanced up to her, and his face reddened. "I beg your pardon. I was ogling your leg. How rude. Please forgive me."

The incongruity, his expression, the humor of it all swelled into a burst of laughter.

"What's so funny?"

Lillian couldn't talk. She waved a hand in front of her face. "No one has ever—ever ogled that leg."

Arch grinned. "Well, I find it interesting. I was trying to figure out how the foot returns to position after each step, and then it occurred to me how it must look to a passerby. 'Why, that officer is ogling that lady's legs. Shame on him.'"

When her laughter receded, she stretched out her artificial leg. "The ankle is hinged. A spring inside returns the foot to position after each step."

"A spring. I should have known. So why doesn't it work with skates?"

"It . . . it just doesn't."

"I don't see why it wouldn't. No spins or jumps, of course, but gliding should be fine."

Lillian studied a skater's feet. "I don't know. I never thought about it."

"Would you like to try?"

"Goodness, no."

Arch tucked his hands in the pockets of his navy blue overcoat. "I thought you were the adventurous sort."

"I—I was." That's why she had only one leg.

"What's the worst that could happen? You could fall. I've already fallen twice."

Could she do it? She hated falling in public, but here everyone took spills.

He nudged her with his elbow. "I'll skate backward in front of you, hold your hands."

She glared at him.

He laughed and inspected the trees behind them. "All right then. I'll find a stick. You hold one end, and I'll hold the other. You won't have to touch me and catch my diseases."

"Oh brother. That's not necessary. We're wearing gloves." She folded her legs beneath her and stood up on the pier. "Come on. I need to rent skates."

"That's the spirit." Arch glided beside the pier. "Nice gloves, by the way."

"Oh, these?" Lillian inspected the russet leather. "Rather pretentious, don't you think? But they're warm."

"Just for that, I'll make you rent your own skates."

"I wouldn't have it any other way." But oh dear, what had she gotten herself into? Ice-skating? Holding hands with Arch? Once again, her impulsivity caused trouble. When would she learn?

After she rented skates, she sat on the pier to put them on.

Thank goodness Arch didn't offer to help. Instead he stood at an angle that shielded her from gawkers.

Chivalry without flirtation—a strange but potent blend. She concentrated on lacing the boots, not sure what to say. She'd been praying more, trying to open her heart to the Lord, but she had no intention of opening her heart to a man.

"Lillian? What are you doing?" Jim skated up with Mary.

Why were there so many grommets? "I'm going skating."

"But . . . but what if—"

"I promised to help," Arch said. "May I?"

Lillian tugged the bow tight. "I don't need my brother's permiss—"

"May I?" Arch didn't break his gaze with his friend.

Jim's hazel eyes softened, then he smiled. "When Lillian Avery gets it in her mind to do something, you can't stop her."

"Right." She stuffed the ends of the laces inside her boot so she wouldn't trip on them. "If I fall, I'll get up. Same as you. Ready, Arch?"

"Ready." He held out both hands.

"Come on, Jim." Mary tugged her boyfriend's sleeve. "She'll be fine."

He skated away but glanced over his shoulder at Arch. "Take care of her."

"I will." Arch opened and closed his outstretched fingers.

Lillian hesitated, but after her brave speech, she couldn't back out now. She grasped Arch's hands and sucked in a breath at the gentle firmness of his grip.

"Nice and easy," he said.

She set her feet square and pushed to standing, Arch's strength stiffening her arms. She felt strangely tall, and she laughed and looked into Arch's eyes, so bright and close. "Oh my."

"Slippery, isn't it?"

"Yes, it is." Heat rushed into her cheeks. Thank goodness he'd misunderstood her.

"All right. Let's get you moving. I'll skate backward. Keep your feet shoulder's width apart, toes pointing forward, knees soft."

"Knees soft. Okay."

Arch checked over his shoulder and glided backward.

Lillian's feet slipped, and she squealed and leaned forward at the waist to stop.

"Don't fight it." Arch scooted closer. "Keep your feet underneath and let yourself glide."

A ragged breath escaped her lungs. "Don't fight it."

"That's right." His voice held such a soothing quality. "Let yourself follow me."

When he eased away, she forced herself to stay upright and allow him to pull her along. The ice melted beneath her blades, and she moved forward, gasping in equal parts fear and delight.

"That's it." Arch's skates moved in and out, tracing hourglasses on the ice. "Soft knees."

"Soft. Soft." She laughed. "I'm skating."

"Yes, you are." Crinkles fanned out from his eyes. "I'll call you Sonja Henie."

"Sonja Henie? Only if she broke down and had to be towed." But Lillian relished the chilly air on her cheeks. She was moving. She was actually moving. And she wanted more.

The lagoon stretched about six city blocks, spanning the width of the Public Garden, with the little suspension bridge like a ribbon around its neck. "I want to go under the bridge, and I want to go faster."

"All right then." Arch grinned and picked up speed.

Lillian stumbled, but she caught herself. "Why didn't I do this earlier?"

"You didn't want to get hurt. I understand." He glanced back and shifted their course to the right.

"On the other side of the bridge, I want you to teach me to skate."

He lifted one eyebrow. "Jim was right. You are a daredevil. Please remember, I promised him I'd take care of you."

"Oh, he's a fussy old hen. You also promised to help me, and I want to skate like everyone else."

"How can I deny a lady's request?" Arch's eyes glinted, the color magnified by the navy blue of his cover and coat. Why couldn't the Navy use a different color for its uniforms?

She tore her attention away to the bridge, to the stone pillar—straight ahead. "Watch out! The bridge."

"What?" He whipped his gaze over his shoulder, which turned him closer to the pillar.

Lillian squealed.

Arch's back slammed into the pillar. She plowed into the wall of his chest. He caught her around the waist, but her feet scrabbled beneath her, and she thumped onto her backside, her back, Arch tumbling beside her.

"Lillian! Are you all right?" He raised himself on his elbows, his eyes wide.

She pushed up to sitting and inspected herself, head to wooden toe. "My leg didn't fall off. That's all that matters."

He got up to his knees. He'd lost his cover, and the disheveled golden waves of his hair shook. Then he laughed, head back, one hand over his belly.

She never talked openly about her condition, never joked about it, never laughed about it, but now she did, and it felt wonderful.

Arch put his cover back on, braced one hand against the pillar, and stood. "Come on, Miss Avery. Let's get you up before your brother comes after me."

"All right." She took Arch's hands, got up to her knees,

planted her right skate on the ice, then pushed herself up. She wobbled and slipped but didn't fall. "Don't slow down now. I want to go fast. But watch where you steer the ship, Cap'n."

He skated backward with a mischievous grin. "Every captain has a navigator."

She laughed. "You're blaming me?"

"No, no, no. I'm inviting you to boss me around."

"Hmm." She liked that idea, and she tilted her chin to the right. "That way."

"Would you at least say *please*?"

"That way, *please*. A bit farther, *please*. Then teach me to skate, *please*."

"I never knew good manners could sound so sarcastic."

She smiled from the rush of cold air and the warmth of camaraderie. Had she ever felt this comfortable with a man who wasn't an Avery? Not with Gordon. Never with him. Always a weight on her chest, a sense of imbalance, of unease.

"Relax." Arch jiggled her hands. "You've already fallen, gotten the worst part over. Are you sure you want to learn to skate?"

Lillian pushed back the memories. "Yes, I do."

"Good." Arch slowed his motion, tensing his arms to slow her down as well. After they stopped in an open patch of ice, he spun to her side, holding only one hand.

He gazed across the Public Garden. "We couldn't ask for a better day for skating."

"No, we couldn't." The sky spread over them, as blue as Arch's eyes.

"Still not used to seeing the State House in mourning."

As an air raid precaution, the golden dome of the Massachusetts State House had been painted black after Pearl Harbor. "Do you think we're in danger of air raids?"

"Not on this coast. The Germans don't have aircraft carriers as the Japanese do, and they don't have long-range bombers. The hysteria is misplaced. We're focusing on a nonexistent danger while ignoring a real danger."

"The U-boats."

He nodded, his expression distant and aimed east. "We black out the dome but refuse to black out our cities. The U-boats sit offshore at night, and the merchant ships are silhouetted against the city lights. Easy pickings. We've lost dozens of ships, thousands of tons of cargo. Hundreds of men." Arch's hand shivered in hers.

"Are you cold?"

"Cold?"

"Your hand is shaking."

Alarm flashed in his eyes, but then he gave her a flat smile. "A sailor never admits to feeling cold. But let's get moving again, shall we?"

"By all means." Men were such a strange lot.

"Now, I promise I'm not getting fresh, but let me put my arm around your waist, and you put yours around mine. Just until you get the feel of skating."

Despite his innocent expression, her throat threatened to close. "I'd rather not."

"Very well." One nod, and he raised their joined hands. "Then hold tight."

No pressure? No reasoned arguments? No cajoling?

"Keep both feet underneath you at first, like before. And watch me." Arch inched forward. "Put your weight on one foot, then the other. Let me know when you're ready."

Lillian gripped his hand, her forearm braced along his, her other hand free and insecure. "Oh dear."

"Are you all right?"

"I'm fine. I'm ready." She shifted her weight to her good leg, wobbled, then put her left leg back on the ice where it belonged.

"You're fine. Try the other leg."

"But that's my bad leg."

"Bad?" He flipped up a grin. "It's as solid as oak."

She gasped out a laugh. "Arch Vandenberg."

"Am I wrong?"

"No." But she shook her head at his audacity, his delightful audacity. Then she put her weight on her prosthesis and lifted her right leg, set it down, repeated with the right.

"There you go." He squeezed her hand. "Keep it up."

"My word." It was clunky, awkward, clumsy, but she was moving, one leg at a time.

With Arch at her side, encouraging her, supporting her, believing in her.

More than anything, she wanted to let go and escape. Falling on the ice would be safer than falling in love.

"There's Jim." Arch pointed. "Show him what his baby sister can do. Ahoy, Mr. Avery!"

Baby sister? Her shoulders relaxed, and she waved at Jim and Mary and skated toward them in her choppy wooden way. As long as Arch saw her as a baby sister, everything would be fine.

11

Boston
Saturday, February 21, 1942

"Are you sure you don't mind?"

How could Arch say no when Lillian looked up to him with those big eyes? "Not at all."

Next to him on the sidewalk, both Jim and Dan Avery grunted. No doubt they didn't share their sister's interest in the show windows at Filene's.

"Oh, stop it." Mary's voice held more affection than scolding. "The movie doesn't start until seven."

"And I'm dying to show off my work." Quintessa linked arms with her roommates and led them to a large window display. "See? Inspired by our afternoon ice-skating."

"It's darling," Lillian said.

Arch smiled. A mannequin couple skated, and three child mannequins lay in a jumble as if they'd crashed into each other. If only he could spirit Lillian away for another whirl on the ice. Alone.

Her small hands gripping his, her pretty face vacillating between terror and joy, her voice begging him to go faster

. . . his heart goading him to go faster, and his common sense telling him to go slowly. Very slowly.

The ladies chattered about the display, how the fake trees and draped white cloth created the landscape, and how sequins and a mirror on the ground made everything glitter.

Dan and Jim quietly discussed the *Ettinger*'s last cruise. They'd been sent out with a North Atlantic convoy from Nova Scotia to Iceland but had turned back halfway to escort some tankers straggling from a westbound convoy.

Arch didn't mind returning to Boston two weeks ahead of schedule. That day at the Public Garden he'd wanted to ask Lillian her professional opinion about sedatives, then realized he could use that question to entice Lillian into an evening out with him, a plan even Jim had approved. Monday was the day he'd ask her.

"I wish I could do something similar at Dixon's." Lillian crossed her arms, one gloved finger tapping on her coat sleeve. "Clear away the ugly ads and showcase the merchandise."

Quintessa pointed at the window. "Maybe a rotating display so people always look to see what's new."

Lillian's face took on a determined set. "If I could increase sales, my job would be secure. But first I have to convince Mr. Dixon to let me make changes."

Arch dug his hands in his pockets. If only he could advise her.

"Start with the cosmetics," Quintessa said. "Tell him it needs a feminine touch."

"Hmm. That might work," Lillian said.

"Let me show you our cosmetics displays." Quintessa headed for the entrance.

Jim and Dan grumbled again, and Arch frowned to look manly, but he wouldn't mind watching Lillian's eyes light up.

Mary took Jim's hand. "I'm sorry, sweetheart. Why don't you boys get coffee in the restaurant? We won't be long."

"Great idea." He kissed her forehead. "Come on, fellows."

"Yes, great idea." Arch's voice sounded fake, but he followed the Avery brothers.

The men strode through the store to the elevator. "Nothing against Clifford," Jim said, "but I'm glad he couldn't come into town this weekend."

"Now we can talk shop," Dan said.

Arch smiled. Did Dan Avery ever *not* talk shop? "Watch out. Loose lips sink ships."

"True." Dan scanned the busy department store as if ferreting out German spies.

Jim pushed the elevator button. "I hope we don't get another North Atlantic convoy assignment. The U-boats have abandoned that route for American waters. We're needed here."

"Especially around Cape Hatteras," Dan said in a low voice. "And now the U-boats are in the Caribbean."

Arch stepped closer. "Any word from the Eastern Sea Frontier about setting up coastal convoys?"

Dan shook his head. "We don't have enough escort vessels. A poorly escorted convoy is an even greater draw for a U-boat than a solitary cargo ship—all those targets clumped together."

"Especially if they're lit up from behind by city lights," Jim said. "I wish the Navy would exercise its authority and order blackouts. But the cities claim it'd be bad for business."

Arch let out a harsh laugh. "So are shiploads of oil and cargo going to the bottom of the sea." Not to mention bodies washing ashore.

The elevator doors opened, and two ladies exited. The three men tipped their covers to them and stepped inside.

On the bronze elevator panel, Arch pushed a glass button for the eighth floor. "How's the Anti-Submarine Warfare Unit shaping up?"

"Very well," Dan said. "Most of the men served on convoy duty and learned from the British. England is two years ahead of us. We need to study what they do—escorted convoys, blackouts, air support."

Arch unbuttoned his overcoat. "Of course, we don't have nearly enough ships or planes to protect our shipping along the East Coast."

Dan knifed his hand toward the door. "In the long run, the best way to protect shipping is to hunt and destroy U-boats. We need better weapons, better sonar training, and better radar. And we need to install radar on far more ships."

"Buckner would sure like a radar set," Jim said. "He's obsessed with sinking a U-boat."

The elevator doors opened, and Arch led the way toward the restaurant.

Tension wiggled inside him. The desire to open up to his best friend wrestled with the knowledge that it wouldn't be wise or masculine. Besides, he was doing his job, even if Buckner might not agree.

The most frustrating part about leadership was being judged for the performance of others. His men were either jittery or drowsy, and Buckner blamed him.

At Dan's request, the men were shown to an isolated booth in the corner.

Arch slid in across from Dan and Jim, who were as different as brothers could be. Jim, with his sunny disposition, and Dan, with his no-nonsense outlook.

The men ordered coffee, and Arch rested his hands in his lap to conceal the trembling. Perhaps he could try a round-about approach. "I've overheard the men calling Buckner Captain Ahab."

Jim chuckled. "That fits. Down in the engine room, we don't feel Buckner's wrath, but the deck gang sure does."

Here was Arch's opening. "It wears on the men. Constantly

being at general quarters, seeing the carnage from the sunken ships, and getting yelled at because we haven't sunk a U-boat. They're on edge, they don't sleep well, and Buckner just tells them to buck up."

Jim grinned. "Buck-up Buckner."

The waitress poured coffee, the men thanked her, and Arch took a sip. "His approach doesn't work. I preferred Captain Durant's ways. He didn't put up with laziness or insubordination, but he encouraged the men and sympathized with them."

Dan frowned at his coffee cup. "You don't get better than Durant, but you have to work with Buckner, and you have to make the men shape up."

"I know." Arch's jaw stiffened. "For the sake of the war effort, my men need to be alert and quick and competent. I need to make them shape up, but I'm also concerned for their well-being."

Dan shrugged. "Frequent drills and training to build confidence. Appropriate discipline. Plenty of rest and recreation."

"He already does that." Jim nudged his brother and laughed. "We went to the Academy too."

Dan lifted half a smile. "Sorry. I still think of you two as little plebes."

Arch stirred his coffee although he hadn't added sugar or cream. The spoon tinkled around the rim. He'd gone against his father's wishes to attend the Naval Academy. He'd worked hard in Annapolis and ever since. But a negative or lukewarm report from Buckner would stall his career.

If he couldn't pull himself and his men together, all his labor would be in vain.

12

Lillian fluffed the red, white, and blue bunting on the wooden box, then straightened the sign soliciting tin donations. A small step, but important. People wanted to aid the war effort, and they'd take their tin somewhere—why not to Dixon's? Once inside the store, they might remember they needed toothpaste or aspirin.

Mr. Dixon had been swayed, and Lillian had made her first change. She frowned at the ad-plastered windows, her next project if she had her way.

"Looks good, Miss Avery," Albert called from the soda fountain, where he served lunch to an elderly couple.

"Thank you." She began rearranging the shelf closest to the door. With rubber on ration and shortages of nylons and metals, they had fewer items.

The bell on the door jangled, and Arch Vandenberg entered the store in his navy blue overcoat. "Hi, Lillian."

"Arch. Hi." She fiddled with the hem of her hip-length

93

white jacket. "What are you doing here? Are you sick? Is Jim all right?"

"Everything's fine." He took off his cover and smoothed his wavy blond hair. "I have a medical question for you."

"All right." She shifted bottles of pomade to disguise the depletion of bobby pins.

Arch cleared his throat. "Actually, it's a complicated question, involving men on my ship. Would you be willing to meet over dinner tonight to discuss it? My treat."

Lillian spun around too fast and knocked down a little cardboard box. Precious bobby pins scattered everywhere. "My word."

"Sorry. I shouldn't have startled you." Arch squatted to pick up pins. "Don't worry. It's not a date. More of a professional consultation."

"Oh." A rush of relief and disappointment heated her cheeks, and she bent over to clean up her mess.

"Well?" He dropped pins into the box. "Are you free tonight?"

"Yes, I am." As she worked, she let her hair fall over her cheek like a mask.

"How about Durgin-Park down by Faneuil Hall? Jim says it's good. Nothing fancy, just hearty New England fare."

"All right. I could meet you there at five-thirty."

"See you then. I think that's all." He handed Lillian the box.

"Thanks." She'd buy the bobby pins herself, since she was responsible for the loss.

"Thank you for the advice, Miss Avery," he said in a louder voice. "I appreciate your help." A wink at her, then he looked down the center aisle and tipped his cover. "Goodbye."

"Bye." A smile escaped at his blatant flattery in front of her boss.

After Arch left, Mr. Dixon came down the aisle. "Your friend's visiting you at work?"

"My brother's friend." Lillian set the box aside to purchase later and resumed rearranging the shelf. "He had a medical question."

"Your brother's in the Navy too, isn't he?"

"Yes, sir. All three of my older brothers."

Mr. Dixon grunted, his heavy gray brows jammed together. "Let's hope the Navy treats them better than they treated my nephew."

"Oh?" Her hands rested on the shelf. Mr. Dixon never mentioned his family, and she longed to pry the door open. "How is that?"

The pharmacist nodded toward Boston Harbor. "He served on a battleship, in the fire room. One day the boiler exploded. Some of his buddies were killed, and he was badly burned."

"Oh dear. I'm so sorry."

"That wasn't the worst of it." His dark eyes turned soft. "After he healed, he tried to go back, but he couldn't handle being in the fire room. His nerves, you know."

"I can imagine."

"What did the Navy do?" He flung out one hand. "Wouldn't give him medication. Wouldn't train him in a new rating. Just kicked him out, said he was unfit for duty."

"What a shame."

"All his life he wanted to be a sailor. He found a job at the Navy Yard, but it's not the same."

"I understand."

Mr. Dixon's gaze swam back, as if he'd forgotten she was there. "Yes. Well, we should get back to work."

"Yes, sir." She smiled as she did so. Mr. Dixon might turn out to be a teddy bear after all.

★ ★ ★

What a strange subway system. The same station had three names—State for the northbound line, Milk Street for the southbound line, and Devonshire for the east-west line. All located beneath the historic Old State House.

Lillian gazed up at the two-hundred-year-old brick building.

"Out of the way, lady."

"Oh, sorry." She darted away from the door. What a hick she was, gawking at the tourist sites. But how could she help it?

In the light of the setting sun, she got her bearings. The Old State House stood at one of those typical Bostonian intersections with half a dozen streets coming from all angles—the site of the Boston Massacre, no less. To her left sat Faneuil Hall and Quincy Market.

Now to act like a big-city girl. She stuffed her hands in her coat pockets and followed the directions Albert had given her to the restaurant. Pass Faneuil Hall, turn right, restaurant on the left.

What kind of medical question could Arch have for her? The Navy was full of healthy young men, and the Navy's physicians and pharmacist's mates cared for them. Why would Arch need to talk to a civilian pharmacist?

It couldn't be a ruse to get her alone for dinner. She'd ruled that out based on his character. She mustn't allow herself to fantasize about romance or to assign cruel motives to her brother's best friend. They wouldn't have been friends for so long if Arch had pathological tendencies.

Lillian passed the colonial brick structure of Faneuil Hall, then Quincy Market with its granite pillars. On her left. She opened the restaurant door and climbed the stairs to the second floor.

"What do you want?" A plump waitress in her fifties eyed Lillian up and down.

She must look like a saleswoman rather than a customer. She raised a warm smile. "I'm meeting a friend for dinner."

The waitress harrumphed. "Isn't that swell? All these years we've kept the sunshiny tourists away, and now they find us."

Lillian blinked. "I . . . I live here."

"Yeah? One month? Two?"

Not quite two months. She blinked again. Didn't they want her business? "I'm meeting my friend at five-thirty."

"And she's late too. Figures." The waitress marched into the dining room. "Who's your friend, sunshine?"

Lillian followed, gaping at the woman's back. Why would the restaurant allow the staff to be inhospitable?

At a table to her right, Arch pushed back his chair and stood. "Good evening."

"Well, don't that beat all?" The waitress planted her hands on wide hips. "Blueblood sailor boy and happy little country girl. What a pair."

Arch pulled out a chair for Lillian. "May I take your coat?"

Stunned, Lillian allowed him. Then she sat, steam filling her chest.

"Suppose you want menus. Can't get a moment's rest around here." The waitress slapped two menus onto the table. "Let me guess—lobster for the King of New England and possum for the country girl. Sorry. We're fresh out of possum." She stomped away.

The steam whooshed out Lillian's nostrils. "That's it. I'm leaving." She shoved back her chair and moved to stand.

Arch clamped a hand on top of hers. "Sit."

The strength of his hand alarmed her, but not as much as the warmth of it. "We should leave. She's rude."

A slow smile eased up. "It's Durgin-Park."

Lillian stared at him, trying to understand, willing him to move his hand, willing herself to pull away.

Arch chuckled. "They're famous for their rude waitresses."

"You picked a restaurant famous for rude waitresses?" She eased back into her chair.

"Blame your brother."

"Jim?"

"Jim. He said I needed to assure you this wasn't a date, so he suggested the least romantic restaurant in Boston. He told me the waitresses were entertaining."

"Entertaining? Jim would think that."

Arch laughed and returned his hand to his lap. "He knew how you'd react. He knew you'd bolt. His way of making sure the evening would be short as well as unromantic. I've been had."

Long tables spread with red-and-white checkered tablecloths. No music or dancing. And the surliest waitress ever. The steam changed form and burst into laughter.

"I've never been one for practical jokes, but I'll have to get him back." Arch picked up a menu. "Now, I need to choose my entrée, because, sadly, they're fresh out of possum."

Lillian smiled and opened her menu. No possum listed, but lobster was, along with steak, shepherd's pie, turkey, and seafood. Oh, and the desserts! Indian pudding, bread pudding, Boston cream pie . . .

"Know what you want, or you need help reading the menu?" The waitress had returned.

Why not play along? "Well, they never learned me much in that ole country schoolhouse, and them words are mighty big, but I reckon I'll have this here chicken potpie. And some beans. Beans is good eatin', all we get down on the farm."

The waitress raised one eyebrow, and one corner of her mouth twitched as she wrote down the order.

Arch gaped at her, much as he had the night they'd met.

"And for you, Your Majesty?"

"Um, pot roast. The New England pot roast, please. And the Boston baked beans."

Lillian looked up at the waitress plaintively. "Go easy on him. He ain't never had beans at that there palace of his."

"Crazy tourists." The waitress strode away.

Lillian grinned in triumph. She'd played the waitress's game and struck Arch dumb. "So what's your medical question?"

"My medical . . . ?" He made a funny face, ran his hand over his hair, and then gave her a charming smile. "I'm fine, thank you. How are you?"

"You did ask me here for a reason."

"Yes, I did. And thanks to that little exchange, now I know not to get on Lillian Avery's bad side."

"Right. Your question?"

Arch's face sobered, and he folded his hands on the checkered tablecloth. "What do you know about combat fatigue? Shell shock?"

Lillian smoothed the skirt of her burgundy wool suit. "We didn't study that in pharmacy school, but it's a type of anxiety reaction."

"Do you know how it's treated?"

"Not off the top of my head, but other patients with anxiety are treated with rest and sedatives. Why do you ask?"

Arch's mouth shifted from side to side. "Some of my men are jittery. They've seen horrible things, been through horrible things. They can't sleep, and when they do, they have nightmares. They complain about their nerves."

Like Mr. Dixon's poor nephew. "What does your doctor do?"

"We don't have a medical officer. Most destroyers don't. We have a pharmacist's mate, a bright fellow who wants to become a doctor. He also mentioned sedatives, but he can't dispense them unless it's an emergency."

"That makes sense. They're habit-forming."

Arch twiddled his thumbs. "The men don't want to talk

to Doc or to a physician, because the Navy might label them as weak, malingerers, cowards—and they could be surveyed out of the Navy. They don't want that. They want to serve their country."

"I understand." But Lillian frowned. Why was he asking her about this?

In the dim light, Arch's eyes were as navy blue as his uniform. "Here's my question. Some of my men are groggy in the middle of the day. I thought one man was drunk, but the ship is dry, and his breath smelled normal. Then a few days ago, I saw one man pass something to another, like a pill. An hour later, both men were groggy, 'doped off,' as they say."

Lillian rested her forearms on the table. "Do you think they're taking drugs?"

"I don't know. That's what I wanted to ask you."

"Those symptoms are consistent with sedative use. But if your pharmacist's mate isn't prescribing pills, where would they get them?"

"That's why you're here."

Lillian gazed at the ceiling and tapped one finger on her elbow. "They could get a prescription from a Navy doctor, or even from a civilian doc—my word! Dr. Kane."

"Dr. Kane?"

"Yes. Do you remember me telling Jim about a prescription for an unusually high quantity of phenobarbital? Dr. Kane wrote it. He writes lots of these prescriptions."

Arch's eye twitched. "Phenobarbital."

"It's a sedative." She scooted forward in her chair. "My word. What if he's running a mill of sorts, seeing all these sailors and prescribing phenobarbital?"

Arch rested his chin in his hand, his fingers covering his mouth. "Could be."

"Or . . . or he might only see a few sailors, and they distribute to their friends. That would explain the high quantities."

"That's illegal, isn't it?"

"Yes, and dangerous. All medications have side effects, and the barbiturates are habit-forming and can be fatal in overdose, especially when combined with alcohol. I knew something fishy was going on. I just knew it."

Arch's hand slid down to reveal a smile. "You look excited."

Lillian laughed. "Maybe I am. I do like mystery books. Oh, I knew I should have called Dr. Kane. Of course, if he's up to no good, he won't admit the truth, but I have to do something."

"See what you can find out on your end, and I'll see what I can find out on board."

"Are you going to play Sherlock Holmes? I could see that."

"Yes, Watson. For what it's worth. The men won't talk to me since I'm an officer, but one of my sailors is an excellent actor. I'll see if he's willing to make some inquiries."

Lillian held up both index fingers and brought them together like magnets. "You work from your end, and I'll work from mine, and we'll solve this thing."

"Partners, then?" Arch smiled and held out his hand.

She stared at it. She didn't relish the idea of working with him, but as a pharmacist, how could she not get involved?

Lillian shook Arch's hand. "Partners."

13

Off Cape Cod
Thursday, February 26, 1942

All night they'd chased that elusive white whale. No sound contacts. No radio reports. Just ceaseless searching.

In the pre-dawn darkness, Arch climbed down from the pilothouse to quarters. Serving as junior officer of the watch presented an opportunity to interact with the captain and impress him, but Buckner saw nothing but imaginary periscopes in the distance.

Arch yawned. Fatigue this deep should chase away the nightmares. But as he descended, his breathing grew ragged. All those layers of metal like a lid on top of him, locking him in. If only he could sleep on the main deck. He wouldn't mind the wind and the cold.

Perhaps thinking about Lillian would soothe his nerves. This investigation would be good, not only to find out if and how the men were obtaining sedatives, but also to spend time with Lillian alone.

Maybe she'd come to trust him. She seemed trustworthy herself, genuine and unspoiled. No talk of money and shopping and fashion. Besides, if she were a gold digger, she'd be making eyes at him.

She wasn't.

Arch huffed and descended the ladder to the wardroom. Why was the woman so suspicious of him? Sure, most men rejected her because of her leg, but why would she suspect a man who didn't reject her? Why would any hint of flirtation make her bolt?

Jim had mentioned a bad relationship in her past. How bad? In what way? Could Arch persuade her to confide in him? Then he'd know what he was up against.

The alarm clanged. General quarters.

Arch slumped to the bottom step of the ladder, gripping the handrails above him, his heart in a painful staccato. He closed his eyes, breathing hard. He could do this. He had to.

A few officers strode out of their cabins and through the darkened wardroom, pulling on outerwear and life vests.

They couldn't see him undone like this. Couldn't. He stood and forced his feet up the steps.

Lillian said his condition was treated with rest and sedatives. He'd rejected the sedatives, but he longed for rest.

A sense of purpose would help too. If they could sink a U-boat or even chase one away from a cargo ship, morale would rise.

"What do you want to bet?" Ted Hayes's voice rose from below. "I think the sonarmen make up sound contacts just to make Old Bucky happy."

Arch pushed away his anxiety to join in the expected chuckling.

On the main deck, he headed to his battle station, straining through the darkness but seeing only black sea and blacker sky. The *Ettinger* bumped forward over the waves.

Machinist's Mate Third Class Tony Vitucci, the talker, lifted one earphone and greeted Arch. "Sound contact, sir.

About a mile ahead. We're preparing for a depth-charge attack."

"Prepare for depth-charge attack," Arch called out, and word passed down the deck.

The *Ettinger* used depth charges like confetti. At least that meant they returned frequently to Boston to restock.

After a few minutes, Vitucci said, "Two hundred yards, sir."

"Two hundred yards," Arch shouted, planting his feet wide and bending his knees.

Before long, the destroyer's stern heaved up, once, twice, five times. Arch stood firm, scanning the waves for any sign of a submarine.

The *Ettinger* cranked into a tight turn to starboard, and her starboard K-guns fired, launching lighter-weight depth charges abreast. Arch went to the lifeline and peered over the water. Still two hours remained before sunrise, and the moon had already set.

The number two gun mount fired. A flash of orange flame, and a star shell shot into the night sky. In a moment, the shell exploded and floated on its little parachute, shedding bright white light over the sea.

Arch saw nothing but water.

The *Ettinger* straightened her course and charged forward for another run. More depth charges split the ocean, and the destroyer circled the attack site.

No air bubbles, no wreckage, no oil slick. Was it a false contact? Or had the U-boat escaped?

They made a third run and circled again.

One of the sailors whooped. "We did it! Look! Wreckage!"

Arch followed his line of sight to something jagged and gray piercing the waves. "Well done! Vitucci, tell the bridge."

The destroyer stopped, and Buckner raced down from the bridge. "You—haul up a piece. I want to see it, touch it, raise it to the yardarm."

Arch directed the men with their grappling hooks, and Warren Palonsky clambered down the cargo net. More chunks of metal popped to the surface, but no bubbles, no oil.

The men called out as they worked, and Palonsky grabbed a piece of the wreckage, lashed it to the cargo net, and scrambled up to the deck.

Palonsky dried his hands on his trousers and shook his head. "Sorry, Captain Buckner, sir. You'll see. It's covered in barnacles. It's been down there a while, whatever it is."

Buckner dashed to the edge.

Arch did too. The men hauled up a piece of metal about two feet square, pitted and coated with barnacles.

"You numbskulls!" Buckner yelled. "It's nothing but an old wreck. Wasting ammo on an old wreck. What a bunch of good-for-nothings."

He stormed away, berating sailors in his path.

Arch's hands balled into fists. How dare he? The men were only following the captain's orders. And they'd followed them well.

The men muttered to each other, glaring after their commander, shoulders sagging. How could Arch undo the damage without undermining Buckner's authority?

"Don't worry, men," he said. "You did well. You did exactly what you're supposed to do, and we hit the coordinates. We hit a sound contact. If that had been a U-boat, we would have sunk it."

"Yes, sir," the men said, but dejection colored the words.

"Say, fellas." Palonsky hefted the chunk of metal in his big hands. "I vote we do something with this. Carson, you're a shipfitter, a metalsmith. What do you think?"

Carson fingered the scrap and rubbed his chin. "Could make tokens or something."

"Yes," Arch said. "Make tokens for every man on the crew because we hit an actual submerged ship. Then when we sink a U-boat—and we will—we'll make new ones out of Germany's finest steel."

"Yeah," Palonsky said. "Today the wreck—tomorrow the Reich."

"Say, that's good." Arch clapped both Palonsky and Carson on the back. "See if you can fit that on the tokens."

Around his section of the deck, eyes brightened. He and Palonsky made a good team. Maybe his plan would work.

★ ★ ★

"This is not an order." Arch sat sideways at the desk in the ship's office, facing Palonsky. "I'm asking for your help, but you can take it or leave it."

Palonsky shifted in his chair. "Me, sir?"

"I'm having troubles with the men. They're struggling with their nerves."

"Do you blame them, sir?"

"Not at all." Of all people, Arch understood. "We live in constant tension, never knowing when a torpedo could strike. We've seen sinkings, bodies, many of us have survived sinkings. It's a lot for a man to endure. The shakes, the nightmares."

"Yes, sir." He smoothed his dark blond hair. "Not me, but lots of the men are struggling."

Arch rested his elbow on the edge of the desk. "Doc can't do anything for them. If they see a Navy physician, they may be labelled as malingerers or psychoneurotics and be surveyed out of the Navy. These men all volunteered. They love the sea, love the Navy, and they want to contribute to the war effort."

"Yes, sir. I've heard some of the boys talk like that."

"So they treat themselves. On land they get drunk, but what to do at sea?"

Palonsky glanced away and frowned. "I don't know, sir."

"I think some of them might be taking pills."

"Pills, sir?" The sailor's forehead creased.

"The problem is the pills are habit-forming and dangerous, and they make the men groggy. They aren't doing their jobs well."

Palonsky's jaw jutted forward. "You want me to snitch on my buddies? Tell you who's doped up so they'll be disciplined?"

"No." This wasn't going well. "I just want to find out where they're getting the pills. You see, I have a friend who's a pharmacist in town, and she's noticed some suspicious prescriptions. We think there might be a link."

"She?"

Arch fiddled with a pen on the desk. "Lillian Avery, Mr. Avery's sister."

"Ah." Palonsky waggled his eyebrows. "She a looker? Or does she look like her brother?"

Arch chuckled. "We want to find out if there's a shady physician at work, or a black market, or . . . well, we don't know. But something isn't right. The crew is at risk, and the nation needs every one of us working at full capacity."

Palonsky rubbed his palms over his trouser legs. "What do you want me to do, sir?"

"Remember, this isn't an order. For once, you can say no to an officer."

"I like that part, sir."

"Thought you might." Arch rolled the pen in his hand. "You're an excellent actor, and all the men like you, respect you, and trust you."

"You want me to betray that trust?"

Arch winced. "No, I want you to put it to good use. Perhaps you could complain about your nerves to some of the men, see if anything happens."

"See if anyone offers me a pill?"

"Yes. Then we could trace it up the supply line, if there is one."

Palonsky mashed his lips together. "Do you realize what could happen to me if the men found out I was a snitch?"

"Happen?"

"There are things you don't do—like snitch. There are risks."

"They'd hurt you?"

"Don't know. Don't want to find out."

Arch's fingers coiled around the pen. What could he do? Only an enlisted man could help him, and no one was as good as Palonsky. A natural actor, a born leader, liked by the men and trusted by Arch. A man who valued high morale as much as Arch did.

"What if I paid you?"

"Paid me?"

"Twenty bucks a month."

Palonsky whistled. "That's a lot of dough."

"Almost a third of your pay."

"Heard you were rich. Vandenberg Insurance, right?"

"My father's company. Not mine."

The seaman leaned back, crossed his arms, and looked Arch up and down. "Dangerous job like this, I might need me an insurance policy. Thirty bucks a month."

Guilt pinched his heart. He'd vowed never to use his wealth to get his way, and here he was doing that very thing. But this was for a higher purpose, for the men's welfare and the war effort, not for selfish gain.

"Thirty bucks." Arch pulled out his wallet and counted out bills. "We have a deal?"

Palonsky's eyes lit up, and he grabbed the money and kissed it. "That we do."

14

Lillian scooped the last of the ointment from the marble slab into the glass jar, used the metal spatula to put a pretty swirl on top, and wiped the rim with a cloth.

Her knee rested on the stool she'd finally asked Mr. Dixon to allow her to use. A sore was developing on her stump, and she needed to relieve the pressure. Thank goodness, the druggist had barely grumbled.

Albert picked up a box filled with prescription bags. "I'm making my delivery. Think you and Mrs. Connelly can handle this place by yourselves?"

She smiled at him. "We always manage fine."

"Well, I don't like leaving women alone. It's a safe neighborhood, but—"

"Go. Now." Lillian gave him a mock scowl and pointed to the door.

"Yes, ma'am." He grinned and departed.

Now was the opportunity she'd waited for all week. No new prescriptions waited, and the ointment wouldn't be

109

picked up until five. It was Mr. Dixon's day off, and at two o'clock, Dr. Kane's office would still be open.

Lillian flipped through the prescription file and grabbed the most recent prescription he had written for phenobarbital, plus another he'd written for thyroid extract.

Not only had she promised to call the doctor, but it was the right thing to do. When Arch returned from his patrol, she couldn't wait to report what she found out today.

What made her so eager? The investigation . . . or Arch? She couldn't figure out if the man was attracted to her. He was handsome, bright, kind, and he genuinely cared about his crew. What would a man like that want with a broken woman like her?

She shuddered, pushed aside the prescriptions, and wiped down the ointment slab. Gordon had shown signs of darkness and control from the start. She'd overlooked them, thrilled to have found a man who wanted to be with her, only her, all the time. So intoxicating. So dangerous.

She'd never make that mistake again.

Lillian took her mortar, pestle, and spatula to the sink and washed them. Keeping her distance from Arch would be wise, but now she'd promised to work with him on this case. Partners.

Her stomach hopped around. What had she done? So many things could go wrong, and not only with Arch. Mr. Dixon had forbidden her to question Dr. Kane about these prescriptions. What if they were for legitimate conditions? What if the physician questioned her judgment? What if he told Mr. Dixon? She could lose her job. And what if the physician were some huge drug kingpin, and he had his thugs gun her down?

There. She'd gotten the worst scenarios out of her head.

After Lillian laid the equipment on a towel to dry, she marched to the telephone and dialed Dr. Kane's number. The nurse summoned the physician to the phone. Lillian put on her most professional voice. "Good afternoon. This is Miss Avery calling from Dixon's Drugs."

"I don't take questions from clerks, young lady. Put Cyrus on the line."

"Mr. Dixon isn't working today, but I'm a pharmacist too."

Silence, then a long sigh. "All right then."

Not a good start, but Lillian schooled her face into a smile so she'd sound confident. "I'm calling about a prescription for phenobarbital for Mr. Norman Hunter."

"Norman Hunter? Not my patient."

"I have a prescription here from you for a man by that name."

"Impossible. My father's name is Norman, and my mother's maiden name is Hunter. I'd remember that name."

Lillian fingered the paper. "That's strange. It was written yesterday and—"

"Yesterday? I didn't see any patients yesterday. I was conducting a symposium at Harvard Medical School. You must have the wrong number. I'm not the only Dr. Kane in Boston. In the future, please be more careful and don't waste my time."

"Sir," Lillian spat out before he could hang up. "The phone number is on the prescription form. It's a printed form like the others you use, a prescription for two hundred phenobarbital tablets."

"Two hundred? That's ludicrous."

"I thought so too, but this isn't the only one we've received for large quantities of sedatives written by you."

"Me? You're mistaken. They must be forgeries. Someone must have stolen a prescription pad from one of my examination rooms. Does Dixon's Drugs no longer take care when filling prescriptions?"

Lillian winced. She didn't want to get her boss in trouble.

"Sir, did you write a prescription for Marian Zimmerman for thyroid?"

"Yes. I saw her this morning."

"I have both prescriptions in front of me." She peered at them. "They look identical—the form, the handwriting, the signature, even the shade of ink. If it's a forgery, it's an excellent one. That's why we never suspected anything."

"Never suspected? Do you honestly think I'd write such prescriptions?"

"No, sir." Lillian coiled her finger in the telephone cord. "That's why I called."

"See it doesn't happen again. Or I'll send my patients elsewhere." The receiver slammed down.

Lillian sat hard on her stool. A forger. Not a sinister doctor, but an actual forger. That was a crime.

"My word. I need to call the police." She yanked the phone book from the drawer, found the number for the police department, and coaxed her fingers to dial. After a few explanations, she was funneled to Detective Mike Malloy, and she explained the situation.

"Is the suspect in the store?" the detective asked.

"No, he came yesterday."

"And you're just calling now?"

Lillian released a sigh. "It's a long story."

"It doesn't do any good to call after the fact. Not if we want to catch him."

"But I have his name and address right here."

"Miss, do you think he'd use his real name and address?"

Lillian ran her finger over the forged signature. "Some of the prescriptions are for delivery."

"Mm-hmm. That way they can leave the store immediately and not get caught."

"But someone has to receive the delivery, so—"

"So what? The crooks can use addresses for vacant apartments, leave the cash payment in an envelope under the door-mat, and pick up the drugs on the stoop after the delivery boy leaves."

"Oh." She hadn't considered that.

"That's why the suspect needs to be in the store. If it happens again, call us, but don't tip off the suspect."

Lillian rubbed her temple. Mr. Dixon wouldn't like that at all. "I—I will. Thank you, Detective Malloy."

"You're welcome. I'm glad to hear there's a vigilant new druggist in town." He laughed. "But wait till I tell my wife. A girl druggist? What'll they think of next?"

"A girl detective?"

He laughed again, a good, merry sound. "Don't give my wife any ideas."

Lillian grinned. Fewer than 5 percent of pharmacists were women. She might be the world's first female druggist-detective. How fun.

She held up the two prescriptions for comparison. An excellent forger, who had fooled both Mr. Dixon and her.

A chill swept up her arms. A forger this good would be a hardened criminal, and he probably had help. After all, he'd written quite a few prescriptions for a lot of phenobarbital, more than any one man would need. Other stores might be filling these prescriptions too.

This wasn't one drug addict forging for his own use. This was a ring. A good-sized ring. And Lillian stood right in the middle of it.

15

As soon as everyone stepped off the train at the Concord Depot, Quintessa dashed to the pay phone. "I can't wait to surprise Clifford."

Jim, Mary, and Lillian formed a cluster nearby, but Arch hung back. Even the prospect of an outing with Lillian hadn't lifted his spirits.

Quintessa flipped through the phone book.

"Did you forget to bring his number?" Mary asked.

"Oh, he never gave it to me." Quintessa tucked a blonde curl behind her ear. "His mother's very ill. She won't be around long, poor thing, and it distresses her when Clifford dates, so he doesn't want me to call."

Arch frowned. How strange.

Jim rubbed the back of his neck. "Should you be calling, then?"

"We've been dating over two months, and I'm a little tired of this. He shouldn't let his mother control him, even if she's ill." Quintessa closed the door of the phone booth.

Lillian leaned closer to Mary. "If I didn't know better, I'd think he was married."

Mary gasped and covered her mouth with her fingers. "I was thinking the same thing."

Jim draped his arms around the ladies' shoulders. "You both read too many mysteries. It's making you suspicious."

"Last time I was suspicious, I was right." Mary gave him a smug smile.

Arch approached the group. "Think about it. He won't give her his phone number. He only sees her in Boston on Friday evenings and the occasional weekend. Either he's a milksop mama's boy or he's married."

"Not you too," Jim grumbled.

"Oh, Jim. That's why I love you." Mary kissed his cheek. "You always think highly of people. But I'll talk to Quintessa this evening in private."

The phone booth door opened, and Quintessa emerged with a fake smile. "He can't get away. His mother's feeling poorly. I don't want to sound selfish, but now I'm feeling poorly."

"I'm sorry," Mary said.

Arch gave Jim an I-told-you-so look, but Jim just rolled his eyes.

Quintessa pressed her hand to her forehead. "I do sound selfish. His mother's ill, and I'm whining because I can't surprise my boyfriend with a picnic at the North Bridge."

"Nonsense." Mary hugged her. "You don't have a selfish bone in your body. You're just used to being adored by the men in your life, and when a man doesn't dote on you . . ."

Quintessa looked stricken. "That's selfish."

"No," Mary said. "Being used to something and demanding it are two different things."

Arch knew plenty of women like Quintessa. Gorgeous, intelligent, vivacious, accustomed to constant attention. At least Quintessa had a measure of humility and self-awareness.

Then there was Lillian. His gaze swung to the lovely young lady in the green coat. Not only did she not demand attention, she seemed leery of it. He wanted to know why. He wanted to change her mind. But how could he do so when his dark mood had stripped away all semblance of charm?

Arch lagged behind the group as they walked along tree-lined streets past graceful colonial homes. Everyone chatted, and Jim tried to draw him in to conversation, but Arch gave short if polite replies. Jim took the hint and stopped trying.

Lillian fell quiet. Her gait stiffened, and the hitch in her step increased. What was it like for her to walk with a prosthesis, with the stump of her leg bearing her weight with each step, perhaps rubbing in the socket? It had to hurt, yet she never complained.

They passed the Old Manse, former home to both Ralph Waldo Emerson and Nathaniel Hawthorne, and then headed down a long pathway to the North Bridge.

Lillian's shoulders relaxed, but her gait slowed.

Arch fell in beside her as they neared the bridge. "Would you like to rest?"

Her gaze flew to him, bristling with barbs. "I'm not weak."

"No, but you do get sore," he said gently.

Her mouth drifted open, then she looked away. "I—I am a bit uncomfortable today."

"There's a bench up ahead by the bridge. I could use a rest myself."

"I'm sorry I snapped," she muttered.

"Well, if your week was anything like mine, you have reason to snap." Arch plopped onto the bench, exhausted inside and out.

Lillian sat beside him and crossed her ankles a few times, probably seeking a comfortable position. "That destroyer that was sunk off the coast of Delaware, right?"

"The *Jacob Jones*." A sigh flowed out all the way from his

toes. On February 28, the *Jacob Jones* had been searching for survivors from the sunken tanker *R.P. Resor*, when she was also sunk by a U-boat. "One hundred forty-nine men killed. Dick Reinhardt was one of them. We served with him. Survived the sinking of the *Atwood*, but not the *Jacob Jones*. He was married."

"Oh no. I'm so sorry."

Arch stretched out his legs and closed his twitching eyelids. "It just won't stop. We don't have enough warships to run convoys along the East Coast. In the Pacific, the Japanese pick off our ships as if shooting skeet. How many Allied ships were sunk in the Java Sea? How many hundreds of men died? Now Singapore's fallen, and the Dutch East Indies, and tens of thousands of our men are besieged on Bataan."

"It does look bad."

"We've only been at war three months, and it's one defeat after another."

"That's only true on the outside."

"Hmm?" He opened his eyes.

Lillian held up her chin. "We'll rally. We always do. Think of the men who are enlisting, the ships and planes and tanks we're building, the women flocking to work in the factories, everyone pulling together. We just have to keep our spirits up and—and lean on the Lord."

Arch gazed at the anchor necklace at the base of her pretty neck. "'Which hope we have as an anchor of the soul.' I wish my faith ran that deep."

"I wish mine did too." Her eyes searched Arch's. "I—I'm trying to lean on him, but . . ."

Arch's eyes closed again. "I don't know why I don't lean on the Lord more. I trust him. I do."

"Me too." Lillian's voice was soft and pensive.

Something unwound in Arch, and he let it. "Growing up, I trusted in money and connections. My parents warned me not to. Trust in your mind, your character, they said—those things no man can touch. So I did. Now what do I trust in? What do I really trust in? My naval career." That was his way to escape the privileged life and its dangers. But man could take away that career. Then where would he be?

"My career." The wretchedness in Lillian's voice pried Arch's eyes open. She gazed toward the bridge, where Jim, Mary, and Quintessa leaned on the railing, dropping sticks in the water and racing to the other side to watch them float away.

"Your career?" Arch asked.

She shook her head, eyes glistening. "I didn't want to be weak like Lucy. She was sickly as a child, always depending on others, and I hated it in her. After my accident, my greatest fear was ending up like her. I pushed myself, forced myself to walk even when I bled. Then I saw how people recoiled from me. When I grew up, no one would take care of me, and I refused to burden my family. A career was my only hope, and I worked hard for it."

Arch watched her reddening face and reached into his breast pocket for a handkerchief, but she shook her head.

"My family," she said, her voice steady. "They all have such strong faith, but I resisted opening my heart to God. I do believe. I always have. But I kept him at a distance. I'm trying to change, trying to open up." She looked Arch in the eye and shifted her mouth to one side. "I don't know why I'm telling you all this."

He chuckled. "I don't know why I told you my garbage either. I guess you needed to take a load off your feet, and we both needed to take loads off our chests."

"Well, I refuse to be down." She stood. "Come on. We can't come to Concord and not cross the North Bridge."

That optimism drew him to his feet. "Yes, ma'am."

Lillian headed up the wooden bridge. "It might not cheer you up, but it'll take your mind off the war for a moment. I called Dr. Kane this week. He didn't write the prescriptions. They're forgeries."

"He's telling the truth?"

Lillian frowned. "I suppose he could be lying. I hadn't considered that."

He didn't want her to question her judgment. "A forger."

"Yes. I called the police, but they can't do anything unless he's still in the store. Next time, the detective said."

"Wait." At the top of the bridge, Arch stopped and reached for Lillian's arm.

She glanced at his hand and eased away.

Why did she distrust him so much? Even now? His stomach soured, but he let go and focused on why he'd stopped her in the first place. "Don't call the police yet."

"Why not? Forgery's a crime."

"Yes, but what if it's a ring? What if more than one person is involved?"

"I—I think it is a ring. It's too much phenobarbital for only one addict." She glanced to the far end of the bridge, where Jim and her friends stood by the Minuteman statue.

"Then please wait. If you have one man arrested, what will the others do? You could be in danger."

Fear sparked in her hazel eyes, but defiance sparked brighter. "You want me to do nothing while these criminals—"

"I want you to wait." He sank his hands in his coat pockets so he wouldn't reach for her again. "Let's investigate some more, find the links. For one thing, Palonsky and I made progress."

"You did?"

His fingers closed around the folded envelope in his pocket, and he pulled it out. "I asked him to complain about his nerves in front of Hobie McLachlan. He did so. It took a few days, but Hobie pulled Palonsky aside and gave him this." He opened the envelope.

Lillian pulled out a tablet and gasped. "That's pheno-barbital!"

"Thought so." He jiggled the envelope.

Lillian dropped the pill inside. "Palonsky didn't take any, did he?"

"No, but the next day he told Hobie he'd had the best night's sleep in ages." Arch stuffed the envelope back in his pocket. "Hobie offered to supply him with more. For a price, of course. Palonsky agreed. After all, I'm covering his costs."

"Hobie McLachlan." Lillian scanned the clouds. "The name doesn't ring a bell. I wonder where he's getting the med. From a physician? From Dixon's under a fake name? Or from a middleman?"

"He said he had a prescription, but I don't trust him one whit."

Lillian strolled toward the statue. "That's nice of you to cover the costs."

"Plus a monthly stipend." Guilt jabbed his belly. But he wasn't using his wealth to manipulate. He'd hired an assistant, perfectly acceptable.

A breeze rustled the empty branches, and Lillian brushed hair off her cheek. "He should be careful not to spend too much in front of the other sailors. They'll wonder why he's suddenly so rich."

"I told him something similar." Only he hadn't used the word *rich*. "He's saving it. He wants to go to Hollywood after the war, get into the movies. If the war ever ends, that is."

"No more of that." Lillian marched to the statue. "Where'd they go?"

Down on the riverbank, Jim set down the picnic basket, and the ladies spread out a blanket. "There they are. Lunchtime."

Lillian stared up at the statue, head tilted, fingers tapping on her crossed arms. "Look at him. He left his plow behind and picked up his gun to fight."

A smile tugged on his lips. "Just like 1942."

"Exactly." She gave him a determined look. "In 1775, who would have guessed a ragtag group of farmers—untrained, undisciplined, and unorganized—would defeat the greatest military power of their time?"

Arch turned toward the bridge. Those farmers had stood their ground, marched toward the uniformed ranks, and fired "the shot heard 'round the world."

He inhaled freedom and courage and hope. "We'll prevail too."

"Yes, we will."

Arch faced Lillian. She was good for him with her stubborn optimism. If only he could convince her that he'd be good for her as well.

16

Lillian peeled tape off the time-faded ad for Bayer aspirin and savored the afternoon sunshine slanting through the window.

Mr. Dixon handed her a poster of a pilot in his cockpit, proclaiming, "You buy 'em. We'll fly 'em. Defense Bonds and Stamps."

Lillian set it in position. Why did a man who hated paying for electricity block God's own free lighting?

With a few pieces of tape, she secured the patriotic poster. How could she present her ideas to Mr. Dixon?

On a recent Sunday at Park Street Church, Dr. Harold Ockenga had preached about Daniel standing up to the Babylonians so he and his friends could avoid unclean foods. Daniel hadn't acted in angry defiance. With respect and kindness and prayer, he'd proposed an experiment.

An experiment. Lillian sent up a prayer and cleared her throat. "Mr. Dixon, I've been thinking about why we don't sell a lot of cosmetics here."

"What do you mean? We sell plenty."

She smoothed down the last piece of tape. "Not compared to other stores where I've worked. I think we could increase sales with a feminine touch to our cosmetics display."

"Mrs. Connelly." Mr. Dixon marched to the cash register. "Do you think there's anything wrong with the cosmetics display?"

The cashier's eyes widened, then she rearranged rolls of Necco wafers. "Well, it could stand some improvement. It's not the most . . . attractive display."

Mr. Dixon strode to a customer, a woman in her forties. "Excuse me, ma'am. Do you buy cosmetics here?"

She stepped back and stared at him. "Um, well, no. I prefer to buy them . . ." She waved toward the street, as if she didn't want to name a competitor.

He tugged his white coat down over his ample belly. "With a more . . . attractive display, would you shop here?"

Her brows knit together. "I might. This store is so convenient, so close to the El station."

Mr. Dixon's dark-eyed gaze wheeled to Lillian. "A feminine touch."

"Yes, sir." She gave him a bright smile. "Think about it. Spring is almost here. We're itching for it. We ladies are tired of our winter coats, and now the War Production Board has placed limits on fashion, and we just want to feel pretty again."

Mr. Dixon rubbed his heavy jowls. "I don't like change. This is my father's store—"

"Founded in 1878," she said with pride as if she'd helped found it herself. "I only want to make one small change. An experiment. One month. If it doesn't work, everything goes back to normal."

He glared at her. "You haven't told me what you have in mind."

Lillian's heart bounded. In the doorway, she gestured to

her right. "On this side, the soda fountain and cash register, same as always, the window covered with ads and posters."

Mr. Dixon grunted his approval. Of course he did. She hadn't suggested a change yet.

Lillian gestured to the left. "On this side, set up a display on a cabinet, with a mirror. Strip away the ads so passersby can see. In the window, I can drape some pastel fabric—my roommates have remnants I can use. We can show off the latest spring goods. Then the ladies will look inside, see the cosmetics display, and wonder if a new spring shade might cheer them up in these dark times. And once they're inside . . ." She swept her hand toward the rest of the store.

Mr. Dixon's glare didn't diminish, but neither did Lillian's smile.

He grunted and adjusted his glasses. "One month, and it'd better not cost me one cent."

"No, sir. And it won't draw me away from my regular work."

"Better not." He marched down the center aisle.

It worked! Lillian wanted to cheer, to spin, to . . . something. Mrs. Connelly gave her a gleeful smile and mimed clapping her hands. Lillian mouthed "thank you" and headed for the prescription counter in a sedate manner. But in her heart, she cheered and spun and danced.

★ ★ ★

That evening after Mr. Dixon left, Lillian used a quiet moment before the store closed to sketch her plans. If she succeeded, sales would rise, and she'd keep her job. Mr. Dixon hadn't talked about replacing her for several weeks.

She was finally winning him over. This afternoon she'd gotten him talking about how he wanted to buy a cottage on Nantucket when he retired and set up his nephew in a fishing business, maybe a seafood restaurant. His love for the young man warmed Lillian's heart.

A patient approached the counter, a light-haired man in his thirties.

"Good evening," she said. "Harvey Jones, isn't it?"

"Yes." He eyed her. "I need this filled tonight. I'll wait."

Lillian studied it. Three hundred phenobarbital tablets, signed by Dr. Kane.

The blood drained from her face, and she headed for the shelf to conceal her expression.

The forger or one of his lackeys.

What should she do? She'd promised Arch she'd wait to call the police, but how could she fill a forged prescription? Dr. Kane had ordered her not to fill any more barbiturate prescriptions in his name. How could she violate her professional standards?

She couldn't. Arch meant well. He wanted to protect her, but she couldn't fill this.

Lillian took down the bulk bottle and walked to the counting tray. And the phone. Out of the side of her eye, she observed Mr. Jones. The man poked through Mr. Dixon's jar of marbles on the counter. Facing her.

How could she call the police without alerting Mr. Jones?

Her pulse raced. Maybe she could call the physician first. Just make sure.

She grabbed the phone and dialed with quivering fingers.

"Is something wrong?"

Lillian's breath froze. Her finger misdialed. She raised a benign smile. "I want to verify the prescription with Dr. Kane."

"Why? What's wrong with it?"

"Nothing I can see. But it's standard procedure."

"Mr. Dixon never calls." His voice rose, and a customer turned and stared.

She couldn't let Mr. Jones make a scene. She returned to the counter and gave him a sheepish smile. "I'm sorry, sir. I'm young and I'm a woman, and Dr. Kane doesn't trust me yet. He wants me to verify his prescriptions."

His eyes flashed. "Then I don't trust you either. Mr. Dixon shouldn't leave you alone."

Her story was falling to pieces before her eyes. "I'm a licensed—"

Mr. Jones snatched the prescription from her hand. "I'll take my business elsewhere from now on. You can tell Mr. Dixon I said so."

Oh no. What had she done?

The crook had fled, and he'd taken the evidence with him. Now she couldn't call the police.

She'd also lost business for the store. What if Mr. Jones complained? What if he told her boss her stupid story about Dr. Kane not trusting her? Mr. Dixon would fire her on the spot.

She moaned, leaned back against the counter, and pressed her hand to her forehead.

Why had she told that story? Calling Dr. Kane to verify? Mr. Jones *knew* Dr. Kane hadn't written that prescription. Her story was guaranteed to set off the crook's alarms. What was she thinking? She wasn't any good at making up stories like that. She should have thought up something better in advance, knowing this day would come.

Now Mr. Jones wouldn't be back. He'd go to another pharmacy and continue his racket.

Her head spun. If he was part of a ring, she'd tipped them off. Would they think she was on to them? Or just a silly untrustworthy girl? Would they buy her story? Or would they see the truth—that she'd already talked to Dr. Kane about the phenobarbital?

What a disaster.

★ ★ ★

That night on her walk home, Lillian saw dark figures in every doorway. Nonsense. She was overreacting. This wasn't a Hollywood movie with spooks prowling after young ladies.

Still, the streets seemed too quiet, the night too dark, the streetlamps too weak.

She turned right onto Monument Avenue. Ahead of her on the hill, the Bunker Hill Monument towered dark, a finger of accusation.

Arch had trusted her to follow one simple instruction. She'd promised him. And she'd failed.

Yet she longed to tell him. In Concord, she'd spilled her heart before him, and he'd understood, wisdom and compassion deep in those too-blue eyes. She pictured him reaching for her again as he had on the bridge. This time, instead of flinching like a dog who'd been kicked too often, she'd fall into his arms.

He'd hold her. She knew he would.

What would it be like to lean into him, to let him support her, even for a minute?

Her breath quickened. From anticipation—or terror? If she trusted him, what would become of her? The last time she'd trusted a man . . .

Lillian shuddered and gripped her necklace. Dad's favorite hymn said, "My hope is built on nothing less than Jesus' blood and righteousness; I dare not trust the sweetest frame, but wholly lean on Jesus' name."

Arch's frame might be sweet indeed, but she needed to lean on the Lord, not a man.

Footsteps clumped behind her, heavy and masculine. Was she being followed, or was her imagination getting the best of her? If it was Mr. Jones, she'd let him know he couldn't intimidate her.

She flung a pointed glance over her shoulder.

Not Mr. Jones. This man was tall and angular. The tip of his cigarette glowed red in the darkness, and a wisp of gray smoke trailed to his side.

Nevertheless, she picked up her pace and pulled her keys from her purse so she wouldn't have to pause at the door.

Finally, her building, the only one with blackout curtains. Although Boston hadn't ordered a blackout, Mary insisted as a quiet way of declaring the necessity for the men at sea.

Lillian climbed the stairs, jammed her key into the lock, and shoved open the door. The tall man passed by without a glance.

She shut the door and threw the lock. But it had only been her imagination.

"Hi there, sweetie," Quintessa called. "We kept the pot roast warm in the oven for you."

Mary, Quintessa, and their other roommate, Yvette Lafontaine, sat in the living room, smiling their greetings, looking up from books and magazines. On the radio in the background, Cab Calloway sang "Blues in the Night."

Lillian managed to say a cheery "good evening," then escaped to her room to take off her prosthesis and put on her cozy nightgown and bathrobe.

How had a day that started so well ended so horribly?

17

Fog pressed on the *Ettinger*, blinding her and concealing her. Standing by the aft funnel, Arch could see neither bow nor stern. Only gray.

For once, they weren't at general quarters, so the boatswain's mates performed basic maintenance as the ship patrolled between Cape Ann to the north of Boston and Pollock Rip at the southern tip of Cape Cod. The men chipped off paint, repaired lines, and checked tackle and davits, the sounds of their tools hollow in the fog.

Carpenter's Mate Bud Engelman handed Arch his report. "Mr. Vandenberg, sir. I took the daily soundings in the peak tanks and voids. No leakage noted."

Seaman Phil Carey stood beside the petty officer, blinking heavily.

"Very well." Always good to know the hull's structural integrity remained sound. Arch scanned the report, then his gaze flipped up to Carey, who was striking to earn a promotion to carpenter's mate as well. "Are you all right, Carey?"

"Just tired, sir. Not getting enough sleep, you know."

"It's almost noon." Engelman scowled. "He's always tired, sir. Can't get any work out of him."

Was Carey taking drugs too? Arch studied the young man's square-jawed face, but droopy eyelids weren't solid proof. Regardless, he had to do something. "I know you're tired, Carey. We all are. But we have to make do. U-boats are sinking our ships, and we're the only line of defense. You must stay alert."

"Aye aye, sir."

Arch clapped Engelman on the shoulder. "Get the man some coffee, the blacker the better. And let me know if this continues. Next time we're in port, Carey might need a long nap on board rather than liberty."

The striker's shoulders slumped.

After they left, Arch read the report more thoroughly and headed to the bridge to take the paperwork to Emmett Taylor, who was serving as officer of the deck on this watch.

"Hey, watch it, Stein!"

Arch whipped around and glanced up at the torpedo tubes.

"Sorry, Fish. Just some oil. Won't happen again." Seaman Stein handed a rag to Torpedoman's Mate Gifford Payne, nicknamed "Fish" for his work with torpedoes.

Fish wiped his face. "Wake up and watch what you're doing, you clod. I'm adjusting the firing mechanism, and you startled me. Could have been fatal to all of us."

"Sorry, Fish. Sorry." Stein rubbed his eyes as if waking from a nap.

Arch shook his head and headed for the bridge, his conscience niggling him. It wasn't enough to investigate the problems on board. He needed to report them. Captain Buckner wouldn't like it, but Arch had to do his duty as an officer. And soon.

For one thing, the problems seemed to extend past the

deck division into ordnance. Jim hadn't seen any problems in engineering. Down in the engine and fire rooms, they didn't see the carnage.

For the first time since the *Atwood* went down, Arch longed for his old position below decks, blind to the death and destruction around them.

But no, the deck division was better. Up here, at least he wouldn't die trapped.

What were his chances of surviving the war anyway? The Japanese continued to devour the Pacific Islands, now down to the Solomons, a small leap from Australia.

In the Atlantic, only two U-boats had been sunk by the Americans, both by Navy aircraft off the shores of Newfoundland, making no dent in the losses of merchant ships. Adm. Ernest King, the Commander-in-Chief of the US Navy, refused to institute convoys along the East Coast until adequate escort ships were available. The British were planning to send twenty-four anti-submarine trawlers, but the vessels were too slow to do much good.

So many tankers had been sunk that an oil shortage loomed, threatening war production both in the US and in Britain. Just when they needed more ships and shells and bullets.

Arch entered the bridge superstructure and climbed the ladder to the pilothouse.

Lt. Emmett Taylor stood behind the helmsman and smiled. "Reports for me?"

"Yes, sir." He handed them to the chief engineer. "Soundings of the peak tanks and voids. All's well."

"Should be riveting reading. Anything else to report?"

Taylor had more experience. Perhaps he'd have some advice before Arch reported to Buckner. "The usual complaints of sleepy sailors."

"Again?" Buckner's voice sounded behind him, from the doorway to the captain's sea cabin.

Apparently now was the time. Arch wasn't ready, but he drew a deep breath and faced the captain. "Yes, sir. I'd like to speak to you in private."

"Very well." He motioned for Arch to follow him to his cabin, where the CO took a seat at the desk.

Arch stood tall, scrambling to organize his thoughts on such short notice. "I've observed two problems. First, some of my men are jittery and suffer from nightmares."

"Make them buck up. We're at war."

With a slow nod, Arch clasped his hands behind his back to conceal the fisting. "It isn't as easy as it sounds, sir. These are good men, volunteers who want to fight for their country. But constant vigilance is a strain for anyone, and the sights we've seen try the strongest souls."

Buckner raised one dark eyebrow. "I refuse to coddle them. This is a destroyer, not a nursery."

"I understand, sir. However, I fear this might be leading to a second problem." He gripped his hands harder. "The drowsy sailors."

"They're lazy. You need to make them buck up."

Back to that again. "I fear the drowsiness is only a symptom. There is some indication the men might be treating their frayed nerves with drugs."

The captain sat forward, his dark eyes piercing. "Drugs?"

"Yes, sir. I . . . I've heard rumors."

"Who? I need names."

Arch measured his words. If the captain cracked down and arrested Hobie, the investigation would be over and the problems would continue. "As I said, rumors. I've discussed the situation with Pharmacist's Mate Lloyd, and he shares my concerns."

Buckner tapped his pen on the desk, over and over, shaking his head. "No. No, I don't agree. I run a tight ship. Very tight. Nothing like that could occur under my watch."

Yet it was indeed occurring. "Yes, sir, but—"

"No." Buckner jabbed his pen in Arch's direction. "They're lazy. You coddle them. They need stronger discipline, and you need to give it to them."

That was an order, and only one response was allowed. A sigh eased out. "Aye aye, sir."

"Dismissed." Buckner waved him to the door. "I'm beginning to wonder if you should be assigned to shore duty."

"I—I'd rather not, sir. I'll make the men buck up. Don't worry." He strode from the cabin. Shore duty? That would kill his career. If the war ever ended, if he survived, if he didn't lose his commission for his weak nerves, what would remain for him? A polite suggestion that he go to the reserves, that he would be better suited for civilian life.

In Concord with Lillian, he'd realized he trusted in his career. What a flimsy anchor. A doctor could take it away with the stroke of a pen. He had to trust in God as his anchor. Had to.

But without the Navy, who would he be? Just another rich snob, using people for gain. *Oh Lord, not that.*

The simple, wholesome life in the Navy had built his character. If he returned to high society, it would all be undone.

Dear Mrs. Lafferty's face filled his mind. The Vandenberg housekeeper had been so good for young Arch—kindly when he needed affection and firm when he needed discipline. And he'd repaid her with betrayal.

His stomach caved in, and he couldn't see for the frenetic twitching of his eyelid. Never again. *Lord, help me. Be my anchor.*

Arch stood inside the doorway to the bridge superstructure, praying, breathing heavily, his hands groping empty air.

"Excuse me, sir."

Arch sucked in a breath and spun around.

Parnell Lloyd stood in the passageway. "Didn't mean to startle you, sir. Do you have a moment?"

"Yes." Arch wiped his palms on his blue trousers. "Yes, I do."

Doc beckoned him deeper into the passageway. "I overheard Fish yelling at Stein for not paying attention, and Stein complaining of his nerves, not getting enough sleep. Have you . . . have you had any more incidents with your men?"

"Several."

"I've been asking around." Doc glanced behind him. "The men won't talk to me. They insist they can handle it. But you work with them. Who's having the biggest problems?"

Why was Doc acting so suspicious? "Why do you want to know?"

Doc turned back, all wide-eyed innocence. "I'm responsible for the health and welfare of the crew. It's my job to know."

It was also his job to refer men for medical discharge. "I'll let you know if any man's condition seriously interferes with his work."

"No, it's more than that." Zeal shone in Doc's brown eyes. "I want to find out who's suffering, who might be using medication. I want to help them."

Arch studied the man's intelligent face. Were they working toward the same goal—to find the source of medication on board? Or did Doc just want to drum sailors out of the Navy? "How can you help?"

Doc huffed out a breath. "Honestly, sir, I don't know. The physicians have some success with rest under heavy sedation, but not many patients return to duty."

"So once they enter the hospital—"

"I know. I wish I could treat the symptoms on board and keep them on duty."

Apparently that's what the men themselves were trying to do. Arch opened his mouth to tell Doc about Palonsky, about Hobie selling him phenobarbital. But something about Doc's shining zeal shut his mouth.

Did Doc want to supply the men with sedatives? He had access to medications through the Navy. Or he could tap into a ring on shore. What if he were the source on the *Ettinger*? What if he wanted Arch to tattle on the men so he could find new customers?

As much as he wanted to trust Doc as an ally, it seemed wise to treat him as a suspect.

Arch set his hand on the pharmacist's mate's shoulder. "I wish you could help them too. If I hear anything you should know, I'll tell you."

"Thank you, sir." He departed.

Yes, Arch would tell Doc anything he *should* know. Nothing more. He didn't have much information anyway. Hobie sold the drug to Palonsky but wouldn't reveal where it had come from. Arch had Palonsky flush it down the head so he wouldn't be caught with it.

The watch was almost over, so Arch headed to the quarter-deck to brief his replacement.

No progress in the case. No progress in his career. No progress with his nerves. Why couldn't he at least have success with Lillian?

Sure, she'd opened up to him. But then she'd flinched from his touch. She wanted his friendship but nothing more.

When women were interested in him, they only wanted his money. And now a wonderful woman didn't want his money—but she wasn't interested in him. Why couldn't he find someone who loved him for himself?

Arch groaned. Maybe it wasn't possible.

18

Lillian slid the pan of scalloped potatoes into the oven and set the timer.

"Are you sure I can't help?" Mary sat at the kitchen table, her chin resting in her hands.

"Nope. It's my night to cook. Sit and relax."

Mary poked through the bowl of shelled peas. "Now it's your turn to solve a mystery. It's such fun. You need a Nancy Drew name, like *The Secret of the Sedated Sailors*."

Lillian scooted a kitchen chair in front of the counter, rested her left knee on it, and opened the paper-wrapped bundle of pork chops. "*The Affair of the Pharmaceutical Forger?*"

"I like that. Mine was *The Case of the Shipyard Saboteur*." Mary sighed and brushed her dark brown hair off her shoulder. "I miss my notebooks. I kept records of conversations, organized by suspects."

"A notebook." Lillian scooped some grease from the can by the stove into the frying pan. "Maybe I should keep a record.

We have prescription files at Dixon's, but they're arranged by prescription number. It's hard to look for trends."

"Oh yes. You could make a log of the suspicious prescriptions."

Lillian smeared the sizzling clump of lard in the pan. "I like the idea. I could see which doctors are involved. Ever since I scared away Mr. Jones, we haven't had a single sedative prescription in Dr. Kane's name. Now they come from two other physicians. But the patients insist that Mr. Dixon fill the prescriptions. He never asks questions."

Yvette Lafontaine breezed into the kitchen and rummaged in the refrigerator. "I'm sorry, dear ones. The French patriots have an emergency meeting tonight."

"Oh." Lillian scrunched her lips together. "Dinner won't be ready till six-thirty."

"Keep a plate warm in the oven, *ma petite amie*. I'll grab a bite of cheese for now. Those Vichy swine are destroying my beloved France, collaborating with the Nazis. So little we can do from America, but we must do something."

"I understand," Mary said.

"Look at me, turning into an American and eating 'on the run.'" The elegant brunette frowned at the cheese. "Oh well. *Au revoir*." She dashed for the door.

Lillian smiled and plopped the pork chops into the pan. "They're keeping you and Yvette busy at the Navy Yard, aren't they?"

"They sure are. The shipyard is running two shifts a day. There's so much work, so many ships being built and repaired. At least I always know when the *Ettinger* pulls in to port."

"Are they back?"

"No." Mary's mouth curved into a smile. "You look eager."

"Goodness, no." She salted the chops.

"You don't want to see your brother?"

Lillian grabbed the pepper shaker. "Of course I do. I didn't mean it that way."

"I know what you meant." Mary's voice lilted.

She'd backed herself into a corner. All she could do was keep busy. She opened the can of tomato soup, spooned it over the pork chops, and lowered the heat.

Mary's chair squeaked. "I love watching you and Arch together."

"We're not together." Her face heated, and not from the stove.

"I know, but I still love it. Last year when Arch was dating Gloria, he was all smooth charm, but they never had long, deep talks like you do."

"We just talk as friends, mostly about the case." That wasn't entirely true. Once again, she was closing herself off.

Lord, help me. Help me open up. Lillian pushed the chair away from the stove and sat. "I don't know what to do."

"What do you mean?"

Lillian shook her head. She couldn't speak.

"Arch?" Mary said. "Why, you don't have to do anything really. Just show an inkling of interest. He's already besotted."

"Besotted!"

"Besotted." Mary raised a dreamy smile. "Remember how he flirted with you in Vermilion? You gave him the cold shoulder, and he backed off. But he didn't go away. He's approaching slowly, cautiously."

Lillian rested her elbows on her knees and dropped her head into her hands. "Oh no."

"What's the matter? Don't you like him?"

"I do. He's a good friend."

"But you aren't attracted to him."

If only that were true. She moaned. "What's wrong with him?"

"Wrong?"

138

Lillian pressed the heels of her hands against her eyes. She never cried, and she wouldn't start now. "Archer Vandenberg could have any girl in the world. Why would he want a cripple?"

Mary came around the table and hugged Lillian's shoulders. "Because you're pretty and smart and funny and you stand up to him."

Lillian sat up straight and looked Mary in the eye. "You've known him longer than I have. Does he have a dark side?"

"Dark?" She frowned. "He gets morose sometimes, like when he realized Gloria only loved him for his money. But we all have our moods."

"No, I mean dark. Sinister."

Mary's eyebrows drew together, and she scrutinized Lillian's face.

How could she explain without . . . explaining? She covered her face with her hands. "I had a boyfriend in college. He said he loved me, but he only wanted me because I was weak. Not a precious sort of weak, a porcelain figurine to cherish. Oh no. He wanted a marionette he could manipulate, and there I was with my little wooden leg. But I showed him. I cut my strings."

"Oh, honey." Mary drew her closer. "I'm sorry that happened to you."

She didn't know the half of it, but Lillian succumbed to the hug. She'd never told anyone before, not Dad or Mom or Jim. She'd only told them Gordon wasn't the man she'd thought, giving her chin a lift that silenced further questions.

She was good at silencing questions, at shutting people out. Now, collapsed in Mary's embrace, she couldn't remember why she did so. Strange how the more she opened up to God, the more she opened up to others.

Her eyes felt moist, and the smell of tomato soup filled her nostrils.

"The pork chops!" Lillian extracted herself and checked on dinner. Just fine, thank goodness.

"Thank you for telling me," Mary said in a soft voice.

"Don't tell Jim please." What if he told Arch? What if Arch did want a puppet to control? But deep inside, she suspected he didn't.

Even so, did she want to become involved with him? Her throat constricted at the thought.

The front door opened and shut.

"Hi, Quintessa," Mary called. "We're in here."

No response.

Mary frowned at Lillian. "Yvette? Quintessa?"

Footsteps shuffled across the living room floor. Yvette and Quintessa never shuffled.

Lillian's blood ran cold, and her hand closed around the knife she'd used on the potatoes.

Quintessa appeared in the doorway, face pale, blonde curls disheveled. "You were right."

"Goodness!" Mary said. "What happened?"

"You were right," she said in a monotone. "He's married."

"Oh no." The knife clattered to the counter. Lillian didn't want to be right about that.

Mary rushed to her friend. "Oh, sweetheart."

"He . . . he's married. And I—I kissed him." She groaned, clapped her hand over her mouth, and ran to the bathroom.

Lillian and Mary followed, but Quintessa had shut the bathroom door. Sounds of retching filled the air.

"Oh no." Lillian leaned back against the wall.

"Poor Quintessa." Mary mirrored Lillian's posture. "Poor, poor thing."

Lillian stared at the ceiling. Clifford had lied and cheated and manipulated. Her brothers couldn't be the only honorable men in the world, but why did so many men have to be cads?

In a few minutes, the faucet turned on and off, and Quintessa emerged, even paler and more disheveled. She trudged to her room, sank onto the bed, and curled into a ball.

Lillian sat and pulled off Quintessa's shoes.

Mary lay beside her friend and rubbed her shoulder. "Are you certain?"

"A—a lady came to Filene's this afternoon and introduced herself as Mrs. Clifford White. She had pictures. Her girl-friend album, she calls it. She shows it to all his girlfriends. I'm not . . . I'm not the first."

Mary pushed curls off Quintessa's face. "I'm sorry, honey."

"Their wedding picture. They have children. A boy and a girl. Their Christmas picture. It was this year. I know, 'cause she was wearing the scarf I helped him pick out for his—his mother." A sob burst out.

"There's no sick mother," Lillian said through gritted teeth. "Just a sick, sick man."

Quintessa groaned and turned her face to the pillow. "I can't stand it. I was so angry, so furious when Hugh cheated on me with *her*."

Lillian and Mary exchanged a glance. Quintessa hadn't spoken the name of her high school sweetheart since he'd gotten Alice Pendleton pregnant and married her.

"But I'm no better," Quintessa mumbled into the pillow. "I'm worse. He's married!"

"You didn't know," Mary murmured. "You couldn't have known."

"Why not?" Quintessa faced her friend through a tangle of curls. "There were signs. You two recognized them. But I ignored them. Am I that desperate?"

Lillian patted Quintessa's knee, at a loss for words.

Mary stroked back Quintessa's hair. "Shh. Please don't be hard on yourself. It isn't like you."

"It isn't, is it?" Quintessa rolled onto her back, eyes large

141

and stricken. "I'm never hard on myself. But I need to be. I don't know who I am anymore."

Lillian's heart ached for her. She knew what that was like.

Quintessa rubbed her forehead. "Ever since I came to Boston, I've been grasping for adoration. First I came between you and Jim, and now this. A married man! Who am I?"

Mary gripped Quintessa's hand. "You didn't know Jim and I were falling for each other, because neither one of us told you. And you didn't know Clifford was married, because he certainly didn't tell you. You have nothing to feel guilty about. Angry, yes. Brokenhearted, yes. Betrayed, yes. But not guilty."

But Lillian recognized the devastation in Quintessa's eyes, the soul-searching devastation when you realized you weren't the person you thought you were.

Lillian patted Quintessa's knee again, awkward and inadequate. "I know. I know."

19

The *Ettinger* drifted toward the pier at the Boston Navy Yard at a ten-degree angle, her engines still. Arch strode toward the stern, longing to fill his eyes with the city's skyline and his mind with thoughts of an evening with Lillian Avery, but he had work to do.

The deck looked shipshape, the crew in dress blues, the bright work shined, and all equipment and laundry stowed. More importantly, the mooring lines were faked down, laid in neat loops clear for running, with the heaving lines attached and seamen standing by.

The ship edged closer, and a sailor cast the bowline to the pier.

"Cast seven," the talker called.

"Cast seven," Arch repeated, and a seaman heaved the stern line to the pier. One by one the other lines were cast. Commands raced. "Slack one!" "Take a strain, seven!" "Check four!"

Arch leaned over the lifeline to judge the distance to the pier and to guide the lines.

The rudder was put over away from the pier to swing the stern closer, and the engine revved in reverse to stop the headway.

The after quarter spring line drooped too low. "Take in slack on five!" Arch shouted.

Hobie McLachlan manned that line, but he was rubbing the space between his eyes.

"McLachlan!" Arch yelled. "Take in slack!"

"What, sir? Oh." He gathered in the slack, but he was too slow, and the line dipped into the water.

Arch groaned. Once they were moored, they'd have to replace that line. Buckner would have words. "Watch what you're doing, boys."

At least the men in charge of the fender flopped it down in time to keep the destroyer from bumping the pier. When the *Ettinger* rested parallel to the pier, the men doubled up the lines and rigged the gangway.

One night in Boston, then out to patrol again. Over two dozen sinkings in the past two weeks, and the few naval vessels along the coast ran around in fruitless patrols, chasing sightings and rescuing survivors. If this continued, the loss in oil and cargo would seriously hinder the war effort.

Before long, all but a skeleton crew disembarked the *Ettinger* for liberty. Down on the pier, Lt. Dan Avery stood with Mary Stirling, both grinning and waving. Arch waved back. It wasn't like Dan to look jolly. What was going on?

Arch and Jim descended the gangway, and Jim swept Mary into his arms and kissed her.

Impatience wriggled inside. Would he ever get together with Lillian? It shouldn't require this much effort.

Yet she was worth the effort. Tonight they planned to take the ladies dancing. If Clifford wasn't in town, maybe they could talk Dan into escorting Quintessa. Arch would sit out with Lillian or perhaps coax her to dance as he'd coaxed her to skate.

"Best news since Pearl Harbor," Dan said with that grin still in place. "Today Admiral King approved coastal convoys."

"He did?" Arch shook his head to clear his mind and his ears. "We still don't have enough escorts."

"Not by a long shot." Dan crossed his arms. "The plan is for partial convoys starting in April—they're calling them bucket brigades—with full convoys by May or June."

"Bucket brigades?" Jim asked.

"You know the U-boats mainly attack at night," Dan said. "So the convoys will sail by day and put into harbor at night. All the merchantmen will sail together with whatever escorts we can arrange. They're even purchasing private yachts and arming them with depth charges and machine guns."

"Say, Arch." Jim nudged him with an elbow. "You have a yacht."

The idea of a machine gun on the *Caroline* made him laugh. "I'm afraid she's too small."

"They're also releasing seventy Kingfishers for air patrols in the Eastern and Gulf Sea Frontiers." Dan tilted his head toward the open ocean. "Not the long-range bombers we need, but it's a step in the right direction."

"And a cause for celebration." Jim whirled Mary around. "What do you say? Think we can talk Lillian and Quintessa into an evening of dancing?"

Mary's laughter and smile dissolved. "Oh. Not Quintessa. I—I'll explain later."

"Mr. Avery, sir?" A seaman stood to the side with a stack of mail. "A letter for you. And Mr. Vandenberg, you have three."

"From Rob," Jim said with a grin.

Dan peeked over his shoulder. "From Hawaii. I'm trying not to be jealous of our brother. Right in the thick of
things."

Arch flipped through the envelopes—one from his mother,
one from Bitsy—no, two from Bitsy. He groaned and tucked
the two unwanted letters in his trouser pocket.

As they walked down the pier, Arch read the letter from
his mother, skimming through the society news.

> We hope you'll be able to come home for our thir-
> tieth anniversary next month. We're planning a lovely
> dinner on Friday, April 24, with music and dancing.
> We'll understand if you can't come, but we'll be elated
> if you can.
>
> By the way, Bitsy and her friends will be in Boston
> next week to visit her brother. She hopes to see you.
> When you came home in December, she was quite con-
> cerned about your welfare, and she says you haven't
> replied to her letters, which deepens her concern. I know
> you two aren't close any longer—and I don't blame
> you after how she threw you over—but she regrets her
> actions. Please remember the Chamberlains are dear
> friends. If your ship is in town and you don't see her,
> we'll never hear the end of it.

That explained why he had two letters from Miss Elizabeth
Chamberlain. Arch extracted them from his pocket—one
from Stonington and one from Boston.

He opened the most recent one. Bitsy was in Boston through
March 29. She was in town today.

Arch's groan caused the rest of the party to stop and stare
at him.

"Is everything all right?" Mary asked.

He waved the perfume-scented missive. "Bitsy's in town.

My former girlfriend. She'll know we're in port, and she expects to see me. And my parents expect me to see her."

"Guess you have no choice," Jim said.

Arch huffed. "We're only in town one night. I'd rather spend it with my friends. But I don't have a choice."

"We understand." Mary's eyes shone with sympathy, but the tilt of her mouth almost looked smug. "Lillian will understand too."

Lillian would probably be thrilled. He wanted to crumple the stupid letter, but he needed the hotel phone number.

Why did it have to be a Friday? He couldn't take Bitsy and her girlfriends out for coffee. They'd expect a night on the town. It was the right thing to do, but he didn't have to like it.

★ ★ ★

In the lobby of the Parker House, Bitsy held both of Arch's hands and gave him a sly smile. "Archer Vandenberg, if I'd known you'd look like this in naval uniform, I never would have broken up with you."

Her friends, Trudy Sutherland and Helen Whipple, twittered by her side.

Arch extracted his hands. "You three ladies are a vision of loveliness."

Trudy patted her brown curls. "Poor Archie. He never got over you, did he, Bits?"

Helen raised her long chin to Bitsy. "You did treat him abominably."

"I did. But I was a silly child then. I'm all grown up now."

Indeed she was. Every inch a cool elegant beauty. Deep-brown hair hung in sleek waves to her shoulders, the front pinned up in curls. Her golden dress clung to a figure as long-legged and lean as he remembered from his youth, but rounded out nicely.

She was lethal.

And he couldn't let her know. "You said we have reservations for six o'clock?"

"Oh my." Helen swung back her pale blonde hair. "All business. What happened to the legendary Vandenberg charm?"

"I grew up too. Shall we?" He gestured across the hotel lobby.

Trudy chattered the whole way, while Helen lashed her with droll comments. Arch studied the ornate wood paneling as they walked. A mutual friend had once told him Bitsy chose her friends because she looked brilliant in comparison to Trudy and gorgeous in comparison to Helen. A cynical thought, but not unwarranted.

In the restaurant, they were shown to a table. The waiter took their orders and brought out the famous Parker House rolls.

Bitsy laid her hand on Arch's forearm. "It's good to see you. I've been concerned. You looked positively haggard in December, and you didn't stay for Christmas."

"You went out west, didn't you?" Trudy asked.

One corner of Arch's mouth flicked up. "I stayed with my friend Jim's family in Ohio."

"Ohio." Helen raised one plucked eyebrow. "How quaint."

Arch sipped his water. He had once been that big of a snob too.

"Well, I think you look worlds better now." Bitsy gave his arm a proprietary squeeze. "You're still quiet, but we *are* at war."

"We are." They had no idea, none at all. Men were dying in the Philippines and New Guinea and Burma, and hundreds of men were dying at sea, and here they sat at ease, while the piano played "Dancing in the Dark."

Trudy laced her fingers together and rested her chin on top. "Tell us, Archie. What's it like in the Navy?"

"First, I don't go by Archie anymore. Just Arch." He laid his hands in his lap to break Bitsy's grip. "And the Navy is the right place for me to be."

"We *are* at war," Helen said.

Trudy nodded as if she'd had a deep thought. "Yes, we are." How many times would they say that?

"What is it about the Navy that draws you? I want to understand." Bitsy's brown eyes glowed.

So now she wanted to understand. When they were eighteen, she didn't want to hear one word about it.

"The sea? Sailing?" she asked.

"That's part of it." An idea tumbled in his mind, and he grabbed it, molded it into words for the first time. "The sea has always drawn me—magnificent, immense, mysterious, powerful. Now I know why. Those same traits also draw me to the Lord. Especially lately. When I'm at sea, I feel . . . weak. I'm learning the Lord, only the Lord, is my strength."

All three ladies wore flat smiles, and they shot nervous glances at each other. He'd breached the law of propriety in his crowd. Good.

Energy surged through him. Time to drive the wedge deeper. "That's not the only reason I love the Navy. It's the spare simplicity of life. Jim and I share a cabin twelve feet by six. Bunks, a sink, a desk, and a locker this wide." He measured off space between his hands. "Everything I own fits inside. Everything I want."

"All this serious talk." Bitsy clucked her tongue and gave Arch an impish smile. "Come along, darling. Why don't you ask me to dance while we wait for our dinner?"

Once again, he had no choice. He stood, nodded apologies to Trudy and Helen, and offered his arm to Bitsy. "Shall we?"

"I thought you'd never ask." She followed him to the dance floor and nestled in his arms as the piano played "Star Dreams."

Her perfume filled his nostrils, sophisticated and evocative. The supple feel of her waist under his arm and the brush of her hair against his chin brought a rush of memories. Dances and horseback rides and picnics. Bitsy stretched on the *Caroline* in the sunshine, her legs as long as a summer's day. Heated, fumbling kisses whenever and wherever they could steal them.

Bitsy sighed and stroked his shoulder with her thumb. "I do worry. I've never known you to be so serious."

"We *are* at war." He couldn't resist.

She snuggled closer. "I can't bear the thought of anything happening to you. I could never forgive myself."

"Forgive yourself? Unless you're a German spy, you have nothing to fear."

She raised her face only a few short inches away, her brown eyes crowned with long lashes. "I mean, I could never forgive myself for how I ended it with you, for not understanding your patriotism and your love of the sea. I should have supported you, but I was silly."

His feet struggled to remember the dance steps. How he would have welcomed that speech a few years ago.

Her bright red lips trembled, just a touch. "Can you ever forgive me?"

"I forgave you a long time ago."

"Oh, thank you, darling. And I forgive you for not answering my letters. Although you must improve in that matter." A coy lift of her eyebrows, and she nestled closer, making him well aware of her new curves.

Heat rose in his belly. He wouldn't have to work for her trust and affection. She didn't recoil from his touch. A few charming words, and she'd be his again.

Would that be so bad? She regretted her choice. She wouldn't pressure him to leave the Navy after the war, would she? She'd learned her lesson, hadn't she?

The heat turned muggy and stifling. The ceiling pressed on him, the hatch slammed shut, dogged into position.

Trapped.

He knew Bitsy too well. She'd drag him back to their old life, and if he resisted, she'd make him miserable. This woman would never be satisfied with the spartan life he loved.

Besides, he couldn't lie to himself. How could he give his heart back to Elizabeth Chamberlain when it belonged to Lillian Avery? Even if Lillian didn't want it, it was hers.

"Darling?" Bitsy looked up with tiny creases across her brow. "Are you all right? Your hand is . . ."

Shaking. His hand was shaking.

He drew in a long breath. Then he stopped dancing and took both her hands in his. "Yes, I've forgiven you. And I appreciate everything you said. But we're not right for each other."

Hurt flickered in her eyes, then a flash of anger, then it all smoothed into confident composure. "So you say. Things change."

No, they wouldn't. But he gave her a polite tilt of his head. "Shall we finish our dance?"

She laughed and twirled into his arms. "Oh, my darling. Our dance will never end."

He laughed for her sake, to help her save face, but he prayed she was wrong.

20

No prescriptions waited to be filled, Mr. Dixon wasn't coming in until one o'clock, and Albert was cleaning the soda fountain.

Perfect. Lillian pulled her notepad out of her purse in the stockroom, returned to the prescription file, and found where she'd stopped yesterday.

Lillian flipped back until she found another order for a large quanitity of barbiturates, then recorded the date, the patient's name, the doctor's name, the medication, and the quantity.

As suspected, nothing from Dr. Kane since her encounter with Harvey Jones almost a month earlier. Recent orders came from Dr. Mercer and Dr. Tennant. How far back did these prescriptions go? How long had this been happening?

Marian Zimmerman approached the counter.

Lillian tucked her notepad in the pocket of her white coat. "Good morning, Mrs. Zimmerman."

"Good morning, Miss Avery." She set an empty tube on

152

the counter and adjusted her hat over her gray hair. "I need a refill of my ointment. I even remembered to bring my old tube."

"Oh, thank you." The War Production Board's new requirement for customers to bring in old tin tubes in order to buy new ones had gone into effect the day before. "I've already had to send one patient home for his old tube, and Mrs. Connelly and Miss Felton are having a time of it. Toothpaste, shaving cream . . ."

"Well, I don't mind." Mrs. Zimmerman raised a strong chin. "Tin is vital to the war effort, and my grandsons have all enlisted."

"Good for them." Lillian examined the prescription label—a compounded ointment. "This will take me about half an hour."

"I don't mind. I'll browse through your new cosmetics section. I love it. And the window is so bright and cheery, like a show window at Filene's."

Lillian laughed. "My roommate works at Filene's. She gave me tips."

"You did a splendid job." Mrs. Zimmerman strolled down the aisle.

If only Mr. Dixon could hear.

In the file, Lillian located the original prescription. Mr. Dixon had recorded his calculations on the back. Too bad. Lillian loved doing math.

She pulled down bulk containers of salicylic acid, benzoic acid, and white ointment.

The door opened and shut, and Albert grinned at her. "Mrs. Z is raving about your display. I'll pass it on to Mr. Dixon."

"Thank you. It'd sound better coming from you than from me." She smiled as she set up the scales and lined the pans with parchment paper.

Albert went to the stockroom. "Have any plans this week-end?"

"My roommates and I want to see Bob Hope's new movie."

"*My Favorite Blonde*? Sounds like a good one. Maybe I can talk my buddies into a movie. Have to drag them from their favorite watering hole, though." He pulled out a large cardboard box. "So your brother and his friends aren't in town, huh?"

"Not that I know." Lillian placed 1.8 grams of weights in one pan, then scooped salicylic-acid powder into the other pan until it balanced.

"I'm restocking the bandages." Albert headed out to the main store.

"Thanks," Lillian called after him. She funneled the salicylic acid into a mortar, replaced the paper, and weighed out 3.6 grams of benzoic acid.

Her stomach felt as sour as if she'd swallowed that acid. If the *Ettinger* came to port, she wouldn't see Arch anyway. He'd go to Connecticut to see his beloved Bitsy.

Bitsy? What kind of name was that for a grown woman? Sounded like a flibbertigibbet prep school girl.

But Arch had once loved her. Jim said she'd broken up with Arch because he'd joined the Navy and she wanted a rich husband. Well, Miss Bitsy must have changed her mind.

Lillian added the benzoic acid to the mortar and ground the two powders together with the pestle. She had no right to be jealous. Hadn't she discouraged his attention? Didn't she use every opportunity to remind him she only wanted to be friends?

Her throat tightened, and she concentrated on weighing 54.6 grams of white ointment. Then she added a small portion to the mortar and mixed it with the powders.

Besotted. Mary said Arch was besotted with Lillian and was approaching cautiously.

Not anymore he wasn't. She'd been too prickly for too long, and he'd given up.

Lillian transferred the mixed ointment to the marble ointment slab, scraped the remaining white ointment onto the slab beside it, and combined the two piles with her metal spatula, back and forth, back and forth.

A month ago, she would have been elated that Arch's affections had turned. But now she felt as empty and squeezed out as Mrs. Zimmerman's tin tube.

★ ★ ★

"Tomorrow." Mr. Dixon jabbed the letter. "Tomorrow the government is taking my quinine."

"We can keep fifty ounces. And we don't get malaria cases here. Our soldiers in the Pacific need it more than we do." Grief flooded Lillian's chest. The American and Filipino forces on the Bataan Peninsula weren't expected to last the week.

Mr. Dixon grumbled, the closest he'd come to acknowledging she was right. "Your shift is over, Miss Avery. Are you done with your work?"

"I am." Lillian went into the stockroom, hung up her white coat, and put on her taupe suit jacket over her peach blouse. Finally it was warm enough to leave her winter coat at home.

She checked her purse to make sure she had her notepad. At home, she'd transfer the information to a larger notebook.

Mr. Dixon passed the stockroom door, set a paper bag in Albert's delivery box by the pharmacy door, then put the bulk phenobarbital bottle back on the shelf.

Phenobarbital? Lillian held her breath. What if she could trace the delivery? As an employee of Dixon's Drugs, she wouldn't look suspicious making a delivery. Then she could see if Detective Malloy was right about the forgers using

155

vacant apartments and setting checks under the doormat. *Lord, should I?*

Mr. Dixon and Albert stood by the shelf, counting bottles of quinine, their backs to her.

Lillian located the bag Mr. Dixon had placed in the box. On the upper right corner of the bag, he'd written "Monument Avenue. Paid in full."

It had to be a sign. Lillian snatched it up. "This delivery is on my way home. I'll take care of it. It's paid in full."

Out the door and down the aisle she strode.

Albert called after her, "Miss Avery, you shouldn't."

She just waved and smiled. "It's no bother. See you Monday."

When she was out on Main Street, she walked at a brisk pace and examined the bag. For heaven's sake—that was her building. Opal Harrison was the patient.

Lillian groaned. She'd grabbed the wrong bag. Instead of tracking down a drug dealer, she'd tracked down a sweet little old lady. At least Lillian could deliver her medication.

She peeked in the bag and stopped short. Phenobarbital, two hundred tablets, for Opal Harrison. How strange.

Lillian turned up her street, the Bunker Hill Monument lit up in the orange glow of the setting sun. She climbed the steps of her building and rang the doorbell.

Mrs. Harrison opened the door and beamed. "Well, hello, Lillian. You're a few hours early for your piano lesson."

Lillian laughed. "Just a few. I brought your prescription to save Albert the trip."

"Oh, thank you, dear. I'm almost out, and I need it for my rheumatism."

"Phenobarbital?" Sedatives weren't used to treat rheumatism.

Mrs. Harrison stared, then blinked her clear blue eyes. "My joints get so painful, it's hard to sleep."

Lillian frowned. "It's a very high dose."

Those blue eyes snapped. "I've been taking it for years. Mr. Dixon doesn't have a problem with it. Why do you?"

She sucked in a breath. "I—I'm sorry. It's none of my business."

Mrs. Harrison's shoulders slumped, and she covered her eyes with her hand. "I'm sorry. It's been a bad day. My hip's acting up."

"That's all right." Lillian took a step back. "I'll see you tomorrow."

"Nonsense. We can't leave it like this." She held the door open wide. "A little music. That's what I need. Play me 'To a Wild Rose.'"

"If I do, you'll really be angry with me."

"Nonsense, sweet girl." Mrs. Harrison led her into the apartment, which smelled like chicken soup. "Have a seat. Let me get the sheet music."

"I already have it memorized." But not mastered. At the top of the sheet music, the instructions read, "With a simple tenderness," something Lillian lacked.

Mrs. Harrison eased into her armchair. "Take a deep breath and pour your heart into it."

If she varied the volume and held some of the notes, that might do the trick. She launched in, but the song sounded disjointed and stilted.

When Lillian finished, Mrs. Harrison folded her hands over her belly. "You're playing with your head, analyzing how to make it sound as if you played with your heart."

Lillian stood. "I'll try again tomorrow. I had a long day at work."

"Of course, dear. Tomorrow you'll do fine."

No, she wouldn't. Her playing was as wooden as her leg, because it came from her wooden heart.

21

"Now we'll see if these bucket-brigade convoys do what they're supposed to." Jim took a bite of corn bread.

"Mm-hmm." In the wardroom, Arch stirred his navy bean soup. Only Hayes and Taylor were having lunch now, at the far end of the table, while the other officers performed their duties.

Over the next few days, the *Ettinger* and two smaller naval vessels were working their way down the coast, escorting empty cargo ships returning from England, then they'd return north with ships laden with oil and goods from the Gulf and the Caribbean.

Jim wiped his mouth with a napkin. "I'm not too upset we're turning around at Hampton Roads. Can't say I want to see 'Torpedo Junction.'"

Cape Hatteras had earned the grim nickname, a play on words with Glenn Miller's hit song "Tuxedo Junction." Arch scooped up more soup, careful to select a chunk of ham. "Buckner disagrees. Where better to hunt U-boats?"

Jim chewed, eyeing Arch. "Thought the convoy would cheer you up."

"It does."

"You've been glum all week. Ever since your dinner with Bitsy."

"Do you blame me? My only night in Boston, and I spent it fending off my former girlfriend. She made it sound as if she'd changed, but I saw no evidence. Same friends, same shallow talk, same angling."

Jim sipped his coffee, still eyeing him. "You never asked about my evening."

"You already told me. Clifford's married, and Quintessa's heartbroken." Why were men like Clifford safe on land while brave merchant marines died by the dozen?

"You didn't ask about Lillian," Jim said.

"Why? Is something wrong?"

"No, but she was as glum as you are."

"Because of Quintessa? Or did something happen at work?"

One corner of Jim's mouth jerked up. "She was in high spirits until I told her you weren't coming. She was disappointed."

Arch buttered his corn bread, applying an even layer all the way to the edges. "That's the polite thing to say."

"No, it was genuine. And when I told her where you were, she went pale. She covered, but I know her. I'm afraid she's softened up to you."

Buttery crumbs of corn bread rolled in Arch's mouth. That was the best news he'd had in weeks, but he kept his expression impassive and swallowed. "And if she has?"

"What? Do you want my blessing or something?"

Arch fixed a serious gaze on the man who had been his best friend for over six years. "Yes, I do."

Jim laughed and shook his head. "For what it's worth,

you have it. I've been watching. You treat her well, and I think you're good for her. But I warn you, if you hurt her in any way—"

"You'll hurt me worse. I know."

"I'm more worried Lillian would cause you serious bodily damage."

Arch grinned. She was certainly capable of it.

But he tempered his elation and returned to his soup. Just because she missed him didn't mean she'd fall in love.

★ ★ ★

The familiar waters off Narragansett spread before Arch, choppy and gray. He stood on the wing of the bridge in the cool air, taking stadimeter readings.

He gazed through the telescope of the handheld device at a ship in their makeshift convoy. He dialed in the mast height of the merchantman, then turned the cylindrical scale on the bottom of the stadimeter until he aligned the top and the bottom of the ship in his vision. Then he read the scale to discern the distance of the ship from the *Ettinger* and recorded it on his clipboard—seven hundred yards.

Warren Palonsky approached. "Sir, may I have a word with you? I'm off duty."

"Very well. Why don't you look busy and record my readings?"

"Aye aye, sir." He picked up the clipboard.

Arch glanced around, but they were alone on the wing. "You wanted to have a word?"

"Yes, sir." His smile stretched wide. "The case broke wide open."

"What happened?"

"Hobie was lying, no surprise. He got the drugs from someone else, only he didn't tell his source he had a new customer."

160

Arch returned to the stadimeter. As junior officer of the watch, he had duties, and none of them involved drug dealers. He measured the next ship. "Position three-two, distance seven-five-oh yards. Record it there."

"Aye aye, sir. So the guy above Hobie's source—"

Arch whipped around. "*Above* Hobie's source?"

"Yeah. Looks like we've got at least three layers on board. Hard to tell. Everyone's secretive."

It really was a ring. Arch blew out a long breath.

"So the guy above him—he wondered why Hobie's use of the drug suddenly doubled, figured he was trying to put one past him. Hobie's a sneaky one. They told him to 'fess up or they'd cut off his supply. Roughed him up a bit."

Arch's breath chilled, and he leveled a gaze at Palonsky. "You can get out any time you want."

"Are you kidding, sir?" His gray-blue eyes danced. "This is the role of a lifetime."

"Still, say the word and you're out." Arch turned the telescope to the next ship. "Position three-three, distance six-nine-oh."

"Got it. And I got another name—Earl Kramer. He's Hobie's supplier."

"Kramer?" The coxswain was experienced and respected. Hard to believe he was involved in this mess. "Who's above him?"

"Don't know. Best I can figure, there's one big shot, a couple middlemen like Kramer, and each middleman has a couple customers like Hobie. That's where Hobie made his mistake. He wanted to add a fourth layer—me. Only they don't like that. When they get a new customer, soon as they trust him, they introduce him to Kramer."

"Guess they didn't trust you." Arch winked at Palonsky.

"Leave the humor to me, boss." He waved toward the ocean. "Do your officer stuff."

Arch turned dials on the stadimeter. "Position two-one, distance one-three-five-oh."

So who was this big shot? Was it Doc? Or maybe Doc was clean, and the big shot was someone different, someone with a connection on shore, either at the Navy Yard or in Boston. And where was the connection to Dixon's Drugs, if there was one?

He took an invigorating breath of sea air. No tremor marred his movements. If he could break this drug ring and get his men to shape up, he might salvage his career—even boost it.

For the first time in months, hope stirred inside—for his career and with Lillian. An anchor for the soul.

No. He adjusted the dial and his attitude. Hope in the Lord was the only anchor he could trust.

22

Boston
Tuesday, April 14, 1942

Most people disliked working every other weekend, but Lillian loved having weekdays off to run errands.

She washed her breakfast dishes and set them in the rack to dry.

The phone rang.

Oh bother. Was Mr. Dixon calling her in to work? She went to the phone table by the door. "Hello?"

"Do you have plans today?"

Lillian's heart bounced. "Arch? Hi. Mary said your ship came into town yesterday."

"Yes, and do you have plans today?"

Her fingers fluttered in front of her. Why was he asking? "Everyone is working but me. I—I'm going to the grocery and the dry cleaner."

"Would you rather go to the Red Sox game?"

She gasped. "Opening day?"

"Jim and I bought tickets yesterday, but Buckner assigned him to the skeleton crew. Mary said you have today off, and

163

Jim thought you'd enjoy the game. It starts at 1400. I could pick you up at 1200."

She leaned back against the phone table, her thoughts racing. Jim knew she loved baseball more than a woman ought to.

"Just as friends, of course," Arch said.

"Of course." The words caught in her throat. Why did she feel disappointed? And yet . . . opening day! "I'll be ready at noon."

★ ★ ★

The El train clattered over the Charlestown Bridge. Lillian smoothed her new dress, a light gray scattered with miniature strawberries, with a short-sleeved berry-red jacket. "I've never been to a Red Sox game. I've seen the Cleveland Indians play, but never on opening day. How exciting."

Arch leaned against the window in his dress blues and gave her a funny smile with only the corners of his mouth.

"I always wanted to play. Perhaps it's best I had my accident, or I would've been an even worse tomboy." She was babbling, but she didn't care what he thought of her. He had his Bitsy, and that was all right. She had a friend—and a trip to Fenway Park.

Arch shifted his position as the train descended into the tunnel on the far side of the bridge. "I'm sorry I didn't see you the last time I was in town."

"No need to apologize." She flapped her hand, pleased with her breezy tone. "Jim and Mary and I didn't mind. We knew you had a friend in town."

"But I do need to apologize. You're my partner, the Watson to my Holmes."

"I thought it was the other way around."

"Perhaps." His lip twitched. "Or the Laurel to my Hardy, the Abbott to my Costello."

"You're awful." She swatted him playfully on the arm. Oh dear, what had she done? Her cheeks tingled, but she scrounged around for her breezy tone. "How are things at sea?"

"Did you listen to the radio this morning?"

"No, I was . . ." She was trying on every outfit in her closet. "I was busy."

"Down around Cape Hatteras, one of our destroyers, the *Roper*, sank a U-boat right after midnight." He slashed his hand through the air. "Obliterated it."

"The first time."

"I thought Buckner would be angry someone beat him to the punch, but he's never been in such high spirits. Now he knows it can be done."

"What great news."

"North Station." He motioned for her to lead the way off the train, then they worked their way up stairs and through tunnels and onto the next train.

Lillian settled in her seat. "So, Watson, anything new in the case?"

"As Palonsky said, it broke wide open."

"It did?"

"He found out the name of Hobie's supplier—Earl Kramer—and he learned there are at least three layers. One man seems to be the source, he has a few middlemen, and each of them has several customers."

"My word." The ring was so extensive.

"We might have a lead on land. Palonsky says the men frequent a bar in Charlestown—the Rusty Barnacle."

"Barnacles get rusty?"

He laughed. "No, but it certainly sounds rough."

Lillian opened her purse and handed Arch a scrap of paper. "I recorded all the suspicious prescriptions. It started in January '41. Here are the patient names. Do any look familiar?"

"No, although I don't know all two hundred men on the crew." He smiled and pointed to Opal Harrison's name. "No women in the Navy—although they're talking about starting a women's reserve as they did in World War I."

"Mrs. Harrison's one of the patients, but she's innocent. She's my upstairs neighbor, my piano teacher."

His eyes widened. "Your . . ."

"The other day, I saw a phenobarbital prescription waiting for delivery. I wanted to trace it, so I delivered it myself. It was Mrs. Harrison, so no progress made."

"Lillian." A furrow ran up his forehead. "Please don't do that again. It could be dangerous. If anything happens to you, Jim will have me keelhauled."

"It won't happen again." She tucked the list back into her purse. "Mr. Dixon wasn't pleased. The patients tip Albert, and if I make deliveries, I deprive him of tips. I don't want to do that. Albert's always kind to me."

"For once, I'm on Mr. Dixon's side." Arch nodded toward the window. "Kenmore Station. Here we are."

More tunnels and stairs, and then they emerged into the sunshine. Lillian drank in the spring air, so warm and light.

Arch squinted at the buildings, then motioned the way. "Now I'm even more annoyed I didn't see you the last time I was here. I'd rather have spent the evening discussing the case with you."

"It's all right. You had a friend in town."

Arch grumbled and led her across a street. "I wouldn't call Bitsy a friend."

"Oh." Did her voice sound all right—not too pleased, appropriately sympathetic?

"We dated in high school. I thought I loved her, thought she loved me. She comes from old money and wants to marry well. Specifically, she wants to marry the Vandenberg heir."

"But you wanted to join the Navy."

"Yes." His gaze roamed her face, then returned to the sidewalk, which was filling with fans. "She was furious, did everything in her power to dissuade me, but my mind was set. I want a simple life, free from the trappings of wealth . . . the trap of wealth."

She studied his determined profile. It took strength of character and will to make that decision. How could Bitsy have been so blind? "You made the right choice."

He stopped and looked at her with knee-buckling intensity.

"Hey, move it, fella." A man shoved past Arch on the sidewalk.

Lillian and Arch startled and continued on their way. They strode alongside a large brick warehouse, but everyone headed inside gates that looked like garage doors. "Is this it?"

"Doesn't look like a stadium, does it?" Arch's shoulder bumped hers in the thickening crowd. "By the way, thanks for what you said about my decision. Bitsy didn't agree. Neither did Gloria or Kate or any other woman I've dated. To them, I was only a ticket to prosperity."

"I'd rather have a ticket to opening day."

He chuckled and handed their tickets to the man at the gate. "I can do that for you."

Lillian's insides squirmed. He was comparing her to his former girlfriends. What did that mean? Did she like it or not? And why was she letting her imagination run wild?

Arch stayed close to her side as they worked through the crowd toward their tunnel. "All of the women I dated were only interested in my money, my name—the outside, not the inside."

The crowd pressed into the tunnel. Up ahead, sunlight and the open field beckoned Lillian. "With me, it's different. No one has ever cared enough to look past the outside."

He flashed a mischievous grin. "Or you won't let them."

Her throat tightened. "I'm cautious. Nothing wrong with that."

"You've been hurt."

She'd wanted the sunlight, longed for the openness, and now she closed her eyes against it. "Can we talk about something else? Anything else?"

"I beg your pardon. It's none of my business," he said in a tight voice, and he approached a vendor selling pop and peanuts. "I'd like a Coke and a bag of peanuts. What would you like, Lillian?"

"Just a Coke, please," she mumbled. The stadium spread before her, rows of seats, emerald grass, players warming up, and how had she thanked Arch? By shutting him out. Again.

He headed down the stairs, his shoulders straight and stiff. What had she done? The man had opened up to her, and she'd been coldhearted and rude.

Arch stopped at their aisle and motioned for Lillian to take her seat, not meeting her eye.

She stood in front of him, aching for him, for herself. "I'm sorry, Arch. You're right. I have been hurt. I don't talk about it, and I've never been a good friend because I don't talk about things, and I'm so sorry—"

"Stop." The softness of his expression and voice almost undid her.

"I am sorry."

"I know, but please don't beat yourself up." He smiled. "And please take your seat before someone beats *me* up."

"Oh." She glanced back, sent the people an apologetic smile, and took her seat.

Arch handed her a Coke bottle, then pulled out his knife, popped out the bottle opener, and removed both lids.

"Thank you." She took a cold, bubbly sip, then braced the bottle between her feet and settled her purse under her seat. Poor Arch should have invited someone else.

"Here. Have a peanut." He grinned and tossed a peanut into her lap.

She caught it before it rolled down her skirt, and she thanked him, but she had no appetite.

Even if he hadn't admitted it, she'd hurt his feelings. She'd closed herself off so she wouldn't get hurt, and in the process she'd hurt someone who cared about her.

Lillian stroked the rough surface of the peanut shell. *Lord, should I open up to him? Can I trust him?*

If the peanut snapped open lengthwise, she'd speak. If it cracked or crumbled and she had to pry it open, she'd stay quiet. One more prayer, and she pressed her thumbs along the seam.

It popped open, nice and neat, and two little peanuts nestled in their cradles, identical twins.

She drew a deep breath. "Lucy and I never got along."

"Hmm?" He raised blond eyebrows. "Your sister. Yes, I noticed."

"We were so different. She was sickly and needy. I was active and independent. Then I had my accident, all my fault. My brothers didn't want me to play with them in the woods, but I chased after them anyway. I stepped in an animal trap. Lucy said I deserved it."

"Lillian . . ."

She couldn't stand the compassion in his eyes, so she gazed at the field, where grown men tossed baseballs back and forth like boys. "She said now I'd know how it felt. Now I'd understand. But I didn't want to. She loved being weak, but I hated it."

"I don't blame you."

Lillian traced the edge of the peanut shell. "Our brother Eddie was born right after my accident. Mom was worn out caring for Eddie and Lucy and me, and I wanted to lessen her burden. So I worked extra hard to walk again and be independent."

"Just what I'd expect from plucky Lillian Avery."

"That's who I am—the plucky one, the strong one, the one who doesn't need anyone else. That's why I don't open up to people. It makes me feel weak. It—it terrifies me." Her voice broke.

A rumble emanated from Arch's throat, and he cracked open a peanut. "Don't shoot me for saying this, but it doesn't help when people hurt you after you do open up."

Lillian's vision blurred, and she blinked to clear it. "And I—I never told him much. My old boyfriend. I never told him what I just told you. I've never told anyone." A breeze ruffled past her, and she shivered in her nakedness.

Arch lifted one hand from his lap, as if to grasp her hand, but then he returned his hand to his lap. "I won't hurt you," he said in a husky voice.

She couldn't look at him. "I . . . I know."

"I'd only hurt myself in the process."

"Hmm?" She glanced at him, at his adorable half-smile.

"Where would Holmes be without his Watson?"

A giggle bubbled up, wet and strange. "Oh no. I'm Holmes. You're Watson."

"I heartily disagree, my dear." He mimed smoking a pipe, rolling a haughty stare down his nose. "You wouldn't look good with a pipe. But I look rather dashing."

"You look ridiculous." She popped the twin peanuts into her mouth.

"Enough of that. Game's about to start. Have another peanut." He flipped one to her.

She caught it and laughed. "Thank you. What am I? An elephant?"

He took a swig of pop, his eyes sparkling.

Suddenly, she didn't want to be cold anymore. She cleared her throat. "I do mean it. Thank you."

"And thank you for trusting me." He gave her a smile, small but sincere, then faced the field.

Lillian wanted to thread her arm under his and clasp his hand, to lean into his shoulder, to kiss his cheek right where the hint of stubble glowed like gold in the sun.

But she didn't.

She cracked open the peanut, nice and neat.

23

Boston Navy Yard
Thursday, April 16, 1942

Under a cloudy late-afternoon sky, Arch strolled down the pier with Jim and Mary. "Another busy day for our Miss Stirling."

"It was." She leaned into Jim as they walked. "Two keel-laying ceremonies and two launching ceremonies."

Jim kissed her temple. "Four more destroyers for the US Fleet."

"Not for a while." Arch stopped and gazed up at the *Ettinger*. "But look at ours. She's never looked more gorgeous."

Mary laughed. "She looks like an explosion in a bedspring factory."

The men joined her laughter. American sailors had dubbed the gangly SC radar apparatus on the mast a "bedspring antenna." But with that antenna, the *Ettinger* could detect surfaced ships up to four miles away. That type of antenna had helped the *Roper* sink *U-85*.

"Well, gentlemen, I'm tuckered out," Mary said. "Time to go home, enjoy Yvette's beef bourguignon, and collapse."

Arch pulled an envelope from his pocket and handed it to Mary. "Would you give this to Lillian, please?"

Mary's eyes danced. "I'd be glad to."

"It's just a Bible verse I thought she'd like." He crossed his arms. "Say, my parents' anniversary is coming in two weeks. I doubt we'll be in town, and if we are, I doubt we'll get a whole weekend's leave, but they're having a big party with music and dancing and plenty of food. I'd like to invite both of you and Lillian too."

"How lovely," Mary said.

"If we can't make it that weekend, another time this spring or summer."

"Lillian too, eh?" Jim's gaze hardened. "Testing her?"

Arch groaned and gazed at the two new Fletcher-class destroyers in the harbor. "I know. Every time you've seen me bring girls home, I've been testing them. And they all failed."

"Don't—"

"You're missing two important points." Arch held up one finger. "First, Lillian is not my girlfriend. Second, gold diggers start flirting the instant they peg me as wealthy. Lillian? She's never even batted an eye at me. I have no need or desire to test her."

Jim dipped his chin. "Good."

Mary turned the envelope in her hands. "A weekend at the shore sounds . . . romantic."

That's what Arch hoped. The more his hope grew, the less he trembled and the better he slept.

After Jim kissed Mary good-bye, the men climbed the gangway.

"I wouldn't count on your parents' party." Jim pointed to the new antenna. "As soon as that's installed, Buckner will want to take her out for a spin."

"I don't blame him. It's time to even the score." If only the *Ettinger* would be one of the nine destroyers the Atlantic Fleet was required to assign to the Eastern Sea Frontier in April. They were needed here. The situation was so dire, the Navy had ordered a halt to oil tanker traffic along the East Coast.

If the *Ettinger* remained with the Atlantic Fleet, they were overdue for North Atlantic convoy duty. Escorting cargo ships to England would take well over a month. Long past the party.

When Arch and Jim reached the quarterdeck, they saluted Captain Buckner. "I report my return aboard, sir."

"Very well. Report to your stations."

Jim grinned at Arch. "Reporting to the sack for naptime duty."

"Sleep tight." Arch checked his watch. In half an hour, he'd supervise fueling and provisioning. He strolled to the lifeline and scanned Charlestown as if he could locate the drugstore.

Taking Lillian to the Red Sox game had been a brilliant idea. Not only had Boston defeated the Philadelphia Athletics 8–3, but conversation flowed for the length of the game. They compared the hitting of Ted Williams, Dom DiMaggio, and the promising rookie, Johnny Pesky. They exchanged stories from childhood and school. And they shared peanuts, lots of peanuts.

How he'd wanted to kiss her good-bye. Outside her apartment, she stood on the bottom step, her eyes level with his, her mouth level with his. She stammered her farewell, cheeks flushed, as if she wanted a kiss as much as he did. But something told him to respect the opening of her heart by waiting to enter.

Loud voices rose by the aft superstructure. A dozen men marched forward, Earl Kramer in the center, hauling Hobie McLachlan by the collar. What on earth?

"We've got a thief on board." Kramer shook Hobie and muscled him to the quarterdeck.

Arch spied Palonsky at the back of the crowd. The seaman

gave him a slow nod, and Arch returned the signal. They'd talk later.

Captain Buckner wheeled to the mob. "What's going on?"

Kramer's square face glowed with fury. "Sir, I caught this thief red-handed."

"He's lying!" Hobie squirmed in the coxswain's grip, his black hair disheveled. "I don't know what he's talking about."

Buckner glared at the taller man. "How do you address an officer?"

"Sir!" Hobie fought to stand up straight, but Kramer shoved his shoulders down. "I'm not a thief, sir."

"Things have gone missing all week, sir," Kramer said. "Anyone notice?"

"Yeah." Phil Carey shook his finger at Hobie. "The ring I bought for my girl—it's gone."

"The binoculars at the torpedo tubes," Fish said. "Can't find them anywhere."

The captain frowned. "Come to think of it, I can't find my silver cigarette case."

Arch etched the scene into his memory. Hobie and Kramer belonged to the ring. Palonsky was pretending to belong. Arch had seen Carey groggy on the job. Why did he have the funny feeling this incident was related?

Kramer gave Hobie's shoulders a hard shake. "Sir, search his things. I saw him sneaking around. He pulled something out of Mahoney's coat pocket and stuffed it in his own locker."

"I didn't!"

Buckner eyed the men. "Show me."

The crowd entered the aft superstructure and descended the ladder to the crew's quarters. Arch passed rows and rows of bunks.

"Here." Kramer pointed to a locker under a bunk.

"Is this yours, McLachlan?" Buckner asked. "Open it."

"Yes, sir." He knelt and opened the locker.

Arch peered around the group.

Kramer scooped stuff onto the deck. "Binoculars. A jewelry box—look familiar, Carey?"

"Hey, that's mine!"

Hobie ran his hands through his dark hair, his eyes wild. "I ain't seen none of that before. None of it . . . sir."

Buckner picked up a silver cigarette case. "It's engraved with my name, you numbskull. What on earth made you think you could get away with this?"

"I ain't done nothing, sir. Nothing."

"The evidence shows otherwise."

Hobie pawed through the locker's contents. "Hey, where's my . . . ?" His face stretched long, and he stared up at Kramer.

The coxswain raised a triumphant smile. "Thieves pay."

Arch held his breath. The meaning of that interaction ran deeper than words alone indicated. He resisted looking to Palonsky for a translation. He'd find out later. If the men suspected Palonsky was ratting on them to an officer, the case would be ruined—and Palonsky could be in danger.

"Good work, Kramer." Buckner slipped his cigarette case into his breast pocket. "You and I will escort this slimy piece of seaweed to the brig on shore. You—Carey—load up everything from his locker as evidence."

Arch followed the group up to the main deck. Hobie would be court-martialed. If he was found guilty—and he certainly would be—he'd serve two to four years in the penitentiary and then receive a dishonorable discharge.

Tomorrow Arch would debrief Palonsky, but he suspected Hobie had broken some rule or defied Kramer in some way. And he'd paid.

The sun went into hiding behind the city skyline, and the sky grew dimmer. How much power did this ring have? What had Arch dragged Palonsky into?

And Lillian. His face went cold. Had he put her in danger?

24

"Why'd I agree to do this?" Lillian wrung her hands, then stopped herself.

Mary squeezed Lillian's shoulders. "You're just introducing Arch to Mrs. Harrison and going out to lunch."

"But we always do things in a group. This is . . . pairing off."

"He's a good man. That's a rare thing." Quintessa crossed her arms over her stomach. She'd lost too much weight in the past few weeks. "You should snatch him up."

"But I don't want a boyfriend."

Quintessa's blonde eyebrows lifted, as if she'd never imagined such a thing.

The doorbell rang. Too late now. She put on a smile and opened the door. "Ready to meet my Boston grandmother?"

"In a minute." Arch stepped inside and closed the door. "I have news."

Why did he have to stand so close and look so handsome

and smell so good? Like her father's shaving soap, but better. Lillian swallowed. "News?"

He leaned his shoulder against the wall. "Hobie's in the brig, in the hospital, actually, going through withdrawal."

"Oh my goodness. What happened?"

"He crossed Earl Kramer. Hobie served as Kramer's apprentice in the ring. He wanted Kramer's job, so he spread rumors about him. But the big shot on board saw right through. He and Kramer stole items from around the ship, planted them in Hobie's locker, and alerted the captain."

"They framed him." Lillian pressed her fingertips to her lips. What would they do to Arch or Palonsky if they found out what they were doing?

"Kramer needs a new apprentice. He picked Palonsky."

"Oh dear."

"No, it's good. The apprentice is connected to the big shot in case anything happens to Kramer. The big shot is Fish."

"Fish?"

"Sorry." He cracked a sliver of a smile. "Fish is a nickname for a torpedo—and for Torpedoman's Mate Gifford Payne. He's our source on board."

Lillian gasped. "You did it!"

Arch held up one hand. "We still need to find the connection on shore. His name isn't on your list."

"But it's a big step."

"Yes, it is." He gestured to the door. "Now, may I meet the famous Mrs. Harrison?"

"Oh yes. You'll love her." Lillian called out her good-byes to her roommates, grabbed her purse, and led Arch upstairs. "By the way, thank you for sending that Bible verse."

"I'm glad you liked it."

Liked it? If he only knew how much. She'd set the card on her dresser so she could read it twice each day and absorb the wisdom. And to admire Arch's signature and its powerful *A*.

Not a pointy *A*, but an appropriately arched one, with the center line aimed high like an arrow. Clever yet subtle.

"I read it the morning after the baseball game and thought of you."

"I memorized it." Lillian paused outside Mrs. Harrison's door. "'And he said unto me, my grace is sufficient for thee: for my strength is made perfect in weakness. Most gladly therefore will I rather glory in my infirmities, that the power of Christ may rest upon me. Therefore I take pleasure in infirmities, in reproaches, in necessities, in persecutions, in distresses for Christ's sake: for when I am weak, then am I strong.'"

On the threshold, Arch removed his cover. "Only the Lord could make truth out of such nonsense."

Lillian twiddled her purse strap so she wouldn't smooth the blond curl that poked up on top of his head. "And it's true. All my life I've tried to be strong on my own. But lately, the weaker I let myself be, the more God strengthens me."

"Good." Something in his long soft gaze told her he wouldn't use that against her.

Lillian rapped on the door. Even if she could trust him didn't mean she wanted to.

"Oh, Lillian." Mrs. Harrison clasped her hands in front of her chest. "I'm glad you brought your young man."

"He's not—"

"I'm just a friend." Arch offered his hand. "Ensign Archer Vandenberg."

"I'm Opal Harrison." She gripped his hand in both of hers. "Any friend of Lillian's is welcome in my home."

"Thank you." Arch entered the apartment and gazed around. "A lovely home it is. How long have you lived here?"

"Five years now, since Mr. Harrison passed away. But we lived in Charlestown all our married years. Our youngest daughter lives here too, though she scarcely visits." Mrs.

Harrison motioned Arch to an armchair and offered a plate of cookies.

Lillian set her purse on the cabinet by the door and perched on the piano bench, smiling at Arch's easy way with a stranger.

"Your youngest daughter." Arch picked out a cookie. "Do you have other children?"

"Yes, another daughter in Worcester and a son in Salem. They don't visit often either. That's why I'm glad I have my new young friend." She held out the plate to Lillian.

"Thank you." The compliment tasted even better than the cookie.

"But you, young lady." Mrs. Harrison circled one finger in the direction of the piano. "It's time for your lesson. 'To a Wild Rose.'"

Lillian sent her neighbor a beseeching glance. "Not in front of Arch."

"Too hard?" he asked.

"Too easy."

He frowned.

Mrs. Harrison settled into her armchair. "We're working on it. She has to learn to pour her heart into it."

Arch winked. "A recurring theme."

She gave him the same wrinkled-nose glare she gave Jim when he teased, and she popped the last of the cookie in her mouth. Then she faced the keys and her nemesis. As always, the nemesis won.

"You played the song perfectly," Arch said. "Every note in place."

"That's why it's bad." Lillian grimaced at the sheet music.

"Mm-hmm." Arch walked up behind her and set his hands on her shoulders.

She stiffened and sucked in her breath. Why was he touching her? Hadn't he seen her flinch every time he came near?

180

"Stop it. Relax." He kneaded her shoulders. "In fact, slouch."

"Slouch?" The word came out too high. How could she speak with his fingers massaging her? "A—a pianist never slouches."

"Excellent idea," Mrs. Harrison said. "Slouch and close your eyes."

Had they both gone mad? "Close my eyes?"

"You've memorized it." Arch pressed one hand to the back of her head. "Slouch, put your head down, and close your eyes."

"You'll never leave me alone until I prove you wrong."

"So prove me wrong."

"Fine." Lillian shrugged away his hands, smoothed her hair, and adopted the ridiculous posture, groping for the keys.

Arch sat beside her. Why did the bench have to be so narrow? His shoulder and hip pressed against her. How was she supposed to concentrate?

"Here it goes." She launched in, but she had to feel around for the chords, and she missed a note. She started over.

"No, don't start over," Mrs. Harrison said. "Let yourself make mistakes. Don't focus on the notes, but on the song. What does the song say to you?"

"You don't want to know."

Arch nudged her. "Play it over and over. Don't stop."

With her eyes shut, she could only sense the cool keys under her fingers and Arch's warm body next to her. And the music. She played as commanded. It sounded as awful as ever, but with the added glory of botched notes.

Over and over she played the short piece, until a strange sense of relaxation settled on her. Why? From the lazy posture? From Arch's strength? Or from the song seeping inside?

"That was nice. Right there," Arch said.

"Was it?" She sneaked a glance at him, and he nodded.

She turned to Mrs. Harrison's armchair, but it was empty. "Mrs. Harrison?"

"She went into her bedroom a few minutes ago."

"What? I didn't hear her."

"She's wearing slippers."

Lillian's heart dragged down. "Oh dear. I play so poorly, she has to escape."

"Not at all. I think . . . I think she wanted to give us a moment alone."

His eyes were so blue, a shade that made her think of swimming pools and diving in and never surfacing for air. His firm shoulder pressed closer, and his Adam's apple dipped to the knot of his tie and back.

What if she did? What if she dove in? Freedom and joy welled up, but then something cold and sickening coiled in her stomach. Not again. She couldn't let this happen again.

Lillian scooted off the bench. "We should leave."

"Sit." His lips twisted back and forth between impatience and compassion.

She crossed her arms. "I'm not a dog."

He sighed and patted the bench. "Please sit."

"I'd rather not."

"You'd rather not open up to me again."

Her head sagged back, and she groaned. "What's wrong with me? I'm so coldhearted."

"I didn't say that, and I don't believe it. You're just . . . independent."

"Independent." Lillian sank down to the bench. "I've been thinking. My independence is like my prosthesis. I rely on both to get by. Without them, I feel weak. And my stump—it's ugly. The prosthesis hides it."

"I doubt—"

"My independence hides my heart. I—I'm not soft and sweet the way women are supposed to be."

"I like you this way."

She resumed the song, her cheeks warm. This wasn't how friends talked. This was more intimate.

Arch added some chords at the bass end. "I haven't been fair with you."

"How's that?"

His fingers spanned the chords, strong but gentle. "I pressure you to open up while I harbor a secret."

She paused. "A secret?"

"Play or I won't tell you."

Lillian returned to the music, watching his face.

His mouth tightened, and his eyelid twitched. "I haven't told anyone, not even Jim. Well, I did tell a physician once, but I won't make that mistake again. It could end my career."

"What?" Her mind bounced between possibilities and memories.

"When the *Atwood* was torpedoed, the engine room started to flood. When the captain gave the order to abandon ship, we—we couldn't get a hatch open. We were trapped."

"Oh no. How awful."

"We finally opened one, just in time. But ever since, I've had trouble sleeping. I get nightmares. My hands . . ." He held up one hand. "See it shake? I'm not cold. I'm never cold. Just telling the story started it up again."

"Oh, Arch." A better woman would take that hand and kiss away the trembles. "No wonder the case is so important to you. It's personal."

"I know what the men are going through." He stared at the top of the upright piano, and the cords of his neck stood out. "When general quarters sounds, I don't know if I can pull myself together. With God's help, I do my job, but barely. I understand how the men feel, why they want to treat it themselves, why they can't tell anyone."

"If the Navy knew . . ."

"I could lose my commission. The Navy is my life. I've worked too hard for this, and I can't go back to what I was. I don't want to be like that again—superficial, pretentious, manipulative."

Lillian smiled at the deep, genuine, kind man beside her. "You couldn't be like that."

He let out a dark chuckle and played a few chords. "You didn't know me when I was younger."

"Well, you could never be like that again. It isn't in you."

"You don't know how tempting it is, the way of life, the way of thinking that takes over. You think you're sophisticated and cultured and right, and everyone praises you. But you're wrong. That—" He thumped out a chord. "That is why I never want to be rich again."

"What about—well, what about when you inherit?"

"I'm selling it all, giving it all away. I don't want a penny of it."

What a fascinating man. What character to know himself so well. What strength to avoid the thing that tempted him. What sacrifice to forsake what most people craved.

He gave a firm nod. "There. I've shown you my weakness—and it isn't a good sort of weakness—and the ugliness inside my heart. Now we're even."

That cost him, same as telling her stories had cost her. Even more because his story held the power to end his career. How could she tell him how much it meant to her?

She lifted her fingers from the keys, hesitated, then laid her hand on his forearm. "Thank you. Thank you for trusting me."

Arch glanced at her hand, then covered it with his own. "I suppose we've worn out our welcome."

Lillian spun around. "Oh dear. Poor Mrs. Harrison."

"I'd like lunch before my watch, so we should leave."

"Of course." She stood. "Mrs. Harrison? We're leaving now."

"Oh, all right." Mrs. Harrison shuffled out of the bedroom with a satisfied gleam in her eye. The little matchmaker. "I'll see you next week, Lillian."

"Or earlier, I hope." Lillian picked up her purse from the cabinet by the door.

Arch stopped in front of the cabinet, which displayed framed photographs of Mrs. Harrison's grandchildren, and he pointed to a photo of a sailor. "Who—who is this?"

"That's my oldest grandson, Giffy." She picked up the portrait. "Isn't he handsome?"

"Oh yes." Lillian studied the picture. The young man grinned at the camera, his white "Dixie cup" cover at a jaunty angle over dark curls, his lean face confident and mischievous. "You must be proud."

"I am. He's the only one who pays me any mind." She traced the outline of his shoulder in his white uniform with its dark neckerchief. "He's taking me out to dinner tonight."

"I'm glad he's in town. Which ship—"

Arch grabbed her arm above the elbow. Hard.

Lillian glared at him, a retort on her tongue, but the pallor of his face and the intensity of his gaze silenced her. What was going on?

"I'm sorry, ladies. I have to report for duty." Without releasing his grip, Arch smiled at Mrs. Harrison. "Thank you for having us over. It was an honor to meet you."

"Likewise, young man. Please visit any time you're in town."

He bowed his head to her and steered Lillian out the door.

"Good-bye." She tried to shake off Arch's grip as he led her down the stairs, but he wouldn't let go. "Would—"

"Shh. Not yet." He propelled her down the stairs.

She pursed her lips and wrestled down panic with logic. Arch would never hurt her, and he wasn't trying to control her. She trusted him enough to bide her time.

Arch turned up Monument Avenue, still gripping her arm.

"Would you mind telling me what that was about?" She let her voice be chilly.

"In a minute." He led her up to the square, up the bank of granite steps toward Bunker Hill Monument, and onto the grass. "Giffy is Fish."

"What?"

"Giffy. I recognized his picture. Gifford Payne. Fish. Our source on board."

Lillian clapped her hand over her mouth. "Her—her grandson? Oh no. Poor Mrs. Harrison."

Under a large shade tree, Arch set his hands on her shoulders. "You delivered sedatives to her. The prescription was in her name, right?"

His face swam in her vision, mottled by leaves blocking the sunlight, his pale, pale face. "Are you . . . are you saying—"

"She's a link between Dixon's Drugs and the *Ettinger*. She's involved somehow."

Her knees wobbled. "She's getting the drugs for him? For him to sell? Mrs. Harrison? *My* Mrs. Harrison?"

"Maybe she doesn't know what he's doing. Maybe he's using her. He's a slippery fish, that man, the other reason for his nickname."

"Oh no." Her stomach writhed, and she clutched it. "I trusted her."

"Now, now." He squeezed her shoulders. "Reserve judgment. We don't have all the facts."

"Two hundred tablets a month. She's the link."

"One link. Two hundred isn't enough. At least ten men are involved on my ship, and Fish told Palonsky other ships are involved. Plus, you've seen forged prescriptions for other patients. This is only one piece of the puzzle."

"Oh, Arch. What have we gotten ourselves into?"

"Now, now." His hands slipped behind her shoulders, as if to draw her close, but he stopped.

186

A breeze rustled the leaves, scented with spring and green and life, and she wanted to lean on Arch, wanted to trust in someone else's strength for a change.

She edged half a step closer. With a sigh, he gathered her into his arms, and she rested her cheek on his shoulder and circled her arms around his waist, clutching at the dark blue wool of his jacket. So new, so terrifying, so right.

"We have to keep you safe," he murmured. "That's the most important thing."

So this was how it felt to be cherished. She wanted to savor it, but she shook it off. "No. Solving the case is the most important thing."

"My brave girl." He rubbed her back, up and down. "But this is no time for bravery. We need to be cautious. Keep making your log, but don't take any chances. None."

She nodded, not feeling brave at all. "What about you?"

"I'll be careful. But you—keep up your lessons with Mrs. Harrison. Don't let her know we suspect her. Don't act as if anything has changed. Can you do that?"

"I—I think so."

"Whatever you do, don't tell her Jim and I serve on the *Ettinger*. What if she told Fish? He mustn't see the connection."

"All right." Lillian gazed across the expanse of Arch's chest, at his chin before her nose, at the dappled light alternating between dark and bright.

Friends didn't cling to each other. Friends didn't call one another "my brave girl." Friends didn't murmur and caress and sigh. Not like this.

Lillian backed out of his arms. Why did she suddenly feel chilly and incomplete? And why did he look lonely?

Arch tucked his hands in his pockets. "Ready for lunch?"

Somehow she nodded, although she had no appetite. What had they gotten themselves into indeed?

25

Off the coast of Massachusetts
Tuesday, April 21, 1942

Arch tugged his blanket under his chin, but sleep wouldn't come. They'd departed Boston at midnight, bound for Halifax, Nova Scotia, to meet a North Atlantic convoy bound for England.

He punched down his pillow. The North Atlantic convoys had full escorts, even though only a few U-boats had attacked that route lately. Meanwhile, the Eastern Sea Frontier boasted the highest number of sunken ships and had the lowest number of escort vessels.

And the *Ettinger* would be gone for over a month.

Arch flopped onto his back. Lillian had let him hold her, and now he'd be gone for a month. He'd miss his parents' anniversary party and the opportunity to spirit Lillian away from Boston so they could focus on each other, away from the war and the case.

He loved her. This was nothing like his earlier feelings for Bitsy or Kate or Gloria. This felt genuine. A restlessness built in his arms and chest—a need to hold her again.

No. He flipped onto his stomach. The needs of the nation took precedence over his personal needs. And the nation needed him to get some sleep before the forenoon watch or he'd be useless.

The alarm clanged general quarters.

Arch groaned and rolled out of bed, fully clothed. Then a strange lightness filled his chest. He hadn't panicked. He was finally licking this. With God's help, he was licking it.

"What is it this time?" Jim thumped down to the deck.

"Who knows?" Arch slipped on his mackinaw and cover and grabbed his life vest. Other destroyers equipped with radar complained about detecting every little fishing boat and Coast Guard vessel. It would take time to figure out this new technology.

Ted Hayes met them at the top of the ladder inside the bridge superstructure. "We picked up a radar contact. We've closed to one thousand yards."

"Probably a fishing boat." Arch fastened his life vest. Radar only detected aircraft or surfaced vessels.

"Or an unescorted freighter," Jim said.

"With a stupid captain." Emmett Taylor shook his head. All cargo ships had been ordered to put in to port at night, but merchant marines didn't always take orders well.

Hayes flicked his chin. "Captain thinks it's a U-boat."

The junior officers exchanged glances. The odds of contacting a U-boat were infinitesimal.

Arch headed aft on the main deck, following the flow of men and officers to their stations. No moon lit the starry sky, and the *Ettinger* sliced through the waves.

He passed the torpedo tubes and bumped into a sailor.

"Sorry, sir." It was Fish. His alarmed expression changed. The eyebrows drifted low, the eyes pierced, the mouth tightened. "Pardon me, Mr. Vandenberg, sir."

"Carry on." Arch continued on his way, but a sick feeling

filled his gut. Mrs. Harrison had mentioned a dinner date with her grandson. What if she'd mentioned meeting Archer Vandenberg accompanying that pretty pharmacist from Dixon's Drugs? A dangerous connection.

Arch flung up a prayer for Lillian's safety, and he met his repair party on the quarterdeck. Most of them. "Where's Carey?"

"Haven't seen him." Tony Vitucci put on his talker's headphones. "Contact at eight-oh-oh yards, bearing three-two-zero, running at sixteen knots. And zigzagging."

"Sixteen knots? Zigzagging?" Arch peered to port. Too fast for a merchant ship or fishing boat, but just right for a surfaced U-boat. Whatever it was, it knew it was being pursued.

Chief Boatswain's Mate Ralph Lynch grabbed the arm of a passing sailor. "Mahoney, you seen Carey?"

"Still sleeping, Chief. I couldn't rouse him."

Arch sighed. Why did he have a sneaking feeling Carey had taken a phenobarbital tablet to help him sleep? "I'll go down. We have a few minutes until we close the distance."

He strode into the aft superstructure and down the ladder to crew quarters. All the bunks were empty, save one. Arch shook the seaman's shoulders. "Carey! Hit the deck!"

"Don' wanna." He rolled over.

Arch shook harder. "We're at general quarters. Hit the deck and report for duty on the double."

Carey sat up, kneaded his eyes with the heels of his hands, and muttered something Arch didn't want to understand. "Duty. Repair party. Not much fun for a party, if you ask me."

"On the double, sailor."

"Aye aye, sir." He stood up and swayed to the side.

Arch caught his arm. "Or should you report to sick bay?"

Carey turned startled blue eyes to Arch. "No, sir. I'm waking up."

"Very well." Arch led the way up to the deck. This was why

they had to break the ring. Sedatives might help in the battle of the nerves, but they interfered with the battle against the U-boats. There had to be a better way, but what could it be?

Back on the quarterdeck, Arch found Vitucci. "What's the word?"

"We're at three hundred yards, sir, staying off her starboard quarter."

Smart idea to stay out of range of the stern torpedo tube, if it was a U-boat. But why would a U-boat flee on the surface? The only way a U-boat could escape a destroyer was to dive. Either the waters were too shallow to avoid depth charges or the sub was damaged.

A cry went up to port. "Torpedo!"

Arch braced himself against the searchlight platform, his heart careening out of control. There! A phosphorescent streak whizzed along the port side, parallel to the *Ettinger*'s course.

Above him, the searchlight flashed on, the bright beam sweeping the waves until another set of cries rang out.

He'd never seen a U-boat. When the *Atwood* was attacked, he'd been below decks. Terror and fascination drove him to the lifeline. Locked in the circle of light lay the humped back of a U-boat, Buckner's great whale, its pale wake racing behind it.

But where was the harpoon? Why wasn't the *Ettinger* firing? They were well within range of the guns and torpedoes, if the torpedoes were set for curved fire.

Arch whipped around. The torpedo crew stood at the lifeline, and on the aft superstructure, the machine-gun crew stared at their prey, immobile. "Man your guns!" Arch shouted. "Vitucci, has the captain—"

"Yes, sir!" The talker's eyes stretched wide. "He ordered every gun to fire at will, torpedoes too. He's spitting mad."

With good reason. Arch faced the aft superstructure and

cupped his hands around his mouth. "Man your guns! Mahoney! Lubowitz! Captain ordered you to fire at will."

The seamen stared down at him. "Aye aye, sir."

Arch spun around. "Fish! Stein! Man the torpedoes. Captain's orders."

"Aye aye, sir."

Out on the U-boat, dark figures spilled out of the conning tower aimed for the 88-millimeter deck gun that could sink the *Ettinger* with a single well-placed shell. "On the double!"

The forward machine gun opened fire, spraying the U-boat's deck, and dark figures toppled into the sea, but still more appeared, ants from their hive. Too many of them.

The U-boat's gun flashed. Arch cried out and braced himself. In an instant, the deck below him heaved, and he landed on his hands and knees. "We're hit."

Vitucci scrambled to his feet and flipped switches. "Aft fire room took the shell above the waterline."

The fire room. Below decks.

Arch froze. Not again. Pipes bursting, steam hissing, men slipping, screaming. The hatches clanging shut, dogged into place. Trapped.

Machine guns stuttered all around him. The two forward 5-inch guns fired, shuddering the deck.

"Mr. Vandenberg? Mr. Vandenberg! Sir!"

Arch's upper lip tingled with cold sweat. How could he go below decks during an attack? He couldn't. But wasn't he the officer? Couldn't he order the repair party down there while he stayed topside, claiming other duties?

The repair party stared at him, awaiting his orders. What was he thinking? That would be dereliction of duty. Abject, unforgivable cowardice. If he gave such an order, he'd have no choice but to resign his commission.

Lord, be with me. He forced out a choppy breath. "Let's go, men."

Ralph Lynch led the way down the hatch. Hissing steam and shouts rose from the depths of the fire room. Just below them to port, a jagged hole showed where the shell had entered.

Arch paused on the ladder to trace the shell's path—and the damage it had done. A torrent of steam spewed from the underside of the giant pipe leading up from Boiler 3 to the funnel. The pipe from Boiler 4 was intact.

"Shut down Boiler 3!" he shouted below.

"Already done." That was Jim's voice.

A smile trembled on his lips. If he had to die, at least he wouldn't be alone. He assembled his crew on the catwalk. "Once that steam dies down, get to work on the pipe. Lynch, let's see if there's any other damage."

He and Lynch scrambled down the ladder, through the heat and humidity. A muffled roar from the 5-inch guns, and the ladder shook beneath his feet. Down on the lower level, Arch swiped at sweat rolling down his temples, his movements stiff and jerky.

Jim's shirt was drenched. "Minor damage, minor injuries. Could have been much worse. Must have been a dud."

"Let's hope we don't take any more shells." Arch scanned the pipes and valves and gauges he knew by heart. "Wish you were still in gunnery. We wouldn't have had that delay."

"Thanks." Jim squinted up toward the main deck. "I hate being blind in battle."

And trapped. Arch shoved out a breath. "Okay, let's see what we have."

He and Jim inspected Boiler 3, closing valves and taking measurements from gauges, the familiar, ordinary actions like a drug.

"Mr. Avery, sir," the fire room talker called. "The U-boat—she's going down. Either we sunk her or she's diving. She left a dozen men in the water."

Arch and Jim exchanged a heavy glance. The captain

would drop depth charges. He had to. The Germans were known to play possum, even abandoning their own men, and then slip away to torpedo range and sink the attacking ship. Buckner knew better than to fall for that ploy.

But the men in the water? The depth charges would kill them instantly.

A loud low whump sounded, sending shivers through the ship and Arch's soul. The first depth charge. Then another, and a third.

Regardless, he had work to do. "Carson! Engelman! What's the word?"

"Lot of popped rivets in the pipe, sir," Carpenter's Mate Bud Engelman shouted down. "And it wrenched loose from where it exits the boiler. Still too much steam to work on it."

"As soon as it's safe. We need to run this boiler."

"Aye aye, sir."

Droplets fell in Arch's face from the condensed steam, and he wiped them away with the sleeve of his mackinaw. "Lynch, let's join the repair party. See any damage down here?"

"No, sir. We took a lucky shot." He whistled.

Thank goodness it was a dud.

Arch's vision swam, and he felt light-headed. And hot. So hot. He needed to get out. He climbed the ladder as fast as he dared. The steam made the steps and the chains slippery, and his shaking hands didn't grip properly.

A scream above him, and his foot slid off the rung. He caught himself, but his pinky finger jammed in a chain link.

Arch winced. "What happened?"

"Carey, you idiot," Engelman said. "I told you not to touch it."

"What happened?" Arch continued his climb, protecting his sore finger.

"I just wanted to see if it was still hot," Carey cried.

"He put his hand in the hole. Cut and burned himself."

Up on the catwalk, Carey clutched his hand to his chest, blood staining his life vest.

"Get to sick bay," Arch said. If only his sore finger qualified as an injury as well.

"Aye aye, sir." The seaman groaned, hunched around his injured hand.

"Mr. Vandenberg, sir," the talker called up to him. "Mr. Odom wants you on deck if you can be spared. They're launching the whaleboat."

"Thank you. Tell him I'm coming." Arch followed Carey up the ladder.

If they were launching the whaleboat, they must be certain the U-boat was sunk. They were searching for survivors.

On the main deck, Arch rested his hands on his knees and gulped down cold, fresh, free air. He was alive. He wasn't trapped. They hadn't been sunk.

But he had no better control of his nerves than before. None.

The sky had turned a sickly shade of pale orangey blue. Arch made his way down the deck. The rising sun illuminated chunks of wreckage, dark pools of oil, and bodies. So many bodies.

"Kill or be killed," a sailor muttered.

"Yeah, they started it."

"Come to our waters, sink our ships, get what you deserve."

Yet the voices were somber, the faces grim.

By the bridge superstructure, the deck gang lowered the whaleboat into the water by its davits. Lieutenant Odom and Captain Buckner stood nearby.

Mr. Odom hailed Arch. "Damage report?"

Arch detailed the damage in the aft fire room. "We should be able to make the repairs while underway. We'll need further—"

Buckner held up one hand like a witness on the stand.

"We're returning to Boston. They'll want to debrief us, and intelligence will want to interrogate any survivors and inspect the bodies."

"The bodies, sir?"

Buckner gazed out at his trophy. "I told them to bring in as many as possible. They might have papers, diaries, documents."

"Yes, sir." His stomach turned. Depth charges did gruesome things to a man. Would the sight of those dead German boys undo the morale boost that came from sinking a sub?

★ ★ ★

The makeshift sick bay in the wardroom was quiet. Only a few men had received minor injuries. And no German survivors had been found.

Phil Carey snored on a cot, his hand bound with white gauze.

"How is he, Doc?" Arch asked.

The pharmacist's mate shrugged. "The laceration isn't deep, sir. First-degree burn. He'll recover quickly."

"Good."

Doc frowned at his patient. "I gave him a low dose of morphine for pain, but it knocked him out cold. And before he fell asleep, he kept saying, 'I've gotta find Fish. I'm almost out.'"

Arch swallowed hard. "What do you think?"

Brown eyes fixed on him. "I think he already took some medication. A barbiturate, I imagine. He was groggy when he came in."

"We've had complaints about his behavior."

"This isn't the first time I've heard Fish's name connected to this affair. These drugs—I think Fish might be the source. He knows people in town, and he goes to the Rusty Barnacle."

"The Rusty—"

196

"A seedy bar, sir. A lot of our men go there. I think that's where they buy the drugs."

Arch nodded, his neck muscles stiff. Doc seemed to have followed the same leads he and Palonsky had followed.

"Sir, have you heard anything?" Doc asked.

"I'm afraid I have nothing to report to you." That was the truth. "Please let me know when Carey awakens. I'd like to speak to him."

"Aye aye, sir."

Arch headed back to his cabin for a nap. If he could sleep.

He and Palonsky had worked so hard to uncover Fish as the source, but Doc had found him out too. Perhaps they should join forces.

But he couldn't shake the suspicion that Doc was involved. If Arch showed his hand, he'd put Palonsky—and Lillian—in further danger.

After all, Doc could be the kingpin. Unlike Fish, he had the medical knowledge to craft forged prescriptions that wouldn't raise the suspicions of druggists. He had access to Navy medical supplies. And he'd told Arch he wanted to treat the men so they could remain on duty.

In his cabin, Arch shrugged out of his life vest. Why had Doc mentioned Fish? Wouldn't he want to protect such an important link in the chain? Maybe Fish had crossed Doc, like Hobie had crossed Fish and Kramer.

Arch sank to the bunk, flat on his back, his eyelids and heart heavy. *Lord, please don't let anyone else get hurt.*

26

Stonington, Connecticut
Friday, April 24, 1942

Lillian gazed out the car window down the tree-lined lane. Meeting new people always unnerved her, but staying a whole weekend with strangers? And a fancy dinner tonight for the Vandenbergs' closest family and friends, followed by a party for over one hundred? Oh dear.

Was this how Arch had felt when he'd arrived in Vermilion? Shame gnawed at how she'd disliked him back then, how she'd judged him. Meanwhile, he'd been suffering from the sinking of the *Atwood*.

Now the *Ettinger* had sunk a sub and had been damaged. How was Arch doing? She studied the back of his blond head in the front seat of the car.

On the train ride, Jim had told the tale with gusto, but Arch remained quiet and kept his hands tucked under the overcoat on his lap.

For the first time since she'd met him, she longed to get him alone to hear his version. And the thought of being alone with him filled her with diffuse warmth.

What was she going to do? Everything had changed between them. The past week while he'd been at sea, she'd felt unmoored. How had she fallen for him after all her caution?

"Here we are," Arch said.

The house stretched long and white, trimmed with gray stone and black shutters. And so many windows. Jim had said the estate had a tennis court, horse stables, and a pier for the yacht. Like something in a movie.

The chauffeur pulled into a circular driveway. Arch opened her door, and she stepped out, trying not to gawk like a country bumpkin.

A middle-aged couple strolled forward, both as blond and good-looking as Arch.

His mother embraced him. "Archer! I'm so glad you could come."

"I am too. Happy anniversary, Mother. And Father."

"Jim and Mary, it's good to see you again." Mrs. Vandenberg clasped their hands, then turned to Lillian with a warm smile. "You must be Lillian."

She gazed into eyes as blue and intelligent and kind as Arch's. "Thank you for inviting me."

"Come in, come in." Mrs. Vandenberg ushered them through the front door. "Please make yourselves at home. I'll show you to your rooms, then Arch can show you around the house and grounds. Dinner is at five, so you have plenty of time."

Lillian stifled a gasp. The entry formed a vast semicircle, framed by a pair of sweeping staircases and crowned with a crystal chandelier.

Mrs. Vandenberg led the girls up the left-hand staircase and down a hallway. "Mary, we put you in the room you were in last time, and Lillian, right this way."

In her room, Lillian set her purse on the bed with its ice-blue bedspread. "It's lovely."

Men's voices trailed behind them. Mr. Vandenberg laid her garment bag on the bed, and Arch brought in Lillian's crutches and suitcase.

"After you're settled, meet us in the sitting room," Arch said.

"All right. I won't be long."

After he left, Lillian opened the garment bag and removed the gown from her pharmacy school graduation, a floor-length princess-cut dress with short puffed sleeves and a sweetheart neckline, in a frothy pale green chiffon.

"Lillian?" Mrs. Vandenberg touched her arm. "Arch said you'd refuse any offer of help. But I wanted you to know that if you need anything, I'm here for you. Please don't hesitate to ask."

How could she not like this woman who offered both hospitality and dignity? "I have to admit, I need help with the buttons up the back of this dress."

Mrs. Vandenberg laughed. "Why *do* they design gowns like that?"

★ ★ ★

"Thank you for serving as my bodyguard." Arch stood too close in the crowded ballroom, his hands clasped behind his back. "Protecting our nation's officers is vital war work."

Lillian giggled. "I hardly think Bitsy Chamberlain is a threat to national security. She was nice to me at dinner."

"I'm sure she was." Sarcasm darkened his voice. "By the way, you held your own. And Dr. Detweiler was impressed with you."

"He's the nicest man. I have to thank your mother for seating me next to him. And next to your Grandpa Archer. He's adorable."

"Caroline Archer Vandenberg is a master at seating arrangements."

Lillian gazed around the spacious room on the second floor of the Vandenberg home. One wall curved out over the grounds, set with a dozen tall windows, the drapes drawn to meet the new dim-out regulations. A small band played elegant music, and couples danced, the women in gorgeous gowns and the men in tuxedos or in uniform.

None as handsome as Arch. She'd never seen him in dress whites before, and when she'd come downstairs for dinner, she couldn't breathe.

No man had ever looked at her that way. She'd seen her father look that way at her mother—and at his sailboats—with deep appreciation and gentle ownership lighting up his eyes.

Once again, joy and terror wrestled inside her.

"When do you think they'll get married?" Arch said.

Lillian blinked away the memory. Jim and Mary danced to "Rose Room," he in dress whites and she in a long satiny sky-blue gown. "They've only been dating about four months."

His face sobered. "Uh-oh. Three enemy warships approaching, bearing two-seven-zero."

"What are you talking about?" All she saw was three young ladies.

"Bitsy's best friends. But no sign of Bitsy. I smell a rat."

"You're too suspicious."

He shot her a "you're not suspicious enough" look, then raised a smile to the ladies. "Trudy, Helen, Pauline. Always a pleasure."

A tall, sturdily built blonde offered Arch her hand. "Yes, always a pleasure. Was it only last month you and Bitsy and Trudy and I danced the night away in Boston? Seems like ages."

"Ages indeed." Arch clasped her hand. "May I introduce

Miss Lillian Avery? Lillian, I'd like you to meet Miss Helen Whipple, Miss Trudy Sutherland, and Miss Pauline Grayson."

"I'm pleased to meet you," Lillian said.

"Charmed." Helen's cold blue eyes didn't match her words.

"Where are you from, Lillian?" Trudy fiddled with a brown curl cascading from her pinned-up hair. "I don't recognize your accent."

"Ohio."

"Archer darling! There you are." Mrs. Chamberlain swooped over, a dark-haired beauty like her daughter. "There's someone you simply must meet. Please excuse us, ladies."

"Of course." Bitsy's friends waved them away, then formed an arc blocking Lillian's escape.

Arch glanced back over his shoulder and mouthed, "Help me."

Lillian smiled and waved him off too, but she also smelled a rat. Four of them.

Pauline inspected her, head to toe. "So, April, what brings you here from Ohio?"

Lillian gave a tight-lipped smile. "My name's Lillian, not April."

Pauline and Trudy tittered, and Helen patted her arm. "Our apologies. We give nicknames to Arch's girls. You're April—"

"Because it's April," Trudy piped up. "Next will come May, and then June."

Pauline sighed. "Please don't take it personally. It's hard to keep track."

So that was their game. She made her eyes large and innocent. "Are you saying he's a ladies' man?"

Trudy raised one white shoulder. "So they say."

Across the room, Arch talked to an older gentleman and Bitsy, with Mrs. Chamberlain gripping his arm. But his gaze reached out to Lillian.

"Hmm." She tapped her finger to her lips. "*They* must not know him very well. He dated his last girlfriend for over a year, and he hasn't dated since."

"Until you." Pauline gave her a too-sweet smile.

As much as she wanted to protect Arch, she couldn't lie. "We aren't dating."

"No?" Helen glanced toward the band. "So that's why he hasn't asked you to dance."

"No. He knows I don't dance."

"You don't?" Trudy frowned. "Don't they know how to dance in Iowa?"

"Ohio, and yes, they do. But I don't dance."

Helen clucked her tongue. "Such a shame. Archer adores dancing. You should have seen him whirling Bitsy around the dance floor in Boston. A vision."

Oh, they were good, but Lillian had dealt with catty girls all her life. She needed to break away and find someone else to talk to—Dr. Detweiler or Arch's grandparents, perhaps.

"Why don't you dance?" Trudy asked. "Two left feet?"

Lillian stared at the brunette who had served a line on a silver platter. "No left feet."

"No left . . . that doesn't make sense."

"I don't have a left foot." Lillian hiked up her gown over her knees. "This one's fake."

"Oh!" All three women gasped and recoiled.

Lillian marched off through the break in the circle, her skirts whishing around her ankles. The nerve of some people, thinking they could elevate themselves by putting others down.

"Lillian?" Arch dashed over, concern etched into his face. "Did I just see you—"

"Insufferable snobs." She related the conversation in a heated run-on sentence. "Well, I showed them."

The corners of his eyes crinkled with laughter. "Would you like to really show them?"

"Yes." She jutted out her jaw. "Any ideas?"

"Dance with me."

"What? I don't—"

"You didn't ice-skate either. This will be easier. A simple slow dance. Just follow me."

Her cheeks puffed up with air. Did she really want him to hold her again?

"Come on." Arch took her hand, led her to the dance floor, and gathered her in his arms while the band played "So Rare."

When she found her voice, she used it. "I don't remember saying yes."

Arch stood in the dance position and tipped his head to the side, waiting.

"All right, but I fail to see how this will show them." This position was worse than the full embrace because she could see his face. So close. She feigned fascination with the band.

"Follow me. Side to side. Step, touch. Step, touch. Nothing difficult."

"Not for you." She frowned at her clumsy feet, but at least she didn't have to look at Arch. "Now explain."

"Simple. Bitsy wants to marry me. In fact, any of those three would marry me for the Vandenberg fortune."

"They're gems. You should snatch one of them up."

He chuckled. "But I don't want to, and they know it. They see me gazing adoringly at you, yet you won't even look at me."

Her breath hitched, she met his gaze, and she tripped. His arm on her waist set her feet in motion again—but not her lungs.

That expression. The same one he'd given her when she came down to dinner, but closer and more intense.

She jerked her gaze away.

"See?" he said. "I snub them for you, and you snub me for . . . no one. You win."

"Great." She forced out a light laugh. "I won. Thank you for your help. Now you can stop pretending to gaze at me adoringly."

His sigh ruffled her hair. "My darling Lillian. Whatever makes you think I'm pretending?"

Every muscle went taut, then squirmed. "Don't talk like that. Please don't. I trusted you."

"Come on. Let's go for a walk outside."

"I don't want to. I want—"

"You want to speak your mind. Not here. You just won. If you make a scene, you'll lose. Let's go outside, and you can say every word as loudly as you'd like."

Maybe Jim could rescue her. Where was he?

"Lillian, come on. Let's go for a walk."

"Fine." She gritted her teeth and let him lead her out of the ballroom, down a back staircase, and across a patio to the grounds that sloped down to the sea.

Lillian flung away his hand and marched along the pathway under a half moon. "I trusted you, Archer Vandenberg. You said we were friends, only friends. That was the deal."

"I never promised I wouldn't fall in love with you."

Love? Lillian whirled around. He stood silhouetted against the muted light from the ballroom windows, soft music floating past him. "I—I thought you were better than that."

"Better? What are you talking about?" He stepped closer, dark and unreadable.

She strode down the path, her chest straining from the pain. "What kind of man falls in love with a cripple? Normal men don't. Normal men reject me."

His footsteps followed. "I didn't fall in love with a cripple. I fell in love with a beautiful, vibrant, clever—"

"Stop it." She waved her arm behind her, swatting away his words. "No man wants a cripple unless he's crippled inside, twisted, sick—"

"Lillian, sweetheart. What did he do to you?"

She spun around, breath racing.

Arch stopped several feet away. "I deserve to know. You're judging me by what he did, and I don't even know what I'm up against. I—I'm fighting blind, below decks."

Lillian pressed her hand to her forehead, dizzy, knees wobbling. "I need to sit down."

"There's a bench under that tree."

She sank onto the bench with her back to the ocean, the cold of the stone seeping through layers of chiffon. How could she tell him? The story was shameful. She'd never told a soul.

Arch stood at the end of the bench, facing the sea. Silent.

Music drifted to her through the trees, the tune indiscernible. "Why should I trust you?"

"Don't you know me by now?"

"I—I thought I did, but then you said you . . . you—"

"I said I love you. Why would love make me less trustworthy?"

She folded her arms and leaned over them. "He said he loved me too."

Arch didn't move, didn't speak, always the gentleman. If she told him about Gordon, he'd think less of her. Wouldn't that drive him away? Wasn't that what she wanted?

Lillian steeled herself, her forehead inches from her knees. "I met Gordon my first year at Ohio State. He said it was love at first sight. I was overjoyed—I'd never dated before. And he reminded me of that constantly. He said I should be grateful he paid me any attention. No one else would. I should . . . I should . . ."

"Go on."

Her shoulders hunched up. "We'd been going steady for a month. One night he took me on a picnic by the river. The ground was sandy, and sand is bad for my prosthesis.

206

He told me to take it off. He'd carry me. I didn't want to, but he claimed I didn't love him, didn't trust him. Since I—I didn't want to lose him, I let him put my prosthesis in the trunk of his car."

A breeze sent curls across her cheek. "It was October, and it was chilly, and the usual college crowd wasn't around. Gordon got fresh. And he—he wouldn't stop. I couldn't get away. I screamed, but I couldn't see anyone."

"He had his way with you." Arch's voice came out hard and tight.

"He would have. There were three boys farther down, drinking. They heard me, and they stopped him."

"See. Some good men in this world."

Lillian snorted. "You know what they said? They said Gordon was disturbed for wanting a freak like me. They humiliated him into taking me home. I was so furious, I broke up with him on the ride back. Well, that was a mistake, because when he dropped me off at the dorm, he refused to open the trunk. He left me there, dirty, dress torn, hopping on one leg."

"Oh, Lillian."

She wrenched her head to the side, away from his pity. "The housemother called me a—a—she questioned my virtue. And I had to use my crutches to get around campus. People stared even more than ever. Gordon said if I apologized, he'd take me back and return my prosthesis, but I refused. I lasted a week. I needed my prosthesis. I couldn't afford a new one on my own, and I couldn't tell my parents."

"They would have—"

"Don't you see? How could I tell them? So I called Gordon. After he brought back my prosthesis, I broke up with him again. I let myself be weak with him, and he . . . and he . . ."

Arch sat on the arm of the bench and held out a hand-kerchief.

"I don't cry. I never cry." She sat up and pushed back her hair to show him.

"My darling girl." He stroked her cheek, handkerchief still in hand. "I would never take advantage of your weakness. It—it's a gift you've given me. Something to treasure."

The compassion in his eyes undid her. Not pitying compassion, but admiring compassion, mixed with gratitude, mixed with love, mixed with his own weakness. "You . . ." Her voice choked, and she swallowed hard. "You're taking a chance on me too."

His gaze roamed her face, one finger tracing her jawline. "In a way. Every woman I've dated has only wanted me for my money. But you're different. If you ever fell in love with me, you'd be looking past these superficial trappings and seeing me, the real me, who I am inside."

She ached for him. He deserved to be loved like that. He already was. And shouldn't he know it?

In the distance, waves shushed to the shore, stretching and retreating. If the Lord was her sure anchor, couldn't she take the chance to accept love, to give Arch the love he longed for?

He sighed and lowered his hand. "I'm willing to wait. I won't push you."

"I already do." The words tumbled out.

"Hmm?" One eyebrow raised.

Oh, why did her mouth have to be as clumsy as her feet? "I—I already love you. Like that. Who you are."

His chin and his eyelids sank. Silent.

She gripped a handful of chiffon. "I didn't say that right, did I?"

His eyes opened, gleaming in the moonlight. "You said it perfectly. I just didn't expect to hear it so soon. If ever."

"Oh." She tucked in her lips. Now what? He'd kiss her, wouldn't he? Was she ready?

SARAH SUNDIN

From his perch on the arm of the bench, he draped one arm along the stone behind her and set his other hand on her cheek, back into her hair, and he leaned forward and pressed his lips to her—her forehead?

"I love you so much," he murmured against her skin. "We'll be weak together, strong together, you and I."

A puff of breeze swirled between them, too much space between them. Now that she'd made up her mind, now that she'd confessed her love, she didn't want to hold back even a little.

She worked her hand up and over his shoulder and tugged him down to the bench beside her.

He let out a surprised grunt and looked her in the eye, only inches away.

"I told you I love you." Her gaze fell to his mouth. "When I decide to do something, I do it."

He pulled in his lips, and then they parted, moist and inviting.

Lillian drifted closer, and he met her halfway, his lips on hers, warm and gently insistent, his arms wrapping around her, nothing weak about his embrace at all. And she kissed him back, opening every cavern of her heart for him to explore, to own, to love.

"My darling." He kissed her cheek, her nose, her other cheek. "My brave, brave girl."

"Brave?" Her smile melted all over her heated face. "We're not facing drug rings or U-boats right now."

He gave her a playful smirk. "Isn't love the greatest danger of all?"

Two hearts, open and weak and vulnerable before each other. Oh yes, it was dangerous.

"And the greatest joy." Lillian threw herself headlong into another kiss.

27

"Ready for sailing, I see." Arch admired Lillian as she entered the sitting room, fresh and appealing in a blue-and-white striped dress, a red sweater, and her hair tied back in a red ribbon. "Now I can say good morning."

Lillian set her bag and hat on a sofa and took Arch's hands, her face glowing. "You said good morning when I came down for breakfast."

"Not properly." He tugged her hands to draw her nearer and kissed her well.

"Mm." She leaned against his chest and beamed up at him. "I wouldn't mind that every morning." Then her cheeks colored. "I didn't mean—I meant—"

"I know what you meant." He kissed her again. "I wouldn't mind either."

Everything about her was refreshing. He loved the way she'd mixed up her words and yanked him down to the bench to kiss him. Not coy and artful like the other women he'd dated.

With a contented sigh, she wrapped her arms around

his middle and rested her cheek on his shoulder, and Arch nuzzled kisses onto her forehead. He'd seen no regrets on her face today, only pure, open love, and his chest felt full.

"An entire day with you," she said.

"And Jim and Mary." He pulled away at the sound of their voices in the hall, but he kept hold of Lillian's hand, so small and light in his.

"I'm ready." Mary grinned, swinging her bag. "I can't wait to go sailing again."

Jim glanced at Arch and Lillian's entwined hands with the same tight-lipped smile he'd displayed when the new couple had finally returned to the ballroom last night, Lillian wearing the high color and bright eyes of a woman who'd been kissed long and often.

At least Jim smiled and didn't glower. It was a start.

"Shall we go?" Arch gestured to the door.

Jim and Mary led the way across the patio and down the path to the pier, but Arch lagged behind with Lillian.

"It's a lovely day." Lillian smiled up to the clear blue sky. "I know you don't like this place, but it's beautiful."

"I do like this place. Too much."

She strolled along, her shoulder brushing Arch's. "You always say you hate this way of life, but you seem happy here, and your parents are wonderful, not snobby at all."

Arch glanced to his left, across the tennis court to the stables, and his shoulders tightened. "They're good people. They're untouched by all this."

"So why—"

"I *was* touched." His voice came out sharper than intended.

"I thought you were a snob when we first met." She gave him a sly sidelong glance. "But you aren't. You're just refined."

He had to distract her from this topic, and he knew how to do so. "How's this for refined?" He swept her into his arms and kissed her long and luxuriously.

211

"Oh." She pulled back, eyelids low. "That might not be refined, but it was fine."

He grinned, hooked his arm around her tiny waist, and continued on the way. Now to find another topic.

"So if this didn't make you a snob, why does it bother you?"

Arch's jaw hardened. Why couldn't she understand?

Then remorse swept through him. She couldn't understand for the same reason he hadn't understood her aversion to romance. Because the story hadn't been told. But his story—how could he tell it?

Maybe a simple declaration would do the job. "It's more than the temptation to be a snob. It's the temptation to use the power of wealth for selfish purposes."

"I can't see you doing that."

"I did. That's all you need to know."

"Is that so?" She stopped and eased away from him, crossing her arms.

He sank his hands, his stupid trembling hands, into the pockets of his khaki trousers, and he looked across the grounds, anywhere but into her accusing eyes.

"So you have a story, and you think it'd make me stop loving you."

He shrugged. "No one knows. Not a soul. I don't like to think about it. Understood?"

"Yes. I *do* understand." Her tone was pointed.

Under the maple tree sat the stone bench where Lillian had splayed open her soul before him.

His head sagged back. *Why, Lord? Why do I have to tell her?*

"Arch?" She looped her arm through his. "I love you. I'd only think less of you if you didn't regret your actions. But you obviously do."

Those hazel eyes locked onto him. How could he prod her to open up to him and then shut her out?

"Come on." He tilted his head toward the sea and coaxed her into walking. "Mrs. Lafferty was the best of women."

Lillian hugged his arm. "Who was she?"

"Our housekeeper. More than that. She was like another grandmother. She doted on me but never indulged me, never let me get away with anything. I loved her for it."

"She sounds like a good woman."

The muscles in his neck tensed. "When I was twelve, I chafed at her restrictions. The boys in my crowd liked to sneak out at night, but Mrs. Lafferty always caught me. The boys mocked me. Who was in charge? Who was the servant? My best friend said that with my wealth, I should have anything I wanted. And what did I want? I wanted to sneak out with my friends. I wanted freedom. And Mrs. Lafferty stood in my way."

Lillian murmured and stroked his arm.

Arch's hands balled up in his pockets. "I seethed for a while. I fought it. But I couldn't resist. I was the sole Vandenberg heir, and this servant had no right to stop me. So I . . ." His throat clogged up.

"Go on, sweetheart."

He glanced down at those eyes full of hard-earned trust, and he swallowed the thick sludge of shame. "It was the worst thing I've ever done. I planted my mother's jewelry in Mrs. Lafferty's room. When Mother noticed it was missing, I said I'd seen Mrs. Lafferty lurking around. And I—I also said I'd overheard her telling another servant she finally had the funds to retire. Lies and betrayal."

"Oh, Arch." She hugged his arm tighter.

"I didn't think through the consequences. I thought I'd just teach her a lesson and get my way, but of course not. Thank goodness my parents didn't press charges, but they did fire her. After forty years of service to the family, she was fired. The look on her face." Arch squeezed his eyes shut, but the image remained burned on his eyelids. It always would.

"What's worse . . ." His voice ground on his throat. "I was too much of a coward to come clean. Poor Mrs. Lafferty went to live with her sister, but she died a year later. I never apologized to her, never had the chance to beg her forgiveness, and I never—never told anyone what I'd done."

"But you changed."

"I had to. I was appalled at who I was. The stock market crashed right after that. Those boys I worked so hard to impress—they turned on each other. They shunned the boys whose families lost their wealth. Fickle and shallow. I didn't want any part of it."

Lillian faced him and stroked his cheek. "My darling Arch. I think Mrs. Lafferty would be very proud of the man you've become."

He couldn't stand it. He smashed his eyes shut and pressed his forehead to Lillian's. "I don't know. I know God's forgiven me, but—"

"Then you're forgiven. Please forgive yourself." She kissed his cheek. "It takes a good and strong man to admit he was wrong and to change. I love that about you."

Arch pulled his hands from his pockets and folded Lillian in his arms. He didn't care if she could feel the trembling through the fabric of her dress. He needed to hold her.

For months, he'd longed for her love, to be loved for who he was, but he wasn't prepared for how a love like that could reach the darkest corners of his soul, unsettling him, renewing him.

"Arch! Lillian!" Jim's voice rose from the stairs down to the pier. "Are you ever—oh, for crying out loud."

Arch opened his eyes, but Lillian didn't push him away, so he didn't release her.

Jim stood on the path, one hand on his hip, his upper lip curled. "I don't want to see this."

"You gave us your blessing."

"That doesn't mean I want to see it."

Lillian rolled halfway out of Arch's embrace and gave her brother a saucy tilt of her head. "For the past four months, I've watched you cuddle with my friend, and now you have to watch me cuddle with your friend. I'd say we're even."

Jim burst out laughing and ducked his head. "Point taken. Now, are we going sailing?"

"What do you say?" Arch gave Lillian his best roguish smile. "Want to go cuddle on the sailboat? I might even kiss you."

"Oh, I hope so."

Jim groaned and jogged down the stairs. "Hurry up, or we'll shove off without you."

Arch followed. "Never thought the most cheerful man in the world would turn grumpy."

"Grumpy indeed," Lillian said in a loud voice. "Maybe that's what happened to Mr. Dixon. Maybe his sister fell in love with his best friend."

Jim laughed. "All right. All right. Now get moving."

Before long, Arch and Jim put the *Caroline* out to sea and trimmed her sails. Jim and Mary took the helm, and Arch sat with Lillian at the bow, snuggling in the cool breeze.

Lillian chatted about the weather and the homes on the shore and the changes she was making in the pharmacy, and Arch watched her, marveling at the sudden openness.

She loved him. He loved her. Such freedom.

Yet a potential trap. She knew enough to hurt him, even to ruin him.

The gray-blue waves surged by, tipped with white froth. He was drifting away from the safety of port, exposed to the elements.

"This is so relaxing," Lillian said, one amber lock dancing in her face. "Do you really plan to sell this place, the yacht?"

He captured the errant lock and twirled it around his finger. "Yes. You know why."

"I do. And I know why you like the simple life. I like it too. But wouldn't it be lovely to have the estate for a vacation getaway, a weekend retreat?"

Arch stared at his finger, trapped in the golden coil.

"I think you can trust yourself, sweetheart." She kissed his chin. "Trust how you've changed, trust how strong you are in the Lord."

He fought the tightening of his jaw. He had to stop being suspicious. She only said such things because she believed in him.

Lillian teased her hair free and tucked it under the red ribbon. "Either way, whether you keep it or sell, I know you'll make the right choice."

Arch released a breath, absorbed the truth, and nuzzled a kiss on her wind-chilled lips. Yes, he'd exposed his deepest feelings. Yes, he could be trapped. But he and Lillian were in this together, and they weren't alone. God would be with them.

28

Boston
Monday, April 27, 1942

It couldn't be.

Lillian stood outside Dixon's Drugs, where the windows were plastered with ads and posters.

Five minutes earlier, she'd been concerned that her giddiness from the weekend in Connecticut would make it hard to concentrate on her work. Now her concern flipped to something darker.

What happened to her pretty spring window? She'd already planned her next display. With sugar rationing scheduled to start May 5, she'd designed a "Who needs sugar to be sweet?" theme, showcasing perfumes and scented soaps and lotions on a floral background.

Lillian opened the door, setting the bells to jangling. Her window display—gone. The cosmetics display—gone. Why, even the tin collection bin was gone.

"I'm sorry, Miss Avery." Mrs. Connelly stood by the soda fountain, wringing her hands. "Mr. Dixon went on a rampage this weekend. He was in a foul mood."

Beside the cashier, a sign read, "Due to sugar rationing and shortages of metal parts for the fountain, the soda fountain will close May 5."

Lillian's breathing grew shallow. She managed to give Mrs. Connelly an acknowledging nod and to move her feet down the aisle. On the way, she passed Albert unloading boxes. His expression brimmed with sympathy.

She hung up her purse in the stockroom and put on her white coat.

In the prescription area, Mr. Dixon had his back to her, mixing an ointment. "Before you say a word, let me remind you I agreed to a one-month experiment. Your month is over."

"But I thought . . . didn't sales increase?"

"Nothing worth the humiliation."

"Humiliation?"

The metal spatula scraped over the marble ointment slab. "The Chamber of Commerce met on Thursday night, and I got an earful. Mr. Morton, the owner of the store on Winthrop Square—he said he never thought he'd see the day when Cyrus Dixon let a little girl boss him around."

Lillian gasped. "I never—"

"And I found out you disobeyed me. Two doctors—two!—asked about the new girl pharmacist who loves to ask questions."

She pressed her hand over her writhing belly. She only called when necessary, and she was always polite and succinct. "I only called—"

"I told you not to." He threw a dagger of a look over his shoulder. "You went behind my back and made me the laughingstock of the Charlestown business community."

Lillian leaned against the counter for support. "It won't happen again."

"No, it won't. I won't have an employee undermining me,

218

telling me what to do. This is my store, and I'll run things my way."

"I never thought I was—I'll do better, sir."

He grunted. "Well, see if you can behave yourself until June."

"June?"

His shoulders heaved. "Pharmacy school graduation. As I told you in January, I'm looking for your replacement."

"I'm sorry, sir." She hated how her voice shuddered, but she couldn't make it stop. "I didn't think I was doing anything wrong. I was just doing my job."

Another grunt. "Well, get to work. I'm still paying you."

"Yes, sir." Eyes burning, she picked up the next prescription on the counter and rolled a label into the typewriter.

How on earth would she find a new job? It had taken six months last time, but now it'd be worse. A crippled woman who had been fired. The black mark of career death.

She pounded out the prescription directions on the typewriter keys. How had she gone from the most glorious weekend ever to one of the worst days of her life in a matter of hours?

★ ★ ★

Lillian paused outside the door to her apartment, exhausted and drained. She'd hoped her improvements to the store would increase sales and make her indispensable. Now there was nothing she could do. In two months, she'd be unemployed.

If only she didn't have to enter her apartment and run the gauntlet of sympathy. But the past few months had taught her that opening up to friends did help.

She opened the door.

"Hello, Lillian," Quintessa called. "Your dinner's waiting for you in the oven."

"Thank you." Her voice came out limp.

Mary looked up from her novel. "Are you all right?"

Her smile was even limper. "No. I'll tell you after I change."

"You poor thing. Go change and quickly."

In her room, Lillian sank down on her bed. Her prosthesis ached to be removed, as did her fitted suit jacket, but both actions required effort.

Out in the entryway, the phone rang. Lillian shook herself from the stupor and unbuttoned her jacket.

Quintessa knocked on the bedroom door. "Sweetie, it's Arch."

"Arch?" How did he know she needed to hear his voice? She dashed to the phone. "Arch?" Her voice broke.

"Darling, listen. I can't talk long. Buckner allowed me to come ashore to make a call only because it's an emergency."

"An emergency?" Lillian grasped the table.

"Sweetheart, Fish is dead."

Fish? The source. Mrs. Harrison's grandson. "Oh no. What happened?"

"On Friday night when we were in Connecticut, some of the boys were celebrating our victory at the Rusty Barnacle. Fish had too much to drink, and he'd taken at least one pill."

"Oh no." Lillian pressed her hand to her forehead. "Barbiturates and alcohol are a dangerous combination. But only one pill shouldn't—"

"This is where it gets fuzzy. Palonsky wasn't there, but he and I are piecing together the story. Apparently Earl Kramer egged Fish on, dared him. A drinking game, but with pills too."

Lillian squeezed her eyes shut. People could be so stupid.

"He passed out at the bar," Arch said. "They revived him enough to walk back to the ship, but his friends were worried. He didn't look well. So they took him to Doc."

"Your pharmacist's mate."

"Yes. Within an hour, Fish was dead."

"Oh my goodness."

"We don't know what happened. It could have been a simple accident, drinking and sedatives and poor judgment. Or Kramer could have been acting deliberately, trying to get Fish caught or killed, so he could take his place. Or it could be Doc. He has medications, and he was alone with Fish. He could have fed Fish more pills. The man was in no state to resist."

"Oh, Arch, how horrible."

Her roommates gathered around, eyes wild for answers, and Lillian faced the wall since she didn't have any.

"I wanted you to know for Mrs. Harrison's sake. And to warn you to be careful, darling. Very careful. These people are dangerous."

"Poor Mrs. Harrison." She loved her Giffy, the only one who paid her any mind, she'd said. How could her family neglect such a sweet lady?

"I have to go now," Arch said. "I don't know when I'll see you again. Buckner's cracking down tonight—he just got back. And we're sailing soon."

"I understand." She longed to see him, to hold him. She hadn't even told him about her problems, but they'd have to wait.

"I love you, darling. Please be careful. Please."

"You too. And I love you too." Lillian settled the receiver in place and faced her three roommates. "Mrs. Harrison's grandson died this weekend. He served on the *Ettinger*. I—I need to go to her."

"Oh, the poor thing." Quintessa clapped her hand over her mouth.

Lillian buttoned her suit jacket again and ventured upstairs. She was no good at consoling people, but after all Mrs. Harrison had been to her, she had to pay her respects.

A sliver of light under the door announced the poor woman was still awake.

Lillian couldn't put this off until tomorrow. She sent up a quick prayer and knocked.

Mrs. Harrison opened the door, gray-faced and empty-eyed.

"Oh, Mrs. Harrison, I'm so sorry. I just heard about your grandson."

The older woman's face buckled, but she motioned Lillian inside. "It was kind of you to come."

Lillian scanned the apartment, but they were alone. Where was the rest of her family?

Mrs. Harrison sat on the couch, and Lillian joined her.

"He was so young." Mrs. Harrison's gaze reached across the room to her grandson's portrait. "He was so patriotic, so proud to be a sailor. And he was celebrating. His destroyer sank a sub. Did you read about that in the paper?" Her eyes turned to Lillian, hungry for affirmation.

"I did." Lillian gave her a small smile. "He must have been thrilled."

With a fluttering hand, Mrs. Harrison covered her eyes. "He was celebrating with his friends, like boys do. But they say . . . they're saying horrible things. Couldn't be true."

"I know." Lillian clasped the woman's trembling hand, certain of her innocence. "The phenobarbital. He told you he needed it for his nerves. He was afraid he'd get kicked out of the Navy. So he talked you into having prescriptions filled in your name. It wasn't right of him, but how—"

Mrs. Harrison's eyes turned to blue knives.

Lillian clamped her lips together, but the horrid words had already left her mouth. She'd violated two great social laws— "never speak ill of the dead" and "blood is thicker than water."

"Pardon?" The older woman's voice cut as hard and sharp as her eyes.

"I—I'm sorry. I shouldn't—"

Mrs. Harrison yanked her hand free and stood. "How dare you? How dare you come into my home and accuse my Giffy—accuse me—"

"I'm—"

"Get out." She pointed to the door. "Get out and never come back."

Oh, what had she done? Lillian dashed out of the apartment, tossing another futile apology over her shoulder as the door slammed.

She sagged against the wall outside the door. How insensitive of her! Just because something was true didn't mean it needed to be spoken. Especially to a woman in the depths of grief.

Lillian doubled over. She'd thought she'd changed, but she was as coldhearted as ever.

29

Arch climbed the gangway under a moonlit sky. If only he could have told Lillian in person. Not only was it improper to relay news of a death by telephone, but he should have held her.

At the top of the gangway, Arch faced aft and saluted the flag, then saluted the officer of the deck tonight, Lt. John Odom. "I report my return aboard, sir."

"Very well. Captain Buckner has called a meeting of all officers in the wardroom at 2200."

Arch glanced at his watch. Half an hour. "Yes, sir."

"Mr. Vandenberg, sir." Seaman Warren Palonsky greeted him with a salute. "I completed the inventory of the repair party lockers."

Their code that they needed to discuss the case. "Very well. Let's start with number five."

Arch led the way into the center superstructure and into the locker, a small compartment crammed with tools and supplies.

Palonsky shut the door behind them, took off his white "Dixie cup" cover, and ran his hand through his sandy hair. "Sir, I just met with Earl Kramer. He took Fish's position, which makes me the new middleman. I don't like it, sir. I'm supposed to sell to other men. I can't do that."

Arch rubbed the spot between his eyebrows. "I agree. You can't. It's wrong and it's dangerous."

"I'll tell you what's dangerous." Palonsky leaned his hand against the bulkhead by his head, his fingers drumming the steel. "As Kramer's apprentice, I'm supposed to meet the sources on shore."

"Sources? More than one?"

"Yes, sir. Civilians. A group of thugs, sounds like. A leader, a forger, and fellows who steal prescription pads, get the prescriptions filled, and deliver them. Some of the deliveries take place at the Navy Yard, some at the Rusty Barnacle."

Arch set his elbow on a shelf and rested his forehead in his hand. A full-blown ring, just as they'd feared. Far more than Fish's grandmother.

"Sir, I don't like this." Palonsky slapped the bulkhead. "I want out."

If he lost Palonsky, he'd never solve the case. "I did promise you could get out any time."

"The time is now, sir."

Arch puffed out a breath. "We're so close. If we could identify even one fellow on shore, we'd have something to take to the police."

"Sir, they framed Hobie. They probably killed Fish."

"What'll it look like if you back out now? You know too much."

Palonsky cussed. "Then get me out of here. Get me transferred to another ship, far from Boston."

He needed to solve this case to prevent more deaths. "Did Kramer say when you'd meet the sources?"

"After our next patrol. Next time we both get liberty."

"Can you wait until then? Soon as we get a name—just one man—submit your request. I'll see it goes through."

Palonsky scrunched up his face, wagging his head.

Arch needed to buy more time. He swallowed some bile at the thought of what he had to do. "Would more money help?"

The sailor leveled a hard expression at him. "Ten more dollars a month."

"Twenty." Arch shook Palonsky's hand, but his heart sank low in his belly. Once again using wealth and influence to get his way. What was wrong with him?

★ ★ ★

Lt. Cdr. Alvin Buckner stood at the head of the table in the wardroom. "I'm sure you've heard of the death of Torpedoman's Mate Gifford Payne."

The officers murmured their shock and grief.

"The doctors say he died from a combination of alcohol and a sedative called phenobarbital. He had an envelope containing the pills in his pocket. It seems we have a problem on the *Ettinger*. When Seaman Hobart McLachlan was arrested two weeks ago, he had withdrawal symptoms from the same drug."

Arch pressed his lips together. Hadn't he informed the captain about the problem over a month ago? Hadn't the captain told him just to make the men buck up?

Buckner leaned his fists on the table. "Some of the boys claim they saw Fish taking pills, even giving them to others, but no one will name names."

Arch studied his folded hands in his lap. It was too early to report what he knew. He needed at least one source on shore, a link between Dixon's Drugs and the *Ettinger*—a link other than the unbelievably unlikely Opal Harrison. If he spoke now, the investigation would fall apart and the ring would continue, supplying other ships and incapacitating other sailors.

"Mr. Taylor, Mr. Avery," Buckner said. "Any problems in engineering?"

"No, sir," Emmett Taylor said. "Our boys haven't seen as much carnage as the men topside."

"Gunnery obviously has a problem." Buckner turned piercing dark eyes to Lt. Miles Gannett, the gunnery officer.

The knuckles of Gannett's clenched hands turned white. "Fish always did his duties well, sir. Stein, on the other hand . . . Melvin Stein. Bill Jenkins."

"Melvin Stein, Bill Jenkins." Buckner scribbled on a notepad. "Anyone else?"

"Not that I know of."

"Deck division." The captain's upper lip curled. "The worst division on board. What do you have to report?"

Odom's mouth pursed. "As I told you earlier, sir, many of my men have problems with their nerves."

Arch's eyebrows rose. Odom had talked to the captain too?

"No excuse for cowardice and dereliction of duty, much less using drugs." Buckner tapped his pen on the notepad. "Names?"

"Phil Carey, sir," Odom said. "He's always doping off. Possibly Warren Palonsky."

Arch forced himself not to react, to keep his breath even.

"Phil Carey . . ." Buckner said as he wrote. "Warren Palonsky."

"Mind you, no problems with Palonsky," Odom said. "He's a top-notch sailor. But I've heard rumors."

If Arch jumped on board, it would remove suspicion that he and Palonsky were connected. "I've had problems with Carey too, sir. Engelman complains about him all the time. And I've also heard rumors about Palonsky."

"Very well." Buckner tucked his pen in his shirt pocket. "We'll assemble all hands for inspection. But give the suspects extra scrutiny. Each officer inspect your own men."

Chair legs scraped on the deck, and Arch's cheeks went cold. Palonsky didn't have any drugs in his possession, did he? He was supposed to flush them immediately.

Soon all the sailors stood at attention by their bunks while officers riffled through their possessions, feeling pockets and opening boxes and toiletry kits.

Arch wasn't surprised when he found an envelope filled with tablets in Phil Carey's locker.

Carey turned white. "Sir, those aren't mine. They're Fish's. He asked me to hide them for him. I—I didn't know what to do with them after he died."

A cry of protest rose from a bunk farther aft. "I swear those aren't mine, Mr. Gannett. Fish gave that envelope to me, told me to hold it for him. I had no idea what was inside."

So that was the story they'd agreed on. If anyone were caught, everyone else would point to that man and no one else. They needed some explanation for why they didn't have prescription bottles with their names on the labels.

"Looks clean." Odom shut Palonsky's locker.

Arch swallowed his sigh of relief and forced himself not to look at his collaborator.

Buckner strode down the crowded aisle. "What do we have?"

"Jenkins," Mr. Gannett said. "He has some pills, claims they were Fish's."

"I found this envelope in Carey's locker," Arch said. "The same story about Fish."

"I swear it, sir. Not mine." The bleariness in Carey's eyes said otherwise.

Arch handed the envelope to Buckner, and an idea leapt

228

into his head. "Sir, we don't actually know what the pills are. Perhaps we should compare them to Doc's stock."

"Excellent idea, Mr. Vandenberg. Come with me. Mr. Hayes and Mr. Odom, take Carey and Jenkins to the brig on shore."

Arch followed the captain up the ladder and toward sick bay. Was that the first time the commanding officer had approved of something he'd done?

Pharmacist's Mate Parnell Lloyd met them in sick bay, and he gave Arch a strange look—suspicious perhaps, or angry.

Captain Buckner showed him the envelopes. "Do you know what these are?"

Doc peered inside. "Can't say I do. Do these have anything to do with Fish's death?"

While Buckner and Doc discussed the situation, Arch scanned the small compartment. More of Doc's art, each sketch and signature in the style of a master artist.

Arch's hands coiled into fists. So the man was skilled at forgery. He opened the medication cabinet and inspected the bottles. Phenobarbital . . . phenobarbital . . . there it was.

He pointed to the bottle. "May we look inside, Doc?"

"Yes, sir." Doc frowned at Arch and opened the bottle. "Not the same. Why do you ask?"

They weren't the same? Arch peered inside and composed himself. "We were both concerned about the men taking sedatives, possibly barbiturates, you said. Like that."

Doc shrugged. "If those tablets are phenobarbital, they come from a different supplier than the Navy uses. Perhaps they came from a civilian pharmacy—or a civilian pharmacist."

Arch's breath congealed in his chest as he stared into the pharmacist's mate's discerning, intelligent brown eyes.

It was no secret that Jim's sister was a pharmacist. Did Doc think Lillian was involved, that Arch was the link? Or was this a ploy to deflect attention from Doc? And just what had he done to Fish before he died?

"Thank you for your help, Doc." Buckner headed out of sick bay. "I'll turn these pills over to the authorities."

Arch followed the captain. He'd give Doc a wide berth.

30

"Nicer than Dixon's, isn't it?" Arch held open the door to Morton's Drugs on Winthrop Square.

"Much." Lillian inspected the uncluttered windows, the classy displays, and the abundant lighting. "I'd shop here too."

"Snob." He winked at her. "Now go be Watson and ask your questions. I'll wait for you."

"Holmes." She winked back and headed toward the prescription area, past attractive bins to collect tin, waste paper, metal scrap, and rubber scrap, each emblazoned with patriotic posters.

Well-labeled aisles beckoned the customer, and several clerks greeted her. No skimping on staff as Mr. Dixon did.

The past week, several patients had complained about the reversals to Lillian's changes, and some left the store, annoyed that Dixon's had stopped collecting tin. But if sales had fallen—or risen—Mr. Dixon remained silent.

Behind the prescription counter, a middle-aged man with

receding blond hair smiled at Lillian. "Good morning. How may I help you?"

"Good morning. My name is Lillian Avery. I'm the new pharmacist—"

"Yes, yes." He chuckled. "I'm Henry Morton. What an honor to meet the girl who's shaking things up for old Cyrus."

Her smile faltered. Not anymore she wasn't.

"Good for you." He poked a finger in her direction. "Cyrus needs shaking up. That store of his hasn't changed since eighteen—"

"Seventy-eight."

Mr. Morton laughed, big and hearty, then rested his elbows on the counter. "So what brings Charlestown's newest sensation to my store?"

Strange how Mr. Morton's depiction of her varied so widely from Mr. Dixon's. She straightened the jacket of her brand-new green suit. "I was . . . well, I'm asking around. Have you seen a high number of prescriptions for barbiturates? In large quantities, like two hundred tablets?"

"Oh my. No, I haven't. I'd call the doctor about that."

In the six stores she'd visited today, each druggist had said something similar. Lillian's smile rose in vindication. Fat lot of good it would do her when she was fired, though.

"Why?" Mr. Morton asked.

"Oh, it's just that I've seen prescriptions that made me wonder." She leaned closer. "Would you do me a huge favor? Please don't tell Mr. Dixon I came by."

His eyes twinkled. "Going behind old Cyrus's back? I'm on your side, Miss Avery."

"Thank you. It was a pleasure meeting you." When she started applying for jobs in late May, she'd visit Morton's first.

Arch met her partway down the center aisle, so handsome in his dress whites, and he took her arm to stop her. "On our way out, I want you to look down the aisles to your left, casually, as if you were browsing. There's a tall, dark-haired man, probably in his thirties. Don't be obvious, but try to get a good look at him."

"Why?" Lillian whispered.

"I'll explain outside." He led her down the center aisle.

Lillian glanced down the rows, trying to appear non-chalant. Soon she saw the man Arch had mentioned—a lanky man in a work jacket and a newsboy's cap. His angular face jolted her memory. Thank goodness he was reading the label on a bottle and didn't look her way.

Arch led her across the street to Winthrop Square, marked off with a wrought-iron fence. "Recognize him?"

"That's Norman Hunter, one of our phenobarbital patients."

Arch's lips pressed into a hard line. "He's been at the last three stores we've visited."

"He's following us?"

"Yes. We need to solve this case and fast."

Lillian picked up her pace. "We need to shake him too."

"That's easy." Arch held her hand. "We stroll around and act like lovebirds. He'll assume we finished our rounds."

"You just want some kisses."

"Don't you?" His eyes gleamed in the way she loved, and he leaned closer, irresistible.

She didn't resist, even in broad daylight in the middle of Winthrop Square. He wrapped his arms around her waist, ducked under the brim of her new hat, and kissed her.

Oh my. Her knees failed, but how could she fall, braced against Arch's broad chest?

"I'm glad you're back," she murmured against his lips. "Even a short patrol feels long."

"I'm afraid I'll be gone for longer periods." He resumed their stroll, his arm around her waist. "The *Ettinger* was officially assigned to the Eastern Sea Frontier, so no more North Atlantic convoys. But later this month, they'll start full coastal convoys, down to Key West and back. That's us."

"Oh." She rested her head on his shoulder. "I can't be disappointed when convoys will save hundreds of lives. Right?"

"Right. But the timing is bad. Not just with you, but with the case. The answers lie in Charlestown, not at sea."

"Well, I can dig for more clues when you're gone. I want to investigate more of the delivery addresses."

Arch stopped, his eyes alarmed. "That isn't wise with this Hunter fellow following you. Let's use the phone book instead."

"You're right." Lillian frowned in the direction of Morton's, almost obscured by trees. "I'll look up the names of the patients, see if they even exist, if the addresses are the same."

"Mm-hmm. If you're bored, you can scan the phone book for the delivery addresses."

"I'm glad the Charlestown phone book isn't thick." Lillian measured a fraction of an inch between thumb and forefinger. "Maybe I'll find a connection, a real address and a real name."

"Or maybe they're fake names and vacant apartments."

"That's what Detective Malloy said." She sighed and strolled past the Civil War Monument. "I wish I had something to report to him. All I have is a list of prescriptions, one of which is for a—for an elderly lady who gave pills to her sailor grandson."

"She may or may not be connected to the ring. Just in case, steer clear of her."

"She isn't connected." Her voice quavered. "But she won't even look at me. I miss her."

"Oh, darling." Arch folded her in his arms and kissed her forehead. "I'm sorry. Perhaps she'll see the truth about Fish and—"

234

"She loved him, and he died, and I called him a drug addict."

"He was a drug addict."

Lillian played with the brass buttons down the front of his jacket. "I miss our talks. I think she'd be proud of me, how I opened my heart to you."

"I know she would." Arch captured her hand and kissed it. "I'm proud of you too. But mostly I'm just selfishly pleased. I got my girl."

Another kiss that melted her muscles, but she managed to pull away after a minute. "We should have lunch soon. I have to go to work at one o'clock."

"I think we lost Mr. Hunter." Arch gazed around the park. "I wonder if he'll have the nerve to show his face at Dixon's today."

"Depends if he needs his meds." She took Arch's hand and headed toward the apartment, where they planned to make sandwiches. "Looks like the ring only targets Dixon's Drugs."

"Probably because Mr. Dixon never asks questions. The other pharmacists said they'd call."

"'Never turn away a paying customer,' he always says. The forgers take advantage of that. They can't risk a phone call to the doctor. They'd be found out. But I wonder . . ."

Arch swung their clasped hands as they turned onto Winthrop Street. "What do you wonder, my lovely Watson?"

Lillian nudged his shoulder. "Holmes is the one who comes up with the theories. Call me Holmes or I won't tell you."

Arch laughed. "Your brothers did anything you wanted, didn't they?"

"Jim did. But not Dan, and Rob could go either way. Now call me Holmes."

"This had better be good . . . Holmes."

"I do love you." She grinned at him, then sobered. "My other theory. I wonder if Mr. Dixon is being blackmailed. Maybe the gang forces him to fill the prescriptions."

Arch lifted one shoulder. "A bit farfetched."

"Maybe not. I've been thinking. He dotes on his nephew, the only family he has. Albert told me he and this nephew used to run in a bad crowd. They both turned their lives around with Mr. Dixon's help. But what if this crowd is related to our ring? What if they had something really bad on the nephew? A murder, perhaps. They could blackmail poor Mr. Dixon to keep his beloved boy out of the electric chair."

Arch faced her in the shadow of a large stone church. "So now it's poor Mr. Dixon, is it?"

"I do feel sorry for him. He doesn't have anyone other than his nephew. Maybe that's why he's such a grouch."

"I don't feel charitable to the man who's making life miserable for the woman I love."

She stroked her thumb along the back of his hand. "I don't feel miserable when I'm with you."

"You're too softhearted, darling. It'll get you in trouble."

Softhearted? She'd never heard that term applied to her before, and it made her heart feel very soft indeed.

"It's already gotten me in trouble." She kissed his cheek. "It got me mixed up with you."

31

Arch stared at himself in the little stand-up mirror propped on the ladies' kitchen table. He didn't recognize himself in beat-up work clothes and a scraggly salt-and-pepper wig. The stage makeup Palonsky had borrowed from a theater friend in town had transformed him into a grizzled old merchant marine. Palonsky assured him the Rusty Barnacle was so dark and smoky no one would be able to tell they were wearing makeup.

"You need grease under your fingernails." Lillian stretched his hand across the table and rubbed a black makeup pencil around his nails. "Don't forget to slouch. And watch your manners. Don't be such a—"

"Dandy," Palonsky grumbled.

Arch shot him a look.

Lillian laughed. "A gentleman. You're no dandy."

"Still don't think this is smart." Palonsky turned the mirror his way and added smudges under his eyes. "I'm the actor.

I can pull this off. But the fellows at the bar will see right through to your fancy officer ways."

"We both need to be there. You said Kramer's picking up a delivery there tonight. You met two of our sources, but they won't tell you their names. All we need is one name. And I'm the only one who'd recognize the man who followed Lillian."

"I would too." Lillian gave him a mischievous smile. "Why shouldn't I be there? I'm the one who spent hours poring over the phone book. I'm the one who discovered the bar's address is one of our delivery spots. I could dress as a pirate. I already have the peg leg."

Arch grinned. How far she'd come from bristling at the mention of her prosthesis to making jokes about it. "Argh, me hearty. No wench of mine—"

"Mr. Vandenberg, sir. Please don't talk." Palonsky shook his head. "Just grunt and glower. Don't open that . . . gentlemanly mouth. Let me do the talking."

"Then don't call me 'sir,' matey."

"That's as grungy as I can make you." Lillian squeezed his hand and giggled. "I'd kiss you good-bye, but I'd mess up your lipstick."

He gave her his best pirate glare, and he and Palonsky headed out into the night. On the way to the bar, they reviewed their codes and signals. If Arch acted too gentlemanly, Palonsky planned to rap his pinky on the table, code for "I'm gonna smash that raised pinky of yours."

The Rusty Barnacle stank of liquor and cigarette smoke and hardworking men. Arch kept his head down and scanned the dim, smoky interior. Sailors from the *Ettinger* and other ships occupied a couple of tables, and workmen and merchant marines occupied others.

Palonsky headed to the bar. "Two beers."

Arch didn't plan to drink his. Not only did he need his

wits, but he'd never cared for beer. However, a glass made a good prop. He'd just pretend to drink.

Palonsky led him to a table closer to the civilians—but not too close.

A bowl of shelled peanuts sat on the table, and Arch selected a nice plump one.

Three raps of a pinky knuckle. Palonsky dug his hand into the bowl and shoveled in a bunch of peanuts, chewing messily.

Arch mimicked the seaman's actions. A peanut even fell out of his mouth. A nice touch, if he did say so himself.

"Source Two and Easy King," Palonsky said in a low voice. "Bearing zero-six-zero."

Source Two? And Earl Kramer? Arch aimed a glower through the smoky haze toward the coordinates, sweeping well past the target.

Three men sat at the table. Kramer had his back to Arch, thank goodness, but the other two men showed their profiles. A heavyset, meaty-faced man with a cap low over his forehead, and a small man with a dark look about him.

Arch pretended to sip his beer. "Big or little?"

"Little."

Another fake sip. He imprinted both men's features in his mind so he could describe them to Lillian.

The door opened. Arch cradled his glass, watching out of the corner of his eye.

Norman Hunter! "Nan How coming our way," he muttered.

Hunter passed their table and joined Kramer and friends. "Hey, Hank," the smaller man said.

"Hey, fellas. Leave any beer for me?"

They all laughed. "Not a drop."

"Source One," Palonsky murmured into his beer.

Source One, and his name was Hank, not Norman Hunter.

Arch studied the amber liquid in front of him, the same color as Lillian's hair, not that he'd tell her.

Hank. Hank. If only they'd used a last name too. If only Hank had greeted the others by name. Arch tuned his ear to the conversation, but he only heard snippets.

Before long, Kramer left the bar, and Palonsky turned his head away as the coxswain passed.

The door opened again. Hunkered over his beer, Arch stole a glance. A red-haired man approached the bar—that was Albert Myers, the delivery boy from Dixon's Drugs. He greeted the bartender and gave him a paper bag.

What timing! On the way home, he'd give Palonsky a hard time about that. The sailor wouldn't have recognized Albert. "Able Mike from Dog Dog."

Palonsky's eyebrows twisted in confusion.

He'd gloat later. "Delivery from my girl's employer."

Palonsky leaned back, rolled his shoulders, and surveyed the scene. "Bartender, huh?"

"We need his name."

"Leave it to me. Finish the peanuts."

Arch scooped in another sloppy mouthful.

Palonsky took the empty bowl to the bar. His mild limp and heavy gait aided his disguise as a wizened old sea salt. He greeted the bartender with a grin. "Say, can me and my pal here have more peanuts?" He sounded like a fisherman from Maine. What an actor.

"Sure." The bartender filled the bowl.

Average build and height. In his forties. Auburn hair thinning on top and graying around the temples. A name. Arch just needed a name.

Palonsky thrust out his hand. "Hal Miller. Folks call me Lob, for lobster."

"Folks call me Rusty." The bartender shook his hand.

Arch winced. He needed a last name too.

Palonsky chuckled and leaned his elbow on the bar. "Rusty, eh? That how the place got its name?"

"Sure is. Started as Rusty's Bar. Sailors started calling it the Rusty Barnacle. I liked it. Made a new sign."

"Your last name Barnacle too?"

Rusty laughed. "Nope. Carruthers."

Not just an actor, but a genius. The man deserved a promotion.

Rusty filled a glass with beer from the tap. "Ain't never seen you or your pal before. New in town?"

"Yep. We're boilermen on the SS—ah, no you don't, young man." Palonsky wagged his finger. "Loose lips sink ships, you know."

"Have another beer on me." Rusty slid him the glass. "You're wise to keep quiet. We get shady characters in here."

"Not this fellow." Palonsky clapped Albert on the back. "Clean-cut boy like this."

Rusty gave him a mock scowl. "It's the clean-cut ones you gotta watch out for."

The three of them burst out laughing.

Someone bumped Arch's chair from behind, and beer sloshed over the table.

"Hey, watch what you're doing," someone barked.

The nerve. Who bumped whom? Arch sat up straight and fixed a hard look on the man. "Pardon?"

Oh no. It was Hank, his eyes dark slits in his angular face.

The last thing they needed was an escalation into a brawl. Arch's heart hammered, but he hefted up his shoulders and grunted. "Did me a favor. Lousy beer anyway."

Hank laughed and gave him a friendly punch in the shoulder. "Ain't it? Hey, Rusty. Need a rag."

"Clumsy oaf." Rusty fired a rag across the room.

Arch snatched it from the air, glad he'd excelled at baseball, and scrubbed the table in rough strokes, pleased to show off his grease manicure. He'd salvaged that situation.

But Palonsky rapped his knuckle against his thigh. What? What had he done wrong?

The seaman ambled back to the table. "Five minutes. Let me down this beer, then we'll scram. Not a word."

Arch popped peanuts into his mouth to justify the new bowlful, but salt and uneasiness dried out his tongue.

Finally Palonsky jerked his head to the door and led Arch outside, tossing a good-bye to Rusty.

"This way and fast." Palonsky darted up a narrow street. "Never again, Mr. Vandenberg. Never again."

"Nonsense. We have new information, names—"

"Pardon?" He pursed his mouth and looked down his nose like a caricature of an aristocrat. "I do believe you caused me to spill my libation."

Arch groaned. "It wasn't that bad."

"It was a test, sir. Don't you see? Hank bumped you on purpose so you'd look straight at him—and to see how you'd react. Didn't you notice he went back to the table afterward?" Palonsky glanced behind him and steered Arch right on the next street.

The peanuts tumbled in his stomach. "I failed the test. Do you think he recognized me?"

"Don't know. But I guarantee they know you ain't a boiler-man on the SS *Sea Salt*." A sharp left turn. "Take off that wig and cap, stuff them in your coat. We'll come to the girls' place from the opposite way."

"They're following us?"

"Not that I can tell, but they were having a heated talk. Couldn't hear, but it looked like Hank wanted to beat you up, big guy told him, 'not on your life,' little guy backed up big guy. Guess who's in charge?"

"Big guy." Arch sighed. "And we don't have his name or the

little guy's, and we only have Hank's first name. Although now we know Hank was definitely following Lillian because of the drug ring and he's using an alias. And we know Rusty Carruthers is involved."

Palonsky headed left, up the hill toward Monument Square. "And we know Ensign Archer Vandenberg is no actor."

Maybe not, but he'd fulfilled a purpose. Only he could have matched Palonsky's source to Lillian's shadow. Only he could have recognized Albert and discovered Rusty's involvement. He grinned at Palonsky. "So, next week—"

"I'll throw myself overboard. I swear I will, sir."

Arch laughed. "From now on, I'll leave the spying to you."

32

Lillian studied the prescription Mrs. Harper gave her for elixir of aminophylline, and she addressed ten-year-old Denny Harper. "Could you swallow a pill?"

Denny raised anxious brown eyes to his mom. "I hate pills."

"I know." Lillian leaned over the counter. "I hated them at your age too."

"Miss Avery." Mrs. Harper shifted the weight of the little girl she carried on her hip. "I'd sure appreciate an elixir."

Lillian nodded, but she slid the prescription across the counter toward the boy. "Denny, you can read. There are a lot of strange symbols, but what's that word?"

"Sugar. That's too easy. And that one's alcohol and that's glycerin."

"Well, you know sugar's rationed. But did you know they need alcohol to make those big shells the Navy uses on battleships? And glycerin is needed for explosives. The nation is running low on all of these."

"Oh." Denny bit his lower lip.

Lillian shrugged. "I could make this elixir and use up a little more sugar, a little more alcohol, a little more glycerin."

Something fierce flashed in his eyes. "Or I could swallow a pill like a man."

"Like a soldier serving his country."

Mrs. Harper chuckled. "How can I argue with patriotism?"

One quick phone call that even Mr. Dixon wouldn't mind, and the doctor changed the elixir to a tablet. Lillian filled the prescription and placed the bottle of manly tablets in a paper bag. Then she extended the jar of marbles to both brother and sister. Mr. Dixon offered them only to boys, but Lillian knew girls liked marbles too. She certainly did.

After they left, she glanced at the clock. Only eleven. Mr. Dixon wouldn't be in until one, and Reggie, the junior clerk, was stocking shelves. Now she could call Dr. Sharp. The past week she'd worked evenings, and Dr. Sharp's office closed promptly at five.

She grabbed the phone and the prescription she'd set aside, called the office, and waited for the nurse to fetch the physician. What did it matter if Mr. Dixon fired her for calling? He'd fire her in a few weeks anyway. She'd typed up a dozen copies of her resume, and tomorrow on her day off she'd start applying for a new job.

"Dr. Sharp here."

"This is Lillian Avery. I'm a pharmacist at Dixon's Drugs. Pardon me, but I'm new to town, and I wanted to verify a prescription that seems unusual to me."

"All right."

Deep breath. "It's for Harry Carruthers. One-half grain of phenobarbital, three hundred tablets. And the delivery address is a bar, the Rusty Barnacle."

Dr. Sharp sighed. "I suppose that would look unusual.

Poor Harry has a violent case of epilepsy and requires five grains daily. As for the bar, his brother owns it. He cares for Harry. Saddest thing you've ever seen. Rusty keeps the poor man in a room behind the bar so he can help if Harry has a seizure."

"Oh dear."

"That Rusty—he's rough around the edges but has a heart of gold. Most brothers would put Harry in an institution, but Rusty won't hear of it."

Lillian fought to keep inappropriate disappointment out of her voice. "Thank you for explaining. I wanted to be sure."

"A wise choice."

When she hung up, her delayed disappointment seeped out in a sigh. Rusty Carruthers was a red herring. A legitimate prescription, not a forgery. It was merely a coincidence that the same bar was used by the drug ring for deliveries.

What more could she do to solve the case? The men who brought in forged prescriptions used aliases, and they certainly wouldn't divulge their identities to her.

That was all they needed. Names to add to the faces. Hank she recognized, but they needed a last name. The smaller man Arch saw at the bar sounded like the customer who used the alias Arnold Smith, but the larger man didn't sound familiar.

"Lillian Avery, standing around doing nothing."

She whipped around at the familiar voice. "Daniel Avery, standing around being annoying."

Dan gave a rare smile, removed his cover, and smoothed his wavy black hair. "So this is where you've been getting into trouble lately."

He didn't know the half of it. "You realize you've been in Boston three months, and this is the first time you've visited Dixon's."

"Well, you know gas is rationed here on the East Coast."

Lillian burst out in a laugh. "Only for the past week, and

you don't even own a car, and Boston has the best subway system."

"Worth a try." Dan's eyes twinkled, and he glanced around. "You've done well for yourself."

If only it would last. "So what brought the busy lieutenant into my drugstore?"

"Telegram from Mom." He slid her a piece of paper. "Good news."

"Lucy had her baby?" Lillian snatched up the telegram and gobbled it down. "A girl? How fun. They named her Barbara. I like that. I can't wait to see a picture."

"I'm hurt." He flicked the paper in her hand. "Mom says Lucy wants to know when Lillian's coming to see the baby. Not when Dan's coming, or Rob, or Jim. Only you."

Since Dan never had any patience with Lucy's histrionics, Lillian felt free to tell the truth. "Simple. She wants to gloat that she has a husband and baby, and I don't. When I say I can't come home because of work, she'll have another excuse to call me coldhearted."

Dan made a face. "I'll never understand women. That's why I'll never marry."

"Just wait. Someday a special lady will make you change your tune."

He raised one dark eyebrow. "Never thought I'd hear my sensible sister spout romantic hogwash."

She smiled. "Even sensible sisters fall in love."

"Well, Arch is a good man. Almost worthy of you. Do you know where he and Jim are?"

"No. They sailed on the tenth. That's all I know." Eleven very long days.

Dan leaned forward with a glint in his eye. "Coastal convoy. Key West and back."

The proper response was, "It's about time," so Lillian said it, even though her brain was calculating how long the voyage would take, how long until she could savor Arch's brilliant eyes and kind words and vertigo-producing kisses.

"About three weeks total," Dan said, his eyelids fluttering in annoyance. "Looks like love has made my sister much less sensible."

"And much happier." She gave him a beaming smile just to see him grimace.

He did. "I'd better get back to work, and so had you. If you have any work, that is."

"It's been quiet lately." She spied Mr. Dixon coming up the aisle, early for his shift. "There's my boss. Quick—buy some war stamps. We're below our sales quota."

Dan grumbled about already aiding the war effort, but he bought five dollars' worth.

Mr. Dixon paused in front of the counter and inspected Dan. "Just how many naval officers do you know, Miss Avery?"

She laughed. "Mr. Dixon, this is my oldest brother, Lt. Dan Avery."

The men shook hands, but Mr. Dixon looked distracted, and Dan took his leave.

Lillian put away the bulk bottle of aminophylline, but what could she do next? She had so few prescriptions today. With less compounding of elixirs and syrups, she even had less to clean up.

"Miss Avery, I'd like a word."

She winced, but she schooled her expression to neutrality and faced him. Had he hired her replacement already?

The druggist did up the buttons on his white coat. "I sat down with the books last night. No doubt about it. Sales have fallen this month."

"Well, it is spring. Fewer cases of cold and flu."

"No, sales are also down from last May. Since you came."

Lillian's shoulder muscles tightened. He was blaming her? "Don't forget the government's price freeze."

"That's not it." He tugged the hem of his jacket. "However, April sales were significantly higher than March, and over April of 1941. It was due to the changes you made."

Her jaw swung low. "It was?"

"We've had complaints too." He frowned toward the main store. "Mrs. Connelly and Miss Felton say customers have left the store as soon as they saw the tin collection bin was gone. And the ladies miss your froufrou displays."

"Oh." Her heartbeat scampered ahead, but she refused to let her mind catch up.

Mr. Dixon flung his hand toward the front of the store. "Put it back the way you had it. All of it. The window, the tin box, the cosmetics table, anything else you want."

"Anything?"

He lowered thick gray brows at her. "Run your ideas past me first."

Her mind joined her heart in its frolic. "Of course."

"Well, get to it. What're you waiting for?"

Lillian could have hugged the grouchy old teddy bear, but he'd fire her on the spot. "Thank you, sir. I'll get right to work."

"Good. Only reason I came in early."

She went to the stockroom where he'd stashed the tin collection bin with all her fabric inside. Her changes had increased sales! She'd done it. She'd made herself indispensable. He'd never fire her now.

She carried out the box and grinned at Mr. Dixon as she passed. "We'll get you that cottage on Nantucket and a boat for your nephew before you know it."

Something soft washed over those dark eyes, and then he grunted and marched away.

Let Lucy call her coldhearted. It wasn't true. Only warmth could have melted Mr. Dixon's stalwart defenses.

33

Off Cape Hatteras, North Carolina
Friday, May 29, 1942

The seas around Cape Hatteras tossed the *Ettinger*, but not as much as Mother's letter tossed Arch.

The letter had arrived the day they left Boston, almost three weeks earlier. On first reading, Arch dismissed it outright, but each day's reading fueled his doubts. Alone in his cabin, waiting for the first dog watch at 1600, he smoothed the stationery on the desk. Muggy air pressed on his chest.

For several days, I've pondered how to address this. I liked Lillian very much and found her kind and gracious. You know I don't tolerate gossip, but since this came from our trusted friend Dr. Detweiler, it carries weight and bears serious consideration. He never spreads gossip either, and he was quite impressed with Lillian that evening.

His granddaughter Pauline was concerned when you brought home a new girlfriend. She and her friends know you've been hurt by gold diggers, so Pauline recorded their

conversation with Lillian. She showed it to her grand-
father, and he thought you should be informed. Your
father and I concurred. I have enclosed Pauline's notes.

Arch unfolded the second sheet of stationery, steeling
himself, praying Pauline's words would form new and less-
incriminating sentences. But they wouldn't.

Helen, Trudy, and I arranged a private talk with Miss
Lillian Avery. We made pleasant conversation until I
asked how long she and Archer had been dating.
Lillian said, "We aren't dating."
Helen voiced her surprise, since Archer seemed smit-
ten. Lillian stated she was aware of his affections.
Then Trudy asked if Lillian was playing hard to get.
Lillian smirked. "There's a reason playing hard to
get has worked for generations. The man thinks it was
his idea and not yours."
We giggled as if we agreed, and Helen leaned closer
with a conspiratorial whisper. "When a man is used to
being chased for his money, it's important that he does
the chasing."
"Oh yes," Lillian said. "He mustn't think I'm a gold
digger."
I chimed in. "But all this wealth is tempting, isn't it?"
She laughed. "Who wouldn't want it?" Then she con-
fessed she hadn't made up her mind whether or not to
date Arch—until she saw the estate.
An admission of guilt from her very lips. Our first
goal was accomplished, but our second goal remained.
We couldn't allow her to deceive our friend.
Helen pulled herself to her full regal height. "You do
know we'll have to inform Archer that you only want
him for his money."

Lillian lost all composure. It was rather embarrassing. She said we'd better keep quiet. Archer would never believe us anyway. Since Bitsy holds a torch for him, he'd think we were lying to drive Lillian away and let Bitsy have him.

Then she did the most unseemly thing. She said we didn't have a leg to stand on, but she did. She raised her skirts—in public!—and thrust out a wooden leg. Of course, we were shocked at her behavior and rather unsettled. Then she stomped away in a temper like a common fishwife.

I hate to report this conversation, but for Archer's sake, it is necessary.

Arch shoved the papers away, and his hands curled into fists. Someone was a lying schemer—either Pauline or Lillian. Two weeks ago, he'd assumed it was Pauline, but now he wasn't certain.

It didn't sound like the Lillian he knew and loved.

And yet . . .

He trusted Dr. Detweiler. He trusted his parents. They wouldn't have passed on Pauline's letter unless they believed her accusations had merit. And Arch had seen Lillian hike up her skirts and storm off in a huff. Both Lillian's and Pauline's explanations fit the action he'd witnessed.

And the shrewdness of the plan. If Lillian were indeed a gold digger, she would choose a clever approach like that. Chasing Arch would have raised his defenses, but inducing him to the chase caused him to lower his defenses.

And the timing?

Arch groaned and rested his forehead on his fist. One sentence knifed his heart—she hadn't made up her mind until she saw the estate. Was that true? In a way, it was. She did make up her mind at the estate. Was the splendor the tipping point? If he'd declared his love while residing in a filthy tenement, would she have made the same decision?

His stomach whirled, as turbulent as the seas beneath him. Did she love him for who he was? Or had he been deceived yet again?

All the clues he'd brushed aside returned to his memory. Before the weekend in Connecticut, she'd supported the idea of selling his inheritance and giving away every penny. Then the day after the anniversary party, she told him to keep the estate. Now that she could potentially enjoy it.

Every time he saw her lately it seemed she wore a new dress, a new suit, a new hat—and nice ones. Having a rich boyfriend did tend to increase a woman's appetite for the finer things in life.

Arch thrust the letter back in the drawer and bolted to his feet. He hated doubting her. He hated himself for feeling suspicious. And he hated the fact that he needed to test her.

But if he'd been deceived, he could be trapped for life. He'd hate that most of all.

If only he could find out the truth simply by showing her the letter. But if she were innocent, she'd say Pauline was lying. And if she were guilty, she'd also say Pauline was lying. Only a test would reveal the truth.

His peace of mind was worth a few months' salary.

Now he had to set aside that business and focus on his duties. He headed up to the main deck. The mugginess remained, but the winds relieved the suffocating pressure.

Across rough gray seas, North Carolina's shore made its siren call. How many ships had been dashed on those shallow shoals? How many had foundered in sudden storms? And how many more had been ripped asunder by German submarines in their favorite killing ground?

Cape Hatteras had earned her nickname of Torpedo Junction.

Arch got his bearings. The *Ettinger* brought up the rear of the convoy of twenty-two cargo ships, which would pull in to Hampton Roads, Virginia, tonight. The *Ettinger* would proceed north, escorting ships to various ports. East of Boston, Canadian ships would relieve them and escort the remaining merchantmen to Halifax to join a North Atlantic convoy.

Arch strode down the deck, greeting his men as the petty officers supervised the change of watch. No U-boats had bothered them since they departed Key West. As American defenses improved, the Nazis shifted their tactics. This month they'd found good hunting in the Caribbean and off the mouth of the Mississippi.

But no waters were safe in the Eastern Sea Frontier, especially around Cape Hatteras. Frequent sound contacts and too-frequent sightings of broken hulls and burnt life rafts kept the men of the *Ettinger* on edge. Always on edge.

"Good afternoon, Mr. Odom." Arch greeted the first lieutenant on the quarterdeck.

"Good afternoon, Mr. Vandenberg." Mr. Odom scanned a clipboard. "The watch went well. Only had one drowsy sailor."

"An improvement." Arch's dry tone matched Odom's. Captain Buckner's purge had made the men more careful—but no less addicted.

"The glass is falling, and I don't like the look of that sky." Arch nodded at the roiling dark clouds. "Storm's coming."

"Agreed." The first lieutenant pointed toward shore. "Keep an eye on the tanker in position 15. She isn't keeping station. The shipping lane is narrow here, with lots of shoals and submerged wrecks, but she's hugging the shore. She's ignoring our signals."

Arch shook his head. The Navy had finally resumed tanker traffic, and the Allies couldn't afford to lose thousands of gallons of oil during a severe shortage.

After Mr. Odom departed, Arch performed the routine

muster of the lifeboat crew of the watch. Down by the bow, the boatswain's mate piped for the sweepers to begin their late-afternoon chore.

Coxswain Earl Kramer reported on the condition of the motor whaleboat and its provisions, and Arch worked down his checklist. The signalman had his semaphore flags, and the pharmacist's mate had his first-aid kit. The boat's crew stood by, as did the crew to lower the boat to the water. All looked well.

A low thunk sounded closer to shore. The tanker in position 15 shuddered and stopped.

Arch sucked in a breath. No explosion. Was it from a torpedo? Or an underwater collision?

At the starboard lifeline, he scanned the waves. No sign of a periscope.

Up on the wing of the bridge, the executive officer, Ted Hayes, studied the tanker with binoculars. Hayes called to the signal bridge above him, but Arch couldn't hear a word.

Back on the port side, Arch stood so he could see the blinking signal lights. The tanker had grounded.

The destroyer changed course. The convoy steamed north toward the haven of Hampton Roads, but the *Ettinger* remained behind to screen the tanker while she freed herself. Arch glanced at his watch. Three hours of daylight remained. By day, the U-boats liked to hide in the deep waters off the continental shelf. By night, they hunted.

General quarters hadn't sounded, so Arch guided the deck division in the routines of the watch. Signals flashed between destroyer and tanker. The tanker hadn't budged, but murky water churned behind her as she ran her engines in reverse. Since the tide and the barometer were falling, they had to act quickly before the tanker was torn to pieces.

At 1700, the crew performed the routine of closing and checking all watertight doors and hatches, but the men were distracted by the stranded tanker and by the little red Civil Air Patrol plane overhead.

Arch thanked God for the CAP plane as the volunteer civilian pilot flew in circles to seaward. Just the presence of the aircraft would keep U-boats away.

"Mr. Vandenberg?" A talker waved to him. "Captain summoned you to the bridge."

Arch gave his khaki uniform a quick check and headed up the ladder. In the pilothouse, Captain Buckner and Ted Hayes conversed near the helm.

Buckner's steely gaze turned to Arch. "The tanker's stranded. She ran her engines too hard in reverse and fouled her propellers."

Arch winced. "They need a tow."

"We radioed Hampton Roads, but it'll take several hours for a tug to arrive. By then, it'll be low tide."

"With a storm coming, it might be too late." Hayes shook his head. "We need to do the job, but we can't get any closer in these waters."

Arch peered across the distance. "We're too far away to shoot the line-throwing gun. What do you think, sir? Should we send a line across with the whaleboat?"

Hayes smiled. "That's why we called you up here."

Would Buckner give him credit for coming up with the correct solution? Either way, Arch would make the most of this opportunity.

Down on the main deck, he summoned Chief Boatswain's Mate Ralph Lynch and explained the plan. Lynch went to the stern, where he'd prepare the heavy towlines and the lighter messenger line.

Once again, Arch mustered the lifeboat crew, but for an actual mission this time. Parnell Lloyd wouldn't come with them, since first aid wasn't needed. Just as well. Arch avoided the pharmacist's mate.

But he couldn't avoid the coxswain. Earl Kramer, Arch, and five other men climbed into the 26-foot boat hanging by its davits over the gunwale.

Slowly and steadily, the crew lowered the boat. The signalman's eyes grew wider as the water approached, but Arch's pulse quickened with the joy of adventure and purpose.

If this succeeded, Buckner might be impressed for a change. And what if Arch solved the case? How could Buckner fail to commend him?

The boat plopped into the water, and Kramer started the engine. Soon, the whaleboat bumped over the waves, the messenger line stretching between her and the *Ettinger*.

Kramer's square face bunched up in concentration as he manned the tiller in the heavy seas.

Arch studied the bouncing messenger line so he wouldn't study the coxswain, a man who sold drugs but managed to do an excellent job. Thank goodness, this case would soon come to an end.

Kramer had briefed Warren Palonsky on the sources on shore. No names were given, and Palonsky was warned not to ask. The larger man was indeed the leader, and Palonsky was scheduled to meet him at the Navy Yard when they returned to Boston. Kramer had nicknamed him Scar for a large scar on the right side of his face—the side turned toward the wall that night at the Rusty Barnacle.

Since Scar had access to the Navy Yard, he had to be an employee. Over thirty thousand men and women worked there, but how many had similar scars? After Palonsky met with the culprit and got a better description, Arch would ask around. Perhaps Mary Stirling could help, since she worked in personnel. Then they'd notify the police, and the ring would collapse.

The whaleboat drew nearer to the massive tanker. The *Ettinger*'s signalman communicated with the tanker's crew using semaphore flags. The tanker's engines had stopped to allow the whaleboat to approach, and sailors at the stern lowered a weighted line.

Arch peered into the choppy water, praying they wouldn't be grounded also.

Kramer slowed the whaleboat's motor and maneuvered behind the stern toward the dangling line.

At the top of a wave, a seaman reached up and grabbed it. "More slack," he yelled, and the signalman repeated his request.

Arch scooted out of the way as coils of rope dropped into the whaleboat. Two seamen scrambled to bend the line from the *Ettinger* to the line from the tanker in a solid square knot.

"Done, sir."

"Very well. Stand clear." Arch turned to the signalman. "Tell them to hoist away."

The whaleboat crew pulled gear, limbs, and necks far from the lines, and the signalman flashed his semaphore flags while yelling, "Hoist away!"

Sailors on the tanker hauled in their line, and soon the messenger line cleared the deck of the whaleboat.

"Take us ten yards to starboard," Arch told Kramer.

"Aye aye, sir." The coxswain swung the whaleboat away from the swooping lines but close enough to assist if the lines parted.

The *Ettinger* had positioned herself farther south, with her stern facing the tanker's stern. The tanker's crew hauled in the light manila messenger line, which was bent to the heavy wire-rope towing line. Signals flashed between the two ships, asking for slack or strain, until the end of the towing line cleared the gunwale of the tanker.

"Take us home, Kramer," Arch said.

"Aye aye, sir." The coxswain revved the boat's motor and sped over the rising seas under a darkening sky.

Arch had accomplished today's mission, and soon he'd solve the case. His personal insurance policy against a lifetime sentence in the Vandenberg business.

In the war, the United States was finally digging in her heels. The East Coast convoys and air patrols were driving the U-boats farther south, and in the Battle of the Coral Sea, the Navy had foiled a Japanese landing for the first time, although at a heavy cost. The current defensive successes hinted at future offensive successes.

Someday the Allies would win. They had to. And when the war was over, Arch wanted his Navy career firm and settled.

The whaleboat sliced into a wave, and cool water splashed Arch's face. Like sailing on the *Caroline*, with Lillian curled up at his side. The same day Lillian had gushed over the beauty of the Vandenberg estate and encouraged him to keep it.

He groaned and squeezed his eyes shut. Pauline's letter was poisoning his memories. Or was it bringing clarity?

For the first time since he'd met Lillian, he didn't relish returning to Boston, because then he'd be forced to test her.

If she passed, all would be well.

But if she failed, how could he stand it? He loved her deeply, more than any woman he'd ever known. He'd told her things he'd never told a soul. He'd pictured a life with her, raising a family with her, loving her forever.

Dear Lord, please. Please let her pass.

34

Boston
Saturday, June 6, 1942

Lillian lost herself in Arch's kiss, wrapped in his arms in the entrance to her apartment, the door wide open because she hadn't taken time to close it.

"It's so good to see you." She nuzzled her lips on his warm, firm jaw. "Four weeks is too long."

"You counted?" He pulled back with his usual intent gaze, but without the usual sparkle.

Tonight she'd bring back the sparkle. "Twenty-nine days."

He held her by the shoulders. "You look nice. Is that a new dress?"

"It sure is." The kiss had dislodged her new hat, so she turned to the mirror over the mail table to fix it. "When Jim called last night and said we were going to Parker House, Quintessa took one look in my closet and declared I had nothing suitable. She dragged me to Filene's this morning and helped me pick this out."

Lillian jammed a pin into the hat set atop the curls piled on her head, with a little net veiling puffed to the side. She never would have picked out the shade of coral pink, but Quintessa said it flattered her complexion. The cut was so chic, fitted to her figure with a slim skirt, capped sleeves, and a scalloped neckline. And the back! A row of fabric-covered buttons curved down her spine, ending above a bustle-like flounce.

Arch didn't speak. He leaned against the doorjamb in his dress whites, his arms crossed.

Lillian pulled on short white gloves. For once, she felt elegant enough to belong on the arm of Ensign Archer Vandenberg. "It was more than I wanted to spend, but I do have a job. Why should I worry about spending a little money?"

"That's important to you, is it?" His voice, his face showed no emotion at all.

What an odd thing to say. "Don't worry. I'm not turning into a spendthrift."

A flicker of a smile, and he motioned to the stairs. "Are you ready?"

"Yes." She grabbed her purse and led the way to the cab on the dimmed-out street. "It was romantic of you and Jim to insist on separate cabs."

"I wanted time alone with you." He opened the door, then joined her in the backseat. "The Parker House," he told the cabbie.

"Yes, sir."

Arch set his cover in his lap. He didn't put his arm around Lillian or take her hand.

Was he all right? She slipped her hand in his, sighing in relief when he squeezed back. "How was the convoy?"

"Uneventful."

Short. Lukewarm. Her stomach squirmed, but she refused to be one of those women who took everything personally. He was prone to melancholy, Jim had said, and she'd seen it herself.

She leaned against his shoulder. "Considering all you men have gone through, an uneventful cruise sounds like a nice change of pace."

"It was." A tinge of sadness bent his smile. "The only crisis was when a tanker grounded on a shoal and we towed her off. She wasn't damaged badly, though, and she made port under her own power."

Something wound tight around her heart. He hadn't told her everything. She stroked his cheek, smooth and freshly shaven. "Are you all right?"

His cheek twitched under her touch. "I'll find out."

Whatever did he mean? She opened her mouth to ask.

His face crumpled. "Darling, I don't want anything to change." He gathered her in his arms and kissed her, the poignant and hungry sort of kiss seen in war movies when everyone knew the soldier was going to die in the next scene.

Her stomach in knots, she pushed away. "Arch, are you all right?"

His lips and eyes reached for her mouth, and then he looked her in the eye. In an instant, his expression cleared, composed once more. "I didn't mean to startle you. I—I just missed you."

"I missed you too."

He settled back, his arm around her shoulders. "So, Watson, what's new in the case?"

A smile flowed up. "I'm afraid *Holmes* has nothing to report."

"In four weeks?"

She shrugged. "More prescriptions, but for the same patients. And the Carruthers lead was a dead end. I called the doctor, and the prescription is legitimate. The bartender's brother has epilepsy."

"Oh. Nothing else? Nothing at all?"

Lillian fought back irritation. "What more can I do? The

patients don't use their real names, and they aren't about to tell me."

"I suppose not." His brow furrowed.

Somehow she had to turn this evening around. She flashed a smile. "But I do have good news. Mr. Dixon changed his mind. Can you believe it? My improvements had increased sales, and sales dropped when he put things back to normal. So he ordered me to do anything I want."

"You're right. Good news."

"You have to see. Both windows are now clear of ads, and Quintessa helped me design the prettiest summer displays. Since Mr. Dixon had to close the soda fountain, Mrs. Connelly and I set up the cosmetics on the counter with little mirrors, and the ladies can sit on the stools while they shop. Mrs. Connelly has a way with makeup, and she's having a ball."

Arch's lips curved in a soft smile. "Very good."

"Sales are up, the customers are thrilled, and we even met our quota in the War Stamp Drive." She clasped her hands in front of her chest. "And yesterday, Mr. Dixon let me order signs to label the aisles. At last. He actually spent money."

The smile disappeared. "That makes you happy?"

What was wrong with him tonight? "Of course. You know how cheap he is, but I talked him into buying something. Don't you see? I've won him over. It's June, Arch. June. No new pharmacist. The job is mine."

The cabbie pulled to the curb. "We're here, sir."

"Thank you." Arch squeezed Lillian's shoulder. "You're here to stay. That's the best news of all."

But the squirming in her stomach increased as Arch ushered her in to the hotel. She felt as if they were sitting at a piano, playing the same piece of music in different keys.

Why? Had she said something wrong? So she'd mentioned money twice. Was that a great sin? She hadn't said anything out of the ordinary.

She refused to sulk when surrounded by the Parker House's dark wood paneling, bronze doors, and opulent carpets. "Oh, Arch, it's beautiful. You're spoiling me rotten."

"Only the best for you." He spoke to the maître d'hôtel. "Vandenberg, party of two."

"Right this way, sir."

"Two?" Lillian whispered. "What about Jim and Mary?"

"I want some privacy." He motioned her forward. "I don't want to share you tonight."

The weight of his hand on the small of her back felt like lead. Gordon had liked privacy too. Gordon didn't like to share her with anyone else. Ever.

Her breath hitched, and she scanned the restaurant for her brother, her dear big brother. There he was, at a table with Mary, and he sent Lillian a grin and a wave.

She waved back, probably with too much enthusiasm. Nothing could happen when Jim was here.

Arch held out a chair at a table to the right side of the room.

"Thank you." She sat and rested her gloves and handbag in her lap. What was wrong with her? Why was she turning a romantic gesture into a sinister threat?

Arch slipped something out of his trouser pocket and took his seat. He set a rectangular box in front of her. "I brought you a gift from Key West."

"Oh, you didn't have to bring me anything." She stroked the black leather jewelry box with its gold lettering, and her throat tightened.

"I wanted to." His gaze stretched to her, earnest and vulnerable.

Everything felt right and good again. This sweet man thought of her even when off to war, and he looked to her as if pleading for her approval, her love. He already had it.

"Thank you." Her voice came out ragged, and she opened

the box. A bracelet lay inside, glittering and bright. "How pretty. The flowers—is that coral? Why, it looks like it was made to go with this dress."

"Yes, that's coral."

She lifted it, appreciating the heft. "And the green jewels for leaves, and the sparkly little rhinestones. It's the prettiest—"

"Those are emeralds," he said. "And diamonds."

"Real . . ." She must have sounded like a hick. "My word."

Real emeralds. Real diamonds. So many of them. And the design was delicate and beautiful and feminine.

For her?

This was the kind of gift a man gave a woman he held precious, a woman he cherished.

"Would you like me to put it on for you?" He reached for her hand.

She nodded, her throat too clogged to allow words to pass.

Arch fastened the bracelet around her wrist, his fingers brushing her skin, his every move tender. Beyond all their loving words and sweet kisses, this moment meant even more to her, fulfilling a dream she'd shoved away, a dream she hadn't believed she'd deserved. To be seen as precious instead of shattered.

And if he'd spent that much on her—she hated to think how much he'd spent—he was serious about her.

Arch released her hand, his eyes awash with hope and fear and questions.

Was this why he was acting so strangely? Was he worried she wouldn't like the gift or the message behind it?

Lillian swallowed to clear her throat, and she drew her jeweled wrist close to her heart. "I can't tell you how much I love it. Thank you. Thank you so much. It's beautiful. I've never had anything this nice, this expensive—oh dear, I hate to think how much it cost. I can't even imagine. And you did it for me. You thought I was worthy—"

Arch raised one hand. "That's enough. You needn't gush."

"But I do. It means so much to me."

"Please don't be gauche." He glanced away, over the dance floor, his face impassive.

Lillian's jaw dangled, then closed, set like granite. "Gauche? Don't be a snob. Since when is it gauche to say thank you?"

"You said thank you. Now why don't we look at the menu? You must have the Boston cream pie. It was invented here at the Parker House." He opened his menu.

At that moment, she had no appetite, even for Boston cream pie.

He didn't look up from the menu. "Shall I order for you?"

"Absolutely not." She snatched up the menu. Gordon had insisted on ordering for her, controlling even the food that entered her mouth. She wouldn't let Arch do that.

By habit, she looked to the bottom of the menu, the most affordable items, but something cold and willful made her want to order prime rib and lobster and all the fixings. Maybe she'd chew with her mouth open. She'd show him gauche.

Arch laid his menu down. "We do have a break in the case."

The case? How could men do that? How could they change subjects without blinking? She kept her voice as impassive as his had been. "Oh? What is that?"

"Palonsky's scheduled to meet the leader of the ring tonight for the first time—the big fellow we saw at the bar. They call him Scar. Kramer says he has a large scar covering the right side of his face."

"That's more than we had before." Lillian rested her hands in her lap, shielding the bracelet with her fingers, as if its feelings had been hurt too, as if to tell the bracelet that, yes, it was worthy of gushing over.

"We're so close," Arch said.

"But we still don't have his name. We can't get anywhere without that."

"Not yet, but he works at the Navy Yard. Palonsky will get a good description tonight, and then we can track him down."

How many thousands of men worked there? "I hope it works."

"I hope so too. The other day Doc said he'd heard rumors about Palonsky taking pills. He's asking questions. I know he's involved. We need to finish this quickly."

The waiter approached the table. Lillian compromised and ordered a steak from the middle of the menu, and Arch ordered some fish thing with a French name from near the top.

After the waiter departed, Arch stood and offered his hand. "Shall we dance?"

She stared up at him. "You know I don't—"

"You danced with me at my parents' party. You went skating. This is a slow song, and you can do it. I'm not asking much of you."

Not asking much? That's how Gordon enticed her to the river. That's how Gordon talked her into removing her prosthesis. Lillian sat back in her chair. "I'd rather not."

His shoulders slumped, and his eyes softened. "Please, darling. This evening hasn't started well. I'd like to turn it around."

She slipped her hand into his and let him lead her to the dance floor. But why? Why was she letting him push her into doing something she didn't want to do? Perhaps she should remind him it was gauche for one-legged women to make spectacles of themselves.

Instead, she let him take her in his arms. Why couldn't she go home and go to sleep and forget about tonight and wake up to find the man she loved back to normal?

"Please don't give up on the case," he said. "I saw it in your eyes. You've done all you can do, and you think we're on a wild goose chase."

At the front of the room, the piano player plunked out "All or Nothing at All" in a low, steady rhythm. "I can't do anything more."

"I—I need you on my side." His grip on her waist intensified. "You know how much I need to solve this case, to make a name for myself in the Navy so I can make a career of it."

"So you don't have to work for your father."

"I couldn't handle that. I couldn't."

"Would it really be so bad?"

Arch pulled away, and his gaze bored into hers. "Why? Do you want me to?"

"I don't care either way. But you need to trust yourself more. I think you're strong enough to handle it."

He put on a strange smile, polite and flat and aimed all around the room. "Why don't we go to the hotel lobby? The air is rather stale in here."

Why? Because an argument was brewing and he didn't want to make a scene? Part of her wanted to make as big a scene as possible, but she didn't want to give him more reason to call her gauche.

She took his arm, as stiff as it was, and he led her out to the lobby, where the air felt no less stale.

He motioned to a plump chair and strode a few paces away.

Lillian stood. He couldn't tell her whether or not to sit.

Arch faced her in his dress whites, silhouetted against the dark oak paneling. "Tell me the truth. Do you want me to work for my father? Do you want me to be rich? If you only want me for my money, I need to know now."

How could he say such things after all they'd shared, all they'd gone through? Lillian's heart frosted over, coiled up to protect the loose ends from the pain. "I thought you knew me better than that."

He barked out a laugh. "Know you? I don't even recognize you. What happened to the girl who wore her graduation dress to the anniversary party so she wouldn't have to buy something new? That's the girl I fell in love with."

Her head spun, and she pressed a hand to her temple to right her world. "I haven't changed. What are you talking about?"

Arch flung a hand toward her. "Nonsense. Now that you have a rich boyfriend, you dress up like a model in *Vogue* magazine. That dress, that hat, your hair all done up, that . . ."

She waved her jeweled wrist. "What, Arch? That fancy bracelet *you* just gave me? You're going to fault me for that?"

His eyes narrowed. "You liked it too much, liked how expensive it was. Next you'll beg for the matching earrings and necklace."

What on earth? She injected her voice with sarcasm. "Well, who wouldn't want that?"

Arch drew back his chin, his gaze like a razor ripping her new dress to shreds.

Gordon had tried to control her wardrobe too. "Are you going to tell me what I can wear? Do I need your approval before each purchase? Or am I even allowed to buy clothes?"

"I thought you were different." His eyes shut, and his head slumped forward. "But now you want me to work for my father. Now you want me to keep the estate and the yacht. I thought you didn't care about money. I thought—I thought you loved me."

Just like Gordon. How dare he? How dare he play to her sympathy in order to bend her to his will? Why hadn't she seen it? Why had she opened up to him? He wanted to force her into weakness so he could control her, own her, hurt her.

Not if she could hurt him first.

What a horrible thought. She refused to be that girl anymore, the girl who could make Lucy cry with one pointed sentence. She drew in a steadying breath. "I thought you loved me too. But you don't even know me. How cold do you think I am?"

His harsh laugh answered her question, and he glanced to the side, stuffing his hands into his pockets. But not in time.

The tremor.

He was scared. Scared to be trapped with a gold digger.

Well, she was scared too. Scared to be trapped with a controlling cad.

That frosty coil in her chest snapped into a solid immovable mass. Oh yes, she could hurt him, and she would before he destroyed her.

35

Inside his pockets, Arch pressed his hands flat against his thighs to stop the trembling. How cold did he think she was? Cold enough to scheme to trap him. Cold enough to conceal her true nature until after she'd stolen his heart.

"You think I'm a gold digger." Lillian thrust up her chin, her eyes glinting like diamonds. "What if I am? What if I do want to be rich? I saw your estate. I saw the yacht and the stables and the tennis courts and the gigantic house like something in the movies. Who wouldn't want that?"

Like a knife slitting him from throat to belly. *"Who wouldn't want that?"*—the precise words Pauline Grayson had transcribed from their conversation in Connecticut. All along, Lillian had been scheming, playing hard to get, making him fall in love with her.

She'd betrayed his trust. A rusty taste filled his mouth— he'd bitten his cheek—and he swallowed hard. "You admit it. You only want me for my money."

Lillian's chin worked from side to side. "Why else would I want you? You're gloomy half the time, and you . . . you have weak nerves."

Acid in the wound, burning and bubbling. He'd confided in her, and she was using it against him. The ultimate betrayal. But she must never know how much she'd hurt him.

He gave her a polite nod. "I'll not be seeing you again, Miss Avery. But a gentleman never abandons his date. I'll escort you back to the restaurant so your brother can see you home."

"Is—is that why Jim and Mary are here?" Her voice rose, so unseemly. "You knew you were going to break up with me?"

"I had a strong suspicion it would be necessary. I'm only sorry I was right."

"You . . . you . . ." Her face reddened and contorted, and she clawed at the bracelet. "Take it. Take it. I don't want it."

The quaver in her voice almost sounded authentic, but he strolled past her toward the dining room. "Keep it. I refuse to take it back. A small price to pay for the truth."

Her footsteps sounded behind him. "You know what? I will. I will keep it. To remind me never to trust a man again."

Perhaps he'd spared another man a similar fate of deception and betrayal. He stopped at the maître d'hôtel's station. "I'll take care of the bill for the Vandenberg table now."

"Yes, sir." The man crossed the room to the kitchen.

Lillian breezed past Arch and faced him. "Not one step farther. I won't let you take me to Jim as if I were a naughty child." She marched away.

"Very well. I only wanted to do my duty as a gentleman."

"A gentleman?" She spun to him, and her eyes shot icy green darts. "Oh yes. You showed impeccable manners as you broke my heart."

Then she lifted that chin and flounced away, a slight hitch in her step.

Just like the night they met.

The night he'd offended her by staring. Except tonight the offense had been earned.

As he watched her leave, an ache filled his chest. What had gone wrong? Why couldn't she resist the temptation of wealth? Why did she have to change?

★ ★ ★

Arch asked the cab driver to drop him off at Boston Common. For two hours, Arch wandered in the dark, avoiding the rowdy sailors, steering past the amorous couples.

What signs had he missed? Memories pummeled him of dinners and walks and ice-skating, of Lillian watching him with guarded eyes as if he were a predatory wolf. Yet all along she was the predator. He'd been too blind to see.

He stared at the sky, devoid of the moon's light. Conversations played in his mind, but no clues surfaced. Until he'd taken her to Connecticut. Until she'd seen the grandeur of the estate.

Arch strode down a path that sliced diagonally across the grassy slope. For the first time, Dan Avery made sense. The oldest Avery brother had sworn off women as a distraction from his naval career. Arch had an even better reason to do likewise.

He'd lost. How many times had he fought this battle in vain? Women only loved his looks and charm, his money and position. No one would ever love the real man inside.

Who could? *"You're gloomy, and you have weak nerves."*

His empty stomach churned. Usually two hours of mulling cleared his mind after he broke up with a woman, but not tonight. For Arch, his relationship with Lillian had moved past an amusing dalliance into genuine open love. He'd told her everything.

"You have weak nerves." Would she use that against him

one more time? Would she tell Jim? Jim had never been vindictive, but blood ran thicker than water.

As an only child, Arch only had water. He had no champion to stand beside him come what may. Not only had he lost the woman he loved, but he would lose his best friend.

Another two hours wouldn't bring peace, so Arch headed for the subway station across from Park Street Church.

No blood. No water. He had no one.

★ ★ ★

In the darkness, two men stood on the pier by the *Ettinger*'s gangway. One had Jim Avery's familiar posture, and Arch steeled himself for the confrontation.

The other man jogged toward him. "Mr. Vandenberg? Mr. Vandenberg, sir?"

"Palonsky?"

The seaman didn't answer but gestured for Arch to walk in the other direction. "I have that report for you, sir."

Arch groaned. "That only makes sense on board."

"Yeah, I know." Palonsky led him across railroad tracks and between two workshops. The Boston Navy Yard buzzed with activity now that three shifts worked round the clock, but this location was secluded.

"I met him, not even an hour ago." The sailor faced Arch, close in the darkness, his voice low. "Scar, the big man we saw in the bar."

"Did you get a good look at him?"

"As good as I could in the dark." Palonsky spoke with a thick Boston accent, slow and grainy. "Big man, about six foot, two hundred pounds. Blond hair, what I could see under his cap. Doughy face, tries to hide his scar by not looking you straight in the eye. But it's there, the scar, covers most of the right side of his face, shiny and ugly."

"That's a new accent for you."

"It's his. He's from Boston. Charlestown, if I had to bet. Doesn't say much. I asked a lot of questions—"

Arch winced.

"Don't worry, boss. Not too many. Just being a curious, friendly sort of fellow." His grin flashed white in the dim light.

"No name?"

Palonsky waved his hand as if cleaning a blackboard. "Knew better than to ask. But I'll find out Monday night."

"Monday?"

"Scar said he likes me, hears good things about me. He invited me to join him and the boys at the Rusty Barnacle. Told me not to tell anyone, especially Kramer."

"Why not?"

Palonsky leaned his hand on the brick wall. "He ain't happy with Kramer, says he wants someone friendlier to drum up more business."

Arch rubbed his mouth. "I don't like it."

"I don't either. I'm not going to drum up new customers, and it won't take long for them to find out I'm an imposter."

"Very well. I'll talk to Buckner right away and get you transferred—"

"Not till Tuesday. On Monday I'll get names. You know me. You know I can get those fellows to chat, especially if I buy some beers. If I can get full names for Hank or Shorty or Scar, we're finished. Tuesday morning, you and me and Miss Avery go to the police, and it's over."

As if a swinging boom struck his chest. Lillian was no longer his partner, his Watson, his Holmes, his anything.

What could he do? He needed the information Lillian had gathered. Somehow he'd get word to her. Surely she had enough personal investment in the case to follow through.

"What do you say, boss?" Palonsky asked in his Scar accent.

Arch clapped him on the back. "Tuesday morning—no matter what—I'll get you out."

They headed back to the *Ettinger*. Now Arch had to deal with Jim.

His former best friend stood at the base of the gangway. Arch motioned for him to follow, and he led Jim toward the same secluded location. He didn't want a scene in front of the crew.

Jim stomped behind him. "I told you not to hurt her."

Arch turned the corner between the workshop buildings. "In retrospect, I should have asked for an exemption in case she hurt me first."

"Lillian? She couldn't hurt—"

"Out of curiosity, what did she tell you happened tonight?" Arch faced him and crossed his arms.

Jim spread his hands wide. "Nothing. She closed up. That's what she does when she's hurt. She said you'd broken up, and all she'd say was, 'Archer Vandenberg isn't the man I thought he was.' The same words she used when she broke up with her boyfriend in college."

Clever ploy for sympathy, linking Arch to that Gordon. "So from that single statement, you conclude I'm to blame."

"I saw the bracelet. You tested her."

"And she failed."

The fist came from nowhere. Pain cracked through his left cheekbone, and stars shot in his vision.

Arch slammed into the brick wall, righted himself, and struck the fighting stance. How many times had he and Jim squared off in the boxing ring at the Academy? Evenly matched. Never once had they exchanged blows in anger.

Jim huffed, hunched over like a bull.

With fists ready, Arch forced a calm tone. "If you care to keep your commission, I'd suggest you don't throw another punch."

Jim wheeled away and paced across the walkway, arms swinging loose and wild. "She failed? Failed?"

Arch tracked his opponent, prepared for the charge, his cheek throbbing.

"Let me guess." Jim flung his hand toward the sea. "You took her to your fancy house, and she had the nerve to like it. You took her to one of Boston's finest restaurants and—shame on her—she liked it. Then you gave her a ridiculously expensive bracelet and—heaven forbid!—she liked it. What is wrong with you? Huh? How can you honestly expect her to share your . . . your neurotic hatred for wealth?"

A grumble scraped Arch's throat. "More than that. She admitted she was a gold digger."

A scoffing laugh. "Lillian? You're crazy. Flat-out crazy."

His fingernails bit into his palms. "She said those very words. She said she wants it all—the house, the stables, the yacht. She told me outright she only wanted me for my money."

"That doesn't even sound like her. What is wrong with you? Why couldn't you listen to me? I warned you. I told you to stay away from her."

"Believe me. I wish I had. I wish I realized the warning was for my own protection."

Jim lunged, but Arch brandished his fists. This time he'd get in some solid blows of his own.

With a snort, Jim stopped, and he thrust one finger at Arch. "I never want to see you again. Tomorrow morning, I'll apply for a transfer."

The idea seized Arch. "Don't. I'll transfer. I don't want to see you, I don't want to see that sister of yours, and I don't want to see this city ever again."

Silence gaped between them. Almost seven years of friendship, and it ended like this.

"Very well." Jim marched away. "This time you'd better keep your promise."

"Tuesday morning. Don't ask why the delay. Tuesday morning."

Jim gave a dismissive wave over his shoulder.

Arch leaned back against the brick wall and probed his pulsating cheek. He'd have a bruise, probably a black eye, but it was better than being trapped.

On Tuesday morning, he and Palonsky would submit their transfer requests. For once, he didn't care if he was assigned to a dead-end desk job. At least he'd escape.

36

Boston
Monday, June 8, 1942

Lillian nibbled the piece of toast, but despite the blandness of the breakfast, her stomach turned. Since Saturday night, she'd barely eaten or slept. How was she going to get through her shift?

Mary and Quintessa and Yvette bustled around the kitchen, and she tried to block the smell of eggs and oatmeal and sausage.

Yesterday, she'd wanted to be left alone in her righteous anger, but Jim and Mary had insisted she attend church with them.

In the historic Park Street Church, with its white steeple pointing over Boston Common, Lillian sat in the pew and tried to absorb the sermon. The topic seemed unusual for a nation rejoicing over America's recent naval victory at Midway, the first real cause for celebration in six months at war. After all, Romans 12 emphasized living at peace and not repaying evil for evil.

Yet that was the point. While the country had just reasons

to fight, the people mustn't let vengefulness and hatred poison their actions, or they would be no better than the oppressive regimes they battled.

The verses drilled through Lillian's skull: "Recompense to no man evil for evil . . . If it be possible, as much as lieth in you, live peaceably with all men . . . Vengeance is mine; I will repay, saith the Lord . . . Be not overcome of evil, but overcome evil with good."

Lillian hadn't tried to live peaceably with Arch. She'd chosen vengeance. Evil for evil.

Yvette sat at the table with an omelette. "Lillian, you must eat something. It is not good to go hungry."

Mary joined them. "Sweetie, I know it hurts, but it's not your fault. He wronged you."

A piece of crust crumbled between Lillian's fingers. She hadn't opened up to her friends. She'd only told them it was over. Then Jim saw the bracelet, and she let him draw his conclusions. "But it is my fault."

"Nonsense." Quintessa poured milk into her oatmeal. "He accused you of being a gold digger, which is—"

"No." Lillian pressed her fingers to her dry, burning eyes. "I mean, yes, he accused me, but I didn't handle it well. Not at all. I didn't try to understand why he reacted so strongly. I didn't reason with him. What did I do? I lashed out in anger. I wanted to hurt him so badly he'd never come near me again. And I succeeded."

Yvette sniffed. "He deserved everything you said."

"No one deserves that. No one." She lowered her fingers, her vision blurry from the pressure on her eyeballs. "You know what I said? I told him I *was* a gold digger. I told him I *did* love him only for his money. All a lie, but I knew it would hurt him most. And I—I betrayed a confidence. I belittled him. I was cold, vengeful, cruel."

Her roommates fell silent, staring at their plates.

Now the sheer ugliness of her heart would drive her friends away too. Just like Arch and Mrs. Harrison.

She pushed away from the table. "I need to go to work."

Quintessa captured her hand. "No, honey. You need to stay home and have a good cry."

"I can't." Tears only came from soft hearts.

"Mr. Dixon would understand," Mary said.

Lillian shook her head. What would she do if she stayed home? She'd wallow in guilt and grief and hurt. She'd finger the bracelet that mocked her with its beauty, because she wasn't worthy of being cherished after all. She'd read the note in Arch's hand reminding her that God's grace was sufficient for her, that his strength was made perfect in weakness. She'd remember how she chose to act in her own brittle, feeble strength.

"No, I need to work." She needed to get on with her lonely life, the life she deserved.

★ ★ ★

Only half an hour remained in her shift. Lillian surveyed the aisles and greeted a few customers.

"When did you put those up?" An elderly woman pointed to the signs Albert had installed, so sleek and modern.

"This weekend." Lillian's lips tingled, her vision went dark, and she gripped a shelf. The handful of saltines she'd forced down for lunch hadn't been enough.

"Now I can find what I need. Dixon's is such a pleasant place to shop now."

"Thank you." But she couldn't look at the signs she'd coaxed Mr. Dixon to buy.

No wonder Arch would take her statement the wrong way. He was used to girlfriends who really would wheedle him into buying the matching earrings and necklace. Of course he was sensitive to the notion that Lillian would use her wiles to induce a man to spend.

"Are you all right, dear?" The lady settled her gloved hand on Lillian's arm and gazed at her with kind brown eyes. "You look pale."

"I'm fine." Her smile wobbled. What was one more lie after the whoppers she'd told Arch? "Thank you for shopping at Dixon's."

Lillian headed for the center aisle.

A man strode toward the prescription counter, lanky and tall. Hank!

She pretended to straighten the bottles of aspirin. Another forged prescription to add to her records. But why bother? Without her partner, the investigation would die.

Lillian peered down the aisle after the suspect. All she needed was his last name. One single word. Then she could go to the police. The detectives could contact Arch to fill in his section of the puzzle.

They'd have to contact him quickly. After church, Jim had said the *Ettinger* had received a new assignment and would ship out soon. He'd also said Arch planned to apply for a transfer. He'd be leaving.

The loss hollowed out her heart, but purpose filled in the hole.

"Thanks, Mr. Dixon," Hank said.

"You're welcome. I'll have Albert deliver it later."

Lillian realigned bottles of cough syrup until Hank left the store. Poor Mr. Dixon. Shame on those criminals for taking advantage of him, maybe even blackmailing him. If she could get them locked up, he'd be grateful forever.

Back behind the counter, she filled two more prescriptions, then cleaned up after herself. Five o'clock at last.

Albert headed for the door. "One last delivery and I'm done for the night. See you tomorrow."

Only one bag sat in Albert's box by the door, Hank's phenobarbital.

Something rash swept through her. What if she followed Albert? Then she'd find out if Hank used a real address or a vacant apartment as Detective Malloy had suggested. If it were a real address, the phone book could reveal Hank's last name. Arch had forbidden her to trace deliveries, but he couldn't boss her around anymore.

A surge of freedom and a thrill of adventure. She could solve this case tonight.

"I'm also done, Mr. Dixon. Have a good evening."

"You too."

Lillian darted to the stockroom, and her vision darkened. She groped for the wall and almost knocked down the flashlight Mr. Dixon hung by the door in case of a power outage. "Sorry."

"Be careful. Bull in a china shop."

A bull who hadn't eaten anything of substance in over forty-eight hours. She'd force herself to eat dinner.

Lillian shrugged off her white coat, grabbed her purse, and left the store. She couldn't lose Albert.

Out on Main Street, she scanned the road. There he was—one block away. A perfect distance.

She matched her pace to his. Up Main Street they continued until Albert reached a square with a little park.

A man stepped out from the trees and approached Albert. "Hey, Bert."

"Hiya, Hank."

Lillian gasped and slid behind a tree by the sidewalk, but neither Albert nor Hank looked her way. What was going on?

Albert handed Hank the bag, Hank gave Albert an envelope, and then they strolled up Main Street. Together. Chatting.

They knew each other? Her heartbeat picked up, and she fell in behind them, careful to keep a block away.

The men turned right.

"Bother." Lillian didn't want to rush to catch up, but she didn't want to lose them. She rounded the corner just in time to see them turn left down another street.

Her prosthesis chafed her stump, but she kept going. So Albert and Hank were friends. Were they acquainted because of the frequent deliveries? Or had they known each other awhile? Albert had said he'd run with a bad crowd when he was younger, and Hank ran with the worst of crowds now.

The men climbed the steps to a house on her left. Lillian crossed to the far side of the street and edged closer, careful to keep the line of trees in front of her. All she needed was the house number. There it was—126. She hadn't paid attention to the street name, but she'd catch it later.

The front door opened, and a large man in a newsboy cap greeted them. "Hey, what do you think you're doing, coming together? Get in here."

"Aw, don't blow your top, Chuck." Hank sauntered inside, and Albert followed.

The big man leaned forward and peered up the street away from her, the late-afternoon sun illuminating a shiny scar on the right side of his face.

Scar!

The tree wouldn't conceal her. Lillian strolled back down the street, trying to look like any other young lady on the way home from work, while her heart ricocheted off the walls of her chest.

Would he recognize her? She'd never seen him before. But what about her stupid, glaring wooden leg? Had Hank told Scar about her? And what about Albert? He was part of this too.

Lillian zipped around the corner and leaned back against the building's clapboard siding. She pressed her hand over her roiling stomach, and sparkles danced in her vision.

Oh no. Albert was involved. Dear, kind Albert. Was that why the forgers had chosen Dixon's? Because of Albert?

He'd said Mr. Dixon had given him a chance. This was how he repaid the pharmacist's faith in him?

She groaned and bent over at the waist, trying to catch her breath. Tomorrow this would end. Now she had one full name—Albert Myers. And she had Hank's first name. And Scar's first name was Chuck. And she had a street address.

Tonight she'd scour the phone book, entry by entry, until she found that address, found out who lived there. Then tomorrow after work, she'd—

No. Tuesday she worked the closing shift. At home in the morning, she'd make sure her notebook was complete. At the drugstore in the evening, she'd gather the forged prescriptions. As soon as the store closed, she'd call the police.

It was a plan. A good plan.

She straightened up and pushed the hair off her face, her heart as empty as her stomach. If only she didn't have to execute this plan alone.

37

The Boston skyline slid away, gray and gold in the morning sun. The *Ettinger* had shoved off at 0800.

Without Warren Palonsky.

Arch's stomach writhed as he stood at the stern of the destroyer. Something had gone wrong. At 0600 Palonsky was supposed to relay what had happened at the Rusty Barnacle so they could notify the police before they shipped out.

But Palonsky hadn't returned from liberty. Absent without leave.

"Lord, keep him safe." Arch had known the plan was dangerous. He should have forbidden Palonsky to go. As an officer, he had the authority to do so, and he had the responsibility to protect the men under his command.

Instead, he'd yielded to the old temptation to use his wealth to obtain what he wanted. Information. Prestige. Security for his career.

And he'd had the nerve to accuse Lillian of succumbing

to the lure of wealth? How arrogant. "Remove that plank from your own eye, Vandenberg," he muttered.

Arch strode down the deck, greeting his men as they stowed lines and gear, preparing for another three weeks of convoy duty, down to Key West and back.

Three long weeks. If only he could have submitted his transfer request before he shipped out. But he'd been waiting for Palonsky.

His gut wrenched. *Oh Lord, what have I done?*

Emotions shredded him—worry for Palonsky, heartache over Lillian, tension with Jim, uncertainty over his career, and even the return of his nightmares.

After the *Atwood* sank, in his nightmares he was trapped below decks while the ship went down. But the last few nights, he'd had a new nightmare. He was on the deck of the *Ettinger*, under attack by U-boats. Lillian was there, and she went down to the engine room and dogged the hatch behind herself. Arch clawed at the hatch, screamed after her, desperate to get below. Waves crashed over the deck, threatening to sweep him overboard. No one heard his cries. He was alone.

Each time he woke in a cold, shaking sweat. This nightmare was worse than the previous one, and he didn't know why.

Arch headed into the bridge superstructure and down to the office to fill out his morning reports.

If his greatest fear was being trapped with a gold digger, shouldn't he feel peaceful and justified now that he'd broken up with Lillian? Shouldn't the nightmares lessen?

Arch plunked down at the desk and shuffled papers. He felt no peace. Saturday night's fury had dissolved into Sunday's doubts and Monday's ache. A great, gripping ache.

Now on Tuesday, the clarity finally arrived. And he hated it.

Alone in the office, Arch rested his forehead on his fists. In the nightmare, he experienced his moment of greatest terror when Lillian slammed the hatch.

She'd shut him out of her life.

That's what she'd done. That's what she did to people who hurt her. And Arch had hurt her with his accusations and his deliberately snobbish comments. *"Don't be gauche . . . Shall I order for you . . . ?"*

His stomach filled with the chilled slime of certainty. She'd lied. Declaring herself a gold digger didn't sound like Lillian, but shutting him out sounded just like her.

Because he'd hurt her. Because he hadn't trusted her. Because he chose to believe Pauline Grayson over the woman he claimed to love. Because he never let her defend herself, and he wouldn't have believed any defense she'd given.

His black eye and swollen cheekbone throbbed from Jim's well-deserved punch. Arch had claimed Lillian had betrayed him, but he'd betrayed her first by giving in to his old suspicions.

"Oh Lord, what have I done?"

★ ★ ★

Arch poked at his ham-and-macaroni salad. Conversation around the wardroom table this afternoon sounded clipped, as if the loss of Arch and Jim's joviality affected all the officers.

His former friend loomed on the other side of the table, silent and stony. He didn't look at Arch, and Arch didn't dare look at him.

At last, the stewards cleared the table. With the nation discussing the possibility of food rationing, throwing away a full plate seemed criminal. But how could he eat?

Captain Buckner cleared his throat. "Before you leave, I need to give you some bad news. One of our crewmen was killed last night."

Palonsky. Arch's blood slowed to a stop. *Dear Lord, no!*

"What happened?" Ted Hayes asked.

"Early this morning, someone found the body of a sailor behind a seedy bar in town. He'd been mugged and stabbed."

The Rusty Barnacle. Arch's hands coiled around his linen napkin, twisted it into a rope.

"There was no identification, so the police called around to the local bases and ships. We'd already shoved off. About an hour ago, we received a radio message. The description matches a sailor of ours who failed to return from liberty last night—Seaman Warren Palonsky."

Arch's groan joined those of his fellow officers. Why hadn't he stopped him? Why had he pushed him? Why had he paid him?

"What a blow," John Odom said. "The men will be upset. Everyone liked him."

Hayes scrunched up his face. "Great guy. Always joking, cheering people up. I can't believe it."

Arch could, and his shoulders contracted in a hard mass, his hands mangling the napkin. He had to tell the police everything he knew. He had to warn Lillian. "We're heading back?"

"No." Buckner frowned at him. "We have a convoy to escort."

"But the police will need to talk to us for—"

"Why? This happens all the time. Drunken sailor wanders into a bad part of town, gets jumped by hoodlums. It's a local police matter."

That was exactly what Scar wanted people to think. That's why he told Palonsky not to tell anyone where he was going. Except Palonsky told Arch. Now Arch was the only one who knew who had killed Palonsky and why.

He shoved the napkin away. "Captain Buckner, may I have

a word with you in private? It's about the murder. I have important information."

The captain's frown deepened. "I need to assemble the crew for the announcement."

"Sir?" Hayes said. "Perhaps I could make the announcement."

Buckner regarded his executive officer. "Very well. You have a better way with the men than I do. Mr. Vandenberg, come with me."

"Arch." Jim's voice sliced across the table. "Is my sister—"

"Yes."

The look on Jim's face said more than a thousand cuss words, and Arch deserved it. He'd used his money and rank to have his way, and Warren Palonsky had paid the price. And Lillian was in danger.

Arch followed the captain to his stateroom. For the next hour, the two men sat at the captain's desk, and Arch outlined everything they'd done in the investigation. Buckner listed names and drew circles and arrows, and Arch showed where all the arrows pointed.

After Arch finished, Buckner laid his hands flat on his notes. "Is that all?"

"No. Lil—Miss Avery—she has a list of all the forged prescriptions, and she can verify that the men who filled the prescriptions are the same men Palonsky identified. She's the link. She needs to be notified right away so she can go to the police." So she'd be on guard.

Buckner ran a finger over the circle he'd drawn for Dixon's Drugs. "As you know, we have to observe radio silence now. When we arrive in New York tonight, we'll send word to Miss Avery. In the meantime, write up a report of all you told me. We'll have you speak to the police in New York, and it'll go faster if you have a report. We can't allow them to delay us. Wartime needs take precedence over civilian matters."

"Aye aye, sir." If only he could shout his warning across Massachusetts Bay.

The captain's lips set in a thin line. "Why didn't you tell me earlier?"

"With all due respect, sir, I tried. You wouldn't listen." He'd crossed a line that would destroy his career, but it didn't matter. Arch had sent a good man to his death, and the Navy had every right to strip him of his commission.

Buckner's eyes went as hard as onyx, but then he blinked, revealing a wash of regret. He sniffed and jabbed his finger at the list of names. "Earl Kramer is in deep. Do you think he's to blame for the murder?"

No, Arch was. He sighed. "Scar told Palonsky not to tell Kramer. I don't think he knew."

"But he could have. He could have ordered Scar to use those exact words. I don't trust the man. I'll lock him up until we reach New York. Anyone else?"

Arch scanned the list of names. "Most of these fellows only used the drug. They didn't sell it. They need medical help, psychological help, but I don't think they're dangerous. This fellow, though—he was right below Kramer. I'd watch him. And Doc too."

"Doc?"

"Parnell Lloyd."

Buckner's gaze roved over his notes. "You didn't mention Doc. How is he involved?"

"I don't know." Arch rubbed the back of his neck. "I can't figure out where he fits in, but he does. From the start, he's asked a lot of questions. And he knows too much. Either he was investigating or he was involved."

Buckner crossed his arms. "I need more than suspicions if I'm to lock up a respected member of my crew."

Arch drummed his hands on his thighs. "He was very concerned about the men's anxieties and wanted to treat them, and he was angry at how the Navy handles men with combat neuroses."

"Yes, he told me that."

"He knew I was concerned too. He asked me to keep tabs on the men who showed signs of either anxiety or drug use."

"That's his job as pharmacist's mate."

Arch pointed at the circle with Fish's name. "He told me Fish was involved. Not long after that, Fish was dead. Doc was alone with him when he died. Then last week, he told me he'd heard rumors that Palonsky was involved, and now Palonsky—" His voice broke. "Now Palonsky's dead."

"Okay." Buckner scribbled more notes.

"I think he's the forger. Someone in the ring has to have the medical knowledge to write prescriptions. Miss Avery said they were credible—the terminology, abbreviations, everything. The other suspects are sailors or shipyard workers, but Doc has the knowledge. And . . . and you've seen his sketches, the different signatures he uses. He has a gift with a pen—he could apply it to forgery."

"Those are excellent—"

Someone knocked on the stateroom door.

"Enter," Buckner said.

Ted Hayes stepped in. "Sir, Doc would like to speak to you about Palonsky's murder."

Arch and the captain exchanged a glance.

"Very well," Buckner said.

Doc burst in. "Sir, I need to warn you about—" His gaze landed on Arch, and he blanched.

Arch eyed him. Hard to believe such a pleasant, earnest fellow could be a cold-blooded murderer.

Doc stood at attention and addressed the captain. "I need to warn you about Ensign Archer Vandenberg."

"Pardon?" Arch said.

"He's responsible for Palonsky's murder."

Arch sprang out of his chair and stood at his full height. "I beg your—"

"Mr. Vandenberg." The captain motioned for him to take his seat. "I ask you to keep silent. You've had your say. Now it's Doc's turn. Go ahead, Lloyd."

"Sir, Mr. Vandenberg is dating a civilian pharmacist. She has access to phenobarbital. She knows how to write a prescription. She could have told the forger what to write."

Buckner narrowed his eyes at Arch. "Miss Avery? You didn't mention you were dating."

Arch sank into his chair. "It isn't relevant to the case. And we're not—we're not dating any longer."

"Mm. That explains the cold front between you and Jim Avery. Does it explain that shiner?"

The bruise throbbed. "Yes, sir. It does."

Buckner looked up to Doc with heightened interest. "Continue."

Behind his back, Doc twisted his hands. "Sir, Mr. Vandenberg came to me several months ago asking about combat fatigue and how to treat it, which drugs we use. I thought he was concerned for his men, but now I don't think his motives were so pure."

Arch mashed his lips together, determined to keep silent as ordered.

Doc shifted his weight. "I found out Fish was involved, sir. I told Mr. Vandenberg, and right after that, Fish died."

How could he keep silent? "Captain, I was out of town that weekend."

"Convenient alibi, sir." Doc glared down at Arch. "That doesn't mean a murder couldn't be arranged."

Buckner raised a hand as if to cover Arch's mouth. "Anything else?"

"Yes, sir. This is the worst." Doc bent closer to the captain, his brown eyes wide. "Last week I told him I'd heard rumors that Palonsky was involved. Now he's dead. Sir, Mr. Vandenberg ordered those thugs to kill him to keep him quiet. I know it."

Waves of panic set Arch's fingers to trembling. He never thought he could be implicated. And Lillian? How could anyone implicate her?

Buckner's gaze bounced between the two men, revealing nothing. "I appear to have a conundrum."

Arch's eyes slipped shut. If anything happened to Lillian, he could never forgive himself.

38

Six o'clock. If only the clock's hands would move faster. Lillian couldn't gather the evidence until after Mr. Dixon left, and she wouldn't call the police until after the store closed. Why disrupt business more than necessary?

"Man the counter, would you?" Mr. Dixon lugged a box out from the stockroom. "With Albert home sick, someone's got to stock those shelves. I'll have to stay late. Boy, am I going to have a word with that Reggie—not even answering his phone."

Lillian murmured her understanding and tapped out the instructions for Mr. Robertson's digitalis on the typewriter. How suspicious for Albert to call in sick the day after his meeting with Chuck and Hank. But what a relief. How could she face him knowing he was involved?

Her finger slipped on the D key and struck the S key as well, and the type bars tangled. Lillian huffed and pried them free, trying not to get ink on her fingers.

Scar's full name was Charles Leary, the phone book had revealed last night. Now she had evidence Detective Malloy could use. The police could contact Arch for his side of the story.

Her heart seized. Again. He wouldn't be by her side tonight when she called the police. He wouldn't hold her and encourage her.

Nor did she want him to. As much as she missed him, as much as she regretted her cruel words, when it came down to it, the man didn't trust her.

What was wrong with him? Maybe in his strata of society it was impolite to appreciate beautiful gifts, but Lillian had been taught it was impolite not to. Did he expect her to say thank you, heave a bored little sigh, and stuff the bracelet in her jewelry box with dozens of other extravagant baubles? Honestly.

After all, the bracelet was the loveliest gift she'd ever received. The most meaningful.

A wave of grief crashed over her, but after it receded, Lillian plucked the prescription label from the typewriter and fixed it to the bottle.

Arch might not even be in town. Jim had said they'd sail soon. Since Mary worked at the Navy Yard, she'd know when the *Ettinger* departed.

One last inspection of the prescription bottle, and Lillian called Mr. Robertson.

The older gentleman peered through reading glasses at the label. "Same as before?"

"Yes, sir. One tablet every day." Lillian rang up his purchase and gave him his change.

"Thank you." He tipped his fedora to her. "Be careful out there, young lady, with a murderer on the loose."

"A murderer?"

"Haven't you heard? Of course it's not in the paper yet, but everyone's talking about it."

"No. I haven't heard." Lillian gripped the edge of the counter.

"They found a sailor stabbed to death behind the Rusty Barnacle this morning."

Dizziness rolled through her head. "The Rusty Barnacle?"

"Not the kind of place a nice young lady like you would know about."

But she did, and her face went numb. "Who—who was it?"

Mr. Robertson shrugged. "It'll be in the paper tomorrow. Some boy in the Navy, probably got in a fight over a girl."

Or over a drug ring. Was it Earl Kramer? Or—no, please, not Warren Palonsky. Was that the purpose of the meeting at Scar's house last night? To plot a murder? Oh goodness, Albert was involved. Was that why he'd called in sick?

She felt more than a little sick herself.

Mr. Robertson's mouth puckered with concern. "I shouldn't have worried you, miss. As long as you stay out of the bad parts of town, you'll be safe."

Lillian worked up a smile, but how could she be safe with Scar and Hank and Albert on the loose?

After Mr. Robertson left, Mr. Dixon returned to the prescription area. Although Lillian wanted her boss to leave so she could gather evidence, a horde of patients arrived, and she was glad she had help. After all, the news of the murder made concentration difficult.

Mr. Dixon poured tablets onto the counting tray. "Sure is busy in the evenings now with all the women gone to work during the day."

"It is." Lillian gathered an armful of bottles to return to the shelves. "We could almost use a third pharmacist."

"If sales continue to climb like this, I might consider it."

On any other day, the news would have made her giddy. But now it only buffed the pain and worry, taking off a few sharp edges.

In the back corner of the store, Lillian climbed a step stool and replaced a bottle on the top shelf.

"Uncle Cyrus! Uncle Cyrus!"

Lillian climbed down from the stool and peered around the end of the shelf. She'd never met Mr. Dixon's nephew, didn't even know his name.

A young man leaned over the counter, his face red and wild-eyed and mottled by a scar.

Charles Leary! Scar!

She ducked behind the shelf, pulse thrumming in her ears. What was Scar doing here?

"What are you—I told you never to come here." Mr. Dixon's voice came out hard but quiet.

"It's an emergency. Just got off work, got here as fast as I could." Scar sounded frantic. "Hank botched it up last night."

"Shut up," Mr. Dixon said.

"And Stan quit. He ran away and enlisted. Don't you see? It's all over without—"

"I said shut up." Mr. Dixon's voice shook with quiet intensity. "Get out of here. Call."

The silence clawed at Lillian's ears. What were they doing?

Footsteps headed down the aisle. Scar must have left.

Lillian leaned against the shelf and shut her eyes, her mind spinning. *Lord, help me, help me, help me.*

How should she respond? Mr. Dixon had to know she'd heard. How would she respond if she knew absolutely nothing about the drug ring?

She'd inquire with friendly curiosity. Yes, she would. Ignoring the situation would be an admission that she knew too much.

Lillian grasped the anchor necklace at her throat. *Lord, be my strength.*

With an airy smile, she returned to the counter. "Was that your nephew? I was up on the step stool. Shame I didn't get to meet him."

Mr. Dixon grunted and dumped pills from the counting tray into a bottle. "Yes. That was my nephew."

"I couldn't hear the conversation, but he sounded upset. I hope everything's all right." Her voice actually carried the right note of innocent concern.

"Just some problems at work."

Lillian picked up the next prescription on the counter, as if she were capable of reading it. "He works at the Navy Yard, doesn't he?" Where he could arrange deliveries to sailors.

"A good job. He's glad to have it."

"I'm sure he is. After the Navy . . ." After he'd been burned in a boiler explosion. That explained the scar. "Such a shame."

"Yes."

Something told her to stop. Just enough curiosity, not too much.

She forced her eyes to read. Lithium carbonate. She could do this. Her legs obeyed and carried her to the correct shelf, and her hands found the correct bottle. She checked twice.

"I'm going to straighten out the stockroom," Mr. Dixon said. "Albert left a mess."

"All right." Lillian rested her forehead against the shelf.

Scar was the perfect man to lead the ring. He used to run in a bad crowd, so he knew thugs to recruit. He worked in the Navy Yard, so he had access to ships and sailors.

And Mr. Dixon . . .

Lillian stifled a groan and hugged herself. Mr. Dixon was involved. Deeply involved.

He knew correct prescription terminology, so he could give the forger the precise wording. He had samples of handwriting from real physicians. He could tell the thugs which doctors to target to steal prescription pads.

And he could fill hundreds of prescriptions for thousands of tablets of phenobarbital—legally.

That's why he insisted Lillian never call the doctors. That's why he didn't want her to make deliveries. All along, he was involved.

That's why no other pharmacies were targeted. He wanted all the prescriptions, all the money.

Cyrus Dixon loved only two things—money and his nephew.

Nothing else mattered.

No one else mattered.

Certainly not a crippled girl pharmacist who knew too much.

"Oh, Lord," she whispered. "Keep me safe."

39

South of Long Island

Confined to quarters, Arch wrote hard and fast, every detail he could remember. A tremor distorted his handwriting, but he didn't care. The same fury and grief that intensified the tremor fueled his urgency to finish the report.

When the *Ettinger* arrived in New York later that evening, he and Parnell Lloyd and Earl Kramer would be taken into custody for interrogation. A complete written report could help the police capture Palonsky's murderers.

Stabbed.

Arch convulsed as if the knife had pierced his own chest. The image ripped through his mind of his friend attacked, in pain, bleeding, abandoned.

The thugs in the drug ring must have discovered he was a snitch. If they had, how much else did they know? Did they know Lillian's role?

He couldn't protect her right now, but maybe his report could remove her from police scrutiny. It didn't matter if Arch was locked up—he deserved it. But not Lillian.

Arch planted his elbows on the desk and rested his forehead

in his hands. Wooziness washed over him, as if he were adrift in a storm, tossed by wind and wave and current.

"Lord, please anchor me." He needed that stability. "For Palonsky's sake, bring his killers to justice. For Lillian's sake, show the police why she's innocent, why she needs their protection."

He stared at his notes between his elbows. He and Lillian had started their investigation in late February. She'd noticed unusual prescriptions as soon as she'd started her job in early January.

He shuffled through his notes. If only he had more details from Lillian's end of the investigation.

"January! Of course!" He jabbed his finger at the date. He didn't know when the problems had started on the *Ettinger*, although the ring seemed established when Arch joined the crew. But Lillian had traced the prescriptions at Dixon's back to January 1941. When she was at Ohio State.

He shoved away from his desk. This proved she couldn't have masterminded the plot. Since Doc's case hinged on Lillian and Arch's relationship and her medical knowledge and access to drugs, it might remove Arch from scrutiny as well.

"That doesn't matter." He pounded on the door. "Pardon me. I need to speak to Captain Buckner immediately. I have new information on the case."

"I'm sorry, sir," the guard said. "I can't leave my post."

"I don't expect you to. Please alert the next man you see. Please. It's urgent."

"Aye aye, sir."

At the desk, Arch raced through his report at flank speed. How dare Doc accuse Lillian? Even if she was a gold digger—which he now doubted—she wasn't a criminal.

What was Doc trying to do? Deflect attention from his own involvement? Or . . . ?

302

The look on his face when he saw Arch at Captain Buckner's desk. He was scared . . . of Arch. Did he believe his own story? Maybe he and Arch had been investigating in parallel, avoiding each other out of mutual suspicion.

Arch groaned and plunged into his report.

The rhythm of the ship changed. The rpms slowed, and the ship tilted into a turn to port. Why to port? That would take them south instead of west. Were they changing sea lanes to avoid shipping traffic off Long Island? They weren't due to arrive in New York until 2100, and it was only 1900.

Without a porthole in the cabin, he couldn't accurately judge direction. But the duration and tightness of the turn indicated a 90- to 180-degree turn.

Arch tapped his pen on the desk, attuned to the vibrations after nine months in the *Atwood*'s engine and fire rooms.

The turn leveled out, and the speed picked up, the destroyer bounding over the waves. Flank speed.

His jaw clenched. Although general quarters hadn't sounded, something had happened—a radar contact, a sound contact, a distress call. Trapped in his cabin, Arch had no way to know the situation.

If they did go into battle, the last place Arch wanted to be was locked in his cabin. If the captain ordered abandon ship, all prisoners would be released. But what if he forgot? What if it was too late?

Arch's pulse galloped. He had to get out. Somehow he had to get out.

★ ★ ★

Boston

From the corner of her eye, Lillian watched Mr. Dixon in the stockroom. Her hands itched to pick up the phone and call the police, but he'd never let her get through.

How could she endure the next two hours until the store closed? If Mr. Dixon left before nine o'clock, she'd call from the store. But if he stayed until closing time, she'd call from the safety of her apartment.

Lillian's fingers beat on the typewriter keys. She'd already ruined two labels for this medication, and she had to get this one right. She couldn't look nervous or he'd know.

The phone rang, and she jumped.

"I'll get it." Mr. Dixon darted to the phone. "Dixon's Drugs, Mr. Dixon speaking."

With effort, Lillian completed the label and centered it on the box of suppositories. "Mrs. Schaeffer, your prescription is ready."

A brunette carrying a new baby came to the counter. Lillian told her how to use her medication and cooed over the newborn, pretending not to listen to her boss. He only said yes and no anyway.

Lillian stroked the baby's silky soft cheek. "My sister had a baby about three weeks ago. She lives in Ohio, so I haven't met my new niece yet." Her voice choked. What she wouldn't give to be in Vermilion right now.

"I hope you can visit them soon." Mrs. Schaeffer gave her a sweet smile, paid for her prescription, and departed.

Another patient stood in line. A steady stream of work kept her from thinking about her situation too much, yet her situation made it hard to focus.

Lillian inspected the next prescription for codeine tablets and plucked the bottle from the shelf.

"That plan we discussed," Mr. Dixon said. "No, the last resort . . . Yes, that one . . . Tonight . . . Yes, that's right . . . Yes." He hung up and returned to the stockroom.

What was he planning? Would he skip town? Hardly seemed likely, since the store was his fortune.

The store. After she called the police tonight, her boss

would be in prison and she'd no longer have a job, nor would the other employees.

Lillian jerked her mind back to the prescription. Patient safety came first. That was her role as a pharmacist, to care for patients.

She counted the codeine tablets, checked her work twice, dispensed the prescription, and took in the next one.

Sounds of boxes scraping over the floor came from the stockroom.

Where had Mr. Dixon gone wrong? Scar had been kicked out of the Navy for his nerves, and Mr. Dixon railed at the injustice, at how the Navy failed to treat his nephew's condition. Had he taken his nephew's care into his own hands and supplied him with phenobarbital?

What if Scar had met with some of his old sailor buddies—at the Rusty Barnacle, perhaps—and his friends complained about their nerves? What if Scar slipped them some tablets? And they liked them?

It could have grown from there. With Mr. Dixon's knowledge and Scar's naval and criminal connections, they could have formed the ring. Mr. Dixon might think he was helping the sailors, but he wasn't. They couldn't perform their duties. Poor Mrs. Harrison's grandson had died.

Now they were murdering sailors.

Lillian blinked hard and stared at the prescription in her hand. *Lord, don't let me hurt any patients tonight.*

Mr. Dixon emerged from the stockroom with a clipboard. He didn't talk to her or look at her, but he walked around the prescription area, taking notes.

What was he doing?

Lillian read the prescription for cough syrup, and she groaned. Not only would she have to do calculations and measurements in her addled state, but she'd use up precious rationed sugar.

The last thing she wanted tonight was to draw Mr. Dixon's ire for any reason. Was she in danger? What exactly did he know about her?

He knew she'd questioned prescriptions at the beginning and had taken a delivery to Mrs. Harrison. He knew she had dated Arch, and Hank had seen Arch and Lillian visiting other pharmacies. They had to know Arch served on the *Ettinger*.

Had Scar seen her outside his home last night? If he had, he'd know she'd followed Albert and Hank, which would be disastrous.

Lillian gave her head a firm shake and gathered her ingredients and glassware.

No, he couldn't have recognized her. And it had been worth the risk. How else could she have learned Scar's name? Arch didn't know his name or his relation to Mr. Dixon. Only Lillian did.

What if Mr. Dixon realized she'd put the puzzle together?

Icy prickles raced up her arms. Scar's gang had killed once. Would they kill again?

40

South of Long Island

A rap, and the cabin door swung open. Arch sprang to attention. "Captain Buckner, sir. Thank you for coming."

"I was already on my way when Mr. Avery found me."

Arch's cheeks heated at the thought of the entire crew knowing of his incarceration. "Sir, it's about Lillian Avery. She moved to Boston from Ohio this January, but the prescriptions date back to January 1941. They're filed at Dixon's Drugs. This proves she couldn't have—"

"The police will want that information, and you'll have the opportunity to give them your full report, but for now I'm releasing you and Doc. That's why I came."

Relief coursed through him, tinged with dread. "Both of us, sir?"

Buckner leaned against the open door. "Earl Kramer is upset about Palonsky's death. The man you call Scar asked Kramer a lot of questions about Palonsky, friendly questions, mostly about Palonsky's acting. Kramer thinks Scar realized the boy was acting, that he was a snitch."

The destroyer yawed, and Arch widened his stance. Had

307

Scar recognized Palonsky from the night they went to the Rusty Barnacle in disguise?

"Kramer wants Scar and his comrades to pay. He confessed to everything, and his report is consistent with yours and with Doc's. By the way, he laughed at the idea that you or Doc might be involved."

Small comfort. But at least Kramer would be able to provide better descriptions of the culprits, maybe some names.

"You and Doc aren't off the hook yet," Captain Buckner said. "The police need to do their work. But for now I need both of you on duty."

"The change in course. We're heading east, aren't we? And the seas are picking up."

The captain crossed his arms. "We received a distress call. Eastern Sea Frontier wants us to investigate. No merchantmen are supposed to be in that area and the call letters aren't listed in the records, but that happens often enough. And yes, we're heading into a squall."

Arch put on his mackinaw and life vest. A cargo ship could be in trouble, or a U-boat could be luring them into a trap. Either way, the *Ettinger* had to be prepared for an attack. "Where do you want me, sir?"

"Junior officer of the watch." He tipped up a smile. "On the bridge, where I can keep an eye on my prisoner."

"I'll try to behave, sir." He grabbed his report from his desk. "May I ask a favor? Would you please place my report in the ship's log?" If anything happened to the *Ettinger*, the crew would do their best to save the log.

"Excellent idea. I'll do the same with Doc's and Kramer's reports."

The captain led the way up to the bridge. The sun had set, and heavy clouds blocked the stars. Captain Buckner relieved Ted Hayes at the conn, so the executive officer could go to emergency steering toward the stern.

Arch's eyes would take half an hour to fully adjust to night vision, so he reviewed the ship's log and entered his data for the change in watch. Since the ship was nearing the coordinates of the distress call, they had slowed to two-thirds speed to allow for sonar readings. Rain tapped on the portholes, hard and fast.

The captain ordered a call to general quarters, and sailors scurried to their battle stations on the rolling deck.

"Captain Buckner, sir?" The radarman leaned out of the radar room behind the pilothouse. "We picked up something."

The CO motioned for Arch to follow him into the dark room, lit only by red light bulbs. A neon green line stretched across the round black "A" scope, and a blob of light pulsed down the length of the line and sent up a spike toward the end.

"See, sir? Six thousand yards." The destroyer's SC search radar could detect planes and surfaced vessels to about sixty-five hundred yards.

The radar pulsed again, but the pip at the end split in two. "What does that mean? The double pip?" Arch asked.

"We're pretty far away, sir," the radarman said. "It might be due to the weather. Or it could be two targets—a cargo ship broken in two, a fleet of fishing vessels, or—"

"Or a tanker and a U-boat," the captain said. "Even a wolf pack of U-boats."

"Yes, sir."

"Send the range to the gun director. We need to be prepared."

"Aye aye, sir."

Back in the pilothouse, Arch logged the time and radar contact. Six thousand yards—just over three miles. They'd arrive in about ten minutes, and they'd come into sonar range at twenty-five hundred yards. Soon they'd have visual contact—and they could also be seen.

Arch flexed his fingers to ease the tremor, and he took slow breaths. *Lord, whatever this night holds, see me through for the sake of these men.*

"Sir!" The talker whirled around in his telephone headset. "Forward lookout spotted what looks like a lifeboat off the starboard bow."

"Engines to one-third speed," Buckner said.

The helmsman rotated the handle on the engine order telegraph to the appropriate speed, which would be transmitted to the corresponding telegraphs down in the engine rooms.

Arch recorded the information in the log.

The captain stepped onto the wing of the bridge and scanned the ocean with binoculars.

"Sir," the talker called out. "Forward lookout spotted the primary target on the horizon."

"Yes. Yes." Captain Buckner peered ahead. "I see it too. Mr. Vandenberg, have your eyes adjusted? Has it been long enough?"

Arch glanced at his watch in the red light of the pilothouse. "Only a few minutes short, sir."

"Take my position." He held out the binoculars.

Arch took his place. A driving rain beat down, the ship bucked beneath him, and his stupid tremor distorted his vision through the binoculars. He shook out his damp hands, huffed a breath, and tilted the binoculars to the eastern horizon. Soon he made out the target, nothing but a dark mass on the dark sea under the dark sky.

Friend or foe?

"Sir, the lookouts say the lifeboat appears to be empty." The talker's voice floated out, muted, from the pilothouse.

"Very well. We'll come back later to verify. Steady on course."

Over the next few minutes, the target's shape became more distinct but not recognizable in the rain. Low to the heaving waters, divided, jagged—probably a wreck.

"Sir, the sound room reports multiple sonar contacts, several at the target coordinates, plus a stray contact bearing zero-four-five, range two thousand yards."

Arch frowned. Submerged wreckage, most likely. And the stray contact—a broken-off section of hull, a whale, a pocket of cold air . . . or a lurking U-boat?

He leaned into the pilothouse. "Sir, the target appears to be a wrecked ship."

"Very well. Left ten degrees rudder. Train the searchlight on the target. If a U-boat is in the vicinity, they've already seen us anyway. And we need to see what's out there."

"Aye aye, sir." The talker relayed the orders to the helmsman and the searchlight crew.

The *Ettinger* made a gentle turn to port, and the searchlight's beam sliced through the rain, destroying night vision but illuminating the scene.

The target pulsed in and out of vision as the destroyer rose and fell. Two or three giant pieces of wreckage, but no oil on the surface, no men or small craft in the sea. It appeared to be an older wreck. So where did the distress call come from?

One piece of the wreckage drew his eye, smooth and cylindrical, rather than jagged and tilted.

Arch's heart thudded to the floor of his stomach. "Sir! A conning tower! Surfaced U-boat bearing zero-one-five."

His voice was overpowered by shouts from starboard, a call for left full rudder, orders called out in the pilothouse.

The destroyer veered to port. On the main deck, sailors leaned over the lifeline, pointing, shouting, "Torpedo!"

Arch braced for impact, gripping the railing in one hand and the binoculars in the other.

A phosphorescent streak glanced by, stern to bow. It came from the south, not the east.

A second U-boat.

They'd fallen into a trap.

★ ★ ★

Boston

Another prescription for terpin hydrate with codeine cough syrup? Lillian glanced at the clock—8:46. She had to fill it, so she forced a smile. "That'll be about fifteen minutes."

"I'll wait." The middle-aged gentleman turned and covered a cough.

Mr. Dixon hadn't left yet. He was still poking around in the stockroom and writing on his clipboard. He'd stay until nine, and then she'd have to call from home. What if he stayed after she left and destroyed the evidence? In fact, that would be smart.

Lillian pulled out the graduated cylinder she'd just washed and set up weights on the scale.

"Finally done for the night." Mr. Dixon came out of the stockroom with a paper sack and his clipboard. "I'll send Miss Felton home. You can ring up the final purchases."

"All right." Her sudden relief lent a nice note of cheer to her voice. "Have a good night."

In jail.

Without his presence making her nervous, Lillian compounded the cough syrup quickly. Thank goodness the patient didn't have any questions, and she sent him on his way.

Five minutes until she could close the store. She grabbed the phone and dialed the police department. "May I speak to Detective Malloy?"

"He's gone home for the day. I'll have him call you in the morning. Name and number?"

"No." Lillian pressed her hand to her forehead. "That won't do. This is Lillian Avery at Dixon's Drugs on Main Street by City Square. I just found out my boss, Cyrus Dixon, is running a massive ring that sells drugs to sailors. His nephew, Charles Leary, is the source at the Navy Yard. The ring is connected to the murder of the sailor this morning. All the prescriptions, the evidence—it's here at the drugstore. I need someone to come here immediately."

"All right then . . ." The officer sounded confused.

Lillian winced. Her story must sound bizarre. "Please, sir. I think Mr. Dixon might leave town tonight. Or he might come back after the store closes and destroy the evidence. It can't wait until morning."

The policeman sighed. "Listen, lady. All our officers are busy. I'll send someone as soon as possible, but it could be a few hours."

She peered down the aisle. "The store closes at nine, and I'm leaving. I'll take the prescriptions with me to protect the evidence."

"No, ma'am. Don't do that. Go home, but do not disturb the evidence. Why don't I tell the officer to meet you at home?"

That would have to do. Lillian gave them her address and hung up.

Two minutes before nine. Close enough. The prescription area was clean and neat, prepared as if someone would actually work there in the morning.

In the stockroom, she took off her white coat and grabbed her purse, with her evidence notebook tucked inside. Then she locked the stockroom, the door to the prescription area, and the side exit in the main store area.

Down the aisle she strolled, glancing down each aisle, but no customers remained. Miss Felton would have locked the front cash register, so Lillian only had to turn off the lights and lock the front door behind her.

One last customer stood in the front display area, a shorter gentleman in work clothes, inspecting an item on the shelf.

Keys in hand, Lillian checked her watch. Nine o'clock

sharp. Thank goodness. "Excuse me, sir. Would you like to make a purchase?"

He didn't face her. "Why? Is it closing time?"

"Yes, sir."

"And I'm the last customer in the store."

"That's right, but—"

He spun around and waved out the window.

Lillian's breath turned to icy shards in her lungs. The man—Arnold Smith, one of the phenobarbital patients.

Another man jogged across the darkened street.

Lord, no! Help me. She lunged for the door.

The man in the street got there first. Tall, lanky—Hank! Deep inside, a scream welled up.

A hand slapped over her mouth. The shorter man yanked her to his chest and jabbed something hard into her rib cage. "Shut your trap, sister. That's a gun."

Oh no, oh no, oh no. Lillian's breath huffed over the man's gloved fingers, and she groped the air in front of her.

Hank shut the door behind him and snatched the keys from Lillian's hand. "Get her to the back. I'll hit the lights."

"Move it, sister." Her captor shoved her forward, his hand and the gun firmly in place.

Help me, Lord. Help me, help me, help me. Lillian stumbled toward the back of the store. She had no choice. If she broke away or collapsed to the floor, he'd shoot her.

"Got the clipboard, Hank?"

"Sure, I got it."

"Dixon said follow it to a T, or Chuck kills us slow and painful."

"Relax, Shorty. You worry too much."

Hank unlocked the door to the prescription area, and Shorty pushed Lillian inside.

"Don't turn on the lights," Shorty said. "Flashlight by the door to the stockroom, Dixon said."

"What do you say, girlie? Do we need to gag you, or will you keep your mouth shut?" Hank shone the flashlight in Lillian's face.

She slammed her eyes shut and tried to nod in Shorty's tight grip.

"See, if we don't gag you, and you scream, we'll take our time killing you, have our fun. Promise not to scream?"

Lillian nodded.

Shorty eased his hand away from her mouth.

She wiped her tingling lips. "Why do I have a hunch you're going to kill me anyway?"

Hank laughed and pressed his index finger to her forehead like a gun. "Sure, but you be a good girl and be quiet, and it won't hurt a bit. You scream, and it'll hurt a lot."

"Come on, Hank. Hurry up. We've got a lot to do to make this look like a robbery gone bad. Get the twine and tie her up."

"Who made you boss?" Hank set the flashlight on the counter, pulled a coil of twine out of a sack, and wrestled Lillian's arms behind her back while Shorty pressed the gun barrel to her ribs.

Lillian's throat swelled. She was all alone. Her boss had betrayed her and ordered these men to murder her. Her family loved her, but they weren't here. Her roommates didn't know she was in trouble. The police wouldn't come for hours, and they'd go to her apartment instead of the store. And Arch . . . she'd driven him away forever.

The rough twine bit into her wrists.

"Now her feet. Sit." Shorty shoved her down.

Her knees struck the wooden floor, and she bit back a cry.

"Hey now." Hank shone the beam at her legs. "We don't have to tie up her feet. We just have to take one off."

"For once, you're thinking. She can't run away on one leg."

The men laughed together. They pushed Lillian onto her

backside, yanked her feet in front of her, hiked up her skirt, and untied the laces of the leather harness around her thigh.

Lillian jerked her head to the side, her chest burning with fury and humiliation.

Shorty tugged off her prosthesis and groaned in disgust. "That's the ugliest thing I've ever seen."

"When'd you last look in the mirror?" Hank laughed at his own joke. "But hey, the rest of her ain't bad. What do you say me and you have a little fun before we knock her off?"

Lillian's stomach convulsed, and she squeezed her eyes shut.

"What's wrong with you? She's a freak. Even you can do better than that."

With a loud grumble, Hank shoved the prosthesis aside. "Fine."

Lillian curled up against the wall by the door to the stockroom. Just like the night with Gordon by the river. The night he'd conned her into taking off her prosthesis. The night he'd tried to have his way with her. The night the college boys shamed him into leaving her alone.

They'd called her a freak. They'd told Gordon he could do better.

She pressed her cheek to the wall. Without her prosthesis, she was weak and incapacitated. Without her prosthesis, her stump was cold and ugly.

Just like her heart.

And it was all over.

41

South of Long Island

The torpedo sliced by the bow of the *Ettinger*. No contact.

But no time for Arch to catch his breath. He dashed into the pilothouse. "Surfaced U-boat, bearing zero-one-five."

"Two of them." The captain addressed the talker. "Forward guns train on forward target. Aft guns train on starboard target. Commence firing when ready. Fire at will."

Arch gripped the threshold, his breath spotty and ragged. Not again. Not again.

All around, men hustled, thinking well, acting well. And Arch stood frozen. *Lord, get me through.*

If he couldn't overcome his combat neurosis, the ship would be better off with him confined to quarters, where at least he'd be out of the way.

He had a job to do. A job. What was it?

Junior officer of the watch. The log. He had to keep the log.

Arch shoved his feet forward, dried his hands on his trousers, and made notations for contact with the enemy, his handwriting barely legible.

"First target approaching from behind the wreckage."

Arch glanced through a rain-smeared porthole. The searchlight illuminated the sleek hull of the submarine. Small figures scrambled out of the conning tower. "Sir, they're manning the deck gun."

"Number one, number two, commence firing on the double."

The talker relayed the message to the gun captains, and more orders flew—to the helm, to the damage control parties, to the radio room to send an "SSS" message.

A loud rumble, and the aft guns fired, rocking the ship. Toward the bow, the forward guns rotated, and the barrels rose. Circular orange flashes, a blast of noise, and both guns fired.

Two shells splashed into the water beyond the U-boat. Arch winced. They'd missed. In the gun director above the pilothouse, gunnery officer Miles Gannett would be adjusting fire.

And still the figures remained on the U-boat's deck, hunched around the gun. Why wasn't that first sub firing torpedoes? Maybe she was at the end of her tour and had used them all. The two U-boats had probably hoped to lure an unsuspecting tanker with the fake distress call—not a destroyer.

The *Ettinger*'s .50-caliber machine guns opened fire.

Light flashed from the U-boat.

A crash of noise overhead.

Arch landed on the deck on his side, and his sore cheek struck his outstretched arm. He scrambled to his knees. The pilothouse was intact. Most of the personnel had fallen.

Captain Buckner pulled himself to standing. "Report casualties. Mr. Vandenberg, check on the signal deck and gun director."

"Aye aye, sir." On the wing of the bridge, Arch glanced up, shielding his eyes from the rain. The gun director sat like a steel cap on the bridge superstructure. The forward top corner was peeled open, wicked teeth biting the wind. "Gun director hit, sir! Send damage control and medical parties."

He climbed the ladder to the signal deck. Wind whipped by. Rain slashed his cheeks. The aft 5-inch guns fired one after the other, and Arch struggled to stay on his feet. Two men lay sprawled on the signal deck, while their buddies performed first aid.

"How many injured?" Arch said.

"Two, sir."

"Medical party's coming." He stepped into the gun director housing and climbed the ladder. "Damage? Casualties?"

The rangefinder operator looked at him, spatters of blood on his face, his eyes wide and haunted. "Mr. Gannett—he's dead, sir. His head—right there in the corner . . ."

Arch squeezed his eyes shut against the pain. "Any wounded?"

"Only minor wounds. We lost director control. Guns are on local control."

"Telephone working?"

"Yes, sir."

"Tell the bridge Mr. Gannett's dead, two seriously wounded on signal deck, minor injuries in director. I'm heading to the bridge. We'll send someone to remove . . . Mr. Gannett."

Arch made his way back to the pilothouse. Machine-gun fire shattered the air, a German shell whistled overhead and splashed into the sea, the destroyer veered to port, someone screamed about a torpedo miss off the starboard bow.

In the pilothouse, Captain Buckner spun to face him. "You didn't get my order. Back to the director. Replace Mr. Gannett."

"Aye aye, sir." He turned for the door and paused. Arch had been trained in gunnery, but he'd rarely served there. In time of battle, they needed someone excellent. Someone like Jim.

But Jim was in the engine room, deep in the bowels of the ship. If Jim went to the director, then Arch . . .

He pressed his shaking hand to his twitching eye. "Captain Buckner, sir? Send Mr. Avery to the director. He knows gunnery well, far better than I do."

"We need him in the—"

"I know engines. I know them well." Arch lowered his hand and faced his captain. "I'll take his place. It's for the good of the ship."

"Very well. Forward engine room, on the double." Buckner waved him to the door, then turned to the talker. "Tell Mr. Avery to report to the gun director on the double."

Arch descended to the main deck. What had he done?

He'd chosen to trap himself.

Through the pelting rain, Arch strode to the hatch to the forward engine room, dodging sailors. This was the right thing to do, for the sake of the *Ettinger*, the crew, and Jim as well. If the ship sank, Jim would want to go down with guns blazing, not fighting blind below decks.

Machine-gun bullets whizzed overhead, and the 5-inch guns heaved shells toward the enemy.

Arch cranked the hatch open and stared into the abyss.

Everything in him screamed not to enter. But he had to. He had to show God he trusted him enough to allow the anchor to drag him to the bottom of the sea.

Maybe this was how he was meant to die.

"So be it," he whispered.

★ ★ ★

Boston

Hank held open a sack, and Shorty scanned the shelves with the flashlight, checked Mr. Dixon's clipboard, and scooped prescription bottles into the sack.

Hunched against the wall in the darkness, Lillian watched them, helpless. When she was weak, then she was strong?

God promised he'd be strong for her. For what reason? So she could die well?

Die well . . .

An incongruous joy lightened her chest. She was going to die tonight, so why not make some good of it? But how?

"This is taking too long." Hank jiggled the sack. "All these long words and Dixon's stupid map."

"Idiot." Shorty grabbed a bottle and tossed it into the sack. Glass clanked on glass. "We gotta do this right. Get the drugs and the cash to make it look like a robbery. Get the prescriptions to cover our trail, make sure they don't find Stan's forgeries. Then kill the girl to shut her up."

Lillian's jaw tightened. Shut her up? Maybe she should scream after all. She'd alert anyone in the vicinity. Hank and Shorty would kill her, but they might be caught, or maybe they'd panic and leave some of the evidence behind.

Then she'd die well.

But what if no one heard? What if the thugs didn't panic? Then Dixon and Scar and the rest of the gang would get away with it.

Staying quiet would buy her time to think. *Lord, if your strength is made perfect in my weakness, then you have the perfect opportunity.*

Somehow she had to make sure Dixon was arrested. She was the only one who knew his role. She'd told the police officer on the phone, but he hadn't asked her to repeat her story, so he probably hadn't taken notes. When they found her dead in the morning, would the police remember any details from her call?

If only she could write a note. It wouldn't have to be long: "Dixon runs drug ring. His nephew, Charles Leary, is Scar. Talk to Arch Vandenberg, USS *Ettinger*." Then Arch would make the connection and fill in the rest of the details.

Could she write with her hands tied behind her back?

Lillian twisted her bound hands around to her hip bone. If she put a piece of paper on the floor beside her and leaned back a bit, she could write. It wouldn't be pretty, but it would get written. Then she could stuff the paper in the back of her skirt waistband for the police to find.

The wooden floor creaked beneath her. Hank and Shorty didn't even look at her as they gathered more bottles from the shelves. They thought her so weak they had nothing to fear.

A little smile poked up. That was indeed a strength. They underestimated her.

How to get paper and a pen? The wastebasket sat in front of her by the door to the main store area. Even a small piece of paper would do. She could back over there on her rump and stick her hands inside. But would that make too much noise?

What about a pen? She peered around the dark pharmacy. If only she were still wearing her white coat. She had a pen in the breast pocket—she could pull it out with her mouth.

She also had a pen in her purse. Her purse? There it was—on the counter by the door. Hank must have tossed it there when he tied her up. She could scoot over, stand up, and find her pen. And her notepad was in her purse. She could record her message inside with the rest of her notes.

"*When I am weak, then am I strong.*" Adrenaline galloped in her veins. They thought she was completely incapacitated. They didn't know she could stand up without her prosthesis.

"That's all the drugs," Shorty said. "Now for the cash. Dixon said the key for the cash register is on a key ring hanging in the stockroom."

Hank unlocked the stockroom door without looking down at Lillian. "Are you sure we shouldn't raid the front cash register too?"

"Right by the window? Idiot. Dixon said get the stuff, knock off the girl, and leave through that side door."

Lillian smiled, as invisible to them as her strength in her weakness. They didn't know what she could do.

Maybe she could make a break for it. They'd left the door to the prescription area open. She might be able to make it to the side exit in time.

No, she'd make too much noise, and the exit was locked. They'd shoot her. Then no one would know about Mr. Dixon.

Hank swore. "I can't find the—there it is." Out he came with the key ring.

The note. Lillian needed to write a note. But all that motion and rustling paper would draw their attention.

She groaned inside. If only she could call the police. She could imagine twisting her hands over by her hip and dialing 0 for Operator with one finger. There were two phones in the store, one by each cash register. One was too close to her captors, and one was too far away from her. They'd never give her enough time.

Lillian sagged against the wall. Maybe it was hopeless after all.

In her head, she could hear Dad singing his favorite hymn while he puttered in the boatyard: *His oath, His covenant, His blood support me in the whelming flood; when all around my soul gives way, He then is all my hope and stay.*

She was never without hope. Christ was her hope, even now.

Coins tinkled down into Hank's sack, and Shorty tossed the bills in on top. "Now the prescriptions. Dixon said get all of them from '41 and '42, just to be safe."

Safe. Lillian hauled in a deep breath. *Lord, asking you to keep me safe seems futile. But please don't let me die in vain. Let me take down the drug ring.*

Safe. Why wouldn't the word leave her mind?

Safe. There was a safe in the stockroom.

Lillian tilted her head and frowned. Why didn't Mr. Dixon

tell Hank and Shorty to clean out the safe? Wouldn't thieves do that?

Unless the safe was empty. Mr. Dixon had spent a lot of time in there, and he'd left with a paper sack—full of cash?

Thoughts zinged through her head, aligning in perfect order. The stockroom had only one door and no windows. The door locked from the outside, and Hank had left the key in the lock.

Shorty dumped a stack of prescriptions into the bag. "Dixon told me to burn these tonight. And his instructions too. He wrote our full names on the clipboard just to make sure we burn it. Then me and you skip town."

Lillian's breath came quick and shallow, pumping the adrenaline even faster. She had one chance. *Lord, make it count.*

"Don't forget the safe," she said.

"What?" Hank shone the flashlight in her face.

She turned her head away. "Don't forget the safe in the stockroom."

"It's not on Dixon's list," Shorty said.

"I'm sure it isn't. He keeps his life savings in there, doesn't trust the bank."

Hank aimed the beam toward Shorty. "I've heard him say that."

She let smugness enter her voice. "I guess he doesn't trust you either."

"Hey . . ." The beam came her way again.

"Any thief with the slightest bit of intelligence would try to crack that safe. And you wouldn't even have to try. I know the combination."

"Yeah," Hank said. "If this was a robbery, we'd torture the combo out of her."

A rumble from Shorty, and he marched over to her. "Don't you see? She wants to cut a deal. We ain't cutting a deal. She's gotta die."

"I know that," Lillian said.

"Then why would you help? I smell a rat."

"Simple." She sat up tall and glared at Shorty. "He's my boss. I trusted him, and he ordered you to kill me. Well, I want to hurt him back. The only thing he cares about is money, so how better to hurt him?"

"Nah." Shorty swatted the air between them. "We steal from him, and we pay."

"You won't steal. You'll give it back—for a price."

"Like a ransom." Hank's voice lit up. "Say, that would work."

Lillian lifted one shoulder. "Maybe 10 percent. Enough to hurt him, but not enough to make him hurt you. Sounds fair for making you do his dirty work. I bet he doesn't pay you enough anyway. And who's taking all the risk?"

"We are." Shorty's voice ground out like a truck on gravel. "And she's right. Won't look like a robbery if we leave the safe alone."

"Come on." Hank headed into the stockroom. "Dixon owes us. That Palonsky kid bled all over my nice new shirt last night."

Oh no. Grief welled up. Not Warren Palonsky. The poor man.

"Hey, sister. No funny business." Shorty stuck his thumb under Lillian's chin and tipped her head back hard. "You try anything stupid, and I'll let Hank there do some carving with that knife of his."

Eyes watering, Lillian managed to shake her head. "No. No funny business." Nothing funny about it at all.

42

South of Long Island

Arch dogged the hatch above him, trapping himself below decks. "Be with me, Lord."

After all, how was dying in the engine room any different from dying on the bridge? If he was meant to die tonight, he'd wake up in heaven, and it wouldn't matter whether he'd entered through drowning, explosion, or fire.

He climbed down the long ladder into the engine room, the familiar noise overpowering the screaming voice in his head, the familiar vibrations melding into his tremor.

Jim would be climbing up the ladder on the starboard side. No time for Arch to ask his forgiveness. No time to pass his regrets to Lillian.

On the upper level, Arch strode along the steel mesh catwalk, ducking around sailors and pipes. He stopped at the gauge board with its wall of gauges and meters. "Damage? Casualties?" he asked the upper-level man.

"No, sir. But we're having problems with the reduction gear."

"I'll take a look." Arch passed the turbine that turned

steam into power. Beside the turbine sat the reduction gear, which reduced the power from the turbine to the lower speed required to rotate the propeller shaft.

For a few minutes, troubleshooting with the machinist's mates and making mechanical adjustments blunted his anxiety. Changes in course, the rolling deck, and the rumbling guns overhead reminded him of the battle and storm.

Why had he dreaded the engine and fire rooms? Being blind to the battle and doing good hard work had advantages.

A loud hollow explosion astern shook the destroyer. Arch and his men braced themselves.

Depth charges. Captain Buckner must have driven one of the U-boats to dive.

Another depth charge exploded.

Something popped, and men shouted.

Arch whirled around. The pipe leading from the condenser to the deaerating feed tank had snapped, and hot water poured out.

He jogged over. They couldn't interrupt the cycle. Steam from the boiler flowed to the turbine and then into the condenser, which converted the steam back to liquid. The deaerating feed tank removed air from the hot water and fed it back into the boiler.

"Come on! Let's get this fixed." Thankful for his leather gloves, Arch lifted a sagging end of pipe, while a machinist's mate grabbed the other end, both careful to avoid the streaming hot water.

Another depth charge rattled the ship, but Arch kept his footing. His men wrapped the broken pipe with mounds of insulation and electrical tape, a temporary fix, but it would do.

"Mr. Vandenberg!" someone shouted from the lower level. "Hull's leaking!"

"Get it sealed!" A destroyer's thin skin and rivets didn't

always stand up to the explosive power of her own depth charges—especially in a storm. He peered through the mesh decking. A fine spray of seawater spurted along a vertical seam. If they didn't seal it soon, the breach would widen.

He passed the gauge board. "What's the news?"

"One U-boat submerged, either sunk or damaged. The other's still attacking on the surface, but she's falling behind."

"Tell the bridge the hull's leaking, no casualties. Send damage control party." Arch scrambled down the ladder. He had to keep the engines running at flank speed to outrun the U-boat.

A thin layer of water coated the lower deck. On the starboard side, sailors pressed steel plating over the breach, water spurting around the edges.

"Where's the welder?" Arch called.

"Coming, sir." The sailor pulled on his leather helmet.

"Get an—"

Noise ripped through the hull overhead, crashed into the condenser behind him.

A shell!

Arch spun to inspect the damage.

A chunk of metal zipped toward him.

He flung up his arm, ducked. Too late. White-hot pain exploded around his left eye.

He cried out and fell to the deck. Slicing, bulging pain. Right where Jim had slugged him.

Arch covered his eye with his hand, but the pressure made him cry out again. He sat up to get out of the water, and he opened his eye, but he only saw red.

"Sir!" The welder lifted his mask and stared down at him.

Head wounds bled profusely. Everyone knew that. It wasn't as bad as it looked. Or felt.

A sailor handed him a rag, and Arch cupped it loosely

over the wound. The pain radiated from his cheekbone up to his eyebrow, the whole eye socket throbbing and prickly.

Regardless, he had a job to do. He got to his feet and gazed around with his good eye. Three other men were bleeding from arms, chests, backs. Shrapnel wounds. "Can you work? Do you need help?"

All three said they could work.

A cloud of steam billowed from the top of the condenser. "Shut down the condenser!" Arch called.

"Already on it, sir."

He turned back to the breach in the hull, which ripped higher now, and he beckoned the welder. "We need to fix that on the double."

"Aye aye, sir." The welder lowered his mask.

Arch pointed to the drenched men holding the patch in place. "Get an extra piece of plating to protect those men from the sparks."

Two men grabbed a large sheet of metal and wrestled it into position.

A new kind of shaking took over Arch's limbs, and a wave of dizziness made him stumble. But he had work to do.

The crackling sound of sparks from the welding torch added to the noise of the engine room. All around him, men cranked valves shut.

With the rag covering the explosive heat around his eye, Arch sloshed through the water to the talker. The dizziness swelled into nausea, and the shaking intensified, numbing his fingers.

He waved his cold, quaking hand at the talker. "Tell the bridge . . . the shell damaged the condenser. We're shutting it down. Shut down the forward engine and boilers. Have to do it."

The talker's dark eyes stretched wide. With his gaze fixed on Arch, he repeated the words into the telephone.

The nausea, the spinning, the pain. Arch bent over and retched, his throat flaming.

"Sir! You need help."

"No, I need to do my job." The words burned in his throat, and he wiped his mouth with a corner of the rag, but it was already soaked through, bright red. "Head wounds. They bleed."

"I—I know, sir."

Arch stumbled forward, splashing through the water. "Shut down the engine. Shut it . . . down."

His vision darkened, and he braced himself, leaned over, retched again.

If only he could sleep. His head felt so heavy, so full. This time he'd sleep well. No nightmares of being trapped below decks, because there was nothing to fear.

His vision went black, his legs gave way, and water washed over him, soothing the pain.

Nothing to fear at all.

★ ★ ★

Boston

"What's the combo?" Shorty followed Hank into the stock-room.

Lillian scooted on her bottom over the threshold. The door opened into the stockroom, and she needed to position herself under the doorknob. And she had to stall the crooks.

The flashlight swept to her. "The combo?"

She ducked from the blinding beam. "It's 40-27-38."

"Here. Hold the flashlight." Hank spun the dial. "Forty . . ."

Lillian eased herself up to her knees, her heart thumping.

"Twenty-seven . . . thirty-eight."

"No," Lillian said. "You mixed up the numbers. It's 40-28-37."

Shorty grunted. "Listen, Hank. Open those stupid big ears of yours."

Hank grumbled, and the dial spun. He'd have to start all over.

Lillian planted her right foot on the floor.

"Forty . . . twenty-eight . . ."

One more diversion. "Not forty. Fourteen. Please listen."

Shorty cussed. "Sounded like forty."

"It's fourteen. With an *N*." Lillian centered her weight over her right leg and prayed for balance. If she fell or made too much noise, she'd be dead.

The dial spun, clicking.

In one smooth motion, Lillian pitched herself slightly forward and rose to standing.

"Fourteen . . ."

She felt tall and conspicuous, but the flashlight illuminated the lock of the safe and two faces intent on cracking it.

"Twenty-eight . . ."

Behind her, Lillian groped for the doorknob and wrapped her fingers around it, careful not to bump the dangling keys. *When I am weak, then am I strong.* Lord, *please make this work*.

"Thirty . . ."

Three quick hops, and she yanked the door shut behind her.

"Hey!" Shorty yelled.

Gritting her teeth, she sandwiched the key between her thumb and the knuckle of her index finger, and she rotated the key, clicking the lock into place.

To the phone, the front phone so she'd be closer to the exit if they escaped.

She hopped to the door, lost her balance, and caught herself on the counter. The jar of marbles rattled—and inspired her.

Cussing and footsteps sounded from inside the stockroom.

In the darkness, Lillian found the door to the prescription area and pulled it shut behind her. Out in the main store area, she leaned over the counter and bumped her forehead into the jar of marbles, tipping it over the edge into the prescription area.

It shattered on the floor, followed by the staccato of hundreds of marbles bounding over the wood.

Hank and Shorty cried out.

It did sound a bit like machine-gun fire. Lillian headed for the main entrance.

More cursing, and they rattled the doorknob.

She hopped down the aisle, picking up speed as she went, guided by the dim light from the street. More than anything, she wanted to fly out that door to safety, but she wouldn't. She had to call the police, the sooner the better.

A loud thump on the door, another, and another. They were trying to break down the door.

At the front of the store, she found the phone on the counter. With her elbow, she knocked the receiver from the cradle. She wrenched her bound hands as far to the side as she could, dug her index finger into the dial at zero, spun the dial all the way around, and released it.

Then she leaned over the dropped receiver on the counter.

"Operator—"

"Help! Send the police. Dixon's Drugs on Main Street. Two men with a gun. They plan to kill me. Hurry!"

A shot rang out.

Lillian screamed.

"Ma'am!" the operator yelled.

"They're trying to shoot out the lock. Do you have a pen, paper? I need you to take this down."

"Y-yes."

More thumping and rattling in the back.

332

Lillian squelched the urge to run. She had to pass on the message, even if she died. "Write this down. Dixon runs the drug ring. Charles Leary is Scar. Talk to Arch Vandenberg on the *Ettinger*."

The operator repeated back, her voice shaky.

Another shot, a thump, a crack, a slam of a door against a wall.

Oh no. They'd gotten out. Her breath raced.

A scrabbling sound. Two screams, two thumps. Hank and Shorty moaned and cussed. They must have slipped on the marbles. Good.

"I'm leaving now. Please. Send the police." Lillian worked her way around the counter. To the door, to the door.

"The gun," Hank groaned. "Where's the gun?"

"Can't see." Shorty cursed the broken flashlight.

Lillian found the doorknob, but it was stiff. "Lord, help me!"

"Gotta get that clipboard. It's got our names on it. Where'd it go?"

More foul words. "That girl. I'm gonna kill her."

She strained her fingers to get a solid grip, and she leaned to the side to get enough rotation on the doorknob. There! It twisted open.

Outside at last, but hardly free. "Police! Police! They've got a gun! Help me!"

She hopped down Main Street toward City Square, where people might be out this time of night, and she screamed for help.

A middle-aged gentleman poked his head out of a house, then pulled back in alarm.

She must look a sight, one-legged, tied up. "Please, sir. Help me. They have a gun. Call the police."

"Okay." He darted inside, his door open, and a middle-aged lady peeked out.

Lillian hopped closer. "Please, ma'am. Let me in. They're trying to kill me."

She covered her mouth with one hand, then motioned Lillian to her with the other. "Oh no. What did they do to you?"

Two men came running up Main from City Square. Police officers, guns drawn.

"Help me!" Lillian tried to wave with her bound hands. "They're at Dixon's Drugs. Two men with a gun. There's a side door as well. Get them."

They stopped and stared at Lillian. "Ma'am, are you—"

"Get them!" She motioned with her head toward the store. "They murdered that sailor this morning. Don't let them get away."

"Yes, ma'am." They ran up the street.

"Miss?" The middle-aged lady inched closer. "What did they . . . what did they do to your leg?"

"They took off my pros—pros—my prosthesis." Her breath quickened, racing out of control. "Please. Please untie me."

"Let's get you safe inside, honey." She looped her arm around Lillian's waist and helped her to the steps of the house.

"I can't—I can't hop up stairs. I need—I need to sit." Lillian turned and sat hard, bumping her tailbone. "Please. Please un . . . un . . ."

"Yes, honey." Her voice cooed, and she worked on the knot in the twine. "Everything's going to be all right now. Everything's going to be all right."

Her hands free, Lillian hugged her knee and hunched over, her breath chuffing. She was going to live. She was actually going to live. "Thank you. Thank you, Lord."

43

Pain awakened him. Deep, aching pain throbbed in his head.

Soft voices broke through, male and female, and the tinkling sound of silverware on tin plates.

Arch opened his eyes. A blur of muted whites, and he blinked to bring them into focus. White walls, pale white light through tall windows, and rows of white beds. A hospital.

How did he . . . ? Yes, on the *Ettinger*. The engine room. The shell from the U-boat. The shrapnel hitting him in the face.

His vision seemed flat—only from his right eye. He extracted his hand from under the blankets. A thick mass of bandages bound the top and the left side of his head.

They were wound too tight. The pain. His skull would crack like an overboiled egg.

He moaned and worked his fingers under the bandages to loosen them.

"Mr. Vandenberg?" A pretty brunette in a white nurse's uniform leaned over the bed. "Good morning, sir. I'm Nurse Green."

"Too tight. Hurts."

The nurse pulled his hand away from the bandages. "Would you like more morphine?"

After all he'd seen the past few months, his instinctual reaction was to refuse the drug, but the pain sickened him. "Yes, please. And loosen the bandages."

She probed the rim of the dressing with cool fingers. "They're fine. Remember, you took quite a blow to the head. You've had a bad concussion, fractures, and surgery. I'm afraid you'll be in pain for a while."

"Surgery?"

Her smile faltered. "Dr. Kendrick did a marvelous job. I—I'll go get him. He's been waiting for you to wake up."

"How long?" The words vibrated more pain through his cheekbone.

"Let's see." She picked up a clipboard. "You were injured on Tuesday night, had surgery yesterday morning. Today's Thursday."

"Well, look who's awake." A silver-haired man stood at the foot of Arch's bed, wearing a white coat and a stethoscope over the Navy officer's blue trousers and white shirt. "How's the pain?"

Arch moaned.

"I was about to get him some morphine." Nurse Green headed down the aisle.

Dr. Kendrick rounded the bed and inspected Arch's bandages, his black tie flopping in front of Arch's face. "Yes, yes. No signs of bleeding or infection. Healing nicely."

Surgery? Arch's mind swam. How bad were his injuries? How deformed was he? While he'd never been vain about his looks, he did enjoy being considered handsome. Of course, deformity would drive away some of the gold diggers. "What happened, sir? How bad?"

"Yes. Well. This is never easy." The physician wrote on his clipboard. "You had extensive fractures around the eye

336

socket. We were able to repair the bones, pin them in place, good as new. But we did have to remove the eye."

Arch clapped his hand over his left eye. "My eye? Removed?" It was . . . gone?

"Not as bad as it sounds." He continued to write in the chart. "In a few weeks when the swelling goes down, we'll fit you with an orbital prosthesis, a glass eye. They're quite realistic. No one will be able to tell by looking at you."

A glass eye. Two-dimensional vision for the rest of his life. Yet only one thought took hold, swirling into nauseating certainty. "The Navy."

Arch closed his eyes—no, his only remaining eye. He already knew the answer. His weak nerves hadn't cost him his commission, but this would. The Navy had no use for one-eyed officers.

His moan settled deep into his soul.

"Here you go, sir." A cool hand rotated his arm and something cold rubbed inside his elbow, followed by a prick of pain, a rush of warmth.

He didn't care. He'd lost the only thing he had left in this life.

"This is always hardest on the Academy boys," the doctor said. "But don't worry. A bright young man with a war record like yours will have no trouble getting a job."

Arch groaned. He *would* get a job. That was the trouble.

★ ★ ★

"Pardon me?" Arch touched the sleeve of Nurse Holloway, the afternoon nurse. "Do you have any word?"

She smiled, plain-faced but kindhearted. "When I hear, I'll tell you."

"Thank you." All day, between bouts of nausea, drug-induced grogginess, and unrelenting pain, he'd been trying to find out if Lillian had been warned. If she was all right.

Even the loss of his eye and his career seemed unimportant once he remembered the drug ring. He was already responsible for Palonsky's death. How could he bear it if anything happened to Lillian?

"Dr. Kendrick?" Nurse Holloway called. "Mr. Vandenberg is asking again."

"Is he oriented enough?"

The nurse's pale cheeks turned pink. "He wants to know, sir."

"Do you have any news?" Arch pushed himself up on one elbow, wincing from the redistribution of pain in his skull. "I need to talk to the police, get word to Lillian—"

"The police wish to speak to you, but I told them you're in no condition—"

"Please, sir. It's a matter of life and death."

The doctor held up one hand. "Your captain said to tell you that he gave the police your report. He's waiting outside with another officer. I wanted to send them away, but they insisted I ask—"

"Send them in." The volume of his own voice provoked a wave of pain, but he bit back his groan. The other officer—it had to be Jim. "Please, sir. I need to see them. My ship. The case. I need to know. I—I'll heal better if I know."

Dr. Kendrick chuckled. "I see his mental faculties are intact. I'll send them in."

"Thank you, sir."

Nurse Holloway eased Arch up to sitting and placed more pillows behind his back. "How is that, sir?"

"Better. Thanks." Being slightly vertical felt more dignified.

It had to be Jim. It had to. Whatever grief Jim gave him would be a small price to pay for news about Lillian.

Two officers came down the aisle of the ward in dress whites, one short with a purposeful stride, one tall with an easygoing gait. Captain Buckner and Jim.

As soon as they reached the foot of his bed, Arch pushed himself higher. "Lil—"

"As you can see, the *Ettinger* made it through." Captain Buckner grinned.

It was only polite, only right to inquire about his ship and crew. "What happened? I passed out, I'm afraid."

"We sank one of the U-boats and drove the other away. She used up so many shells, she'll have to go back to Germany." The captain clapped Jim on the shoulder. "Thanks to some excellent gunnery from Mr. Avery. I'm grateful for your suggestion to send him to the director."

"He's the right man." Arch gave his old friend a nod.

Jim returned the gesture, his gaze unnaturally inscrutable. "I'm sorry to tell you we lost three men. Mr. Gannett and two signalmen. And about twenty men were wounded."

Captain Buckner clasped his hands behind him. "The ship will be at the Brooklyn Navy Yard for repairs for a while, but she'll be back in the fight before you know it."

Arch had waited long enough. "And Lillian?"

Jim's lips thinned to a straight line. "She's alive."

"Alive!" Arch jerked up to sitting, and pain stabbed. "Alive? Why? Is she hurt?"

"Praise God, no."

The two officers took the chairs offered by Nurse Holloway, thanked her, and sat.

Arch listened in stunned disbelief as Jim related Lillian's story. How she'd discovered the elusive Scar was Mr. Dixon's nephew, and that Mr. Dixon—Mr. Dixon!—ran the whole operation. How the pharmacist had sent two thugs to stage a robbery and kill her. How Lillian had foiled them with quick thinking and a great deal of courage. And how Mr. Dixon, Scar, and the two thugs were in jail and several other men were under investigation.

Arch sank back to the pillows and thanked God for keeping

Lillian safe, for helping her think straight, and for putting an end to the whole mess. "Are you sure she's all right?"

"I saw her myself," Jim said. "We pulled in to New York early yesterday. I called, found out what happened, and caught the next train to Boston. I came back a few hours ago. She's a bit shaken, but she's resilient. She'll be fine."

She was more than resilient. Lillian Avery was the best woman he'd ever known, and he'd pushed her away. And he'd endangered her. "I'm sorry I got her into this."

Jim sighed and stretched out his legs. "You? I'm the one who got her that job—with a criminal for a boss."

"Maybe, but I'm the one who started the investigation."

Captain Buckner cleared his throat. "Because you did, the ring is broken and four criminals are behind bars. The work you and Palonsky did was vital. With your testimony, Miss Avery's, and Earl Kramer's, convictions are guaranteed. Palonsky's death was not in vain."

Nausea oozed around, and Arch pressed his hand to his belly. Palonsky's death might not be in vain, but it wouldn't have happened at all if Arch hadn't waved dollar bills in the man's face.

"We should let you rest." Captain Buckner stood. "I'm sorry about your injury. You served well on the *Ettinger*, and I've put you in for a commendation."

Arch shook his hand, but what good was a commendation without a commission? Nothing but a medal to stuff in his dresser drawer.

"I hope our paths cross again." The captain turned to leave.

"Jim," Arch said. "I'd like to speak with you in private."

Jim looked to his CO, who gave a nod of approval, and Jim returned to his seat.

Arch waited for the captain to depart. "I need to apologize for what happened with Lillian. For breaking her heart."

Jim shrugged. "It wasn't going to work anyway. You're too different. Better it ended early before you got too attached to each other."

Too late for that. "I suppose you're right."

"I also need to apologize." Jim gestured to Arch's face. "Your eye. That's right where I hit you."

"You only gave me a bruise."

"Maybe I weakened the bone."

"You overestimate the power of your own fist."

Jim cracked a smile, the first Arch had seen from him since that fist had been thrown. Then Jim sobered. "Anyway, I'm real sorry about the Navy. You're a good officer, and I know how much it meant to you."

Misery intensified the nausea, and Arch glanced away, along the line of beds filled with the wounded.

"I should go." Jim's chair creaked. "I guess we won't see each other again."

Arch sucked in a breath, but then it seeped out. Nothing connected them anymore—not the Navy, not Lillian, not even the long years of their friendship. It was all gone.

Jim stood tall and snapped a salute, his eyes dark with emotion. "It was an honor serving with you, Mr. Vandenberg."

Arch's salute touched his bandages and his heart. "And it was an honor serving with you, Mr. Avery."

With military precision, Jim turned on his heel and strode out of the ward.

In less than a week, Arch had sent a good man to his death and he'd lost his eye, his commission, his best friend, and the woman he loved.

All that remained was his wealth. And he knew what that would do to him. He didn't deserve any better.

44

Lillian poked at the cool mound of chicken salad resting on a bed of tomato slices. The perfect meal for a balmy evening.

She had to eat. Too many days with too little food were taking a toll.

Her brother Dan wiped his mouth with his napkin. "That had better be your last day with the police."

Mary and Quintessa murmured their agreement.

"It's all right." Lillian cut a tomato slice in half. "Detective Malloy is very kind. He lets me stop when—when I need to."

The police had caught Hank and Shorty in the store—sack, clipboard, gun, and all—evidence that landed them in jail beside Mr. Dixon and his nephew. They were also questioning Albert and a man named Stanley Jackson, the forger. From Mr. Jackson's picture, Lillian identified him as the man who used the alias of Harvey Jones. Apparently he'd wanted to get out of the ring so badly that he'd run away to enlist. Now he was cooperating with the police.

Lillian had spent the last two days at the police station

and in Dixon's Drugs, helping the officers decipher the mess. It was hard to see the store again and remember what had happened. It was even harder to talk about Arch and remember the joy of his friendship, of working together, of the protective way he'd held her.

He'd lost his eye! That meant he could no longer serve in the Navy. He had to be devastated. On top of that, he was dealing with Warren Palonsky's death and all the nasty things Lillian had said to him.

"You had some phone calls today."

She blinked and forced her eyes to focus on Quintessa.

The blonde slid a piece of paper to her. "Good thing I had the day off from Filene's to serve as your personal secretary."

Lillian stared at the list of drugstores and phone numbers. "Five stores?"

"They all want to hire Boston's plucky girl druggist."

That's what the newspapers had dubbed her.

She pushed away the list and her plate. "I don't want to be in Boston anymore. I want to go home."

"I don't blame you. Go home, sweetie." Quintessa patted her arm. "What you need is rest and relaxation and pampering from your mama."

Dan snorted. "I disagree. Interview for those jobs. Take the best offer and start immediately. Work will take your mind off all this. Leaving town would make things worse, cement your fears."

Lillian rubbed her hollow stomach. "I should visit Lucy. And I can't stand Boston right now. I just can't."

"How about a compromise?" Mary slid Lillian's plate back in front of her. "Go home for a week, be pampered, hold that baby niece of yours, and clear your mind. Then you can decide—Ohio, Boston, California, Texas—wherever you want."

The doorbell rang.

343

"I'll get it." Mary set her napkin on the table.

Lillian scooped chicken salad into her mouth. It did taste good. If only it would stay down.

"Lillian?" Mary said. "It's Mrs. Harrison."

Mrs. Harrison? Her neighbor hadn't spoken to her in almost two months. Lillian went to the door.

Mrs. Harrison stood on the landing, twisting her hands, her eyes watery. "I—I saw the newspaper today."

"Please, come in." At last she had a chance to apologize.

"No, no. You have company. Would you . . . would you be willing to come to my apartment?"

"Of course." Lillian said good-bye to her brother and roommates and followed her neighbor upstairs. "I'm glad you came. I need to apologize—"

"No. You were right about Giffy. I just couldn't hear it."

"But it was wrong of me, so coldhearted. You were grieving. I was awful."

"Well, I was wrong too." Mrs. Harrison opened her door. "I shouldn't have treated you as I did."

Lillian inhaled the sweet familiar scents of furniture polish and chicken broth and lavender. Then she looked into Mrs. Harrison's blue eyes. "I truly am sorry about your grandson. I know how much you loved him."

Her lips pressed together, her cheeks reddened, and she blinked over and over. "It was a double loss. I lost the sweet little boy I adored. And I lost the upright young man I believed him to be. He . . . he was using me. Deep inside I knew it, but I told myself I was helping him."

"I'm so sorry." Lillian pulled her handkerchief from her pocket.

Mrs. Harrison shook her head and dabbed her eyes with her own hankie. "When I saw today's paper—oh! That gang of hoodlums Giffy got himself involved with—they tried to kill you. And they killed that poor sailor. And what about that handsome officer of yours? I saw his name in the paper too. He could have been hurt. How is he?"

The piano bench—she and Arch had sat there not so long ago, shoulders pressed together. "I—I don't know. Oh, it was horrible. I fell in love with him, and he with me. I opened my heart, but then I slammed it shut and drove him away. Now he's been injured, and he's out of the Navy, and I'll never see him again."

"'To a Wild Rose.'"

"What?"

"You need to play it." She motioned to the bench. "And I need to hear it."

Why bother arguing? It would only delay the inevitable. Lillian plopped onto the bench, so alone. Although she hadn't played the piece for weeks, or even thought of it, she played it by rote. Once through, mechanical, note by note, just as written.

The last chord sounded, and it resonated, tingling through Lillian's soul. So poignant. So wistful, full of longing and loss.

She started again. Arch had sat next to her with vulnerability in his brilliant eyes, compassion in his deep voice, and strength in every fiber. She'd loved him so much, and now he was gone from her life forever. And Warren Palonsky was dead. Funny, bright, talented—murdered. And her own boss, the man she'd worked with for six months, had cared so little for her that he'd ordered her death. And those thugs—they could have . . . they could have . . .

Her chest heaved, and something wet splashed on her thumb. Then another droplet landed on middle C. She was . . . crying?

She hadn't cried since she lost her leg. Not one tear.

"Oh, you poor, sweet child. It's all too much, isn't it?" Mrs. Harrison sat beside her on the bench and gathered her in a hug.

345

Something broke inside, and great sobs convulsed her, creaking and rusty, and Mrs. Harrison rocked her back and forth in her lavender-scented embrace.

Two sets of sobs mingled together, for young life lost, for love destroyed, for trust betrayed, for friendship forsaken. And they rocked each other and comforted each other and mourned together and healed together.

After a few minutes, Lillian pulled back with a sniffle and fumbled for her handkerchief.

"That was lovely," Mrs. Harrison said, drying her own eyes.

"My tears?" Lillian grimaced at the ugly mess she'd made of her hankie.

"The song. That was the most touching version of the piece I've ever heard."

"It was?" She couldn't even remember how it sounded.

Mrs. Harrison squeezed her hand with her wrinkled, arthritic, beautiful fingers. "Now you've experienced great love. Now you've suffered great loss. Now your heart is truly open."

Lillian pressed her free hand to her chest. Why did an open heart have to hurt so much?

45

US Naval Hospital, Brooklyn
Saturday, June 20, 1942

Mother leaned over and kissed Arch's cheek, then held his face between her hands, her eyes brimming with concern. "I'm so glad you survived. It could have been much worse."

Sitting up in bed, Arch nodded so he wouldn't have to speak. His bruising and swelling had receded, and the bandages had been reduced in volume. On the outside, he seemed barely altered.

Father shook his hand. "You look well, son. You'll be up and around in no time."

"Yes, sir." He swallowed a bitter taste. At least his father hadn't said, "I told you so." All those years he'd run from Vandenberg Insurance, and now he was thrown back in.

"It's good to see you, Archer." Bitsy kissed his cheek too. A white pouf of netting on her hat veiled her dark eyes. If she'd intended to look like a bride, she'd succeeded. But the veil didn't conceal her averted gaze. Was she afraid of what she'd see? Or would she put up with the gaping hole in his skull as long as she was surrounded by opulence? He knew

347

the answer. She wouldn't visit him in the hospital unless she was willing to wear his ring.

His parents and the woman who wanted to be his wife sat in chairs at the foot of his bed.

This was his fate, and he had to accept it. Sure, he could look for another job, but he had a hunch all other doors would be slammed in his face because he belonged in the family business. It was time to stop running.

"I have a proposition for you." Father removed his fedora. "As I've told you, business is booming. I'd like to open a branch in Boston and put you in charge."

"Yes, sir." Was this fate so bad? He had a job for life, and he'd earn more money than he could ever spend. He'd have the beautiful wife and be able to buy her the ornate home and yacht she expected.

"You'd spend a month or two with me learning the ropes, but you already know a lot about the business, more than you think you do."

"I'll do my best to learn quickly."

Father's blue eyes lit up as his dream of his son following in his footsteps came true, a dream Arch had denied him for too long. "I'll pay you handsomely. And you can stay in Boston. I know you have friends there."

Arch winced. Not anymore.

Bitsy smiled and tipped her head coyly. "It's a splendid opportunity."

"Yes, it is." She'd never love him for who he was inside, but he didn't deserve it anyway. Lillian had loved him like that, but he'd driven her away with his suspicion and his tests.

And now he would become everything he hated. Now he could hire and fire at will. He would manipulate people and use them, he knew he would, just like he'd used Palonsky. Who could love a man like that?

More bitterness, harder to swallow this time.

Fifteen more minutes passed, filled with Father's giddy plans for the family business and Mother's giddy plans for his homecoming and Bitsy silent and smiling.

Finally they left.

Arch groaned, stood, and paced. The sooner he accepted his fate, the better. So why did he chafe? Why did he long to escape this hospital and catch a train to Boston to see Lillian?

This fate would be more bearable with her at his side.

A louder grumble, and he wheeled and strode in the other direction. She'd never speak to him, and he didn't blame her. He hadn't been fair to her. Why had he insisted she despise wealth as he did? Wasn't it enough that she didn't crave it? Jim was right. Arch had a neurotic obsession, and he'd punished the woman he loved for not sharing it.

And he did love her. He still loved her. And he missed her.

Arch stopped, and his head sagged back. How could he marry Bitsy when he loved Lillian?

"Why are *you* so glum?" John Simmons glared at him from a slit in the bandages that swathed his head and torso. "Did I hear right? Your father's offering you a plum job?"

He sighed. "I don't want it."

"You have a job, and you're complaining? Some nerve. What about the rest of us? Who'll hire us? No one."

Arch had heard the doctors and nurses. Simmons had suffered severe burns that would leave him covered with disfiguring scars.

The man was correct. Arch had no right to complain. He shook off his self-pity and stepped closer to the officer's bed. "What did you do in the Navy?"

"Gunnery officer. No need for that in civilian life."

"How about working for an ordnance manufacturer?"

Pale blue eyes stared from that slit. "They'll never look past the scars."

Arch rubbed his chin. If Lillian had a hard time finding a job with her disability, how much harder would it be for John Simmons?

Or for Bob Carmichael across the aisle, who sat in a wheelchair, both legs amputated above the knee?

"Carmichael? What did you do?"

"Executive officer," he said in a dull voice, not meeting Arch's eyes.

"And you?" Arch marched over to Harlan Dyle, whose minor injuries and weak nerves were getting him drummed out of the Navy.

Dyle didn't look up from the paper he was writing on. "Supply officer."

Arch stood in the aisle and turned in a slow circle. So many intelligent, educated men, whose talents would be wasted due to scars and missing limbs and persistent tremors.

They had no hope, nothing to cling to. Neither did Arch.

Wait, what was he thinking? He pressed the heel of his hand to his bandaged forehead. He knew better than that, but he'd never truly put it into practice.

As a youth, he'd put his hope in his wealth. As a man, he'd put his hope in his career. Both had failed him.

What would it be like to put his hope in God, not just for moments of decision or turmoil, but day to day? With the Lord, he'd been able to descend into the engine room during battle for the good of the ship. And he'd done his job.

But working for his father?

The night he and Lillian broke up, she'd said he was strong enough to handle it. He wasn't. He was weak. But with God . . . ?

Why wouldn't the Lord help him descend into Vandenberg Insurance . . . for the good of others?

Arch took another turn, studying the men around him, his two-dimensional vision filling with possibilities.

"Simmons!" He pointed at the man. "You're good with numbers, aren't you?"

"Well, yes."

"Of course you are. And Carmichael? You're good with people, a leader. And Dyle—all you need is a quiet space to work. Am I right?"

The patients stared at him, baffled.

Arch couldn't help it—he burst out laughing. He could do this. With God, he could handle anything.

46

The Avery family strolled home from church in the summer sunshine. Ed and Charlie led the way, then Dad and Mom, then Martin and Lucy carrying baby Barbara, and Lillian brought up the rear.

Lillian turned right onto Liberty Avenue by Glenn's Sohio Station, gazing behind her on Liberty toward the Ritter Public Library, where she'd spent many hours exploring distant lands and times through stories.

Two weeks she'd been home. Two weeks she'd been pampered. Two weeks she'd rested and relaxed. She'd helped Dad in the boathouse and Mom in the office. They'd gone sailing on Lake Erie, watched the regatta on the Vermilion River, and enjoyed a fancy meal at Okagi's. While people with Japanese ancestry living on the West Coast had been sent to relocation camps, those living in the rest of the nation remained free.

As much as Lillian loved her home, two weeks was enough. Pampering was like a drug, sedating and habit-forming and incapacitating, and she needed to wean herself off.

Her brothers' laughter drifted back, mixed with her parents' chatter and Lucy's whining.

Lillian studied the storefronts in brick and in brightly painted clapboard, the solid bank building on her right and cozy Hart's Drug Store to her left on the corner of Main.

Mr. Hart had always encouraged her, and he'd trained her well when she'd worked for him in high school. But his son, Jim, had just graduated from pharmacy school at the University of Michigan, and Lillian wouldn't have a job in Vermilion.

Everyone insisted she'd have no trouble finding work anywhere she looked. All she'd have to do was show the article from the *Boston Globe*.

But where did she want to go? Lillian followed her family up Main Street toward Lake Erie.

Could she return to Boston? Could she face the scene of the crime? No matter where she went, God would be her sure refuge.

She did have ten job offers in Boston, including one from Morton's, the lovely store on Winthrop Square. She still had an apartment, she had friends, and Jim and Dan would be in town, at least for a while.

And she wouldn't have to worry about seeing Arch.

The familiar ache twisted inside her. Where would he go? Back to Connecticut to work for his father? Surely he wouldn't have to do that. A man with his attributes could land any job he wanted.

The ache hollowed out. Since he and Jim were no longer friends, she'd never find out what happened to him.

Lucy stopped on the sidewalk and hefted her daughter higher on her shoulder. "Mom, would you please carry the baby? My arms are going to give out."

"May I?" Lillian gathered the month-old infant in her arms.

"Watch her head. Keep the sun out of her eyes."

"I know." For the baby's sake, she bit back the testiness in her voice. "Hello, Miss Barbara. It's your Aunt Lillian again."

That sweet little face squinted at her from under a lacy bonnet.

Lillian laughed. "I know. I look like Mommy, I sound like Mommy, but I'm not Mommy. You'll just have to make do." She nestled her niece on her shoulder and continued down the road.

Lucy stuck to her side. "You're wearing that bracelet again. I think you've worn it every day since you came home."

"I have." The sunlight warmed the coral and sparkled on the emeralds.

"But Mom said Arch gave it to you."

"The night we broke up."

Lucy's eyebrows sprang high. "Isn't that a bit . . . macabre? Are you pining for him?"

"No, that's not it." Lillian patted the baby's back. "The morning I left Boston, I looked at it one last time. I planned to hide it away forever. Seemed a shame. It's so lovely. Why should it be abandoned because of a painful history? It has intrinsic beauty and worth, and it deserves to be worn and loved."

She could still feel Arch's fingers as he fastened the bracelet around her wrist, still see him longing for someone to see his intrinsic worth and love him for who he was, rich or poor.

She'd given him that love, but then she'd stolen it from him. If only she could tell him the truth. But what would it accomplish? Right now he thought she was a calculating gold digger. If she told him the truth, he'd realize she was the sort of woman who would betray a confidence and tell lies just to protect her heart.

"The bracelet deserves to be loved?" Lucy let out a long sigh. "You talk as if it has feelings, as if you feel sorry for it."

Lillian nuzzled Barbara's soft neck. "I do feel sorry for it."

"Why do you have more compassion for that bracelet than you do for people?"

Her muscles stiffened. When Barbara squirmed in her grip, she forced herself to relax and speak calmly. "You don't know me as well as you think you do."

"Well, you don't know me at all. You never even tried."

Lillian wrestled with a lifetime of frustration and annoyance and hurt, but the bracelet circled her wrist, its warmth seeping inside and melting her resistance. She stopped on the sidewalk until her sister faced her. "No, I don't know you as well as I should. But I'd like to."

Lucy gaped at her. "Pardon?"

"You and I have a history, and a lot of it is ugly. You were sickly, and I ignored you because I was strong. I was rude to you."

"I'll say." She crossed her arms and glanced up the road toward the lake.

"And all my life you've called me coldhearted and cruel. That's hard to hear and dangerous to believe."

Lucy gasped, a retort practically visible on her tongue, but then she pressed her lips shut. "I was . . . I was hurt."

"So was I. Now, we can spend the rest of our lives arguing about who wounded the other the most. Is that what you want?"

Tears welled in Lucy's eyes, and she shook her head.

Lillian jiggled her wrist and made the sparkles dance. "Or you and I can decide that our sisterhood has intrinsic beauty—we're twins, for heaven's sake. We can decide to forgive each other for the past and love each other for who we are. I'm willing to do that. Are you?"

Lucy wiped tears from her red cheeks. "It's all I ever wanted. A sister."

A sigh ruffled the baby's bonnet. "All right then. As of today, we're starting over."

"I—I'd hug you, but the baby."

Lillian laughed, shaky and damp, and her sister joined her, the rhythm of their laughter melding, identical yet unique.

★ ★ ★

US Naval Hospital, Brooklyn
Tuesday, June 30, 1942

Arch forced himself to look in the handheld mirror at his flattened eyelid and the void filled with a flesh-colored composite. In a few weeks, a shell-shaped glass eye would rest over the rounded implant. The sight was rather disturbing.

"The war has raised some challenges." Lieutenant Schneider sat on a stool facing Arch's exam chair. "The art and science of making ocular prosthetics was developed in Germany, and the process has always been a closely guarded secret. Now we've lost our supplier."

Arch murmured his understanding and laid the mirror in his bathrobe-covered lap.

The ocularist held out open palms. "The Navy is researching other materials, but in the meantime, we have to work with the supply in stock. We should have the right size, and we can polish it to fit. We'll match your eye color as best we can."

"How much longer?"

"You're healing well, Dr. Kendrick said. Another two weeks for the swelling to resolve, then we can start fitting you. You should be able to go home in three weeks."

Late July. "The sooner the better."

Lieutenant Schneider grinned. "Raring to go? I'm sure it's difficult to sit still and do nothing."

Arch returned the grin. "Actually, I've been quite busy."

"Good." He stood and offered his hand. "I'll see you next week."

"Thank you, sir." Arch shook the man's hand—after a miss. How long would it take to adjust to a lack of depth perception?

After Lieutenant Schneider left, a nurse came in and replaced Arch's bandages, mostly so he wouldn't shock people.

Arch thanked the nurse and headed for the recreation room. Yesterday he hadn't minded creating shock.

Bitsy had visited again, and alone this time. He'd shocked her four times. First, he told her his plans for the Boston office of Vandenberg Insurance, which made her brow wrinkle. Second, he told her his plans for his salary, which made her gasp. Third, he informed her that Pauline Grayson had told malicious lies and he'd already written to his parents to refute them, which made Bitsy blanch.

Fourth, he removed his bandages, which made her recoil and beg him to have the decency to cover up.

He hadn't done it to test her, but to show her the truth—he wasn't the man for her.

In a huff, Bitsy declared something was seriously wrong with him, and then she'd left.

He'd become skilled at driving women away.

Arch peeked into the recreation room, where patients in matching pajamas and bathrobes played pool and chess, discussing how Ted Williams of the Red Sox had enlisted in the US Marines.

In the hallway in front of him, a pay phone beckoned.

While he'd never regret driving Bitsy away—and in time she'd be glad—he'd always regret driving Lillian away.

The urge to speak to her had grown inside like a painful tumor. The only way to feel better was to excise it. He would have preferred to talk to her in person, but three weeks was too long. A phone call would be better than nothing.

He checked his watch. At 1800, someone would be home. Had Lillian taken a new job? What was she doing now?

Arch plunked a coin into the phone and dialed the operator. While she made the connection, he gathered his courage and his words.

"Hello?" That was Mary's voice, and it warmed him.

"Hello, Mary. This is Arch."

"Arch! I'm so glad you called. How are you? I've been praying for you."

"Thank you. I'm doing well. The doctors plan to fit me with a glass eye, and I'll be released in three weeks."

"That's wonderful news."

Arch leaned back against the wall by the phone. "Is Lillian there?"

"No, I'm afraid not. She went home to Ohio."

He frowned. "For a visit or . . . ?"

"We don't know." Mary's voice was soft and sad. "The incident at the store was traumatic for her. Jim and I don't think she'll return to Boston. She paid her rent for July, and she promised to let us know by July 1, but we still haven't heard from her."

Oh no. She'd retreated. She'd closed herself off from the world.

"Arch? If she calls, would you like me to give her a message?"

"No." His answer came out too fast. "No, don't tell her I called. Don't tell Jim either. I don't want him to think I'm hunting down his sister."

Mary sighed. "He misses you, although he'd never admit it."

"I miss him too, but don't you dare tell him."

Mary chuckled. "Men are such strange creatures."

Arch hated this, hated saying good-bye to people he cared for. "I wish you both all the best."

"Thank you. And I'll keep praying for you."

He settled the receiver on the hook to hang up, then picked it up again and dug in his bathrobe pocket for more coins.

Any intelligent operator would be able to connect him to the Avery residence.

What a warm home, cozy and filled with laughter.

A picture filled his mind, and he hung up the phone.

He'd step off the train in Vermilion wearing a civilian suit and his brand-new glass eye. He'd knock on the front door of the Avery home. She'd be shocked to see him.

He had no illusions that she'd take him back. That wasn't his purpose.

All he wanted was to show her she was worthy of a long journey, worthy of an apology, worthy of love.

She didn't have to accept any of it, but she needed to know.

47

US Naval Hospital, Brooklyn
Saturday, July 4, 1942

"It's good of you to visit our boys on the Fourth of July." The Red Cross volunteer at the hospital front desk smiled at Lillian. "Don't forget the barbecue on the back lawn at six o'clock. Only two hours from now. Friends and family are invited."

Lillian managed a smile, but she was neither friend nor family, and she wouldn't be staying that long.

The volunteer traced her finger down a piece of paper. "Vandenberg . . . Archer Vandenberg . . . Yes, go down this hall to your right, up the stairs, down the hall, second ward on your left."

"Thank you." She sorted the directions in her mind and straightened the jacket of her green suit. She could do this. She had to.

"Miss?" The volunteer gave her a sympathetic smile. "It's difficult to see our young men maimed, but we urge our visitors to conceal their shock and control their tears. It's best for the boys."

"Yes, ma'am." Lillian headed down the hall. If only the

sight of Arch's injury were her only concern. She, of all people, could handle that.

Instead she dreaded seeing either his hot hatred or the cool condescension he'd shown the night they broke up.

On that night, she'd acted in her own strength, and she'd failed. Today she'd accept her own weakness, admit her sin, and stand in God's strength, the strength of the truth.

Up the stairs, down the hall, her shoes tapped in beat with Dad's favorite hymn:

> When darkness veils His lovely face,
> I rest on His unchanging grace;
> In ev'ry high and stormy gale
> My anchor holds within the veil.
>
> On Christ, the solid Rock, I stand.
> All other ground is sinking sand,
> All other ground is sinking sand.

The ward stretched long. Tall windows brightened the beds on either side of the aisle. Men in pale blue pajamas milled around or lay in bed, and white-clad nurses and pharmacist's mates took care of their needs.

Lillian made her way down the aisle, searching for Arch, hugging her purse to her stomach, her right wrist bare and forlorn.

A familiar laugh drew her eye. Arch sat on the side of a bed with his back to her, chatting with a man in a wheelchair and two other men on the bed across from him.

Her heart lurched in a bittersweet way at the sound of his voice, the set of his shoulders, and how the bandage around his head made his blond hair stick up.

To her left, a man whistled. "Some lucky dog has a visitor."

Lillian stopped and hauled in her breath.

Every male on the ward looked her way, and more whistles followed.

Arch stood, his face long. "Lillian."

Oh why, why, why had she come? He didn't want to see her, she could tell by the shock on his face. But she'd come to make him feel better, not herself, so she wrangled up something close to a smile.

Arch gave his head a quick shake, waved her over, and turned to his friends. "Excuse me, gentlemen."

"Choosing her over us." The man in the wheelchair clapped his hand to his chest. "A mortal wound from which I'll never recover."

"Enough, Carmichael." Arch grabbed a chair, set it next to a bed, and looked at Lillian.

She hadn't moved. She couldn't. All her speeches had fled.

Arch raised a slight smile. "If you came all the way to New York, you might as well come the last ten yards."

Her cheeks warmed, but she coaxed her feet down nine of the yards.

He blocked the way to the chair. "It's good to see you."

"It's good to see you too." She stood painfully close to him, painfully far from him. "How are you?"

"You first." He sat on the side of the bed in blue pajamas and slippers, a bandage around his head, his right eye as blue as ever. "Jim told me about Mr. Dixon and how you caught the whole gang. That must have been—"

"They're in jail, and I'm alive. That's all that matters." Lillian sat in the chair and rested her purse on her lap. She hadn't come to discuss the case.

Arch's mouth worked as if chewing words and rejecting them. "What's next? You're in New York—did you take a job here?"

"No." She twisted the purse strap. "I went home to Ohio for a few weeks, but now I'm back in Boston. Well, not today, but . . ."

"I know what you mean."

Why couldn't she ever speak straight? "On Monday I start my new job at Morton's Drugs."

"That store you liked."

"Yes, on Winthrop Square." The square where Arch had kissed her breath away. She studied her cream-colored purse.

"That'll be nice."

Why did she feel his absence from her life more keenly in his presence? "What about you? I'm sorry about your eye and the Navy."

A grin spread. "Don't be. It's the best thing that could have happened. I'm going to work for my father."

Lillian blinked to clear her vision, but the sight remained—Archer Vandenberg happy about joining the family business.

Arch chuckled and rested his elbows on his knees. "I know it sounds strange, but now I see God's plan. I was meant to work for Vandenberg Insurance. The Navy was only a stepping stone—a very good one. I served my nation and became my own man, but it was for another purpose. For this."

That blow to his head must have been harder than they thought. "Are you . . . are you all right?"

"Never been better. Father wants me to set up a new branch in Boston."

"Boston . . ." Maybe she should have searched harder in Ohio.

"I told him I'd only accept the offer if I could hire wounded servicemen." Arch gestured around the ward, and his face glowed. "See these men? They have the intelligence and leadership skills to serve in the Navy. But with their scars and handicaps, no one will hire them. Except me. I've been recruiting. They get great jobs, and I get some of the brightest men in the nation."

Now she saw the reason for his joy. "Oh, Arch. That's brilliant."

"The men I was talking to when you arrived—they're working with me. We were making plans."

"That's such a great idea." Her love for him grew. Not only had he come up with an innovative plan that helped others, but he'd embraced a situation he should have hated.

"I may have to receive a high salary—Father won't budge on that—but he can't control how I spend it. I'm using the bulk of my income to start a foundation. The Warren Palonsky Foundation."

"Oh . . ." Everything melted inside her.

Arch looked at his hands between his knees, his cheeks red, and he cleared his throat. "I want to help—" His voice came out strangled, and he cleared his throat again. "I want to help men with combat fatigue. I'm talking to the staff here about what I can do—research into treatment, helping the men after they're discharged—we're working on options."

Lillian's chest squeezed. That was the most wonderful idea she'd ever heard. "Warren would be proud."

He met her gaze. "I think he'd be pleased his work wasn't in vain. The drug ring is broken, the criminals are behind bars, and we'll help sailors and soldiers with combat fatigue."

All this conversation felt good and right, as if angry words hadn't been spoken between them. But they had, and she'd come for a reason, and she had to get on with it.

Lillian sat up straight and drew a deep breath. "You're probably wondering why I came."

"I am." A slight smile.

"I don't want you to think I came here to throw myself at you. Things are over between us, and that's for the best. We both know it didn't work."

Arch's face flattened. "I know."

"I came to apologize—"

"Don't." He held up both hands. "No need to apologize. I'm the one—"

"Please listen. I do need to apologize. When we broke up, your friendship with Jim ended too. I feel horrible about that. He was like a brother to you."

"I'm making new friends." He motioned to his business partners.

"I'm glad." She opened her purse and pulled out the jewelry box. "I also came to give this back to you."

He flinched as if she'd slapped him. "I'd rather not see that again."

"And I wish I *could* see it again."

His one visible eyebrow rose.

Her breath caught. "I love it. I think it's the most beautiful thing, and it deserves to be worn and loved, despite its history."

"So why—"

"I kept it for the wrong reason. I told you I'd keep it to remind myself never to trust a man again."

Arch lowered his head, and the tendons on his clenched hands stood out.

She held out the box to him. "That was wrong. I refuse to go back to who I was. I refuse to shut people out. I want to trust. So I have no other reason to keep the bracelet, not in good conscience."

"I bought it for you." His voice was strained. "I want you to have it."

Lillian stood and placed it on the bed beside him. "I want to give it back for another reason. Because I lied to you."

Arch frowned up at her, close enough for her to lean over and kiss those lips.

She stepped back and fastened the latch on her purse. "You thought I liked it because it was expensive."

"I was wrong, and—"

"I was hurt, and I was scared because I thought you were trying to control me, telling me what to wear and how to act and what to eat—like Gordon did."

Arch's mouth dropped open.

Lillian slung the purse strap over her shoulder. "I chose to ignore everything I knew about your character, and I chose not to trust you, and I chose to hurt you worse than you'd hurt me. So I lied about only loving you for your money."

His mouth and his eye closed, and he nodded slowly.

"I gave back the bracelet to show you the truth—it *is* possible for a woman to look past your wealth and love you for who you are. Someday a wonderful woman will do just that. But I also gave it back to show you another truth—you chose to love the wrong woman, a woman who betrayed your trust, deliberately hurt you, and destroyed what we had. And I'm sorry."

"Lillian, I—"

"Please don't." She glanced toward the door, her eyes hot and prickly and damp. She was going to cry again, but not in front of him. "I didn't come to rehash the argument, and I didn't come to beg for a second chance. It's over, and that's for the best."

"For the best." His voice sounded stiff.

"Good-bye. I wish you well." Choking back her emotion, she aimed for the exit. As soon as the door shut behind her, a sob escaped.

There. She'd done it. Now he knew the truth, and he could get on with his life.

She wrapped her fingers around the golden anchor at her throat. Somehow the Lord would help her get on with her life too.

48

Arch sat in stunned silence on his bed. What just happened? Lillian had whipped in and out like a summer thunderstorm.

Bob Carmichael wheeled over. "Who was that?"

"The woman I love. But it's over."

"She broke up with you . . . here?" His square face contorted into a grimace.

"No, we broke up several weeks ago."

"So why did she come?"

Why indeed? She certainly hadn't come to give him a second chance. She'd reminded him repeatedly that it was over. For the best, she'd said.

His hand settled on the leather jewelry box. "She came to give this back."

"What is it?"

Arch flipped open the lid and cringed at the sight.

Carmichael whistled. "You really do have money, don't you?"

"I do." But he hadn't used it well. That was going to change.

He fingered the gold fittings, as delicate and strong as Lillian Avery. Why had he let something so beautiful become contaminated by suspicion?

For some reason, she'd loved the bracelet despite everything it represented.

The emeralds—they sparkled like her eyes when the light hit just right.

She'd said she really had loved Arch in spite of his wealth. And . . . she didn't say she no longer loved him.

He stroked the smooth coral, as pink as her cheeks after he'd kissed her.

She'd said he'd loved the wrong woman. Not at all. He couldn't imagine a woman more right for him.

A woman he still loved. A woman who was walking out of the hospital this very minute.

Arch snatched the bracelet from the box and stood. "Excuse me, Carmichael. I have unfinished business with Miss Avery."

He charged down the aisle and into the hallway. At the end of the hall, the door to the stairway shut. Arch jogged down the hall as fast as he could in slippers, and he flung open the door. The stairs made an attractive rectangular spiral, and the central space opened to a skylight. "Lillian?"

A feminine gasp directly beneath him.

Stairs presented a challenge without depth perception, so he grabbed the banister and came down a few steps until he could see her on the landing behind him.

He grinned at her startled look and held the bracelet up to his temple. "I need to give this back to you. It doesn't match my eye. Though I could ask them to make my new eye green."

The startled look broadened to outright concern. Then she ducked her chin and marched down the stairs. "Tell the doctor to decrease the dose of your pain meds. I told you I don't want it."

His smile built in strength, and he followed her. She wouldn't bristle if she didn't care. "Now, now, you just said you love it. So I'll tell you what. When they let me out of here, I'll take the train down to Key West and buy you the matching earrings and necklace."

She wheeled around and glared up at him. "I don't want you to spend money on me. I never did."

"I know, but I want to. I want to buy you the biggest house, the best yacht, the most glamorous wardrobe, the—"

"Are you making fun of me? What is wrong with you?" Her voice shook in a way he'd never heard before, and she stomped down the stairs.

Second time this week a woman had spoken those words to him. "What's wrong with me? I'm deeply in love with you. I love you so much I'm willing to sacrifice the modest life I desire."

"I don't want to be rich. I never did."

"I know you don't, and neither do I. But I trust God to help me even if I become the richest man in the world. And when I trust God, I can trust myself and I can trust you. For richer, for poorer."

"Please stop." She opened her purse and pulled out a handkerchief.

The pause allowed him to gain on her, to study her. "You're crying?"

"Yes." That syllable rose like a wall.

Arch planned to scale it. "You said you never cry."

She wiped her eyes and continued on her way. "I didn't. I started last month, and I can't seem to stop."

"Because of me?"

"Not just you. Everything. Now, please let me leave and let me keep my last shred of dignity."

Arch's steps descended, but his hopes ascended. If he'd made her cry, she really did care. "I'll let you leave if that's what you want."

"It is."

"But I won't stop pursuing you."

Lillian stopped at the door, her hand on the knob, her gaze fixed on Arch.

He went down the last flight. "I'll be in Boston. I'll visit you every day and tell you how much I love you until you agree to go out with me or until you convince me you don't love me anymore."

"I don't—" Her eyes flew open, and her mouth slammed shut.

He couldn't contain his grin. "You still love me."

She wrestled the door open. "I didn't say that."

He laughed. "So you do love me."

"You had a concussion. Your brains are addled." Out the door she went, onto the back lawn. She gazed around.

He came alongside her on the green grass under a warm sunny sky. "Where are you going in such a hurry?"

"I—I—to my hotel. Where am I?"

"You went out the back door. Why don't you stay for dinner? We're having a barbecue right here on this lawn. No fireworks with the dim-out, but you can see the East River and the city skyline. I'd like you to meet my friends, the men I'll work with in Boston."

Lillian looked at him with reddened eyes. "What medications are you taking?"

He laughed. "I haven't taken anything for a week. This is the real me."

Her gaze wavered.

He grasped her elbow. "Please stay, Lillian."

Her face crumpled, and she swayed. "Oh, Arch. I do—I do love you."

"So stay." He folded her in his arms, and a contented sigh flowed out. "I can say my apologies to you. I owe you a boatload. Then we can kiss and take a walk and kiss and eat hot dogs and kiss."

"You already said that."

"I plan to do a lot of it."

Her shoulders bounced—in laughter or tears? "I—I've never kissed a man in pajamas."

"If I'd known you were coming, I would have dressed for the occasion."

Her hands felt warm on his back through the thin cotton. "I missed you so much."

"I missed you too. Now, would you like your bracelet back?"

"Oh, I would." She stepped back and wiped her eyes. "I hate crying. It's so messy."

"You've never looked prettier." The mottled cheeks and moist eyes showed her love. He wrapped the bracelet around her wrist and attempted to fasten it. "This isn't easy with the shakes. I've realized God might not take away my combat fatigue—but he'll help me live with it."

"He will. And he's already using your condition for good. You'll help others, I know it."

His cheeks heated at her praise, and he finally fastened the clasp. "Not easy with one eye either."

"You're doing well." She smiled up at him with admiration. "So well."

Arch set his hands on her slender waist and drew her close. "I may have lost an eye, but I've never seen more clearly."

"Oh . . ." Her pupils widened, and her eyelids drooped slightly, an irresistible invitation.

Since he planned to spend the rest of his life kissing her, why not take his time today? Slowly, trying to judge the distance and not dislodge her hat, he lowered his lips to her brow.

"My girl," he murmured. "My brave, warmhearted girl."

"My boy." Her kiss warmed the tip of his chin. "You . . . you smell so good."

He chuckled and trailed kisses down her temple. "So do you."

Lillian slid her hands up his chest, around his neck, into his hair, and she tugged him lower.

How could he resist such eagerness? He sought her lips, found them, captured them, savored them. Never again would he give in to his suspicions. Never again would he allow her to shut him out. Never again would he let her go.

"Oh, Arch." She laid her cheek on his shoulder. "I'm glad you'll be in Boston."

"Think you can get used to seeing me in a civilian suit? And . . . and a glass eye?"

She pulled back. "May I see?"

His stomach muscles tightened. "I don't have it yet. It's—"

"I know. May I?"

He hesitated, but didn't she deserve to see? Didn't he trust her to love him as he was? He shoved the bandage up to his forehead.

Lillian studied his face. Sympathy softened her eyes, but no fear or disgust warped her features. Then the corners of her mouth turned up. "There. I'm used to it."

He couldn't speak around the thickness in his throat, and he fumbled with the bandage.

"You don't have to put it on for my sake," she said. "Unless you need it to prevent infection, or if it feels strange."

What felt strange was having her look unflinchingly at his disfigurement. He hauled in a breath and tugged off the bandage. "Being here, going through this, seeing the challenges the other patients face—well, now I understand better what you face."

"I'm sure you do." She planted a kiss on his left cheek, right below his missing eye. "Oh, I'm so excited about your new job and what you're doing for these men."

"I am too." The breeze cooled his face, but her enthusiasm warmed his insides. While he'd miss being in the Navy—the spare living, the camaraderie, and the direct contribution to the war effort—this new venture energized him. "Something good came out of this injury."

"Two good things, I hope." A tilt of her head, a gaze through her lashes, a hand weaving into his hair—snaring him forever.

He was trapped, and he couldn't be happier. "And many more good things to come."

Dear Reader,

Thank you for sailing with Arch and Lillian. I want to assure you that the drug ring in this story is purely fictional and not based on historical incidents. However, the treatment of combat fatigue (now known as post-traumatic stress disorder) at the time is accurate. Great strides were made during World War II, as physicians and commanders slowly came to see it as a medical condition rather than cowardice or "weak nerves," but treatment remained difficult.

The USS *Ettinger* is a fictional ship, but the situations she faced were typical. When Germany sent her U-boats to American waters for Operation *Paukenschlag* ("Drumbeat"), the United States was not prepared. Blackouts were considered but not ordered, due to cities complaining about decreased business. Too few escort vessels were available to form effective convoys, and too few aircraft were available for air patrol. Infighting among the various commands didn't help. In the first six months of 1942, one hundred merchant ships were sunk in the Eastern Sea Frontier (off the US East Coast), killing thousands of merchant marines and passengers. The merchant marines and the officers and sailors of the US Navy and Coast Guard showed outstanding bravery and determination.

The sinkings of the *Norness* and the *Traveller* follow the historical record, although the survivors of the *Norness* were actually rescued by the destroyer USS *Ellyson*. The incident in chapter 25 is loosely based on the sinking of *U-85* by the destroyer USS *Roper*.

All characters are fictional other than Dr. Harold Ockenga, pastor of Park Street Church, restaurant owner Mr. Okagi, pharmacists Albert and Jim Hart in Vermilion, and historical figures.

If you're on Pinterest, please visit my board for *Anchor in the Storm* (www.pinterest.com/sarahsundin) to see pictures of Boston, destroyers, Lillian's dresses, and other inspiration for the story.

Please join me for the third novel in the Waves of Freedom series. The last thing no-nonsense officer Lt. Dan Avery wants to see on his radar is fun-loving Quintessa Beaumont—even if she has joined the WAVES.

Look for Book Three of the

WAVES *of* FREEDOM

★ ★

Series

★ COMING **SPRING 2017** ★

1

A touch of kindness and enthusiasm could transform a person's spirit, and Quintessa Beaumont delighted in participating in the process.

"This is lovely on you, Mrs. Finnegan." Quintessa lined a box with tissue paper on the counter at Filene's.

Her customer giggled and tucked a gray curl behind her ear. "Listen to me. I sound like a schoolgirl. All because of a blouse."

"Not just any blouse. The perfect blouse for you." Quintessa laid the floral fabric in neat folds in the box. At first, Mrs. Finnegan had struck her as drab and tired and dowdy. Shame on her for thinking that way—so shallow. But as Quintessa had assisted the older lady in her search, she'd sensed a sweet dreaminess. Mrs. Finnegan deserved a blouse that reflected who she was inside, something to make her happy and confident. Quintessa had found it.

She settled the lid on the box and handed it to Mrs. Finnegan. "Thank you for your purchase. It was a pleasure meeting you."

"The pleasure was mine. You certainly have a gift, Miss Beaumont." Mrs. Finnegan strolled down the aisle with a new bounce in her step.

Quintessa returned to the sales floor. No customers, so she straightened racks of summer blouses, which needed to be sold soon to make room for autumn merchandise.

Filene's fifth floor boasted fashionable women's apparel, all designed to meet the War Production Board's standards to limit use of fabric. For the past ten months, Quintessa had rotated among Filene's various shops, learning the business and the wares. When her year in training was complete, she could finally put her business degree to use in the offices.

A few ladies browsed the racks. With so many women working now due to the war, business was slow on weekday mornings.

A figure in white caught her eye—a naval officer with a familiar determined gait. Quintessa's heart lurched. Dan Avery? What was her roommate's oldest brother doing here?

She smoothed her blonde curls but stopped herself. Why bother? The man was already married—to the United States Navy.

Although his stride didn't waver, he gazed from side to side like a lost child, frowning and squinting. Then he spotted Quintessa, and the frown and squint disappeared.

He was looking for her. Another lurch, with a tingle this time, but Quintessa shoved it aside. She tilted her head and raised one eyebrow. "Lieutenant Daniel Avery. Whatever brings you to Filene's better blouses?"

"My mom's birthday." Dan rubbed the back of his neck and eyed the clothing racks like a fleet of enemy vessels. "I tried to bribe Lillian to do my shopping for me, but she refused. Some sister. Told me you'd help me find something."

Quintessa loved her roommate's forthright nature. "Does the bribe apply to me too?"

He didn't smile. He rarely did, and she didn't think she'd ever heard him laugh, but his dark eyes twinkled. A no-nonsense man, but not humorless. "I imagine Filene's disapproves of employees taking bribes."

"I'll settle for the commission." Shifting her thoughts to her former Sunday school teacher, Quintessa contemplated the summer blouses. "Let's see. Your mother is about Lillian's size and coloring."

"Plumper and grayer."

No wonder the man was still a bachelor. "We would never say that here at Filene's. She's more mature."

"I'd hope so. Raising the seven of us, she's earned her gray."

Quintessa smiled and flipped through the blouses. Mrs. Avery handled the business end of her husband's boatyard, and she was neither frilly nor frumpy.

"How about this?" Quintessa held up a tailored cream blouse with a brown yoke and short brown sleeves. An embroidered green vine with delicate yellow flowers softened the border between cream and brown.

"I'll take it."

"Let's see what else we have."

"Why?" Dan gestured to the blouse. "Is it her size?"

"Yes."

"Do you think she'll like it?"

"Well, yes, but—"

"I'll take it."

The man certainly knew his mind. One of many things she found attractive about him. "All right then."

Quintessa took the blouse to the cash register and rang up the purchase. "How are things at the Anti-Submarine Warfare Unit?"

One dark eyebrow lifted, and he pulled out his wallet. "We're making progress, but personally, I want to get back out to sea."

"That's where the excitement is."

"And the real work. We finally have convoys along the East Coast, and we've pretty much driven the U-boats away. But they're back to their old hunting grounds in the North Atlantic, and they're wreaking havoc in the Caribbean and the Gulf of Mexico. The battle's constantly changing, and we have to stay on top of it."

Quintessa focused on making change. Concentration was always difficult when Dan Avery spoke about the war or ships or the Navy. Passion lit the strong lines of his face and animated his firm mouth. If only he'd remove his white officer's cap and run his hand through his wavy black hair. The wildness of it.

She puffed out a breath. "Here's your change. Let me wrap that for you."

"Very well." He slipped the coins in the pocket of his white trousers and glanced at his wristwatch.

Quintessa gritted her teeth as she pleated the tissue paper inside the box. What was wrong with her? She'd always been drawn to men who showered her with starry-eyed adoration. Now she was drawn to a man who looked right through her as if she had nothing of substance to stop his gaze.

Shame shriveled up inside her. How could she blame him? He had to know she'd come to Boston to throw herself at his younger brother Jim—who turned out to be in love with her best friend, Mary Stirling. Dan had also been in Boston when Quintessa was dating Clifford White—who turned out to be married. Surely Dan saw her as a silly, selfish woman with poor judgment.

He'd be right.

She worked up a smile and presented him with the wrapped package. "Here you go. Thank you for your purchase."

"And thank you for your help. I'm sure Mom will love it." He tipped his cap to her and strode away.

Just as well. She needed to set her head on straight before she started another romance anyway. The past year had turned her topsy-turvy.

Miss Doyle arrived to relieve Quintessa for her lunch break, but Quintessa headed up to the offices on the seventh floor instead. Her former boss, Mr. Garrett, had retired last week, and she'd only briefly met his replacement, Mr. Young.

First she slipped into the restroom, powdered her nose, freshened her lipstick, and straightened her chic golden-brown suit jacket. She smiled at her reflection. Pretty and feminine, but smart and professional. Perfect for this meeting.

The business offices buzzed with a tantalizing sense of purpose. Mr. Young's office door stood open, and she lightly rapped on the doorjamb.

Her boss raised his salt-and-pepper head, grinned at her, and stood to shake her hand. "Miss Beaumont, isn't it? Yes, yes. I don't have the final sales figures for July, but you're in line to be one of the top salesgirls again. A true asset to Filene's."

An excellent start. "Thank you, Mr. Young."

He crossed his arms over his charcoal-gray suit. "What can I do for you today?"

"I wanted to speak with you about the next step in my training program."

"Training?" He narrowed one eye. "You're the last person who needs sales training."

A sick feeling settled in her belly. Hadn't Mr. Garrett told Mr. Young why she was here? "Mr. Garrett hired me to work here in the business offices, but—"

"You're a secretary?"

Somehow Quintessa maintained her friendly professional smile. "No, sir. I have a bachelor's degree in business. Mr. Garrett wanted to give me a year of sales experience before starting here. He felt it was important for his assistant—"

"Assistant?" Mr. Young winced as if he had a toothache.

"That might have been Mr. Garrett's plan, but I just hired a man. These offices are no place for a young lady."

"Unless she's a secretary."

"Yes, I'm glad you understand." His face brightened. "Besides, you're excellent at sales. Why would we waste your talents on boring old numbers and paperwork? And why would we hide that pretty face of yours behind office doors?"

A pretty face. That's all she was. Only good for decoration.

"Now, off you go." Mr. Young set his hand on her shoulder and guided her out his office door. "That's a good girl. Go make Filene's proud."

Quintessa trudged down the hallway. She'd come to Boston for nothing. She'd worked for her degree for nothing. *Lord, what's the reason for all this? What do you want me to do?*

Patriotic posters by the elevator reminded employees to put part of their paychecks into war bonds. The nation was at war, and everyone was working together. Her roommates Mary Stirling and Yvette Lafontaine worked at the Boston Navy Yard, where American warships were built and repaired. Her other roommate, Lillian Avery, worked as a pharmacist, freeing men to fight.

But Quintessa Beaumont was only good for selling blouses.

★ ★ ★

After a day like today, Quintessa needed this. She opened the door to Robillard's Bakery and inhaled the scents of bread and pastry and hospitality.

"*Bonsoir, ma petite* Quintessa." Madame Celeste Robillard raised a plump hand in greeting.

"*Bonsoir*, Madame Robillard."

"I will be with you in a minute," the bakery owner said in French, Quintessa's father's native tongue.

"*Merci.*" Her French roommate, Yvette, had introduced

her to Robillard's, a gathering place for Boston's French ex-patriates and refugees.

With sugar on ration, Robillard's carried fewer pastries and more breads, but today a row of éclairs called from the glass display case. Why not? If she were fat, Mr. Young might *want* to hide her in the business offices.

Maybe she'd buy two éclairs. Or three.

Guilt zinged through her. No, she'd buy four, one for each roommate. How could she forget her friends? After all, she planned to indulge in their sympathy this evening. Didn't they deserve compensation in pastry form?

"Oh, *ma petite*. You are sad." Madame Robillard's brown eyes crinkled.

Quintessa refused to cry. She waved her hand in airy dismissal. "Nothing an éclair can't fix."

"*Oui*." Madame Robillard opened a pink pasteboard box. "Four, *s'il vous plait*."

"You are so kind. Such a good friend."

That's what everyone thought.

Madame Robillard stopped and studied Quintessa. Wiry curls in brown and gray framed her face, escapees from the loose bun at the nape of her neck.

Quintessa propped up her smile.

"Come, come." Madame Robillard abandoned the éclairs, shoved open the half-door in the counter, grabbed Quintessa's arm, and guided her to the back wall. "Paris is the cure for sadness."

Quintessa had to smile at the Philippe Beaumont lithograph of the Pont Neuf, from Papa's youth in Paris, before he'd come to America in 1910 and had fallen in love with Mama. His early work sparkled with color and light, influenced by the Post-Impressionists.

Madame Robillard squeezed Quintessa's arm. "Are you sad because of Yvette?"

"Yvette?" Quintessa blinked at the tiny woman. "Why? Is something wrong?"

"Have you not noticed? She is not herself. At our last meeting, she said not a word."

Quintessa had never attended one of the meetings with Yvette's French friends, but it wasn't like Yvette to keep her mouth shut. "I think she's preoccupied with Henri."

"Henri Dubois? *Non*." Madame Robillard fluttered her hand in front of her chest. "They are like brother and sister."

"Not anymore." Quintessa smiled. "Last week she told me they've fallen in love."

"*Non*, it cannot be. A woman in love is happy, not suspicious, always looking over her shoulder. Yvette is jumpy. Like a little flea."

Come to think of it, last night while cooking dinner, Yvette had jumped when the egg timer dinged. Quintessa patted Madame Robillard's hand. "I'm sure she's fine. Aren't we all blessed to have another mother here watching over us?"

"You are too kind." The baker pressed her hand to her chest. "You young people are far from home with no one to look after you. And here I am, far from my Paris and my sons and my grandchildren. We must be family for each other. And now I must get to work."

Quintessa followed her back to the counter. An evening newspaper lay in an untidy mess on an empty table, so Quintessa picked it up.

The headlines made her shudder. Eight German saboteurs had landed in the US by U-boat in June and they were under trial for their lives, with the verdict expected any day. And the Nazi army was advancing rapidly in the Soviet Union, unstoppable.

Awful, awful. She folded the paper to hide the madness.

"Navy making WAVES." She stood still and read the article. Earlier that day, President Roosevelt had signed a bill establishing Women Accepted for Voluntary Emergency Service, a women's naval auxiliary.

Back in May, the Women's Army Auxiliary Corps had been formed, and magazines showcased young ladies in olive-drab uniforms. Now young ladies would parade in navy blue.

Purposeful women contributing to the war effort, selflessly serving the nation.

"*Ma petite?* Are you all right?"

"Yes." Quintessa's vision cleared. "I know what I'm going to do."

Acknowledgments

When you work on a novel for a year, you owe gratitude to many people. Many thanks to my family for enduring the extremes of author craziness and for constantly inspiring me. Dave, your fearless campaign against shady prescriptions inspired the mystery plot for this novel, with a hefty added dose of "what if" paranoia.

While I already had this book plotted out when our daughter, Anna, began to fall in love with one of her brother's best friends, it was great fun for me to watch life imitate art. And even more fun to watch their happy ending/beginning. As I write this, their wedding is in my future. When you read this, they will be close to their first anniversary.

I am extremely grateful to some wonderful professionals who aided my research from afar. The amazing staff at the Ritter Public Library in Vermilion, Ohio, downloaded photos of microfiche copies of *The Vermilion News* from 1941–42. The bits of local color helped so much—and I was delighted by the story of Mr. Okagi and his restaurant.

Likewise, Margaret Dyson at the Boston Parks Department answered my obscure question about ice-skating in

Boston—complete with public records and photographs! Thank you so much.

When I was in Boston, my aunt, Ginny Siggia, took me to Durgin-Park, where we enjoyed delicious New England fare, including Boston cream pie. A few days later, Dianne Burnett and Kate Burnett of Christian Book Distributors informed me of Durgin-Park's reputation for delightfully surly waitresses . . . which has toned down in recent years. I'm afraid our waitress was rather polite.

Thank you to my Facebook friends for suggesting "To a Wild Rose" for Lillian. And extra-special thanks to Amy Drown for helping me avoid a musical mishap.

As always, I appreciate my brainstorming and critique buddies, who help me build my stories and polish them. Cathleen Armstrong, Judy Gann, Sherry Kyle, Bonnie Leon, Ann Shorey, and Marcy Weydemuller—I love you ladies.

I'm especially thankful for all the people who make these books come to pass. My agent, Rachel Kent at Books & Such, for shepherding the business end of things. My editors at Revell—Vicki Crumpton with her insight and wit, and Kristin Kornoelje with her eagle eye. Cheryl Van Andel and the cover team for one stunning cover after another. Michele Misiak and Claudia Marsh for creative and diligent marketing and publicity. I love this team!

And how I love my readers! Thank you for your touching emails and for your prayers and encouragement. Please visit me at www.sarahsundin.com to leave a message, sign up for my quarterly newsletter, or read about the history behind the story. I hope to hear from you.

Discussion Questions

1. Had you heard about the U-boat war off the US East Coast in World War II before reading this novel? What did you find interesting or shocking?

2. Lillian Avery lives with a visible physical disability. How does it affect her? What negative consequences does she experience because of it? How is she stronger because of it? How have things changed for people with disabilities since 1942?

3. Arch Vandenberg fears being rich. What did you think about this? When you learned his history, how did this affect your opinion? What did you think of his decision at the end of the story? In general, what are the benefits and dangers of wealth?

4. At the beginning of the story, Lillian dismisses Arch as a snobby society boy. Then Arch challenges her: "I believe in judging a person on words and actions and character. Not on background or appearance." In what ways do both Lillian and Arch struggle with judging, suspicions, and lumping people into categories? In what ways do you struggle?

5. Arch suffers from combat fatigue, what we now call post-traumatic stress disorder. Were you surprised at how the condition was treated—or not treated—during World War II? Do you know anyone with this condition? How did Arch's story give you insight into their struggles?

6. Mr. Dixon is not the most pleasant boss, but Lillian does her best to win him over. Have you ever worked for a difficult person? How did you handle it?

7. As Arch and Lillian investigated the drug ring, whom did you suspect?

8. Lillian struggles to open her heart—to God, to Arch, and to her roommates. How does her relationship with Opal Harrison challenge her and cause her to grow?

9. Both Arch and Lillian cling to their careers for security. In what ways is this acceptable? In what ways is this misguided? How do they change?

10. Lillian is close to her brother Jim but has a strained relationship with her twin sister, Lucy. What sort of dynamics do you see in the Avery family? In your own family? Do you think Lillian and Lucy will ever be close? Why or why not?

11. Arch tells Lillian, "We'll be weak together, strong together, you and I." Do you find that to be true in your deepest relationships? In what ways?

12. Discuss the meaning of the anchor.

13. "Blood is thicker than water"—how does this saying apply to Jim and Lillian? To Mrs. Harrison and her grandson? To Mr. Dixon? How have you seen it in your life?

14. In what ways did the weather mirror the characters' journeys?

15. If you read *Through Waters Deep*, did you enjoy following up with Jim Avery and Mary Stirling? The third novel in the Waves of Freedom series features Lt. Dan Avery and Quintessa Beaumont. From what you've seen of these characters, what might you expect?

Sarah Sundin is the author of *Through Waters Deep* as well as the Wings of the Nightingale and the Wings of Glory series. Her novella "I'll Be Home for Christmas" in *Where Treetops Glisten* was a finalist for the 2015 Carol Award, and her novel *On Distant Shores* was a double finalist for the 2014 Golden Scroll Awards. In 2011, Sarah received the Writer of the Year Award at the Mount Hermon Christian Writers Conference. A graduate of UC San Francisco School of Pharmacy, she works on-call as a hospital pharmacist. During WWII, her grandfather served as a pharmacist's mate (medic) in the Navy, and her great-uncle flew with the US Eighth Air Force in England. A mother of three, Sarah lives in northern California, and she enjoys speaking for church, community, and writers' groups.

War is coming.
Can love carry them through
the rough waters that lie ahead?

"With her trademark knack for blending historical research with lyrical prose, Sundin weaves an exciting story of intrigue, faith, and character development."

—*CBA Retailers + Resources*

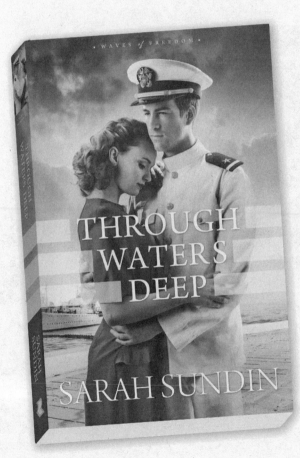

"Sarah Sundin seamlessly weaves together emotion, action, and sweet romance."

—*USA Today's* Happy Ever After blog

"A gripping tale of war, intrigue, and love."

—*RT Book Reviews* review of
A Memory Between Us